THE SHELTER OF HIS ARMS

Sybilla awakened, surprised by Guy's whiskered cheek in the hollow of her neck. She'd no recollection of how she'd gotten into his bed. But he'd kicked off his covers, rolled onto his side, and thrown his arm across her chest. She'd lain there for hours, listening to him breathe, allowing herself the luxury of his warmth, his strength and the intimacy of his slumbering embrace. When at last she forced herself to rise, she did so with regret, the kind of regret one feels when one awakens too soon from a wonderful dream.

Praise for DARK RIDER, also by Kathrynn Dennis

"Kathrynn Dennis's debut romance, DARK RIDER, will dazzle readers with its beautifully crafted characters, vividly detailed medieval setting and captivating plot rife with passion and intrigue!"
—*Chicago Tribune*

"Dennis's debut marks the entrance of a powerful voice into medieval romance. The era comes to life in fresh, vibrant expression as her strong, engaging characters tackle vicious enemies and engage in wild adventures. This hard-to-put-down novel will keep you up all night."
—*Romance Times* (four-star review)

"An extraordinary debut! DARK RIDER is a spellbinding tale of sensuality, adventure, betrayal, and romance that I couldn't put down. Kathrynn Dennis is a shining new talent."
—Lorraine Heath, *New York Times* bestselling author

"DARK RIDER by Kathrynn Dennis is a story that transports the reader back in time with its passion and medieval action. It is a definite keeper that will be read again and again!"
—*Romance Junkies* (five-blue-ribbon review)

"Kathrynn Dennis's DARK RIDER has everything I love in a medieval romance . . . Dennis will soon be a fly-away favorite for fans of the subgenre, if this well-written medieval romance is anything to go by!"
—*Heartstrings Reviews*

"DARK RIDER is an adventurous tale of two outsiders who must stop a powerful enemy. The fast pace of the story continues until the last page. Will Robert and Eldswythe survive and have the chance to love? You will need to read DARK RIDER to find out!"
—*Romance Reviews Today*

SHADOW RIDER

KATHRYNN DENNIS

ZEBRA BOOKS
Kensington Publishing Corp.
http://www.kensingtonbooks.com

ZEBRA BOOKS are published by

Kensington Publishing Corp.
850 Third Avenue
New York, NY 10022

All Kensington titles, imprints, and distributed lines are avail-
able at special quantity discounts for bulk purchases for sales
promotion, premiums, fund-raising, educational, or institu-
tional use.

Special book excerpts or customized printings can also be
created to fit specific needs. For details, write or phone the
office of the Kensington Special Sales Manager: Attn. Special
Sales Department. Kensington Publishing Corp., 850 Third
Avenue, New York, NY 10022. Phone: 1-800-221-2647.

Zebra and the Z logo Reg. U.S. Pat. & TM Off.

ISBN-13: 978-1-4201-0048-8
ISBN-10: 1-4201-0048-3

First Printing: October 2008

10 9 8 7 6 5 4 3 2 1

Printed in the United States of America

To William and Annah.
I love you to the end of the universe and back.

Prologue

Baldwin Forest, England
December 1390

If a man could sell his soul to the devil for an hour, Sir Guy of Warwick was prepared to strike the bargain.

Pray, let that hour be tonight.

Heedless of the icy wind that stung his eyes and cheeks, he spurred his destrier into the beckoning darkness. There he could lose the demons that raged inside him—or find them. There in the ancient woods, where the midnight air smelled of rotting leaves and death, Sir Guy of Warwick searched, as he had every night for weeks, driven by hatred and despair.

He kept his sword ready. Blue-black shadows moved through the moonlit forest, flickering through the snow-dusted trees like lost souls. He'd hunted them before to no avail, but tonight he would not give up. Instinct told him the killer would return, and Guy of Warwick would be ready when he did. Bargain with the devil or no, Guy would find the man he wanted and send him straight to hell.

From the corner of his eye he glimpsed a lurking shadow.

Wheeling his destrier around, he thundered toward the fleeing phantom. "Hold there!"

The racing figure stumbled, tripped by a fallen log. A man, skeletal and bent, but definitely human, scrambled to his feet. He cowered, cradling a rag-wrapped bundle in the crook of his arm.

Guy reined his horse to a halt. "Stay where you are."

"Shadow Rider, hear me out!"

"Who are you?" Guy bellowed, his sword ready. No man ventured into this part of the woods alone at night. Not without a reason.

"James Cobbler, from Halvern village."

"What's in the bundle?"

The cobbler quaked. He held up a scrawny brown hare. "There's no game left in any other wood. Folks won't come here since . . ." He cast a worried glance into the forest.

Guy leaned forward. "Are you not afraid, cobbler? What if the killer who murdered my sister and her babe returned?"

"I should hope the Shadow Rider finds him first, sir, and lets me be."

A freezing wind whirled around the little man. His face turned ghostly white. He ducked and shielded his head with the hare. "Don't let them get me!"

Guy scanned the woods. He felt their presence as he always did, his sister's and his nephew's ghost. They were the reason he patrolled at night, waiting for the killer, searching. He felt no fear when they were near, only restlessness and regret.

He took a deep breath. "Go home, cobbler. Keep the hare for your supper. No more poaching."

Wasting no time, the cobbler tucked the hare beneath his arm. "The hare is not for me. I'll trade her to the seer for the potion that will cure my sickly wife. Bless you, Shadow Rider. You've saved a life tonight." Without another word, he slipped into the darkness, weaving his way through the trees.

Guy sat perfectly still, his gut burning, the words spoken by the cobbler ripping through his heart. If he'd been here in the woods just a month ago, he could have saved more lives, his sister Roselynn's and his nephew's, a newborn babe named John.

Rage swelled inside him. Night after night he'd come here seeking, waiting for a sign, searching for their killer. He'd turned up nothing. What more could he do?

He clenched his fists. He'd seek the counsel of the seer, the Lady Morna, just like the desperate cobbler, though intuition told him 'twas better to bargain with the devil than with her. She had a way of throwing salt on old wounds and bringing back memories he'd just as soon forget.

The icy night went deathly silent. Twigs snapped. Footsteps approached. A dark form raced into the circle of stones, darted behind one and then another, hiding.

Guy wound the reins around his fist and steadied his mount.

Every sinew in his body taut and battle ready, he raised his sword. If the cobbler-poacher had returned, the man was a fool. If the footsteps were from one who walked this earth only in the night, so much the better. He relished the opportunity to tussle with a demon.

The single shadow, shrouded in a black cloak with a pointed hood, stooped and scratched the earth with its long pale hand.

Human. No poacher this one. This one was digging.

Guy leapt from his horse and bounded o'er the snow-encrusted earth. He growled a violent sound that ripped from his throat and echoed off the stones as he lunged, reaching for the hooded figure.

Fabric shredded, slipping through his fingers. He landed with a thud on his knees, his arms outstretched and reaching, his hands empty.

The figure vanished, leaving nothing behind but a ghostly imprint in the air and trail of snowy footprints quickly swept away by the wind.

Guy of Warwick sat on his heels and roared into the darkness, his heart beating hard against his chest. "Be you man or demon, I *will* find you. I swear it!"

Chapter One

Forbidden by the village priest to be here, she'd still do what she had to do. Sybilla Corbuc, at twenty years of age, unmarried and unspoken for, could not help herself.

Tonight, it was simply worth the risk.

She lifted her faded blue gown over her head and tossed it into the straw. The icy night air sucked her breath away as the feeble layer of warmth between her gown and her thin chemise vanished.

Better to remove the garment and suffer the cold than risk soiling it with telltale stains.

She folded her arms beneath her breasts and willed herself not to shake.

"Etienne," she whispered, "are you certain the night watch did not see you? The moon is bright tonight." Her warm breath, cloud-like and vaporous in the icy night air, rushed past her lips.

A boy with eager eyes and downy whiskers on his upper lip stamped his feet and rubbed his hands together.

"No, mistress. They were all a sleepin' afore I left ta fetch you."

Sybilla shivered. Thick, wet snowflakes floated down and stuck to her cheeks and forehead. She wiped her face with the back of her hand and looked up. Sparkling snow drifted through a pie-sized hole in the roof.

She moved closer to Etienne. "I saw boot prints along the road. Someone is about. Please, snuff the candle. For this, there is light enough." She slipped her arm from her chemise.

Shadows fell across the boy's face, but not before his cheeks flamed red and his eyes grew wide. Was it possible he was both embarrassed *and* afraid?

His voice trembled. "What will they do if they catch us, mistress?"

"To you, nothing. But to me . . . prison. I'll be tried and branded as a Separate, and cast out naked in the woods."

A gasp slipped from Etienne's mouth. "'Tis a death sentence," he squeaked.

Sybilla shuddered at his words. "Tell no one about tonight, Etienne."

She clutched her half-removed chemise to her chest, wishing she had some goose grease, or a little dab of butter to help with the task at hand. "I'm forced to risk my life and work in secret, else I'll starve," she whispered, her voice low.

Etienne glanced down at his feet. "Why won't they let you help with the livestock birthings anymore?"

"The bishop has barred all women from working in the stables. He lost fifty of his foal crop this season, all aborted, slipped from the mares without warning. He does not understand what happened, so he blames the deaths on witches."

Etienne blew on his cold-shriveled hands. "Were it witches, mistress?"

Sybilla shook her head. "Nay. 'Twas a contagion. There was nothing anyone could do."

She dropped to her knees. "We'd best get on with it."

The old horse resting in the straw beside them rolled her eyes upward and stared at Sybilla, pleading.

Without another word, she plunged her arm into a bucket, a bucket filled with water so cold it stung like nettles. She gasped and sat back on her heels. A cloud of sweet mold and straw-dust billowed upward, then settled on her lips and eyelids. She pressed her face into her bare shoulder and held her breath. *St. Genevieve, I beg you, just this one last time, do not let me be discovered.*

And then she sneezed.

A wet, head-splitting sneeze. A sneeze loud enough to roust the pigeons from the rafters. Fear streaked though her as Etienne clamped his hand across his mouth and turned his head toward the door.

Sybilla sat as still as a statue and held up her freezing arm. Water ran in rivulets to her elbow and steam wafted from her soaking skin.

Minutes passed. She sat in silence while the wind whistled through the roof hole. Pigeons cooed and skittered in the loft above. Beams moaned and the whole structure overhead seemed to shift. *Mother Mary. Would the rearrangement of half-starved pigeons be enough to bring the building down?*

The withered barn suddenly creaked. The ancient beams groaned and settled without collapsing. The night watch, apparently, had not heard the ruckus.

Sybilla let out her breath and stroked the swollen flank of the downer horse, a faded sorrel mare with a sunken croup, a broomstick tail and an udder which was not as full as it should be. What little nutrition the old mare had taken in had gone to keeping herself warm and not to making milk. Even if the mare survived, the foal might not.

Sybilla patted the mare on the rump and scooted round behind her. "God's peace, Addy, why did you have to do this on the coldest night since Michaelmas?"

She slid her arm into the mare's velvet warmth and probed to find a tiny hoof trapped behind protruding pelvic bones. Wrapping her fingers around a small fetlock, she looked at Etienne, his youthful face pinched with worry. "Don't fret," she whispered. "This will be easier than I thought."

With one strong tug, she pulled as the mare pushed and grunted. The tiny limb straightened and the foal slithered out in a gush of shiny fluid, black hair, and legs.

Sybilla wiped the mucous from his mouth and nostrils. "Aren't you a handsome one?" she said softly, as she traced the perfect white stripe that began between his soulful eyes and ended with a splash across his muzzle.

She raised her eyebrows and pointed to his feet. The hair there was solid white, right up to his fetlocks, on all four hooves. "Mother Mary. You look like you danced in chalk-paint, or you robbed the nuns at St. Bertone's an' stole their stockings. But you're a beauty."

She glanced at Etienne and her joy faded.

His mouth agape, he took a step back as he stared at the newborn. "Mistress, he's marked like the magic horse from Hades! The one the seer told us would be born at Cornbury. You don't want this one, mistress. He'll bring you nothing but trouble."

"Etienne, that's tittle-tattle, a tale told by a seer to earn pennies at the fair. She'd say anything to earn coin to buy food." She ran her hand along the foal's graceful neck. "Marked as he is, he's mine. I spent my last chink to buy his mother. He's sired by the Duke of Marmount's champion Spanish stallion. I shall call him my *Regalo*, God's gift. Safely delivered, sent from heaven, not from hell."

Sybilla's words surprised her. She'd attended the births of hundreds of foals, but for this one, she felt an unprecedented sense of ownership.

Addy nickered and staggered to her feet. The remnants of the afterbirth clinging to her tail, she sniffed the foal and snorted her approval. Pray to the saints, her milk would come now that she'd seen and smelled her foal.

The foal, surprisingly alert for just a minute old, lifted his head and looked around. His bright eyes flickered with unusual acuity and with an eagerness that made Sybilla take a second look. He rolled himself upright, folded his legs beneath him, and boldly met her gaze. A whinny pealed from his throat, as if to say he would get up when he was damn near ready, but for now, he preferred to sit like the prince he knew he was.

Sybilla smiled. "Praise the saints, you're healthy." She splashed water on her freezing arm and mopped it dry with the hem of her chemise. "You are a fine colt, even marked as you are. I could not have hoped for better."

She tossed her braid behind her shoulders, and nudged Etienne. "Go and fetch your mother. She'll know what to do from here. I daren't stay any longer."

A pensive Etienne slipped out of the barn without bothering to close the doors fully. Through the crack, Sybilla watched him go, a boy on the verge of manhood. He raced across the snowy yard to the tiny mud-and-wattle house with a thatched roof and a crooked chimney. How his mother, the widow Margery, managed to feed all six children through the winter was a wonder, having not a penny or a man to help. They all might still starve to death. The April fields had not been planted, the ground still blanketed with a crusty mix of ice and mud. Even Sybilla was down to her last cabbage.

The foal floundered, struggling at his first attempt to stand. His muscles shook from the effort but, when at last he hoisted his gangly legs beneath him and stood squarely on all fours, he swung his head around and looked at Sybilla. His big round eyes filled with pride.

Sybilla grinned. She, too, had her pride. She was a free woman, cold and hungry, but free. Her parents, God rest their souls, had been freemen, too—her stepfather born that way, her mother blessedly released after years in servitude.

Sybilla took a deep breath, wondering how she would survive. If she could last another week or two, spring would be here. She'd planned to earn her keep by helping farmers with the foalings. But now what would she do? She'd been warned once already to cease practicing her trade.

"Mistress Corbuc," the wiry Father Ambrose had yelled one sunny day last spring, when he'd found her with her arm inside a mare who struggled to deliver her twins. "The church bars women from the practice of surgery and ministrations on animals. It cultivates the keeping of familiars and cavorting with the devil. I forbid you to be a midwife to a horse. 'Tis indecent."

Sybilla prickled. If she were caught tonight, they'd arrest her without witness or defense.

She put her hand to cheek, the place where they would hold the branding iron and burn the mark of a Separate into her skin . . . She'd seen it done to other women—heard their screams, and smelled the nauseating scent of burnt flesh. 'Twas even worse if they scorched to the bone.

Her stomach roiled at the recollection. God in heaven,

she had to leave Cornbury—to go anywhere a woman with her skill was free to earn her keep.

A squeal erupted from the foal, jolting Sybilla from her dark thoughts. He pranced and nipped at the glittering snowflakes drifting through the roof hole. The sparkling white powder that dusted his finely sculpted head gave him a definite aura, a spirit-like quality not of this world.

He was different, though she couldn't quite say why. But in that instant, she knew they shared a common bond. She would defend him with her life.

Heavy footsteps suddenly crunched across the frozen yard and headed toward the barn. Sybilla spun around and faced the door. Panic shook her heart. Those were not the feet of Etienne, or his mother!

Choking back a yelp, she shoved her arm through the sleeve of her chemise and dove beneath the feed trough. Shards of rotting wood snagged her scalp and cobwebs whisked across her mouth and lashes. She drew her knees to her chest and let the shadows fall across her face as she watched the scene unfold before her.

Men's voices shouted. Hinges squealed and the barn doors swung fully open. A blast of wind blew powdery snow across the threshold and she watched as a knight, a stubby man with a rounded belly and an icy red beard, stumbled inside, his short mantle swinging like a bell. He surveyed his surroundings. "This will do," he grumbled. He shoved his hood back, and brushed the snow off his shoulders and his red-topped head.

A second knight strode in past the first one, his cloak billowing around his powerful legs. The ice-glazed spurs at his heels glinted like crystal. His hood obscured the details of his features, but he was tall, towering, and the way he held his strong back, erect with assured purpose, suggested he was mayhap twenty five or thirty years of age—and the kind of man who could keep a woman safe—or destroy her.

He took a deep breath, expanding his hulking chest, his shoulders as wide as a church door. His presence filled the space around him like that of someone accustomed to taking and doing exactly what he wanted.

He rested his hand on the hilt of his sword as he turned his head slowly and scanned the barn. Stomping the snow from his booted feet, he strode toward the shadowy stall where Sybilla huddled.

She didn't dare breathe.

The tall knight stopped, pushed off his hood and coif, and ran his fingers through his dark hair. He looked up and studied the column of snow that fell through the roof hole and spiraled down, swirling in the dim ray of light not two feet from Sybilla.

"'Tis a poor excuse for a barn, Simon," he called across his shoulder, his deep voice resonating bravado. "But it keeps out the wind, and given that we've lost our horses, it matters not."

"Hell to the devil, Guy. Hamon set us up. Those men were his soldiers, not common thieves. They waited for us and 'twas more than just our horses they meant to take. You should have finished off the one you pinned, not given quarter. Do you have to be so bloody noble?"

The tall knight ignored the comment and leaned across the stall boards. "Hah! There is actually a beast in here." He offered up his open palm and clucked. "Old girl, would you like some company tonight?" He patted Addy's neck while the foal, trembling on his spindly legs, took a few cautious steps and sniffed at the intruder.

The tall knight chuckled and let the foal lick his glove. "This one's just hit the ground. Within the hour I expect." He squatted and peered between the stall boards. "God's teeth, Simon. Look at it! Four white socks and born in Cornbury. It's him. My horse. Marked just like Morna said he would be."

Simon squinted. "Blessed saints. Would you look at that?"

The foal nickered, flagged his tail and stared, unblinking, at the knights.

The tall knight stood and faced his friend. "I am not a superstitious man, but I do believe I have found my horse, the one who will help me on my quest."

Sybilla's breath caught in her chest. *Her* colt? His *quest*?

Simon grunted. "You of all people should know you cannot trust the Lady Morna. The colt's got a white blaze down his forehead, like she said he would, but marked with four white feet, every horseman from here to France knows he won't amount to much. You know that too, but you've had too much to drink."

Sir Guy frowned. "Or Hamon's robber-man-at-arms knocked me silly." He rubbed his swollen cheek and studied the foal.

The wicked lump beneath his eye was so prominent it was visible even in the shadows.

Sir Guy spun around and slapped Simon on the back. "But I have a feeling about this colt. A feeling that I did not get with any of the others. This one is The One."

Simon furrowed his brow. His small eyes darted 'round the barn as if he sensed they were not alone. "You said that about the Lady Constance, and Mary Tanner, and the butcher's daughter, too. Proving that you cannot recognize a decent woman . . . or decent horseflesh either. This wobbly-legged farm colt is not The One. His rump is higher than his withers and his ears curl like a lady's slippers. Now let's bed down afore the sheriff finds us. He'll be looking for the man who stole Lord Hamon's emerald."

Sir Guy scowled. "You know I didn't pinch Hamon's necklace. I am many things, but I am not a thief."

Simon strode a few steps back to the barn door and looked through the crack, his gaze assessing. He spread his cloak out in the straw and laid down, but kept his sword at his side. "You are true and honest, and I know you are no thief. But Hamon is a rich nobleman and we are both poor knights. He considers men like you and me just one step above the peasants. He was looking for a fight and it didn't help that you groped his sister. Bloody all, Guy, why do you provoke him? The rift between you two will never end."

Sir Guy stabbed his sword upright in the soft dirt floor. "I am falsely accused. I've never groped a woman, any woman. Certainly not the Lady Avelina. She's the spiteful type. I refused her advances and she got angry. 'Twas she who stole the emerald."

Simon rose to his elbows. "Why do dangerous women always seem to find you? You can spot a man who plots against the king when no one else suspects. Why can't you can tell the difference between a woman you can trust and one you cannot?"

Sir Guy surveyed the dark barn while he spoke to his friend. "I may miss my mark with the fairer sex, but not with horses . . ." He pulled his sword from the dirt and pointed the weapon at the colt. "This colt is The One. I'll have a horse with four white socks when I avenge my sister's and my nephew's murderers. Morna said so."

Simon spoke, his voice tense. "Morna isn't always right. You've searched for months now, and the killer's trail has gone cold. Guy, give it up."

"Never. Especially, not now that I've found my horse. This horse was meant to be mine."

Sybilla nearly sprang from her hiding place. Sir Guy was talking about Regalo as if *he* owned him.

The wind howled and a shutter beat against the barn.

Simon jumped up from his resting place, his weapon drawn. He raised his face to the rafters and searched the darkness above. "Let's move on. This place is not safe, and that colt is strange, not magic . . ."

Guy shook his head. "We stay. His magic has yet to be revealed. If I'd had more coin to pay Morna, she would have told me what it was."

Simon snatched his cloak from the floor and flung the garment round his shoulders. "Mayhap she told you all she knew. Now let's go. I'd rather brave the wind than stay here. Hamon's men will find us if we don't keep moving."

Guy thrust his sword into a round of brown hay leaning against the wall. Dust swirled around him. "Then let them find us. I feel like fighting. When Hamon and his men stumbled into the inn, I could not resist his challenge." He drew his sword back and held it high over his head. "He weighted his dice. I did not run the cheat through on the spot because we were outnumbered. I will stay the night with the colt. I will fight Lord Hamon and his men should they find us, I will . . ."

Simon swore. He flung his cloak back down. "God's feet, you're as stubborn as a boar. 'Twill be a frost in hell before I go out drinking and gaming with you again."

Sir Guy swung the blade tip 'round to point at the foal. "Imagine, Simon. Imagine being born to greatness in a barn as poor as this one, to a swaybacked mare too long in tooth to live another winter, and with no one to witness the event but the pigeons in the rafters."

Simon crossed himself, but kept one eye on the barn door. *"Jesú*, forgive him. He knows not what he says. He hasn't been the same since you took his sister and his little nephew."

Guy scowled. "'Twasn't God who took them, Simon. 'Twas a man. I intend to find him." He leaned across the railings, and scratched the foal on the rump. "You will never lack for anything, from this day forward, my fine young steed. If it's oats and barley cake you want, you will have them. If you want a saddlecloth of silk, you shall have it. There are wrongs I must set right and deaths to be avenged. You are destined to help me."

Sybilla's blood boiled. *God's teeth, the man presumed too much.*

The wind stopped for a moment, and all was silent, but Simon stood on guard, his jaw muscles tight, his fist wrapped around his sword hilt. "Then I'll take first watch. You get some rest and figure out how you can pay to keep the colt for the next three years or until he's big enough to ride. By then you could be dead, given that you fight like a man who doesn't care much if he wins or loses, or lives or dies."

Guy clenched his sword hilt, his voice low and resolute. "The man who killed Roselynn and my little nephew will pay. I swear it. For the last six months, I've spent my days searching 'cross the countryside for the murderer, and my nights riding, searching in the shadows of the woods where my sister and her son were killed. I've vowed to find the killer but am no closer now than when I started. This colt was born to help me." He pointed to the mare and foal. "We'll take them with us when we leave, first thing in the morning."

Sybilla pressed her lips together to halt a gasp. This

man, the one they called the Shadow Rider—meant to steal her foal?

Sybilla clenched her fists until her fingernails dug into her palms. Shadow Rider or not, she would defy him if he thought to steal Regalo.

Guy ripped an armful of brown hay from the lopsided roll and chucked the stuff into the stall. "Eat heartily tonight, old girl. Tomorrow morn we leave for Ketchem Castle."

The hay landed in the trough above Sybilla. Dust and chaff floated down, coating her face and shoulders. She squeezed her eyes shut and held her breath.

Then she sneezed.

In an instant, Sir Guy leapt across the stall boards, grabbed Sybilla by the arm and pulled her to her feet. As her back slammed against the wall, moonlight streamed down, shining brightly in her face. Cold steel pressed against her throat.

Sir Guy stared, his gaze penetrating, searching. "Who are you, Mistress Green Eyes?" he demanded, his hot breath blowing on her cheek. He eased the blade away, but just enough to let her speak.

Sybilla's mouth went dry. He smelled of barley ale and wood smoke, and he was so close she could see the welt beneath his bruised eye was turning a bloody-purple hue. Fear gripped her heart and limbs, yet she would not yield. He meant to take her foal, her Regalo, and she would not give him up.

She glared at Sir Guy. His dark eyes flamed with an animal-like quality signaling he would react if she so much as flinched. But, Mother Mary, he had the face of the fair St. Michael—with a swollen eye and bleeding cheekbone, but an astoundingly beautiful face—framed by a mass of thick black hair that curled at the nape of his neck.

Her heart pounding, she clutched her shift to her chest. "I am Sybilla Corbuc. The foal is mine. I will not let you steal him."

His brows furrowed. "Steal him? What makes you think I'd steal him? I repeat, Mistress Corbuc, for I am certain you heard me the first time—I am many things, but I am not a thief." He leaned in close. Too close.

Sybilla felt the scorching heat rise up her neck. Her thin chemise did little to conceal her breasts, and the bottom of the threadbare garment had hiked high above her knees. Her woolen hose had slipped down around her ankles, leaving most of her legs exposed. Mother Mary. She was as good as naked and his ready hardness pressed against her thigh.

Sir Guy narrowed his gaze. "What have you been doing, Mistress Corbuc?"

He glanced at the bucket filled with dirty water. "Were not the foal newborn, I would suspect you were up to something else entirely," he whispered. "'Tis too cold to be undressed, though I must admit, the look of you does much to warm my chilled heart." He plucked a sprig of hay from her unraveling braid. "You are filthy and your hair is a mess, but what a color. Dark and golden, like cooked honey."

Sybilla's knees almost buckled. His face was just a hair's breadth from hers, his mouth as close as a whisper. His body radiated warmth and strength, and maleness. For a moment, she wanted him to wrap his arms around her and pull her closer.

Simon's voice rang out, "Guy, you don't know whose kin *she* may be. Remember Lady Avelina. We've trouble enough tonight already."

Guy drew a deep breath. His eyes searched her face, as if he savored one last look. He stepped away. He pulled off his gloves and bowed to Sybilla. "I am Sir Guy of Warwick. Sworn by oath to serve King Richard and by fealty to the Earl of Ketchem. By my honor as a knight, I will not steal your foal."

His face grew intent. "But I can *pay*, Mistress Corbuc. If you are willing to sell." He leaned beside her and draped his arm across the stall boards behind her head. He took her hand into his and interlaced his fingers with hers.

Sybilla stole a startled glance at their entwined hands. The heat from his fingers promised languid warmth, like the golden sun on a lazy summer day, radiant and caressing.

He smiled, his eyes hopeful and meant to charm.

Sybilla's breath quickened. What kind of woman did he think she was?

She ducked from underneath his arm. "The foal is not for sale."

Guy pulled her back. "But I *can* pay, Mistress Corbuc. I am an honorable man. We can strike a bargain."

A strange sensation, tingling heat, raced from her fingertips to her gut. Mother Mary, he was vital and strong and she couldn't help but notice how his breath quickened.

He leaned closer, his voice husky. "I'll give you three times more than you will get for him at Smithfield Market. If you will let me."

Without warning, he placed her palm against the bulging velvet money pouch hanging just below his belt.

Sybilla gasped. *God in heaven, he's missed his mark with me.*

She wrapped her fingers around the velvet bag and yanked. "What can I do with a stolen emerald, Sir Guy? A lowly woman, poor and without a husband. If I tried to sell it, I would be arrested and hanged for thieving."

His brow knotted. "I didn't steal Hamon's em—Hold there!"

She raised her arm, her fist gripping the pouch.

He reached for her wrist. "That's not an em—!"

Before he had the chance to grab her, Sybilla hurled the pouch across the stall. "Now let me go, you lout, else I'll call the sheriff."

Simon spun around to face the barn door. "It seems, Mistress Corbuc, he is already here." He raised his sword. "Guy! To arms!"

Chapter Two

Fighting back a scream, Sybilla ducked beneath Sir Guy and knocked the water bucket over, kicking the straw to cover up the muck.

A deep male voice boomed from outside. "Show yourselves. On the order of the sheriff."

Terror shot through Sybilla. Good saints. *'Twould be better to be accused of fornication than it would to be caught attending to the foal's birth.*

She threw her arms around Sir Guy's neck and with a flying leap, she wrapped her legs around his waist.

He staggered, struggling to gain his footing. He toppled, taking Sybilla down with him. She landed underneath him. His handsome face directly over hers, he rested the weight of his upper body on his forearms and smiled down at her. He didn't look at all surprised, or worried. If anything, amusement danced in his eyes.

Footsteps approached, the sound of boots stomping through crunchy snow. The mare and foal skittered into the corner.

Sybilla pressed her mouth to Sir Guy's and kissed him hard, praying her ruse would be convincing. What did she know of lust and coupling, aside from what she'd witnessed mares and stallions do? She had never lain beneath a man.

Sir Guy took her lower lip between his teeth and gently sucked. "Open your mouth a little," he muttered against her lips. "'Twill make it look more real."

Much to Sybilla's dismay, his tongue pressed its way between her slightly parted lips. He drew his head back for a moment and looked into her eyes. "Mistress Corbuc," he whispered. "You are delicious. And I have a feeling . . ." He lowered his head and planted a searing trail of kisses on her eyelids and across her cheeks.

Sybilla's heart jumped. The stolen kisses from the baker's son three years ago were never like this—so arresting. Sir Guy's passion stirred up something deep inside her—an alarming need for more. Instinctively, she lifted her chin and leaned her head back, allowing Guy to explore her neck, to go dangerously lower with his mouth. The heat from his lips set her skin on fire and sent goose bumps rippling down her arms.

God's breath, what was he doing? What was *she* doing? The night watch was here!

Limbs flailing, she struggled, but her ill-thought effort only caused Sir Guy to shift. He settled his lower body between her legs, his firm shaft pressed immodestly against her mons. A sudden rush of heat flowed over her, starting from her core, spreading, and arousing more than just a hint of maidenly desire. A low moan escaped her lips.

Sir Guy grinned down at her. "If you are pretending your enthusiasm, Mistress Green Eyes, you should know that I am not. The passion that you stir in me is real."

The barn doors banged open and a lantern flooded light into the darkness. From the floor, Sybilla could see the feet of three men: a guard's boots, a priestly pair of slippers, and a finely crafted pair of leather shoes, dyed red, complete with silver buckles.

"What goes here?" bellowed the voice above the red shoes.

Guy lowered his head and whispered into Sybilla's ear, "Trust me. I will not steal your colt—or your virtue. Remember that." He jumped up and pulled Sybilla to her feet.

Trembling, Sybilla lowered her chin, hoping to hide her flushed face.

Glancing up, she watched a sardonic smile spread across Guy's face. He tipped his head at the sheriff. "Good eve, Sheriff. What brings you here?"

The sheriff stroked his pointed black beard. His beady eyes studied Sybilla. "Mistress Corbuc? What businesses have you with this man?" His gaze roamed the length of her.

Sybilla lowered her eyes, wishing she was fully clothed. "I-I . . ."

Guy stepped forward. "Mistress Corbuc and I arranged a meeting. I wanted to see the colt she had for sale. We were just negotiating the price."

Sybilla glanced away, alarmed. She'd never witnessed anyone address the sheriff as though he were no more than a beetle on a dung heap.

The sheriff cocked a well-groomed eyebrow. "She has no colt, unless the old mare has given birth. And you, Sir Guy, have no money left, having gambled everything you owned and lost. Unless of course, you plan on paying with a stolen emerald, the one belonging to Lord Hamon."

Sybilla shot a glance at Guy. Good Lord, the man gambled like her father.

Guy narrowed his eyes. "Lord Hamon's emerald? His sister stole it. I do not have it. You can check my person. If you dare." His tone was calm, but the muscles in his jaw were tight.

The sheriff sneered, dimpling his cheeks. "Then you have stashed it somewhere and I intend to find it." He peered inside the stall. Letting out an irritated breath, he wheeled around to face Sybilla. "The foal is not an hour old, Mistress Corbuc. The mare still has the birth sac hanging from her tail. Were you here, attending the delivery?"

Her whole body shook with denial. "No. I was only—"

The priest crossed himself. "Saints preserve us. The foal has four white socks. A familiar if there ever was. And Mistress Corbuc here delivered it, of that I can be certain. The watchmen checked the smith's shed where she's been sleeping and she was not there. That was an hour ago."

The priest pushed his black hood from his head. It was Father Ambrose, who somehow had managed to grow fatter over the winter. He glared at Sybilla, his face flushed, his horse hair undershirt visible at the neckline of his black cassock. He looked warm and not at all like he was suffering a penance.

Indignant, Sybilla scooped up her blue dress and pulled it on over her head. She smoothed her tangled hair and faced the sheriff. "Good sir, the foal was born before the sun went down. He was already here when I checked after my supper. The afterbirth is there, but some mares will carry it for hours." She pointed to Guy. "And the only devil I have cavorted with . . . is him. I confess. I left my bed an hour ago. He wanted to see the foal, having heard I would sell it. I did not know he had no money, or I never would have met him."

She lowered her head. "I beg forgiveness for my carnal weakness, Father, but that is my only sin tonight."

The ease with which she lied amazed her. Guilt stabbed at her stomach as she glanced at Guy's bemused face.

In the momentary silence, Etienne and his mother strode into the barn, the determined Margery in the lead. She was a small woman, with button eyes and a severe mouth permanently puckered with determination. Her mouse-brown hair was thin and her eyes were sunken, like someone who had not had a decent meal in months. She pushed her way between the men and pulled her tattered woolen shawl around her frail shoulders.

Sybilla swallowed. Margery was never one to hold her tongue. Even when she tried to help, she had a way of making the situation worse.

Margery pointed at the priest. "You said, sir, that I should pray for a way to feed my children, that God would help me. Well, he did. He sent the Mistress Corbuc here to deliver this mare of a colt that was trapped inside her. She is my mare, Father. Mistress Corbuc an' me, we struck a bargain. She said I could have the mare iffin I would give the 'orse shelter in my barn until the foal was weaned. The old mare woulda died, had not Mistress Corbuc helped with the birthing. My mare," she repeated, "the one that's gonna feed my children."

A chill washed over Sybilla. Addy to slaughter? Margery had never mentioned that.

Margery knelt and bowed her head before the priest. "God bless the Mistress Corbuc. Have mercy on her. She's saved more souls tonight than you have in a multitude of sermons."

Sybilla groaned inwardly. *Margery, say no more!*

Father Ambrose's face turned the color of a pomegranate. "She has broken the law."

The sheriff nodded to the guard. "And so we have a witness, Mistress Corbuc. The widow Margery has just confirmed your crime. From this hour on, you will spend your days in Gambolt prison and await your trial." He lifted the manacles from the guard's hands. "If you are convicted as a Separate, you know what happens next." He clucked as if he were disappointed. "Pity, to mar that lovely face."

Margery's mouth dropped open. "Corpus bones, Mistress Corbuc. I dinna mean to tell 'em what they wanted to 'ear."

Sybilla squared her shoulders. "It's all right, Margery. Sooner or later, they would have arrested me. I've long been like a burr beneath the Father's cassock."

Chains rattled. Iron cuffs opened wide.

Guy grabbed Sybilla's wrist. "Hold, Sheriff. You have no say here."

The sheriff glared at Guy. "By order of the bishop, I do, Sir Guy. I keep the law in Cornbury for the church and for Lord Hamon. And what's this woman to you? As of this moment, she's in my custody and the colt goes with me until he's weaned. But, I am a fair man. Not unkind. I will let the Mistress Corbuc keep her dress and shoes. She will be transported to the prison first thing in the morning. She should be grateful she will not go there naked. I've a right to strip her now and drag her there before her trial, so egregious is her crime."

He held the manacles out as if he expected her to put them on herself.

Guy kept his grip on Sybilla, but moved his other hand to his sword, his face stark with determination. He stepped toward the sheriff, the movement a calculated threat. "The disposition of Mistress Corbuc is not under your jurisdiction. The foal is nearly worthless, marked as it is. But she agreed to sell him to me for a half a shilling. And Mistress Corbuc has conscripted to work for me. I've employed her for three years' worth of room and board. Her life is already mine, as is the foal's. And I agreed to send a shilling to the widow for the old mare."

Margery looked up, her eyes wide, her head bobbing in agreement.

Sybilla's palms turned clammy. Sir Guy of Warwick just claimed her foal, and he had just claimed *her*—as his indentured servant—for three years!

God's breath. She'd sworn to her mother she'd never be a servant. She'd seen the scars on her mother's back, scars from a brutal master who'd beat her senseless and left her in a ditch to die. Bless the wicked master's God-fearing wife. The woman feared her husband had committed murder—and demanded he set her mother free as penance. Her mother had kept the blood-stained servant's dress in a chest for years thereafter as a reminder of what servants had to endure.

Sybilla shuddered. Sir Guy of Warwick could not truly expect her to give up her freedom. And she'd not part with Regalo, the colt who was her future, not for any price.

"No!" she blurted.

The word slipped out before Sybilla saw Margery's pleading eyes. The poor woman looked stricken, as if she'd been given a brief reprieve, then ordered to the gallows. Addy wasn't worth a shilling, even by the pound, but with that kind of money in her pocket, Margery could feed her family for a year.

Sybilla drew a deep breath and bit down on her lip. Giving up her freedom would save Addy, Margery, and her children. And it was the only way, at the moment, to avoid a stint in Gambolt prison. Her parents had died in that disease-infested place. They had not been criminals, just poor folk who could not pay their debtors. God's bones, even if she lived through Gambolt prison, she'd be sentenced as a Separate. She'd not the courage or the strength for that.

Her heart raced. 'Twas best to play along with this ruse and survive.

She squared her shoulders and looked at Sir Guy. "I mean, no, Sir Guy, you agreed to give the widow Margery two shillings, not one."

A sly grin spread across Sir Guy's face. He spread his hands apologetically, as if he was sorry he had tried to cheat.

Sybilla bowed her head, feigning acquiescence. "And give her the half a shilling for my foal. I owe her for the hay."

Guy opened his mouth as if in protest. He snapped his jaw closed and shrugged. "As you wish, Mistress Corbuc." He nodded to Simon. "Sir Simon, pay the widow Margery. Use my winnings from the gaming tables, the coins I gave you for safe keeping last night."

Simon swore an oath beneath his breath. He cut the small leather pouch from his belt and tossed it to Margery. "You're lucky that he saved some back, but it's all he's got." He shot a look at the sheriff, as if the last few words were meant for him.

Sybilla arched an eyebrow, surprised.

The sheriff folded his arms. "Sir Guy, I've orders from the bishop to arrest the Mistress Corbuc and Lord Hamon commands I find his stolen necklace. What do you suppose I should do?" He drummed his fingers on the leather purse buckled to his silver belt and cast a furtive glance at the priest. The priest bowed his head as if preoccupied with prayer.

Guy's eyes locked with the sheriff's. "Tell the bishop he will no longer be troubled by Mistress Corbuc. She has found employment as a servant to Sir Guy of Warwick and she will be leaving Cornbury. Tell Lord Hamon you could not find his necklace. You searched everywhere, even through the hay bales and the stall." He said those last words slowly, hinting. He pointed his sword at the sheriff's heart. "But know that I'm no thief, Sheriff. I do not take such accusations lightly. If you or Lord Hamon dares to challenge me on this, I relish the opportunity to settle, sword to sword. Man to man. No need to wait until the fighting season."

The sheriff stepped back. "I will search the bales and stall myself. I promise I will find that necklace, Sir Guy. And if you and Mistress Corbuc are still in Cornbury at morning's light, I'll send ten men with pikes to hunt you down, if Hamon and his guard don't find you first." He thrust his fist at Sybilla and rattled the manacles. "Good riddance, Mistress Corbuc—that is, until we meet again. Given that you have cast your lot with this man," he said, gesturing to Sir Guy, "you are just one step short of prison. You know the price for what you've done. You have escaped it, for now."

Sybilla inwardly cringed, but she forced herself to stay composed.

The foal emerged from the shadowy corner. He sniffed the sheriff's red shoes, spun around, flagged his tail and farted.

Sir Guy smirked at the sheriff. *"Voilà.* It appears my colt holds a rather low opinion of you, too." He bowed with a flourish and touched the flat side of his sword to his forehead in mock salute.

The priest, Margery, and Etienne froze in silence, but

Simon doubled over, hooting as Sybilla pressed her hand across her mouth to hide her grin.

The sheriff spat and planted both hands on his hips. "That colt is as common as a mule, Sir Guy. I know the rumors planted by the seer. She's a Separate and a heretic. And Mistress Corbuc here has swindled you, for certain. The colt's not magic and with four white socks, he is as worthless as she is. But 'tis a satisfying way to end my night. 'Tis clear you and Mistress Corbuc deserve each other. Get out of Cornbury before the cock crows.

With that he spun on his heels and left, the indignant priest stumbling behind him, scratching at the hay stuck in the seat of his cassock.

Chapter Three

Guy banged on the cottage door. "Smith? Open up," he bellowed. The fog from his warm breath puffed from his mouth as he spoke.

He listened for an answer and watched Sybilla shift and stamp her feet beside him. They'd hiked a mile in ankle-deep snow to the smith's and she'd not complained, but her face was pale and her lips had taken on a bluish tinge. Her golden hair and faded blue dress were dusted with a light coat of snow and in the pre-dawn light she looked like a woman from a mystic world, too young to be a ghost, but too fair and ethereal to walk the earth.

He pulled his cloak off and tossed it to Sybilla. "Put this on," he ordered, annoyed he hadn't thought to give it to her sooner. Turning, he pounded on the door. "Get up. We've need of your services and we're freezing."

The cottage door cracked open. Warmth seeped invitingly across the threshold and a man whose head was like a melon with bleary red eyes, stumbled forward.

The smith pulled a woolen blanket over his shoulders and squinted. "By the devil, who the hell are . . . Mistress Corbuc?" He cocked an eyebrow. "What are you doing with these men? I do not want trouble. An' I already told you, you can sleep in the shop, but there's no room for your mare and foal."

Sybilla shook her head and lowered her eyes.

Guy glowered at the smith. "Mistress Corbuc says you have a horse for sale. I want to buy it."

The smith narrowed his eyes. "I know you . . . Sir Guy of Warwick. And you too, Sir Simon."

Simon grinned and saluted the smith.

The smith lifted his chin and studied Guy. "I was on the battlefield at Balmont. You fought like a madman and saved King Richard. You're poor but noble knights. And you've nothing on you now that makes me think you can pay for a horse." He pointed to the mare and foal and shook his head. "I'm not looking for a trade. The colt's a straggly one and marked as he is, he'll bring bad luck." He sniffed and held up his hand as if he antici- pated an argument. "Aye, I've heard the tale about a magic horse, to be born this winter hereabouts. But this colt is not The One. Wouldn't trade a goat for him."

Guy stood up to his full height. "I am not here to trade, but I need another horse." He put his hand on his sword and stepped toward the man.

"No." Sybilla clutched Guy's forearm. "He let me sleep by his firing grate these last two weeks. Otherwise, I would be dead from the cold. If he doesn't want to sell the horse, we can walk. *I* will walk."

Guy looked at Sybilla as she shivered; her fingernails had turned blue. She wouldn't last long on foot. He re- moved and lowered his sword and offered the hilt to the smith.

The smith's eyes grew wide. "That's the weapon King Richard gave you. I recognize the stone in the handle. 'Tis the biggest rock o' lapis I ever seen. For that sword,

I'll trade my horse, an' I'll throw in a little bag o' last year's oats."

Guy shook his head. "You get the stone, but not the weapon."

The smith stroked his chin and studied the handle of the sword. "'Tis a bargain. But you get what you get in horse tradin'."

Within the hour, the smith wore the blue stone around his neck. He hurried to the barn and reappeared, leading a burly horse. Grain spilled from the animal's mouth and he snorted bits of hay from his nose. The smith handed the lead rope to Guy. "You be doin' me a favor ta take him. He eats like every mouthful is his last."

The stocky courser, a stallion with a winter coat as black as soot, coughed and rubbed his face on his wide knees. He had a plug's head, but by the looks of his belly, he hadn't missed a meal all winter.

Guy frowned. "He's sound?"

The smith nodded. "He ain't pretty, but he's a solid ride. His name is Bacchus."

Taking Addy's lead from Sybilla's hands, Guy tossed the rope to Simon. "The mare is your mount."

Simon pulled a horse face. "Why can't I ride the stallion? I can't be seen riding on this bag-o'-bones. I'm a knight, too, you know."

Suppressing a grin, Guy shook his head. Simon had a gifted sword arm, but he was not a knight who could boast his talent as a rider. He hated riding without a saddle.

Guy jumped onto Bacchus' back, and hauled a cold-stiffened Sybilla up to sit behind him. He winked at his friend. "Two of us will have to share a horse. I'd rather ride with Mistress Corbuc than with you." He reached toward the smith. "I'll take those oats now."

The smith tossed the oats to Guy. "Mistress Corbuc, what have you done? Have you sold your soul for a warm bed and whatever scraps this man will give you? 'Tis a pity. He'll put a babe in your belly, then turn you out. You coulda stayed here and kept your freedom. We could have come ta some agreement." He smiled and scratched his crotch.

Guy bristled at the thought of Sybilla sharing hearth and bed with this man. He was a greasy fellow and smelled of soured straw and piss.

He turned Bacchus toward the road. "Mistress Corbuc has conscribed to be my servant. The choice was hers to make."

Sybilla called down to the smith. "Thank you for your kindness for these last few weeks, good sir. Aye, I am a servant now, but my heart and soul are free."

He felt her stiffen and lean away from him. The gap of cold air that rushed across his back made the fine hairs on his neck stand up.

Guy exhaled and rubbed his forehead. What was he doing taking this woman, an old mare, and a gangly, un-proven foal back to Ketchem?

Damnation. He could not afford to pay the board on two more horses and he needed a servant like he needed head lice. For the past six months, he'd slept in a stone cell in the bottom of the castle and eaten with the other knights in the great hall, even though the Earl of Ketchem Castle and his wife, Lady Claire, had offered him a warm apartment and a place at the high table. He preferred the solitude and the privacy of his darkened cellar room.

What would he do with Mistress Corbuc?

He would set her free, he decided, as soon as he was certain she was safe. He'd keep the foal, but it would be hard to part with Mistress Corbuc. God's breath, she was a comely woman with no husband or protector, but full of pride and independence, determined to survive. He knew what it was like to be alone, with nothing much to live for except your freedom and your horse.

Guy spurred Bacchus into a gallop, jostling Sybilla. She grabbed his waist and fell against him. Her softness felt good against his back and he breathed in her earthy scent, of horses and of hay.

Hell to the devil. He got that feeling again. The one that made him stop and think, for just a moment, that he wanted something more than the life of a knight-for-hire. He'd had a taste of home and hearth, and of the kind of love that once filled his widowed sister's house. He'd grown accustomed to her boisterous home, the squall of his infant nephew, and the antics of their one-eared cat that made him laugh. Every now and then, he craved that life and blamed himself for having lost it.

Having lost them.

He clenched the reins, guilt and regret burning in his stomach. He'd sacrificed it all to be a knight. King Richard's wars had cost him dearly. Had he not left his widowed sister and her child for the call to battle, he would have been there to protect them when the raiders came.

The foal whinnied. His coltish squeal pierced the wintry silence. Armor clattered and hoof beats thundered in the distance. Sybilla straightened and tightened her arms around Guy's waist.

Guy drew Bacchus to a halt.

Crimson banners shimmered in the morning sun and a retinue of mounted soldiers, all dressed in red and black, stopped in the middle of the road ahead. A fair-haired nobleman on a white horse rode to the front of the pack.

The massive destrier reared and snorted, his rider's

brilliant blue cloak, emblazoned with his crest, an eagle with a sheaf of wheat clutched in his talons, draped over the horse's rump and haunches like a king's parade robe.

Guy moved his hand to his sword. "Lord Hamon," he said, his voice detached. "I trust you are well rested?"

Lord Hamon drew his sword. "Guy of Warwick and Simon Portney, impoverished knights, pretending to be noble. I am not surprised to find you fleeing Cornbury at the crack of dawn. I want my emerald." His eyes narrowed and his covetous gaze settled on the foal. "That colt. I want him, too. Yield them both and I'll let you live."

The sound of swords flying from their scabbards rattled in the air as the men behind him drew their weapons. Lord Hamon's horse pawed and the animal tossed his head as though he had a hornet up his nose.

Simon sidled Addy next to Guy's black courser. The foal, wedged between them, stood quietly, as if he understood the danger.

Before Guy had the chance to stop her, Sybilla slipped his cloak off her shoulders and dismounted. Her golden hair shining in the morning sun, she strode across the icy road and stood directly in front of Lord Hamon's maniacal horse.

Arms akimbo, she squared her shoulders and glared up at Lord Hamon. "Let us pass, my lord. The colt is not for sale and Sir Guy doesn't have your emerald. We are on our way to Ketchem Castle. You will be rid of me forever."

Lord Hamon's fair cheeks flashed with red. "Mistress Corbuc, you are as comely as your mother was, but you test me sorely. I don't mean to buy the colt, I mean to take him. And retrieve my emerald. Now step aside. I have business with these men and no quarrel—today— with you."

Sybilla glanced across her shoulder at Guy. He watched

as her gaze rested on the foal for a moment. She turned and faced Lord Hamon. "No. I will not step aside. I have stepped aside for you for years. Let us pass, or run me through."

Lord Hamon inched his horse a few steps forward. "Mistress Corbuc, 'twould be a pity to separate your lovely head from your lovely neck. Step aside and do not force my hand." He lifted his sword.

Sybilla didn't flinch. She tipped her head slightly to the left and lifted her chin. "Kill me, Lord Hamon . . . and know that you have murdered the only seed to ever spring from your infertile loins."

A hush fell across Lord Hamon's soldiers. Even his great white horse stood still and ceased his incessant snorting.

Simon raised his eyebrows and looked at Guy.

Guy rubbed his forehead and moaned. *Good God, what a way to start the day.*

A flash of steel glinted in the sunlight as Lord Hamon swung his weapon—just as Regalo bolted, kicking and squealing, raced to Sybilla's side.

Lord Hamon's horse pinned his ears back. Teeth bared, he lunged at the foal. Hamon's blade slashed the space just inches from Sybilla's head.

Sybilla screamed and Addy, her broomstick tail sticking straight up, whinnied and spun around, nearly flinging Simon from her back.

The old mare bucked. Both rear feet shot out behind her, aiming at Lord Hamon's horse. They clipped the destrier across the muzzle and a broken tooth went flying.

The white horse, his mouth bloodied, whinnied and reared. Hamon grabbed the reins to keep from falling. Jerking backward, he threw his mount off balance.

The great horse twisted, his head pulled to the left, his

feet scrambling on the ice until his massive bulk came crashing down. Lord Hamon landed underneath his mount, his foot trapped beneath the horse's hips. His voice cracked with pain. "Get him off me!"

Soldiers jumped from their horses. Three men put their shoulders to the horse's white rump and heaved, while another two grabbed the animal by the mane and pulled.

Regalo darted from the road and headed for the field. Addy raced to follow. Simon's beefy arms strained against the reins, but she had set the bit between her teeth and he could not hold her back.

Hamon's face contorted with agony as the white snow beneath him turned red. He beat the ground with his fists. "Bind my ankle before I bleed to death, you fools. The bone is through the skin!"

At the sound of Hamon's voice, Addy seemed to gallop faster. With Simon clinging to her bony back she raced, gaining on her foal with every surging stride.

Guy galloped Bacchus forward and hauled a shocked Sybilla up and into his lap. "Mistress Corbuc, whatever possessed you to—"

"Sir Guy!" a boy's voice called from across the field. "Your emerald. Found your bag afore the sheriff got it. I ain't opened it. Brought it straight to you!"

Sybilla snapped her head up. "Etienne?"

Guy clamped his arm around Sybilla's waist and spun Bacchus on his heels, pointing the horse toward the field. "Bloody hell, boy—not now!"

Etienne's small form tromped across the field, through snow drifts as high as his knees. He raised the pouch and shook it, waving it proudly in the air. He cupped his hand around his mouth and called louder. "Your emerald, Sir Guy. I got it."

He shook the bag high above his head.

Bacchus' ears pricked. His nostrils flared and he swung his head around to look at Etienne.

Lord Hamon yelled, "Get them. I want that colt. And the boy with my emerald. Kill the girl."

Horses whinnied and swords clattered. Bacchus squealed and bucked, his stomach rumbling, burping like a hollow drum filled with gas and water. He reared and landed facing Etienne. With the speed of the wind, the great horse charged into the field.

Etienne stopped waving. Panic swept across his face as his eyes shifted from Addy and the foal thundering toward him, to the furry black stallion not far behind them.

With the force of Bacchus' stride, Sybilla's head slammed against Guy's chest. "Etienne! Get out of the way!"

Guy wrapped his arms around her and laughed. "Hold on tight, mistress. I do believe Bacchus thinks the bag is full of oats and if the boy runs, I think we all might escape."

Sybilla twisted in the saddle to look behind her, her white-knuckled fingers threaded through Bacchus' wiry mane. "Give the horse his head and they'll not catch us."

Guy slackened the reins and leaned forward. "Woo-hay! Here we go."

Bacchus powered on, clods of snow-pack flying from his feet. He galloped into the field, roundly overtaking Addy, Simon, and Regalo.

Sybilla cried out, "To the woods, Etienne!"

Guy craned his neck to see behind him. Lord Hamon's men had fallen lengths behind, their mounts slipping spread-eagled in the snow. Not a horse could run full out and neither did they seem inclined to try, lacking, apparently, the proper motivation.

He grinned and leaned into the icy wind that whipped

his hair and stung his eyes. Hell to the devil, the fiery Mistress Green Eyes would defend her friends and her possession against Lord Hamon, or go down trying. She could ride a horse like she was born in the saddle. What a woman! The kind of woman who could defend his hearth and home—if he had one. God's teeth, she made him feel alive, made his blood rush from his heart and his breath explode from his burning lungs.

He leaned close to Sybilla and laughed, his lips against her temple. "Hail to Bacchus, mistress! He has a demon's appetite and when he's hungry, he thinks his feet can fly!"

Chapter Four

Gray clouds filled the hazy midday sky and snow floated down, settling on the trees. The air crackled with winter's bite and the frozen ground crunched as it gave beneath the horses' footsteps.

Teeth chattering, Sybilla sat close against Sir Guy, unable to resist his warmth, but she kept a close eye on Regalo. Not yet one day old, he struggled through snow drifts as tall as his chest. He showed no signs of fatigue, but it was only a matter of time before his little legs would give out. She would have been right there beside him, had Guy not ordered her to stay mounted, promising he would carry the little beast if needed.

Sybilla pulled her cloak around her shoulders. Mother Mary, what had she agreed to? Was she really a servant now, and officially not the owner of herself, or of Regalo? Sir Guy had saved her life and her foal, and she wasn't ungrateful, but the bargain they'd struck in the stables was just a ruse. He could not hold her to it. At first chance, when she was far from Cornbury, she would thank Sir Guy and Simon and depart, taking Addy and Regalo with her.

She closed her eyes and let Sir Guy's solid warmth

offer comfort. She hadn't counted on that slight hitch
in her breath every time she touched him or held his
gaze too long. Even thinking about him now, the power
in his legs and the feel of lap against her backside, made
goose bumps ripple up her back. Mother Mary, he was
handsome. It would be hard to leave.

Sybilla snapped her eyes back open and straightened.

Such thoughts were ridiculous, of course, and may
prove to be dangerous. A penniless freeborn woman on
the run from prison should be careful with her feelings,
especially about a man she barely knows and one with
such an enigmatic reputation.

By late afternoon, the dull gray sky had darkened.
They'd stopped to rest deep in the woods, where the
frozen trees and thickets offered cover from the worst of
the biting wind and from their enemies.

Sybilla stood beside Regalo, her teeth clattering, rat-
tling like pebbles in a box. She rubbed the colt's neck
with her bare hands, attempting to warm him. He stood
quietly with his head down, his foggy breath blowing
from his nostrils. Guy fed Bacchus, while Simon picked
the snow-pack from the great horse's hooves, and Addy
stood quietly with her eyes closed.

A youthful voice pierced the air. "Ho there! I've found
ye!"

Etienne emerged, jogging from his hiding spot in the
woods. Breathless and pink cheeked, he handed Guy the
pouch.

Without so much as a word to Etienne, Guy shook the
contents into his gloved hand. Sybilla craned her neck
to see.

A string of prayer beads spilled out. The shiny black

beads, obsidian mayhap, were as dark and glittering as Regalo's eyes. A delicate wooden cross, covered with mother-of-pearl roses, dangled at the end of a leather cord. Guy squeezed his eyes shut for a moment and his fingers closed over the beads. Grief flooded over his face and he mouthed the words *thank you* to Etienne, before he turned away.

Sybilla lowered her eyes. God's breath! There was no emerald in his pouch. Had she known the contents were so dear, she never would have ripped the little bag from his possession and hurled it across the darkened stall.

Simon patted Etienne on the shoulder and smiled.

Etienne stroked Addy's neck reassuringly, but his gaze roamed the woods as if he wasn't sure he was entirely safe. He'd always been a superstitious lad. He shivered, no doubt as much from fear as from the cold. A Separate, Joan the hayman's wife, had died not far from here, months ago. Poor Joan had been blamed when Will Talbot's cow birthed a one-eyed calf. Drunken Will, as he was known, had blubbered to the sheriff that Joan helped with the birthing. She'd been arrested, tried, and branded within an hour. 'Twas the beating that ended her life. Her naked body had been dragged into the woods and left unburied, as an example to anyone who defied the law. 'Twas said the dead woman's ghost still wandered in the woods, looking for her grave.

The thought of dying here, alone, exposed, and unable to fend off the wolves, made Sybilla tremble.

Guy spoke softly. "Time to leave. Hamon will send more men to search." He offered her his hand.

On impulse, Sybilla reached out, glad for the comfort of his touch. Suddenly, she halted. She scanned the wooded cove for Regalo. He was never far, but now the little colt stood not fifty feet away, like a hound pointing at a rabbit hole.

His ears pricked forward. He kept his sad eyes focused on the thicket in front of him. He turned his head when Sybilla called his name, but otherwise, he did not move.

Sybilla walked slowly toward him. Beneath the twisted, frozen branches of the thicket, where the wind whirled close to the ground, she caught a glimpse of a human form, or part of one, leg jutting from the snow.

Her heart almost stopped.

She covered her mouth with her hands and stepped back, unable to tear her eyes away from the sight— a woman's leg, the frozen flesh marred by wolves, the bare foot missing most of the toes. Though she could not see the woman's face, tufts of familiar coppery-red hair poked through the snow.

A gust of wind broke through the trees and snaked around Sybilla. She fought back a scream, her body shaking.

She wanted to run, to flee as fast as her feet would go to take her to—to where? She was safe nowhere. Not in Cornbury, not anymore, and mayhap not in the neighboring villages, or further. The bishop's law applied to all of England and news of her near arrest and of Regalo's strange markings would travel like fire over dried grass.

She felt Guy's arm wrap around her. He pulled her close, his warmth and strength enveloping her like a blanket. "Come away from here, Mistress Corbuc," he whispered.

Sybilla's heart beat hard, so hard she could hear it thumping in her chest. She motioned to the snowy corpse. "'Tis Joan the hayman's wife. I heard her screaming when they branded her. She was my friend. If I am not careful, there lies my fate."

Not waiting for his response, she pulled away from him, turned and bolted toward Bacchus. "I must not be arrested."

Guy mounted Bacchus and pulled her up to sit behind him, Etienne mounted Addy.

Simon glanced at Guy. "Let the boy come?"

Guy nodded and spurred Bacchus onward, toward a path that lead out of the cove and back into the woods. "The ground is frozen solid and Hamon's men are sure to follow, else I'd bury the hayman's wife for you, Mistress Corbuc. But know this, you've no one to fear. Not while you are with me."

No one but a greedy sheriff, a superstitious priest, and Lord Hamon, a ruthless overlord who'd have put my head upon a pike before he'd call me daughter.

Sybilla kept a close watch on Etienne and Regalo. Regalo dragged along and Etienne huddled close to Simon. The boy's body shook when the wind kicked up. He'd not an ounce of body fat on his skinny frame to keep him warm. Guy and Simon, seemingly impervious to the cold, bantered on about great battles, the superiority of Gascon wine, and the merits of the broadsword over the mace. Their deep voices droned on as if they hadn't a worry in the world.

Her backside stiff and cramping, Sybilla twisted round again to make certain Regalo was still at Addy's side.

Regalo lagged far behind, a good stone's throw from his mother. His head hanging low, his stride more languid and wobbly than it was just minutes before, he ambled, losing ground with every step.

Sybilla grabbed Guy by the shoulders and shook him. "Stop. Now!"

Before Bacchus had come to a complete halt, Sybilla jumped off his back and hurried to the colt. She lifted his head and studied the inside lining of his lower eyelid. The flesh there was pale and turning gray. She called to Guy, who was already stomping through the snow and motioning for Simon to follow.

Sybilla called out to Guy. "Mother Mary, I feared this would happen!" Panting, she scrambled to her feet and dragged the drooping Regalo toward Addy. "He needs to nurse, Sir Guy. Pray Addy has some milk."

Guy wrapped his arms around Regalo and moved him close to Addy. He spoke softly to the colt and nudged Regalo's muzzle to Addy's teat. "We are not far from a place we can rest, Regalo," he said, stroking the colt. "Drink, little one. We cannot linger here." The colt made no effort to latch on.

Sybilla warmed her hands with her breath and reached underneath Addy's belly to massage the old mare's udder. The mare's teats were flat and cold, and her bag was soft, empty.

Sybilla closed her eyes. "'Tis as I feared. She has no milk. Her udder is collapsed. She needed more than moldy hay these last few months." Sybilla glanced at Regalo. His glazed eyes gave his face a vacant look, as though he was in another world. Sybilla lowered her head and took a deep breath. She had the heart-breaking suspicion there was more to his affliction than lack of milk.

She raised her gaze to Guy. "We need to find a nurse mare, or a cow. Even a goat would do. Regalo needs to eat and rest."

"There's smoke rising over the treetops ahead, a crofter's house and a fire. We can ask if they have stock.

But Hamon's men will soon be on our trail. We must make haste."

He cast a warning glance at Simon. Simon turned his face away from Sybilla and wrapped his fingers around his sword hilt. Etienne lowered his eyes, a tinge of pink coloring his pale cheeks.

Sybilla shot a questioning look at Guy. "What lies ahead? Whatever danger, we must risk it. Mayhap the crofter has a cow or goat. Regalo will die without sustenance." She stood up, noting she could no longer feel her own frozen feet. "Regalo can barely walk."

Guy knelt, gathering Regalo up in his arms. "He won't have to, Mistress Corbuc. But you get back on Bacchus and get warm."

With a grunt, he hefted the foal over his head, onto his shoulders. Regalo's spindly legs dangled like broken sticks and he lowered his neck, resting his chin on Guy's chest. Guy straightened. The muscles in his forehead and jaw tightened, yet his stance did not falter.

He gripped Regalo by the fetlocks and spoke sternly to Sybilla. "Do as I ask, Mistress Corbuc. Get on Bacchus before you freeze to death."

Sybilla swallowed. Carrying Regalo was an act of strength and gentleness she'd not expected. The deed sparked her curiosity about the soul that made the man.

She stood unmoving, staring at the battle-hardened warrior, a man with legs like tree trunks, a narrow waist, massive shoulders, and a colt slung across his back. Good Lord, could he carry *her* like that if he had to?

The corners of Guy's dark eyes creased. "Mistress Corbuc, I do not wish for you to sicken, too. Do as I ask. Hurry."

Sybilla bit down on the inside of her cheek. He'd asked her, not ordered her to mount. Surely that meant he did not consider her his servant, or intend to hold her to the ill-thought agreement she made in the barn? She was glad to do as he *asked*.

Sybilla leapt on Bacchus.

As soon as she got to the cottage she and Guy of Warwick would talk.

Smoke curled from the short chimney on the crofter's dwelling. The place was an oblong cottage with a snow-piled roof, a structure large enough for a family and their livestock. But no one came into the yard as they approached.

Guy lowered Regalo to the ground. The colt was so weak, he promptly lay down and rested his head in the snow. Sybilla dismounted and knelt beside Regalo, stroking his neck, brushing away the icicles hanging from his short mane.

"We'll have you by a fire, in just a moment longer, and get you milk," she whispered.

He closed his eyes, and her heart sank while she watched his breathing slow.

Simon and Etienne slid from Addy's back. "Looks safe, Guy." Simon stamped his feet and tucked his hands beneath his armpits. "I say we venture inside." His breath was as thick as fog.

Guy drew his sword, his eyes wary, but before he could answer, the cottage door opened.

A woman stepped across the threshold.

Sybilla stood transfixed.

The woman wore a rich red overdress of fine damask, with dangling sleeves lined with ermine. Her sable hair, unbound, tumbled down her back, framing a regal face with smooth skin and full crimson lips. Dark, arching eyebrows swept upward over luminous brown eyes. She was no crofter's wife, or huntsman's woman. Her elegant bearing bore a stark contrast against the humble cottage.

Guy smiled a slow but knowing smile.

The woman held her hand up in greeting as she surveyed the rest of the traveling party. Simon craned his neck to look around her, attempting to see inside the cottage. Etienne turned pink and looked at his feet.

Sybilla endured the woman's scrutiny. Guy was not a stranger to this woman.

Guy glanced back at Sybilla, a look of contrition on his face, almost apologetic, yet at the same time, asking for her trust.

"Greetings, Lady Morna." He addressed the woman as though they were at high court.

Sybilla shifted on her feet. So this was the famous Lady Morna—the gifted seer, renowned for her beauty, and cast off by her noble husband? Sybilla had never dared to get this close. 'Twasn't safe for horse midwife to be seen with a seer who lived on the edge of churchly persecution, too.

Lady Morna smiled.

Turning her gaze to meet the woman's dark eyes, Sybilla saw the mark—the small, blackened half-moon, no bigger than a thumbprint, burned into her left cheek—the mark of a Separate.

The mark did not mar the Lady Morna's dark beauty, but a chill rippled up Sybilla's neck. She clenched her fist to keep from touching her own cheek.

By the saints, what had this gentlewoman done? And how had she survived? By her dress and well-kept cottage, Lady Morna lived far better than most peasants. She had some means, mayhap a wealthy patron of noble birth who did not fear the law. Common folk caught consulting, or bringing food or clothing to a Separate would face a lashing, or worse.

Sybilla shivered. She risked her life by just being in this woman's presence. Sir Guy and Sir Simon might not be charged for consorting with her, but she doubted she or Etienne would escape punishment if they were caught.

Regalo nickered, a small nicker, so weak it was barely audible. Sybilla stroked his head, wishing he'd been born a month later, when the sun would have been warm and Addy would have had the chance to graze on green grass. He looked so frail now, and he had that distant look in his eyes, one that told her he would worsen.

Sybilla struck that thought from her head. A warm fire and a little rest and milk could save Regalo. She would take the risk and shelter with a Separate to get him what he needed if that would save his life.

Lady Morna glanced at Regalo, resting at Guy's feet. She took a deep breath. Her voice tight, she spoke with strained calmness. "Sir Guy, I see you've found your horse."

Guy nodded. "As you said I would, my lady."

Lady Morna turned her attention abruptly to Simon. "Be at ease, Sir Simon. There's no guard inside. No one's waiting for an ambush."

Simon snorted and looked away.

Etienne shuffled, tossing snow with the toe of his shoe.

"And you, young Etienne," she continued. "You want to be a knight like Sir Guy? Lurking by my cottage hoping to see me naked is not the way. Go home to your mother. Work hard and grow strong so you will be ready when you're called from the fields to battle."

With a sheepish look, Etienne nodded once. As he turned to leave, Guy whistled to call him back. He tossed the boy his overtunic. Delight spread across Etienne's young face. He pulled the garment over his head and scampered off, the hem dragging in the snow.

Simon sighed. "God's teeth, Guy. Your cloak to Mistress Corbuc and your tunic to the boy. Do you *want* to freeze to death?"

Guy ignored his friend. "Lady Morna, your beauty would tempt any man—or boy. You cannot blame the lad for trying. Might we share the warmth of your hearth tonight?" He bowed and with his head down, he winked at Sybilla.

Sybilla pressed her lips together and forced a blank stare. She couldn't help the twinge of jealousy that squeezed her heart. It wasn't a rational feeling. She had no claims on the knight who'd come to her rescue and wasn't even sure she could trust him. Why did it matter if he flirted with the seer?

Sybilla shot Guy her most indifferent look.

Rising, Guy grinned. He took Lady Morna's slender hand. "I'm sorry we parted so abruptly when last we met. I had urgent business to attend to."

Her face serene, Lady Morna didn't answer right away, but her eyes belied calculating insight. She leaned toward Guy and squeezed his outstretched hand, a familiarity that confirmed Sybilla's suspicions. Guy and Lady Morna knew each other well.

Lady Morna spoke in a low voice. "You are always welcome here, Sir Guy. Few knights would risk the company of a lonely noblewoman who's fallen far from grace. Bring your colt and your friends inside. But hurry. Lord Hamon's men are sure to be searching for you." She lifted her long skirts and made a half-turn toward her cottage.

A look of relief swept across Guy's face. He knelt and scooped the fading Regalo into his arms.

Her dark eyes alight with understanding, Lady Morna stopped to study Sybilla. "Mistress Corbuc, be kind in your assessment of me. We both do what we must to survive. I know what saving your colt has cost you. Why don't you tell them what's really wrong with the foal?"

Sybilla's knees went weak. "He needs milk," she replied, shifting from one foot to the other.

Lady Morna shook her head.

Sybilla lowered her eyes. She could name a dozen maladies—twisted guts, water head, jaundice, or navel ill. All grave conditions, but none as lethal as the one she refused to say, the one that was the cause of Regalo's weakening. It would be better for Regalo, and for her, not to reveal his condition. Guy of Warwick might abandon them both and they'd surely die out here in the cold.

She lowered her eyes. "He was fine until the last few hours. He's just tired and hungry."

Lady Morna held her hand out and motioned for her to follow. "Come now, Mistress Corbuc, your knowledge and intuit exceeds those who usually ply your trade. Confess. Tell your friends what the colt's problem really is. They'll see it soon enough."

Sybilla folded her arms to steady her nerves. Lady Morna was right. Soon Regalo would reveal his malady to all. If Guy cast her and colt aside once he heard the news, so be it. She wouldn't blame him. Villagers would stone a foal with this affliction, and probably her too, for bringing him into the world.

She faced Guy straight on. "Regalo has been elfshot."

Guy's mouth gaped open. Simon gasped.

Morna stepped across the threshold, one foot inside her cottage. "Now tell them the rest of it, Mistress Corbuc, so they are prepared."

Sybilla took a deep breath. She squared her shoulders

and locked her gaze with Guy's. "By midnight Regalo will be sitting on his haunches, barking like a dog and staring at the stars. Pray he lives the night."

Guy ran his hands through his hair and let out an exasperated groan. "Elfshot! How? And how long have you known, Mistress Corbuc?"

Sybilla couldn't lie. "From the moment he was born, but I had hoped he was just a sprite and gifted." She took a deep breath. "It happens when a foal is stuck in the birth canal too long. 'Twas no fault of his own, or mine, Sir Guy."

Sir Guy looked mournfully at the foal. The great knight's shoulders slumped like a man whose hope dissolved before his very eyes.

Sybilla rested her hand on Sir Guy's arm. No need to tell him Regalo would soon be as addle-brained as a rabid sheep, prone to wandering and howling at the moon and barking like a dog. Even Addy had begun to distance herself from her foal. She hadn't whinnied for him since they'd left the road in Cornbury.

Sybilla pressed the heel of her hand to her forehead. She should have prepared for this as soon as Etienne told her there was a problem with the birthing. But what could she have done to prevent it? In the end, she could not have changed the outcome.

She braced herself for what was sure to come.

Guy of Warwick would surely cast her and Regalo off. Then what would she do?

Guy locked his gaze on hers. "I don't believe in elves, Mistress." She watched as he knelt and lifted the ailing Regalo into his arms. "Come inside with us. There's food and a fire."

A wave of relief washed over Sybilla, and she quickly fell in step behind Lady Morna, Guy, and Simon.

She scanned the dimly lit interior. A comfortable place, with a finely carved oaken table; thick candles sputtered on the mantle and a graceful tall-back chair and spinning wheel sat beside the hearth. Oaken chests lined the walls and in the far corner, goats baa'd and stuck their heads between the slatted fencing that formed a livestock pen.

Guy set Regalo down by the fire, and Simon led Addy to the pen. The scent of spiced hot stew and warm bread mingled with the smell of animals and herbs.

Guy's deep voice boomed above the livestock noises. "Mistress Corbuc, sit down and eat." He pointed to the table. "A meal will warm you."

Vaguely aware of the steaming bowl of stew Lady Morna thrust into her hands, Sybilla lowered herself to the bench. She watched the foal lying on his side next to the fire, his feet paddling aimlessly. He smacked his lips like a fish and blinked, his eyes staring at nothing. Her heart sank. If Regalo died tonight, all she had to live for was lost.

Guy removed Sybilla's snow-soaked cloak and wrapped a heavy blanket around her shoulders. Warmth settled over her, but she set the bowl aside. Fatigue had claimed her appetite.

Guy stoked the fire, fanning the kindling with a bellows. "Simon would you milk the goat? It's for Regalo."

Simon choked on his spoon. He looked up from his steaming bowl of stew. "Me? Milk the goat? I'm a knight, Guy. Why do I have to——" He clamped his mouth shut, his complaint cut short by Guy's beseeching look.

Guy came to the table and rested his big hand on Sybilla's shoulder, his touch reassuring.

"You rest. I'll feed him, Mistress Corbuc. He'll get

better. Wait and see." He reached for a fur coverlet resting on a stool. He tossed the fur over Regalo.

Lady Morna's gentle voice drifted from the darkened corner. "He won't take milk from you, Sir Guy. He's chosen her." She pointed to Sybilla. "'Tis the way for a colt who's been elfshot. He's lost affinity for the mare and bonded to another—her."

Guy spun around. "Only Mistress Corbuc?"

Lady Morna nodded. "He'll only let her feed him. For days, mayhap weeks. Who knows?"

Guy shot a befuddled look at Sybilla. Sybilla lowered her eyes. What Lady Morna said was true. 'Twas a common thing for an elfshot foal to reject the mare and bond with someone, or something else. She had seen an elfshot foal become attached to a wine barrel.

The goat brayed. Squirting milk hit at the bottom of a pail while Simon grumbled and Lady Morna spoke softly to her animals, and to Addy, though the old mare seemed indifferent.

Guy swore beneath his breath. "Then come, Sybilla. I'll prop him up while you feed him."

The winter chill chased away by the fire's heat, Sybilla could actually feel her toes and fingers. Guy had shown nothing but kindness to her, the least she could do is do what he asked. He seemed just as determined to save Regalo as she.

Sybilla eased from the bench. "His affliction was an act of nature. You know that don't you?"

Guy grunted. "I've no fear of the foal or of you, mistress, if that's what troubles you. Rest assured, I'm not of mind to put you or the colt aside. But if what Lady Morna says is true, as I suspect it is, I will require your company for weeks."

Sybilla sat down beside the foal and slipped her finger

between his velvet lips. He stopped smacking for a moment and made a weak attempt to suckle, his soft lips pursed and his tongue curled at the edges. She sat back on her heels, surprised and relieved he hadn't lost that vital reflex.

"Blessed Mother," she said, her voice more animated than she intended, "he's trying to drink."

Guy propped Regalo upright and Sybilla held a wine skin filled with goat's milk to the foal's mouth. He slurped and dribbled, spilling as much as he took in.

Lady Morna donned her red velvet cloak. "We'll need more firewood." She slipped on her deerskin gloves.

Guy turned to Simon. "Simon, could you—"

Simon held up his hand. "Help her? Why of course," he answered, then mumbled, "Milk the goat, fetch the wood . . ." He pulled his cloak over his shoulders. "Guy of Warwick, if you hadn't saved my arse at Balmont I'd refuse. But the ladies tell me it's a good arse and I'm glad to have it still, thanks to you." Simon winked at Sybilla and followed Lady Morna out the door.

A sharp blast of winter wind sliced through the cottage before the door slammed shut.

Guy nudged Sybilla with his elbow. "Let me try to feed Regalo. You're exhausted and there's still hot stew and fresh bread on the table."

Sybilla shook her head, though the very thought of warm brown bread and rabbit stew made her woozy. "He'll not let you."

Guy took the wine skin from Sybilla's hands and held it to the foal's lips. Regalo closed his mouth, his head weaving, his eyes glazed and vacant. He spit the spout from his mouth and rested his chin on his knees, ignoring Guy.

Guy's brow furrowed. He handed the wineskin to Sybilla and watched, his expression thoughtful.

Sybilla put the spout into Regalo's mouth. He suckled 'til the wineskin had emptied. Apparently satisfied, he rolled onto his side and closed his eyes. Sybilla rubbed the foal's ears, acutely aware of Guy's nearness, of the way he watched her, the way he knelt so close beside her, their shoulders touching.

Reaching across the foal, she pulled a deerskin cover over his haunches. At the same time, Guy reached across her lap for the emptied wineskin. The tip of his nose grazed her cheek.

Startled, she drew back and parted her lips to say, "I'm sorry."

His mouth covered hers before she uttered a single word.

His lips warm and pliant, caressed her, the taste of him pleasingly rich. His arm slipped around her waist and as he drew her closer, her back arched. Her breasts crushed against his solid chest, she could feel his heart thudding, pounding as hard as her own.

His breath quickened and his hand skimmed up her back and came to rest on her shoulder.

Lord help her, but she wanted to wrap her arms around his neck and bury her face in his warmth.

Just as quickly as he'd swept her up, he broke their embrace and drew back.

The door banged open and in stomped a snow-dusted Simon, his arms filled with wood. His eyes flashed with bemusement—and with warning. Lady Morna came in behind him, her dark gaze focused on Sybilla.

Sybilla wiped her mouth and turned away, unable to meet Lady Morna's eyes or to look at Guy. Mother Mary, why had he kissed her? What was it about this man that drew her in?

She gulped. He was now her employer, some would

say her master—which she intended to address, and soon. But, he hadn't introduced her to Lady Morna as his servant.

She touched her lips with her fingers. She could still taste him, a wonderful taste, rich and smoky, all man, a taste that left her wanting more.

Would he expect more?

Heat crept up her neck.

Simon cleared his throat. He dumped the wood beside the hearth and stretched his arms over his head. He yawned. "If I'm done with all my chores now, I'll be turning in." He bedded down, his makeshift pallet a long wide chest stashed against the wall, opposite the goat pen.

In the silence, Lady Morna looked at Guy. "I see," she said, softly, her face impassive. She glanced at Sybilla. "Get some rest if you can. You must all leave here before the dawn."

Guy turned slowly to face the beautiful seer, his eyes apologetic, like a child who'd been caught with his hand in the sweetmeats. "I'm sorry, Morna. We'll leave as soon as we can."

She nodded. Without another word, she ascended the ladder to the loft like an angel dressed in red, with her long dark hair shimmering in the firelight.

Still reeling from his inexplicable kiss, Sybilla steadied her tingling nerves by pulling her knees beneath her faded blue skirt and hugging her legs to her chest. Guy kept his eyes on the loft. When the rustling above ceased, he lowered himself beside her and stared into the fire. Only the sound of Regalo's tiny wheeze breached the silence in the room.

Guy reached to stroke Regalo's cheek. "I apologize to you too, Mistress Corbuc, for kissing you. You've not invited my attentions. I was glad to see Regalo drink, that's all."

Something in his tone told Sybilla he was glad to see Regalo rally, but he wasn't sorry for the kiss. Now that her fate and livelihood were intertwined with his, she best set some boundaries. Her heart told her 'twas time to be on guard.

"Sir Guy, I wish to make it clear, I cannot stay in your employment for three years. I would have agreed to anything in front of the sheriff to avoid arrest. Surely you don't hold me to the agreement we made in the stables. I cannot be your servant."

Guy straightened his legs. Hell to the devil. He'd planned to set Sybilla Corbuc free once they were safely out of Cornbury. But he intended to keep the colt and she was the only one who could feed the little beast. Releasing her was out of the question. And then there was that kiss, that incredibly delectable kiss . . .

He took a deep breath. "Mistress Corbuc, I consider our arrangement binding."

Sybilla's mouth gaped. "But I am a freeman. Pay me an honest wage and I will willingly take care of Regalo while I earn enough coin to buy him back."

The fire crackled and Regalo stirred, switching his tail.

Guy stared at Sybilla. Pay her? Buy Regalo back? How could she be so determined, but uncomprehending?

He leaned toward her. "I can't release you from our bargain. I intend to keep the colt and only you can feed him. I cannot pay you, mistress. I've no coin. No wages until the fighting season starts. Even then, I'll not sell Regalo. Not to you, nor to anyone. I'll provide a roof over your head, clothes, and food, and you will live with me as my servant. For three years. I'll keep my side of our agreement. You are honor-bound to keep yours."

* * *

Guy's words felt like a dagger twisting in her heart. Sybilla sucked in her breath. God's breath, the man had saved her life and Regalo's. She owed him for that, but three years of servanthood *and* giving up Regalo?

She rose to her knees, shaking. "Why is my horse so important to you?"

Simon's snoring skipped a honk.

Guy leaned toward her. "He is the horse Lady Morna says will help me find the murderer I seek. What can be more important than that?"

"I need him. His stud fees will pay the collectors who've claimed my family's horse farm. Without him, I've no way to live. No hope of ever buying back what I have lost."

Guy held up his hands. "No hope? No way to live? *Mais je vous ai sauve, non?* But I have rescued you, no? For three years you will be provided for, and you can help me train the colt. By then he'd be big enough for me to ride and you will have your freedom. But, I will not sell him even then."

Sybilla fumed. His smattering of French annoyed her. She folded her arms. "But he is mine and I was born a freeman. I don't know how to live any other way."

Guy rolled a dazed Regalo into an upright position. "Then you must learn, Mistress Corbuc. It is not too much ask. I saved your life. Now help me save his." He patted Regalo. "Roselynn and baby John were murdered. They were innocents, Mistress Corbuc. Help me avenge their deaths," he added softly.

Sybilla sank down. She was indeed indebted to Sir Guy of Warwick for saving her life, and she sympathized with his loss, even felt the grief in his words. But three years?

A sense of obligation filled her heart. God's bones, Sir

Guy of Warwick had a way of persuading her to agree to things she should not. She pushed the spout of the wineskin into Regalo's mouth. "Three months. Regalo should be weaned by then. Agree I have repaid my debt in three months." She lifted her chin.

"Don't do that."

"Do what?"

"Lift your head like that, slightly to the left with your chin jutting out. You do that every time, just before you say something you know I will not like. It is not the mannerism of a servant. Best not to do it."

Sybilla wiped at an imaginary smudge on her cheek with the back of her hand, a habit she had when she was agitated. "Sir Guy, I implore you, give me leave in three months' time. Agree my debt to you is paid by summer's end."

Regalo stopped suckling.

Guy took a deep breath, his face pensive. "Six months. More time to wean him. But you must understand—six months, or six years from now, I will not sell the colt. And you cannot practice horse midwifery while you live with me at Ketchem Castle. The law there is no more forgiving. For six months you will simply be my servant."

Sybilla felt the blood pool in her feet. "Ketchem Castle? You are taking me there?"

Guy nodded. "It's where I live and train. I am a knight in service to my lord. Where did you think I would take you?"

Sybilla tossed the wineskin aside. Her empty stomach suddenly felt like it was filled with lead. She glowered at Guy. "I hadn't thought that far. I cannot live in a castle. The stink, the noise, the walls. Six months at Ketchem is too much."

Regalo flopped back onto his side.

Guy's eyes darted to the foal. "Three months then. Three

months you will stay and work at Ketchem as my servant, and then you are free to leave." He leaned back, crossed his ankles and stared into the fire. "In three months take your leave, go to Scotland, or to Ireland where it's safe to ply your trade, or take a husband if you choose . . ."

Sybilla looked up, alarmed. Marriage was as bad a fate as servanthood as far as she was concerned. Her mother labored on the farm while her stepfather gambled away everything they earned. And the day the collectors came, she'd sent her fourteen year old daughter from her arms and climbed into the debtor's wagon along with the man she said she loved. That kind of love Sybilla would never understand. She'd never marry, never put her heart, or her fate, in a man's hands.

She sat down, tucking her feet beneath her. "I've no interest in a husband, Sir Guy. I'm better off alone. I've lived on my own since I was girl. It hasn't always been easy, but I am not afraid of hard work. With God's grace and the generosity of Margery, the smith and others, I've survived. I've still got my freedom."

Guy's gaze swept over her and he raised his eyebrows, as if to say he'd seen beggars who were better off.

Sybilla straightened her shabby blue gown, a sack-cloth compared to Lady Morna's garments. Shame tugged at her pride. There'd been a time when she'd owned two fine dresses, and her family had inhabited a cottage much like this one, with a stone floor and finely carved furnishings.

Guy arose. "I'll see that you get a new dress once we arrive at Ketchem."

Sybilla felt her cheeks flush. By the saints, as if she cared if he thought her poorly dressed.

He pulled her to her feet and spun her round to face the table. "You need to eat, Mistress Corbuc. And rest.

I'll wake you to feed Regalo. We leave for Ketchem at morning's light and not an hour later."

Sometime in the wee hours of the night, Guy raised his heavy eyelids. After his last swig of ale, he'd laid his head down on the table, but even when sheer exhaustion plagued his wakefulness, sleep evaded him.

He rubbed his bleary eyes and focused. The fire had long grown dim, and Regalo still slept, his form obscured by shadows. Mistress Corbuc sat next to him, slumbering with her arms sprawled across the table, her chin resting next to a half-eaten bowl of stew and her fingers still clutching a spoon. Her eyes were closed, and thick, pale lashes lay against her fair cheeks. Her golden hair spilled down her shoulders.

She was not much older than his sister, Roselynn, who had been so fair of face she'd captured the attention of a wealthy, landed knight. Sir Walter Highthorn was too old to be her husband, but he was kind and rich and when he offered for her hand in marriage, Roselynn accepted. Like Mistress Corbuc, she'd had the same fiery spirit, and the same sense of pride.

Guy studied the faint freckles scattered across Sybilla's nose. He denied the impulse to touch her, to run his fingertips across her smooth, white cheeks. Part of her appeal was her dogged independence. So like his sister, who'd been insistent she could take care of herself and her son after Sir Walter died. The old knight's heart had simply stopped while he slept by the fire one evening.

It wasn't long thereafter when raiders came, riding in on the cloak of night, hiding in the darkness while they did their murderous work.

At that thought, Guy's belly burned. He grabbed his

gut. He'd brought death to his sister and his beloved nephew as if he'd killed them with his own hands. He'd been too long at war, eight years in France in the service of the king. Morna had begged him not to go . . .

He should have been at home watching over Baldwin Manor.

His heart heavy, Guy eased up from the table and he let his gaze roam the smoky cottage. An eerie sense of foreboding filled the air and his senses stood on guard.

Morna had predicted this strange little foal would lead him to the killer. He'd stop at nothing to keep the colt alive and in his possession. He hadn't expected to be so drawn to the horse midwife who assisted with the foal's birth and refused to let him go. Blessed saints. Why ever had he kissed her? Simon was right. Dangerous women always found him, or rather, he found *them*.

Regalo stirred, rousing Guy from his thoughts. The colt's lips parted with a little grunt and he squeaked. Then a second squeak followed the first, the next deeper. Guttural. The colt sat upright, his front legs extended, his hind legs crooked beneath him. His ears pricked forward and he swung his head around to stare at Guy as if to say *help me*.

Regalo barked. Once. Then again. His eyes rolled back in his head and he lifted his nose, continuing to bark, the eruptions interspersed with dog-like whines that sounded much like howls.

Hell to the devil. The colt was howling and barking like a dog.

Chapter Five

Guy stood unmoving, uncertain what to do. Sybilla bolted from the table, her eyes wide. "Mother Mary! I prayed he wouldn't do this. If anyone sees this, we'll be arrested. Me for witchcraft, him as my possessed familiar. I've no potion that would stop him—"

"Mayhap Morna does. She's been known to dabble," Guy interrupted as he bounded across the cottage, past the goat pen. Like a hawk taking flight, he leapt onto the ladder and climbed to the loft.

He flung aside the piles of fur and damask coverlets. The bed lay empty. Guy hurled his great body from the loft to the floor below. He hit the stones with his booted feet spread apart and his hand reaching for his sword.

He faced Sybilla, grabbed the cloak from the chair beside the fire, and tossed her the garment. "Put this on. We need to leave. Now!"

Simon staggered from his pallet, hopping on one foot while he pulled his boot onto the other. "The devil's arse. What's all the ruckus?" He stared open-mouthed at the barking Regalo. "Holy Mother. He thinks he's a dog."

Sybilla pulled the cloak around her shoulders. Her voice strained, she cried out to Guy, "Where's Lady Morna?"

Guy scooped up Regalo and slung the colt across his shoulders. "She's gone. Simon, get Bacchus and Addy and grab the nanny goat. Let's be off!"

Simon swore. "Damnation. 'Twas against my better judgment to trust a seer. Guy, you have the devil's knack for entanglement with problematic women!"

With Regalo on his back, Guy kicked the door open. He strode into the moonlit yard, mindful that Sybilla followed close behind him. Simon led Bacchus, Addy and the goat from the cottage.

In an instant, Guy caught a glimpse of movement in the trees. The sound of a horse's hooves crunching the snow. A single horse. Not ten. Not twenty.

He swore beneath his breath and glanced at Simon. "Bloody hell, at least she's come back alone."

Without another word, Simon lifted a startled Sybilla onto Addy. He hauled himself up on Bacchus and set the bleating goat in his lap.

Guy faced the approaching rider. Her red velvet hood fell back, revealing her full red lips, the dark, moon-shaped scar on her cheek in stark contrast against her pale skin.

"I'm sorry to have left my guests," she said, dismounting, swinging down from the saddle like a knight just come from battle. "I had urgent business to attend." She looked pointedly at Guy. "The widow Margery has spread the news about the birth of a colt with four white socks. The village is in a clamor. Lord Hamon wants the colt and has sent out a search party. His men are looking for you and Regalo. I could hear the colt barking a half a league away. Make haste to Baldwin Manor. Hamon's men will not ride onto your Lord Phillip's land."

Guy felt the blood drain from his face. Baldwin

Manor. His sister's home, now his, though he hadn't set foot on the place since her death. The house was abandoned and in disrepair, but it was the closest refuge, close enough to walk with a newborn foal on your back and soldiers on your tail and still have a chance.

Lady Morna pointed at Guy's velvet pouch, wet and muddied. "I'm glad you didn't lose it. I know how important it is to you." She tucked the bag into the waistband of his breeches.

He looked at Morna. Pity and regret stirred his heart. Her delicate face hadn't aged since they'd been lovers—years ago, before Hamon took her as his wife, then cast her off, claiming she'd been unfaithful and her gift of prophecy was the devil's work. Her bitter husband hated that she'd taken lovers, but truth be told, her greatest crime was failing to give him a child. He'd needed a reason to replace her, but one which wouldn't bring the question of his own infertility to light.

As if she'd read his mind, she laid her palm against his cheek, and stood on her tiptoes. She kissed him softly on the lips. *"Adieu*, Sir Guy. Don't feel sorry for me. I'll not forget the days we lay together in the meadow watching clouds while I tried to teach you French. Now go. Hamon's men are but an hour's ride from here. Another ice storm is on the way and the roads will soon be impassable. Get to your manor house while you can." She held her hand against his cheek, and Guy felt the wetness on the edge of her sleeve, where the color of her deep red gown had turned black with the moisture. *Blood.*

He sucked in his breath. God's breath. How she earned her living now, or whom she accepted as a patron was not for him to judge, but if she'd been ill-used by Hamon . . .

He clenched his fists. He wanted to take her hands in

his and tell her he would defend her from whatever danger she faced, but he was no longer certain he could protect anyone, not even the woman who once held his heart.

"Have you been hurt?"

"No. But Lord Hamon is badly wounded and in a rage. If he catches you, he'll take your colt and your life." Her voice trailed off and she glanced at Sybilla. "And he means to take the woman who will someday hold your heart." Regret lingered in her words. "Hamon put a price on her head, and you know as well as I, what he will do to a woman who's defied him." Her words fell away and she looked to the woods. "I had to go to him, Guy, to tend his wound. If he died, I could not survive out here."

Guy hissed through his teeth. Damnation. Hamon kept Morna prisoner as well as if he'd locked her in the tower. But he would not lay a hand on Sybilla Corbuc, not ever. Guy would chain her to his side to protect her if he had too. He'd kill the man with his bare hands if he so much as touched Sybilla Corbuc.

Morna turned and hurried toward the barn, her horse in tow. She called across her shoulder. "By the saints! Don't just stand there. Go!"

The blizzard's fury turned the early day into shades of gray and white. The path ahead appeared more like a sinking, snowbound gully than a road. With her legs wrapped around Addy's bony sides, Sybilla hunched against the piercing wind. The air smelled sharp and burned the inside of her nose, and she kept her eyes closed for long stretches at a time to shut out the stinging snow. Every now and then, her knee touched Simon's. He rode beside her, while Guy followed afoot with Regalo slung over his shoulders. He called out every few minutes to make certain she was still astride and not frozen. Simon sat silently on Bacchus, holding the goat close.

Addy barely moved now, the old horse's head bent low against the wind. She walked, but each step seemed weaker and slower than the last. Sybilla let her mind wander with the mare's plodding pace. She relived the warmth of Sir Guy's kiss, the way he slipped his arm around her waist and held her close. The way his mouth descended on hers, his lips so soft and supple.

By the saints, if Simon hadn't entered and interrupted their embrace would she have kissed him back? Or more?

Goosebumps rippled up her arms and neck. Sybilla tucked her chin into the deep hood of Guy's cloak. Blessed saints, Guy wore only his shirt and the snow-covered foal on his back was his only source of warmth. Simon looked as frozen as the goat in his lap. His beard and the goat's were both masks of snow.

Sybilla turned her head to speak to Simon. "How much farther? Sir Guy is cold and fatigued. He lags too far behind."

Snow fell from Simon's beard as he spoke. "It isn't far, Mistress Corbuc. Guy's used to the weather and is as strong as an ox. I've seen him haul a tree stump bigger than that foal when his family needed firewood. It's not the cold or the burden he carries that makes him slow."

"What is it, then?"

Simon glanced back at Guy, as if he wanted to make certain his friend wouldn't overhear. "Baldwin Manor was his sister's house. She and her infant son were murdered, nay slaughtered, not far from here. He can't abide this place, though it belongs to him. Sir Walter had no heirs, and King Richard bequeathed it to Guy as thanks for saving him at Balmont."

Sybilla shifted. A sudden surge of sympathy for Guy

swelled inside her. She swallowed. "Who would kill his sister and her babe and why?"

"Don't know. Marauders attacked at night. We were away, but en route home from fighting Richard's war."

"But Sir Guy must have some idea who did it."

Simon turned his head slowly. "Lord Hamon, though we have no proof."

Sybilla's heart twisted in her chest. "Lord Hamon? But why?" She leaned forward and pushed back her hood, heedless of the flurries. "Why would he?"

Simon glanced back again at his friend before he spoke. "Revenge. He discovered his wife, Lady Morna, proclaimed undying love for a poor knight, Sir Guy of Warwick. 'Twas more than a nobleman of his rank could stomach. The murders were meant as a message for Guy—to stay away from Morna." His voice faded, as if it pained him to speak about the subject further.

The wind that swirled around Sybilla made her dizzy. She grabbed Addy's withers to keep from falling.

Simon's mouth clamped shut and the muffled sound of snowy footsteps moved closer.

Guy's voice bellowed. "Simon, is the goat still breathing?"

Simon raised his finger to his lips, signaling to Sybilla to say nothing of their conversation. He turned and rested a hand on Bacchus' furry rump. "She is, my friend. And your house is just ahead."

Sybilla squinted. Through the snowfall, the two-story, buff-colored manor house appeared, complete with a steep snow-dusted roof. A cob half-wall surrounded a small inner yard, a horse barn, a dairy house and other buildings, all timber-framed with crumbling wattle and daub walls, and thatched roofs in bad need of repair.

She'd not expected such a grand, though neglected, place.

The nanny goat tucked beneath his arm, Simon drew Bacchus to a halt and dismounted. "Guy's fair sister caught the eye of an old but landed knight, Sir Walter. 'Twas his place. He took sick and died right 'afore we got home. Roselynn had just given birth a week before she was made a widow." He lowered his eyes. Snow covered his knees as he trod through the drifts, and wrestled with the hip gate that was hanging askew from a tilted fence post.

Sybilla couldn't take her eyes from the looming house with the tall, narrow windows, two on the ground floor, two on the second, and a chimney as wide as it was thick. The walls needed patching, as did the roof. But the chimney alone promised warmth, and the thought of comforting heat made her want to rush inside.

The goat bleated. Sybilla slid off Addy and patted the mare on the neck. The horse kept her eyes closed. She felt alarmingly stiff and cold beneath Sybilla's hand. The mare needed rest and shelter as much as did Regalo.

Simon hollered, "Guy, are you coming or not?" The goat squealed and squirmed in his arms. He set her down and she scampered close beside him, leaping through the snow as if she'd suddenly come back to life.

Guy didn't answer.

Sybilla turned around. Guy stood fifty paces back, staring at the house, his face as cold and dispassionate as the wind. Regalo lifted his head and, for the first time in hours, he pricked his ears.

Simon took Addy's reins from Sybilla's hands. "Go inside and warm yerself, Mistress Corbuc." He led Bacchus and the mare toward the barn. "I'll put the animals up and get them fed. If the old steward, Dunback, is still here, send him out to help me, though I'll bet he's lost what was left of his wits." He stopped and watched Guy moving through the snow, his approach reluctant and stalling.

Simon took a deep breath. He whispered, "I never seen a man rage like Guy did the night we found the bodies, not even in the pitch of battle. I'll not forget the way Guy broke down when he found his sister and her babe lying in the dirt not far from here, God keep them. Or the way he cradled the lifeless body of his little nephew in his arms and cried. He blames himself for their deaths."

The private look Simon gave Sybilla made her heart ache. Sir Guy of Warwick, a hulk of a man, didn't seem like the kind of man to cry.

The snowfall faded for a moment, and Sybilla watched Guy's back straighten as he approached the gates. He walked toward the house like a man walking into his own private hell—with the sick foal on his back.

She picked up her snow-soaked skirts and fell silently in beside him.

Guy's deep voice rang out. "Could I have avoided bringing you and Regalo to this house, I would have." With his hand on his sword hilt and the other wrapped around Regalo's ankles, he pushed the door open with his foot and stepped across the threshold. He scanned the long dark hallway. "This place reeks of death."

A sliver of light slipped through a crack between the wooden doors that opened into the great hall. Guy's footsteps trod down the hallway, across the familiar glazed green and yellow tiles. His shadow tracked him, moving along thick stone walls, walls devoid now of the tapestries and flax sconces that once lit the place with color and with warmth. The cold air that filled the space smelled lifeless and stale, like the air inside a cathedral during a funeral mass. Guy motioned for Sybilla to follow, glad that the low light would keep anyone from noticing the sweat on his upper lip.

He pointed to the half-eaten bowl of pottage sitting on a long trestle table. "Looks like Dunback is still here. Somewhere." The same beaten long table, serviceable and once of good quality, sat where it always had, in the center of the room. But the hearth that stretched across the east end of the room was filled with broken furniture. A small fire radiated from the fireplace and its golden light looked inviting, despite the source.

Guy set Regalo down beside the fire. The remnants of Roselynn's spinning wheel crackled in the flames, the wooden spokes sticking up like charred fingers.

He swallowed, clenched his fists to keep dragging out what had once been her most prized possession. She'd been sitting by the fire spinning when he'd come to say goodbye. A one-eared yellow kitten at her feet batted at a ball of wool.

"Be careful, Guy," his sister told him, setting her work aside. Then she threw her arms around him, her tears wetting the neckline of his tunic. "Mayhap when you return, you'll have niece or little nephew to tell of your heroics, God willing," she blurted out in a voice she barely managed to control. "Sir Walter and I . . . we'll need your help with the harvest."

Guy knew they didn't need his help. The farm thrived and, even without him, they would do well. He'd made certain of it by recruiting the strongest men from the village, and the hardest workers. Sir Walter paid them well in shares of the crops and in beer.

Guy had kissed her on the top of her head and reassured her King Richard would have the French well beaten by mid-summer.

But he did not return until November—eight years later. Too late for Roselynn and her son.

He closed his eyes. Self-loathing filled his empty soul. He relished the stiffness and strain in his back from carrying Regalo. It distracted him from the pain in his heart.

He leaned on his sword and rubbed his forehead.

Sybilla took the wineskin filled with goat's milk from her shoulder and offered Regalo a drink. He consumed what was left with vigor. Having sucked the wineskin dry, the colt promptly curled up like a hound just returned from a satisfying hunt, and slept.

The front door flung open and banged against the stone wall.

Simon strode in holding Dunback by the scruff of the neck. The old toothless man grinned and stared through glazed eyes.

Simon released the old man. "Look who I found in your cellar, Guy. The man who's supposed to be guarding your reserves, not drinking them."

Dunback smiled apologetically. He stumbled forward, his patched and dirtied woolen tunic reeking with the smell of soured wine. "Welcome home, my lord. We've missed you." He bowed and almost lost his balance as he glanced at the foal sleeping by the fire.

Guy helped the man to his feet. "We? Who in God's name is here besides you?"

A blank look crossed Dunback's hollow face. His foggy eyes lit up with something quite akin to madness. "Why the Lady Roselynn, and her little babe, sir. We've been waiting for you. And the new reeve needs your help. The fields need threshin'."

Every nerve in Guy's skin fired at once, every muscle in his body tensed. Holy Mother, the man was as dolt-witted as a loon. Worse than he was five months ago, when Guy found him cowering in the woods, terrified and ashamed that he'd escaped and survived the night of the murders, when his Lady Roselynn and the baby John had not.

The white-haired, frail-looking steward belched and tittered.

Guy shook his head. This was the man he'd left accountable for running Baldwin Manor in the months after Roselynn's death? 'Twould seem Dunback, once capable and honest, had done little more than drink himself into a stupor while he hid from winter's grip and talked with private ghosts.

Guy searched his soul for patience. The last time Dunback had been questioned about that night, he'd collapsed into a rambling fit and begged for his life. The agony of having one who knew the answers but who could not reveal them, set Guy's blood coursing.

He ran his hand through his hair. The last of his sister's spinning wheel caught fire and collapsed into the ashes.

Sybilla stepped back from the hearth, her eyes wide and worried. She sent Guy what he guessed was a silent plea for compassion.

Guy folded his arms. No sense in harboring ill will toward a mindless old man whose days were numbered, judging by the redness of his nose and the jaundiced pallor of his cheeks. "I must thank you, Dunback, for watching over the place in my absence. Where have you been sleeping? Upstairs?"

"No, sir! You know the Lady Roselynn and her babe sleep up there. I've made my pallet here, sir, where you used to sleep, right here by the fire." He lowered his bleary eyes and wrung his hands. "I only burned what I needed to stay warm," he continued, as if he still had wits enough to know he'd be reprimanded for using furniture for kindling.

He limped over to the foal. "How 'bout I watch him for you? We'll keep each other warm." He patted Regalo on the rump, as if there was nothing odd at all about a foal sleeping hearthside in the great hall. Dunback stretched out beside him and rested his head on the colt's withers.

Sybilla smiled.

Simon pulled the cork from the wine. "Before you leave us for your drunken dreams, where's the food?"

Dunback interlaced his fingers and rested his hands on his chest. "A good hunk of bread, pottage and a little wine is all I need. But I reckon you'll be hungry after fighting for the king. There be dried eel out in the kitchen if you want some. But no eggs. I ate the chickens." He closed his eyelids and his eyes sank deep into their sockets. Mouth open, he snored.

Guy picked his cloak from the floor and tossed it over the old man and the foal. "Simon, we've yet to break our fast. Would you—"

"Get the food? Anything else?" He shot a beleaguered glance at Sybilla, as if to say *please release me from my duties*.

Sybilla averted her eyes, avoiding contact with Guy's. "I'll help. Which way to the kitchen?"

Without waiting for an answer, she started toward the great door.

Guy caught her by the wrist. "Oh, no you don't. It's blizzarding outside and you're already wet and cold. If you catch lung fever, who'll take care of him?" He pointed at Regalo. "Simon knows where the kitchen is. You and I can search for dry clothes and blankets."

Simon pulled his hood up and stomped from the hall. "I'll be back soon. If I'm not, come find me."

Guy lifted a tallow torch and held the cobwebbed rushes to the fire. Raising the smoky light high, he headed for the narrow spiral stairway at the end of the room. "This way, Mistress Corbuc."

He kept his back to Sybilla and paused at the foot of the stairs. Looking up, he gripped the staircase railing with his cold-stiffened hand. At the top of the landing was the private apartment once occupied by his good-hearted sister, her doting, aged husband, and a cantankerous one-eared kitten. The thought of their laughter, the warmth and light that once graced the darkened room made his head hurt.

A shadowy form, ephemeral, feminine and sad, suddenly floated across the landing and disappeared through the door that led into the chambers.

Sweat trickled down the back of Guy's neck. God in heaven, Roselynn's ghost is here—just like Dunback said.

Guy swore an oath beneath his breath. He should leave this place. No need to confront the past. He'd no fear of Roselynn's ghost, but he'd no need to invite the memories back. He glanced over his shoulder. Mistress Corbuc was still there, waiting. If she'd seen Roselynn's specter, she said naught of it.

Guy put one foot on the first step. Then he halted.

Chapter Six

Sybilla's soft voice echoed from behind him. "Is something wrong, Sir Guy?"

Guy's stomach rolled. He was no coward. Hell to the devil if he'd let Sybilla Corbuc know the room upstairs was anything to him other than a sleeping chamber.

"No," he answered, faster than he meant to. He didn't fear Roselynn's ghost, just the aching grief that filled his soul whenever she appeared.

Bracing himself, he pounded up the stairs, every footstep slamming down. The wooden risers creaked and groaned beneath his weight.

Guy flung the door aside and stepped into the chamber.

The faint scent of herbs hung in the air. He stooped as he crossed the threshold, though he could not recall having to duck when he entered this room before. The low, painted ceiling and oaken wall paneling made the room feel smaller than he remembered.

He took Sybilla by the hand and drew her across the threshold, holding the torch high to light the room.

A draft of cold air wafted from the large stone fireplace to his left; its hearth reached from the floor to the ceiling, the opening as big as a giant's gaping mouth. The rope bed, covered with dusty furs, looked as though it had not been disturbed. Roselynn's wooden chest still sat beneath the window and the family's wooden tub, still lined with a swath of cloth, was lying on its side in front of the hearth. Roselynn's green woolen slippers lay beside the bed, as if she had just kicked off her shoes and intended to come right back.

A lump the size of a peach pit formed in Guy's throat.

Sybilla stepped beside him. "'Tis a fine room, Sir Guy. Warm in the winter, I should think, when there's a fire."

He took a deep, bracing breath. Though words escaped him, the memories assaulted like arrows raining down, threatening to pierce the armor which encased his heart.

Aye, 'twas warm enough. And in the summertime the ribbons Roselynn tied to the shutters danced in the cooling breeze and made her kitten play.

Guy took a deep breath. He strode across the room, shoved the torch into the wall sconce. He knelt beside the chest. "Something in here should fit you, Mistress Corbuc." The lid to the chest banged open.

He rummaged through the contents and produced a green woolen gown and a yellow underdress. He held up a linen chemise, a pair of woman's woolen hose, and black ribbon garters.

He lowered the lid. "Take these." He dumped the clothes into Sybilla's arms.

Sybilla stared at the clothes. "These were your sister's?"

Guy drew his eyebrows together. "She's dead, Mistress Corbuc. What does it matter?"

He brushed past her and pounded down the stairs, the air in the little room too thin to breathe.

* * *

Sybilla bit her lip. The Lady Roselynn's clothes were rich and well-made. 'Twas generous of Guy and she'd meant to thank him, but he'd stormed out in a huff before she'd had the chance.

She ran her hand over the soft wool dress and traced her finger round the neckline of the fine linen chemise. Once a year she'd been given new clothes by her mother, the quality and the cut of the cloth inferior to these, but they'd been new and just as clean.

She rubbed her cheeks, hoping to scrub off some of the dirt. She was embarrassed by her filth, the tangled mess of hair that dangled to her waist, and the holes in her stockings. She sat down on the bed.

She'd been poor for nigh on a year now, destitute, worse off than most servants. She wasn't ungrateful for the offer of the dead woman's clothes, it just made her uneasy knowing Roselynn may have died at Lord Hamon's hand—it seemed unfair that his bastard daughter should have the victim's clothes.

The door banged open, and in stomped Guy with an armful of broken furniture. "I'll start a fire. After supper I'll heat the water for our bath. I smell like a horse and you could use a scrubbing."

At the reference to her hygiene, Sybilla's cheeks grew warm. She'd bathed once or twice a year, but never more. No one had ever suggested that she needed to. And surely Sir Guy didn't intend they bathe together? She'd bathed in the river with the other women from the village, but never with a man. No good could come of that.

Bathing—another reason she must find a way out of their agreement.

She tossed the Lady Roselynn's garments in a heap on the bed. "Sir Guy, I will not—"

She halted, startled by the sound that rose up from the hall below. The noise was not the iron hinges on the chamber door creaking, but rather the sound of Regalo barking.

Guy spun on his heels, bounded out of the room and down the stairs.

Sybilla clambered after him, her heart beating like a drum.

Dunback clapped his hands over his ears and ran in circles round the table. "Make him stop! Make him stop." He leapt at Guy, threw his arms around Guy's legs and hung on, cowering. "'Tis the devil's horse come ta take me. Please, my lord. Don't let him."

Sybilla hurried down the stairs to see Regalo standing, staring up at the narrow window. The light from the midday sun filtered down through gaps in the clouds, shining on his big head—a head that looked a good deal bigger than it had when he was born. Mother Mary, the colt looked like he'd grown all over, and added at least three inches in height while he slept.

The wind howled and Regalo howled with it. His mournful wail was punctuated by sharp barks as he sat on his haunches and looked at her, his dark eyes penetrating and pleading.

Guy shook Dunback from his leg and set the man upright. "No need to fear the colt. He's just hungry."

Dunback buried his face in his withered hands.

Sybilla stared at Regalo. *God in heaven, what had set him off?*

She scooped the wineskin from the hearth floor. The

foal stumbled forward. He sat on his haunches at her feet, but he didn't raise his muzzle to the milk. He blinked, the look in his eyes forlorn and lost. She stroked his curly ears.

In three months time, Regalo, I'll be free to leave. I'll work to buy you back from Guy and you'll belong to me.

Regalo howled. He swayed, and then collapsed, limp as a wet rag, onto the stone pavers at her feet.

Alarmed, Sybilla dropped to her knees. Regalo barked and his head writhed from side to the side, his eyelids twitching. When the symptoms subsided, he lay there panting, so weak his scarlet tongue hung from his mouth like a dead fish.

Mother Mary, it seemed as if every time she thought about parting company with Sir Guy, Regalo worsened. Could her thoughts of leaving have been what set him off? Surely not. The little beast could not read her mind.

The door to the hall thundered open and Simon marched in, his cheeks bright red, snow melting in his bushy hair. With a small rucksack over his shoulder and the goat on a leash behind him, he stopped and stared at Regalo. "Another relapse?" He frowned and dumped the rucksack onto the table. "Stopped by the barn to get our supper and Regalo's." He drew the goat to his side and untied her. He gave her a gentle push. The goat wandered to Sybilla and sniffed her skirts before he settled down beside Regalo at the hearth.

Guy ran his hands through his hair. He tipped his head and stared at Sybilla, his eyes questioning. "What's set Regalo off, Mistress Sybilla? Have you any idea? It seems like he's regressing, not getting better."

Sybilla lowered her eyes. It was impossible the foal could be responding to her thoughts. Mayhap her brain was muddled by the cold. "I don't know, Sir Guy. I honestly don't know."

Simon pointed to the sack on the table. "Found a little pickled eel, a cheese, and some prunes. And Dunback missed a few crocks of last year's wine."

Guy poked the fire. "We leave tomorrow. Ketchem Castle is more to my liking." He leaned his head from side to side and rolled his shoulders. The bones in his back crackled. "Damnation, the little beast was heavy. I think he grew a stone while I carried him."

He strode to the table, tore off a piece of cheese, and handed the morsel to Sybilla. "Eat, Mistress. I'll make a fire upstairs and heat some water. I'm ready for a bath and bed."

The cheese stuck in Sybilla's throat. Mother Mary, did he intend they bathe *and* sleep together?

By the time the moon was high and the snow had turned to sleeting ice, Sybilla had eaten two prunes and a thick slice of cheese. Guy had returned from the upstairs chambers an hour ago and he sat on a stool beside the fire in the hall and stared at the flames, speaking to no one, rarely moving except to add snow to a cauldron of boiling water.

Dunback busied himself scooping up Regalo's and the goat's droppings, and tossing them into the fire. Sybilla passed the time coaxing the goat to stand on a wooden chest to let Regalo nurse. There'd been no more barking from the colt since he'd eaten, and now he slept peacefully with the goat curled up beside him.

Guy rose from the stool. "Mistress Corbuc, the water's ready and there's more warming in the hearth upstairs. We've enough to fill the tub." He poured the water from the cauldron into buckets, the steam dampening his cheeks and hair. He motioned for her to follow him.

"You and I will sleep upstairs tonight. Simon, Dunback, and Regalo can make their pallets here." He motioned for her to follow.

Sybilla hesitated. She caught a glimpse of Simon. He set his cup down and mouthed the words, *don't worry.* He settled down on a pile of furs next to Dunback.

Guy's booted feet thudded against the floor. "Mistress Corbuc, make haste while the water is still hot."

Sybilla followed Guy up the stairs and into the small private bedroom. A fire crackled in the fireplace. The room glowed with golden light—and the heat from the hearth made her suddenly aware of the closeness of the quarters—of Guy's nearness.

Her gaze focused on his strong arms and the ripping muscles that strained beneath his shirt, he poured the steaming buckets of water into the wooden bathing tub.

"There's a brush for scrubbing and a drying cloth in Roselynn's chest. Can you get them?" he asked quietly.

Sybilla took a deep breath. She couldn't help it, but he was so unlike any man she'd known, strong, made of solid muscle, and at the same time gentle. Mother Mary, he'd kissed her and made feel things that sparked her curiosity.

"Mistress Corbuc?" Sir Guy set the buckets down and looked at her, his face puzzled, as if he wondered what she'd been thinking.

A warm blush rushed up Sybilla's neck. Silently, she turned and knelt to rummage through the chest. Mother Mary, she wasn't born to be a servant.

Brush and towel in hand, she spun around to face Sir Guy, to tell him she would go back downstairs as soon as—

She froze in place.

God's eyes.

Sir Guy of Warwick was naked.

He was standing in the tub and staring at her, with his long arms hanging at his sides, his powerful legs slightly parted—and there between them, nestled in a matt of thick dark hair, lay his . . .

Oh my.

Sybilla felt the heat rise to her cheeks.

God had certainly blessed Sir Guy of Warwick.

Even though he'd shed his clothes, the blazing fire in the hearth and the steam from the tub made the room feel like a roasting pit.

Guy's gaze moved to Sybilla. Damnation she was a comely woman. He could feel his cock growing just at the thought of her. She stood there, holding the brush and drying towel in her hands, her pink lips slightly parted, her wide blue eyes staring at him as if he'd grown horns. A flush of pink colored her cheeks and long neck.

He cocked an eyebrow. "Is something wrong?"

She shook her head, but kept looking at his groin, her eyes wide.

Hell to the devil.

Irritated with himself, Guy sat down in the tub and nonchalantly used his hands to spoon water into his armpits and down his chest, hoping to distract her. "Mistress Corbuc, my back needs scrubbing," he said, his tone casual. He sincerely hoped she would be willing to do what he asked. His cock throbbed from a different kind of hurt, but his back and shoulders ached from carrying the colt.

He leaned forward. "My back, please, Mistress Corbuc."

Sybilla averted her eyes. "I-I . . . I would rather not."

He splashed water over his face, pushed his hair off

his forehead. "We have an agreement," he said, reining in his disappointment. "You are my servant."

"I am. But you are, er, aroused . . . and I am, er, distracted."

Guy closed his eyes and let out a slow breath. God in heaven, he'd not planned on having an erection, he merely wanted a bath. But when he saw her standing there, looking at him and when her tongue had lightly touched her lips, 'twas enough to light the fire in any man. He had the urge to kiss her again, his loins driving him to think about doing things to Sybilla she would not understand, and may not want. By the saints, he'd keep those thoughts in check, however much it pained him. He'd promised her he would not take her virtue.

"I am sorry, Mistress Corbuc, if I've put you off. At Ketchem Castle there will be little privacy. You cannot be so modest. I suspect you've seen a man's ready shaft before, but I promise not to—"

Her fingers suddenly came to rest against his back, slipping over his wet skin, massaging, soothing out the cords of tension. The warmth of her hands lulled him into a place he'd rarely ventured in the last year, made him think about companionship, about the home he longed for, about lust and love . . .

He leaned his head back and kept his eyes closed, letting her hands work their magic over his shoulders. He needed this, her touch, her gentle spirit, and the kind of comfort only she could offer. God's bones, what was it about this woman that made him ache for her? He should warn her how much she tempted him, and how at times he thought to never let her go.

"Mistress Corbuc," he said, his voice husky as he turned his head to face her. "We should not let this go fur—"

In an instant her lips covered his. She kissed him, tentative at first, then bolder, exploring. Her hands slid down the front of his chest, her fingers awkward and unsure, but skimming lower.

His heart jumped. Christ's bones!

He gripped her face between his hands.

"Sybilla," he muttered against her cheek, breaking off her kiss. "Do not do this. I vowed I would not take your virtue. You are making it too hard to keep that promise."

Sybilla stared at him, her eyes filled with passion. She held her fingers to her mouth as if she couldn't believe what she'd just done.

She lowered her eyes, the rise and fall of her chest as rapid as his own. "I'm sorry."

Rising, Guy wrapped the towel around his waist, though his rod stood at full attention. He took a deep breath. "I should not have pressed you to rub my back." He stepped from the tub, the movement stiff and halting. "I'll get dressed. Your turn to get in."

He shook the water from his hair and handed her the scrubbing brush.

Sybilla folded her arms, hugging her chest. "I think it would be unwise for me disrobe in front of you, Sir Guy," she said with a shaky voice. "You kissed me, and now I—"

Guy suppressed a grin. He whipped the towel from his waist and rubbed his wet hair. "Really?" he said, turning to hide his amusement. *"I* kissed you? 'Tis not my recollection of what just happened."

She didn't answer and the only sound in the room was that of her breathing, hard. "We see things differently then. Still, I should like it if you leave me to bathe alone."

Guy tossed the towel on the bed. If his shaft stood upright, to hell with trying to hide it. He was a man and the thought of Sybilla unclothed, of her sweet smelling skin, clean and warm from the bath, was more than he could bear. By the devil, he'd not had a woman in months, and the maidenly Sybilla Corbuc, virtuous but willing in spirit, tempted him beyond reason. But he would not take her virtue. Look what happened the last time he'd yielded to his lust. His passion had grown to caring. His caring had grown to love—and that had cost him dearly.

God in heaven, he'd paid too dear a price for love. Sybilla Corbuc would not be another Hamon victim because Guy of Warwick had bedded her.

The walls of the chamber suddenly closed around him like a tomb.

Sybilla shifted from one foot to the other. "Will you please leave?" she asked, her tone unsure despite her request.

Her green eyes filled with smoldering passion, and in an instant, he understood that though she asked him to leave, to do the right thing for the both of them, her body had betrayed her.

Guy raked his fingers through his hair. God's bones, he needed to get out. Now.

He spun on his heels and marched to the door. His back held straight, he ignored the cold air against his bare arse and he flung the door open.

"Mais oui. Simon! Save some wine!"

The devil take his nakedness. He hoped the hall was freezing, cold enough to douse his desire and to make him forget about Sybilla Corbuc.

Sybilla hurriedly peeled off her old blue dress, her shift, and her filthy hose. She shivered, in part from the cold, in part from unfulfilled desire.

She sank into the tepid water and drew her knees to

her chest to let the water wash away the lingering warmth between her legs.

St. Genevieve, forgive me for the kiss.

The kiss had been an accident. She'd not meant to do it, but when Guy had turned to face her, his mouth so near, she found him irresistible and all too close. Wanting flooded her brain and turned her resolve to mush.

She dunked her head into the water to cool her cheeks while she scrubbed her hair. Mother Mary, she was grateful Guy had left. She couldn't trust herself not to act on these feelings.

Stepping from the tub, her knees shook as she wrapped the towel around her. She tossed her old blue dress and shift into the water, remembering Sir Guy of Warwick had called her filthy on the night they met. She rarely washed her clothes, because everyone knew the more you washed them, the worse for wear they looked. But for reasons she could not explain, what Guy thought about her cleanliness was suddenly important.

Sybilla gritted her teeth and wrung the water out of her clothes. Her toeless, heelless hose were ready for the rag pile, and the pain of her poverty made her wince.

She grabbed Lady Roselynn's fine white chemise and pulled the garment over her head. Soft and almost seamless, the fine linen fabric skimmed across her skin. She added the yellow underdress and laced the sides. Donning the wide-sleeved, sideless green overdress, the gown landed at her feet with a puff, the weight of the fabric enclosing her legs.

Sumptuous warmth enveloped her, a warmth that smelled of lavender and thyme. She eased onto the edge of the bed and slipped her feet into the umber-colored hose. The softness of the wool should have been reserved for angels' feet.

By the saints, she was no angel when it came to Guy of Warwick. The man made her want to know things, experience the kinds of things she knew happened when a man took his wife to bed. But that kind of exploration might leave her with a babe in her belly, and then where would she be? Knights rarely married beneath their station, and if they did they sought out merchants' daughters or widows who were rich.

"Heaven help me," Sybilla muttered to herself as she tied her stockings up with the black satin garters. "I cannot fall in love with Sir Guy of Warwick. Nothing good could come of that."

She rose from the bed, smoothed her gown, and glanced into the tub of water to see her reflection.

She didn't look at all like Sybilla Corbuc, the horse midwife from Cornbury. Dressed like this, she could be mistaken for a court lady, like the one she'd seen traveling in a painted litter, escorted by her knights-in-service who rode beside her on horses bedecked with saddle cloths in brilliant reds and greens.

Her eyes came to rest on her old wooden shoes. Crudely cut and splintered, they were worn at the heels and cracked. Hardly the kind of shoe a lady dressed in a gown of green and gold would wear. No, a lady would have patens and fine green woolen slippers—like the pair that beckoned from beneath the bed.

Sybilla took a deep breath. The clothes on her back were borrowed. They met a need. But she'd no right to wear the slippers. Guy had not given *them* to her.

She shoved her feet into her clogs and ran her fingers through her damp hair. Damnation, the color, as gold as flax when it was wet, reminded her of Lord Hamon's. Would that she'd been born as dark and as lovely as her mother—who'd had a love match with her husband, despite his failings, despite Lord Hamon's claim to *droit du seigneur*. Sybilla would never overcome her secret shame. She'd be Lord Hamon's bastard daughter, even if she were dressed like a queen. Now, adding to the insult, she was a servant.

She straightened, reminding herself this was a temporary turn of fortune.

I will survive. In just three months, I'll be free to go. I'll take Regalo with me, steal him if I have to, but I will find a way to recover what's been taken from me.

She flung the door open, fearing what she'd find in the hall below. Regalo yipping and a cold, naked knight who'd left his bath too early.

The fire blazed, warming Guy's face and feet to the point of roasting. He flung his cloak aside and took another drink, the wine thick and muddy. It'd been stored too long and kept in the wrong kind of barrel. Birchwood, he supposed, instead of oak. It tasted slightly burnt.

But it didn't matter. He needed a strong drink. Wine helped dull the cold while he waited for Sybilla to get dressed. With every moment he passed in this house, the wound in his conscience opened wider. God in heaven, he'd seen Roselynn's apparition. A sure sign her spirit was as discontent as his.

Let me just get through the night, and we can leave on the morrow.

He finished the dregs in his cup and pulled his cloak back around him. His bath forgotten, his gaze drifted to the window, where sleet spat against the single pane of leaded glass. Frozen roads would make travel impossible, especially with a sickly foal, an old mare and Mistress

Corbuc slowing him and Simon down. But neither could he use the delay to rest. Not here.

He leaned his head back and pinched the bridge of his nose. *Saint Crista, don't send the nightmares tonight. I need to sleep.*

He turned his aching head toward Simon and Dunback, his neck and shoulders as tight as ropes. The two men snored, and every now and then Dunback babbled and fondled the goat, mistaking her it seemed, for Neda, the affable cook who was once in charge of Baldwin's kitchen. No telling where Neda was now. Probably ran off like the woodsman, the brewing maids, and the rest of his vassals. With no Lord of the Manor to collect a tillage, there was no need to attend to their master's demesne.

The wine clouding his thoughts, Guy watched Regalo wander around the hall suckling anything he could get his lips on: the handles on the cupboard, the table corners, the remnants of the rope that once lowered the candled chandelier. The odd colt couldn't tell the goat from a maypole, and twice Guy had shooed him from the foyer, where the poke-brained little beast suckled on the iron latch to the front door. The only thing he seemed to recognize or care about was Sybilla.

No wonder.

Sybilla Corbuc had not been far from *his* thoughts either, not since the moment he'd met her. Beneath the beggar's clothes and dirt he'd seen the face of an angel with searing green eyes, and a pale pink mouth that made him want to kiss her.

He grunted. The thought of her standing in the tub, fully clothed but soaking wet and glaring at him, almost made him laugh.

Almost.

The door to the upstairs chambers swung open hard, jolting Guy from his thoughts—frightening Regalo, or so it seemed, for he jumped, and started that infernal barking.

Guy sat upright, his attention captured by the fair Sybilla, a vision who descended down the staircase, accompanied by the music of Regalo's barking.

Dressed in green and gold, Sybilla seemed unaware how her honey-colored hair, now clean and shining, floated over her shoulders. Her young face solemn, she moved in Roselynn's clothes as though she'd been born to wear them. But where Roselynn had been darkly handsome, her figure soft and rounded, Sybilla was fair, her form statuesque and very slim. Her old clogs tapping on the stairs were the only clue she was not a highborn lady.

Guy cared not what she was at this moment, only that he longed to keep her near him. He pulled his cloak to cover his groin, his shaft as hard as bone.

Simon sat upright and rubbed his eyes. "Mother of St. Marcus, will the beast ever stop that?"

Dunback sat up and grabbed his pewter cup, waving it around like a weapon. "I'll silence the little bugger. One good whack on the noggin should do the trick." Dunback stirred as if to rise, wielding the cup over his head like a mace.

Simon dodged his weapon and caught Dunback by the back of the neck. "Put that down, you old fool, before you hurt someone."

The colt lay down at the bottom of the stairs. His eyes rolled back into his head and he smacked his lips, barked. He went completely still.

Guy bounded across the room. He knelt beside the colt and placed a hand on the foal's chest, feeling his heartbeat jumping beneath his tiny ribs.

"Peace, peace, little one." He stroked the foal's long white forehead with his other hand.

Sybilla knelt beside the foal and ran her hand along his neck. Her eyes glittered with tears and she bit down on her lower lip.

Guy lowered Regalo's head back down. "Tell me, Sybilla, why he does this? Do you know?"

"I was thinking . . ."

"What?"

Sybilla wiped her eyes with the heel of her hand. "Just thinking how I've nothing that's my own. I was thinking about the day I could leave your employ and work to earn coin to buy back Regalo."

Guy stood slowly, pulling his cloak around him. "Every time you contemplate the end of your time with me, or buying back the colt, he has a fit?"

Sybilla nodded. She looked up at Guy, her green eyes glittering with anger. "I know you said you wouldn't sell him, but I find it hard to give him up. I wasn't born to be a servant, even a temporary one. I planned to raise him, somehow."

Guy felt a twinge of guilt. But he'd not give an inch on their agreement. He was fighting, too, for something he desperately wanted. Revenge. But he also wanted Sybilla Corbuc. Mayhap she would come to like him, just a little.

"Our agreement stands, Mistress Corbuc," he said, softly. "Regalo is mine and you are honor bound to be my servant for the next three months. Mayhap after that, I could convince you to stay and help me train the colt to the saddle?"

As quickly as Regalo had collapsed, he got up and wandered to the table where the goat had taken refuge from old Dunback. Regalo nursed, taking two or three long swallows. He settled down on the floor and closed his eyes.

Sybilla spoke in a low voice. "I want my colt back, Sir Guy."

Guy let out a long breath and shook his head. "It cannot be, Mistress Corbuc." He strode across the room to the staircase. "Now come. I'm for bed. We will leave here tomorrow. Tonight you can sleep on a pallet beside the hearth." He held out his hand.

Sybilla didn't move. "On the floor, at your feet. Where a servant should?"

Guy lowered his outstretched hand and set one foot on the first riser. "You will not stay down here," he said softly. "It isn't safe. And yes, you may sleep on the floor on a pallet, unless you would rather sleep in the bed with me?"

Sybilla bit her lip. "No. I couldn't—"

"I thought not." He motioned to Sybilla to follow him up the stairs. "Make haste, mistress. Simon, look after Regalo. Don't let him out of your sight."

Simon moaned. Dunback cackled.

Chapter Seven

Guy shrugged his cloak from his shoulders and flung it on the bed. Sybilla pressed her back against the door, her hands gripping the folds of her gown.

Seeing him like this, gloriously male, earthy, and unadorned, and knowing that they were alone, made her heart beat faster.

The room suddenly grew quiet. He stood motionless and with every breath, the rise and fall of his chest quickened. His eyes locked with hers. His mouth stayed firm, but still sensual and strangely alluring. She did not look away though his gaze burned into her soul and made warmth spread from her belly to her fingertips and toes.

Time stopped and for a moment, Sybilla wondered what it would be like to shed her fine dress and slip inbetween the coverlets with him, to take in his scent, feel the warmth of his skin.

"Sybilla, I . . ." His voice trailed away. He spun around, breathing hard. "I'll don a nightshirt." He flung open the chest.

By the saints, he'd called her by her given name. 'Twas

the first time he addressed her as such, but afterall, 'twas appropriate for a servant.

Hesitant, Sybilla stepped away from the door. "Sir Guy, mayhap it 'twould be better if I slept downstairs. It's warm there by the fire. You can have the chambers to yourself."

Guy frowned, as if staying alone was the last thing he wanted to do. "You are safest here with me. Hamon's men search for us. I can best protect you if you are close."

"What about Regalo?"

Guy frowned. "Simon can take care of him. Hamon's men want you just as much, mayhap even more."

Sybilla's hands grew cold. She was used to watching out for herself at night. But common thieves and drunken villagers were one thing, raiding knights from Hamon Castle were another.

"Hamon hates you," he offered as further explanation. "You insulted him in front of his men and you are a reminder of his failure to sire an heir." Guy added softly, "And now, because you are with me."

She lowered herself onto her pallet beside the fire. "Why should he care if I'm with you?"

Guy eased down to the bed. "Because I loved his wife once, and she loved me. He will kill any woman he believes I care for."

Sybilla's throat tightened. "How could you care about me? We barely know each other."

Guy lay back on the bed and stared at the ceiling. What seemed like minutes passed before he let out a slow breath. "I cannot explain it, but I care about you. More than I expected."

He closed his eyes and exhaled, as if he braced for her rebuff.

Sybilla looked away. To hear his admission touched

her soul and she knew not how to respond. This knight had saved her life and her colt's, and he was man of honor, respected by his friends, loved by his family, and revered by his king. How could she not care for Guy of Warwick?

Sybilla took a deep breath. "I, too, am surprised, Sir Guy. I feel for you much more than *I* expected," she whispered.

Guy rolled on his side, hoping he still might convince her to join him on his cot. Sybilla had already closed her eyes and pulled the covers to her chin. A strand of golden hair resting at the corner of her mouth fluttered as she breathed. By Saint Crista, he found it hard to resist a fair-faced woman, but this one in particular stirred more than his passing interest. A fiery spirit, innocent and intemperate, she'd stirred a need he'd long suppressed, though it pained him to admit it.

Guy threw the covers off, the room suddenly too warm. Guilt crept upon him most often late at night, as it did now, even though the lovely Sybilla slept on the floor beside him.

He sat on the edge of the bed and held his head between his hands. Sybilla wasn't truly resting. Beneath the furs her shoulders shook and she mumbled to herself. Silently, he moved to her side and gently lifted her to his bed. He crawled in beside her and settled close, her body warm and soft.

She stopped trembling and and rested her smooth cheek against his chest. Guy closed his eyes, taking in her feminine scent and warmth. He felt the tension melt from his shoulders and his heartbeat slow.

For the first time in weeks, real sleep threatened to steal his consciousness. He forced his eyes open and shook the fog from his head. His quest for vengeance would be first on his mind and always ruled his thoughts. He'd made sure of that.

As long as he didn't sleep, he knew he could keep Sybilla Corbuc from his mind—and his heart.

With the last of the morning's kindling on her hip, Sybilla stood beside the arched hearth in the great hall and fed the fire. White smoke billowed, carrying last night's ashes and most of the heat up the flue.

She'd awakened this morning surprised by Guy's whiskered cheek in the hollow of her neck. She'd no recollection of how she'd gotten into his bed. But he'd kicked off his covers, rolled onto his side, and thrown his arm across her chest. She'd lain there for hours, listening to him breathe, allowing herself the luxury of his warmth, his strength and the intimacy of his slumbering embrace. When at last she forced herself to rise, she did so with regret, the kind of regret one feels when one awakens too soon from a wonderful dream. Reluctantly, she'd pushed his arm aside and slipped from the bed.

Regalo needed tending. She needed to think. Alone. 'Twas a good excuse to rise and start the day.

The colt met her at the foot of the stairs. He looked like he'd grown still another stone overnight, and yet his eyes had that glassy look, hollow and empty. She managed to get him to drink a little milk from the goat, and finally go back to sleep.

Sybilla swept the floor to pass the time. She knocked the cobwebs from the corners, even managed to clean the smoky soot from the window glass. She'd set fresh rush lights in the wall holders, scrubbed the long table, and fed the goat. She'd found a white linen tablecloth of good quality and clean, and unfurled it over the table.

Simon stirred from his pallet and yawned. He rubbed the sleep from his eyes with his knuckles, and took a seat at the table. His eyes roamed the hall. "Place looks more like I remember it," he said, softly. "Lady Roselynn used to set a bowl of apples, right here in the middle of the table. Guy and I used to eat right here after training. Food never tastes good unless you've got sweat and dirt on your hands." His face filled with a look of wistful reminiscence as he stared into the fire.

Sybilla lowered herself onto the bench and glanced at the staircase leading to the chamber loft. "Sir Simon, what is Lady Morna to Guy?"

Simon broke off a lump of cheese. "I had four sisters, Mistress Corbuc. I know what you are really asking." He smiled. "Morna and Guy were lovers years ago. They were both sixteen. She was forced to marry Hamon. Guy went away to war. For the first few years she sent him letters. But the letters stopped and then there were rumors that she—" Simon broke off and looked up. He studied Sybilla's face, as if he gauged her reaction.

"Go on."

He sighed. "Never mind. Guy rarely speaks about what happened between the two of them, not to me, not to anyone. I think 'tis best to leave that topic alone. But I can only tell you when he looks at her, it's with pity. Hamon cast her off. Had her tried as a Separate."

A wave of panic washed over Sybilla. "What did she do that he could try her as a Separate?"

He took a bite of cheese. "Hamon is infertile, but after years of trying to get her with child, he claimed 'twas she who was barren. He trumped up charges about her prophetic gift and her knowledge of potions, then had her cast out as a Separate so he could take another wife. At Morna's trial all of England learned about her, er, many lovers. Nonetheless, she declared undying love only for Sir Guy of Warwick, partly outa spite for her husband, and partly because in her brain-addled way, she really thinks she loves Guy—hoped when Guy came home they would rekindle what they had. If you ask me, I think she's not in possession of her wits, but Hamon's hated Guy ever since. Got worse when he learned Guy survived eight years of fighting."

Sybilla felt the blood drain from her face. "Lady Morna was stripped and, and—?"

Simon nodded. "A little more than a year ago. Before Guy came back to England. Hamon's a wicked, vengeful man, the kind who could've killed Lady Roselynn and her son."

"But Guy has no proof?"

Simon let out a slow breath. "He doesn't. Mayhap the killers were common thieves—there was more than one judging by their horses' hoof prints. They took the plate, Sir Walter's swords and weapons . . . but the life of Lady Roselynn was what they really wanted, the person Guy loved most in the world." He broke off and raised his wary eyes to the staircase.

Sybilla's heart wrenched. The sick feeling in her stomach choked off her voice.

Heavy footsteps padded on the timbered floor above. Guy called her name, his tone irritated.

Good Lord, had he been listening?

She looked up to see him standing at the top of the stairs, his dark hair uncombed, circles beneath his deep-set eyes.

He pounded down the stairs. "Sybilla, why did you leave?" He scanned the hall and his eyes widened as they settled back on Sybilla. "What have you done? And I presume 'twas you because Dunback is still sleeping and Simon looks like he just got up."

Sybilla swung her legs over the bench, and dusted her skirts off as she stood. She grabbed a broom and started sweeping. "I've been cleaning. There's a squirrel's nest in the eve above the hearth I couldn't reach, and more mice in the cupboard than I could catch. The place needs a cat. And more cheese. The mice have chewed on that one." She pointed to the cheese that Simon held to his lips.

The color in Simon's face changed from sleepless-pale to blanched. He tossed the cheese to the nanny goat and swore an oath.

Guy's voice rang out. "Mistress Corbuc, no need to clean. We leave today, as soon as we've got provisions ready."

Sybilla halted. God's feet, he could have thanked her. He could at least be cordial.

"You're most welcome, Sir Guy," she said with a huff.

"We are leaving." Guy strode to the table and picked up his empty cup. He peered inside, before he slammed it down. "Today."

Sybilla glanced at the window. The thin rays of morning sunlight had already faded and snow threatened to spill out of heavy gray clouds. She put one hand on her hip and held the broom at her side like a weapon.

"More snow is coming. We should stay. Baldwin is not so bad a place. I ran my family's farm with my mother before my father lost it on a bet. I cleaned our cottage, and I worked on the land when I was finished in the stables. Regalo could be your stud colt to earn his keep. Baldwin's fields could still be tilled and there's still time to plant if we—"

Guy's face hardened. "We are leaving. Today."

Simon cleared his throat. He wrapped his cloak over his shoulders and pulled Dunback to his feet. "We'll see to the horses."

Dunback, clear-eyed and surprisingly lucid, sprang to

Simon's side. "By the rood, Sir Guy, if she wants to stay an' bake us bread let her, an' there's deer still in the wood. You could hunt 'em like you used to do. We'd have real food." He hurried out the door with such eagerness and lightness in his step, he looked like a different man.

Regalo wandered up and suckled Guy's thumb. Guy snatched his hand away and redirected Regalo to the goat. He spoke in a low tone to Sybilla. "As I said last night, Sybilla. I care. But I make my living by the sword now. I've no interest in running a farm. I wish to leave. You and Regalo will come with me."

Had she no say in anything?

Her hopes dashed, anger swelled up inside her. Sybilla struggled with the urge to fling the broom across the room. "Rather than stay and face your demons, you run away. I trust there are no ghosts at Ketchem Castle?"

The vessels along Guy's neck and temples throbbed. His fist closed around the handle of his sword. "My ghosts don't haunt me, Sybilla, they comfort me. They remind me of my mission, of what I've yet to do. At Ketchem I can keep you and Regalo safe. There I can train for battle, wait for Regalo to reveal his secret and lead me to the killer."

He drew up to his full height, a proud knight hell-bent on revenge, but the anguish in his eyes belied his turmoil. He'd suffered just by being here, the memories too painful. What she'd said about his ghosts had hurt him.

Sybilla set the broom against the wall. "I am sorry, Sir Guy. I should not have said—"

A shrieking whistle pierced the air. Sybilla twisted to see the front door bang open, a snow-dusted Simon came striding in with a meager armload of firewood, with Dunback straggling behind him, carrying a single flagon of wine. Dunback pulled the cork from the flagon with his teeth and put his lips to the spout.

Simon pulled the flagon from the old man's lips. "Gimmee that." The flagon clacked against the table. Simon chucked his armload of wood beside the hearth. Turning, he pronounced, "That's the last of it. We'll need fresh game if we're to eat. There's another storm coming Guy. We dare not set out without food."

Dunback frowned, his big eyes focused on the flagon. "You'll be leaving me with nothing?"

Guy crossed the room and grabbed his cloak. He kicked the door ajar and a shock of biting wind blew across the threshold.

"I'll hunt," he said without looking at Sybilla. "I'll be back before the sun sets. We may have to stay another day, God forbid." He spun on his heels, his sword swinging at his side. The door slammed shut.

A mournful sound came from the corner, a sound barely above a whimper. Regalo barked.

Chapter Eight

Regalo thrashed, feet flailing, tail beating against the floor. The fit lasted a good ten minutes, maybe more. When he finally stopped, he stared vacantly at the foyer. He breathed, but every breath grew more ragged and weaker, as if each could be his last.

Sybilla's throat tightened.

There was no explanation for Regalo's sudden attack. She'd not been thinking about leaving when the little beast collapsed. She'd rushed outside to call Guy back, but he was gone, far from earshot.

She put her head in her hands and sank beside Regalo.

Simon wrestled the pewter cup from Dunback and sat on the man until he stopped blubbering about the wrath of the devil and a horse with four white socks. "You old fool. The horse just had one of his attacks. Leave him to Mistress Corbuc. And if I catch you trying to whack him with your cup again, 'tis you will get the whackin'."

Dunback spoke as sanely as any man. "She's as strange as the other one, only this one brought a demon colt in here. Sir Guy ain't never known how to pick 'is women."

Sybilla looked up. "Regalo is not a demon colt and I am not Sir Guy's woman."

Simon flicked Dunback on the back of his head. "Pay no attention to him. He's not right in the head."

"I am at the moment. And you're always's stickin' up for Sir Guy. 'Tis time you speak the truth. The women he brings to Baldwin Manor always bring us trouble."

Simon's face reddened. "I'm warning you, Dunback. Don't go on about things you've no knowledge of."

Sybilla stroked Regalo. "Other women?"

Before Simon could distract him, Dunback answered, rolling round so Simon couldn't cover his mouth. "Plenty. But the fine Lady Morna, the seer, she bewitched him. The two of them used to meet fur ruttin' in the woods. Until the godly Lady Roselynn caught 'em. She put an end to that, but it was too la—"

Simon slipped his arm beneath Dunback's neck and held him in a headlock. "That's enough. Another word and you'll not get another drop tonight." He pushed away the half-emptied flagon.

Dunback opened his mouth, but quickly snapped it shut, as if he'd had more to say but thought better of it.

Sybilla sat on her heels and looked at Simon. "Lady Roselynn knew about their trysts?"

A long silence followed. Simon released Dunback. "There are times in a man's life when he's not thinking with his head, at least not with the one on his shoulders. Guy was barely into his whiskers when his sister caught them."

Warmth crept up Sybilla's cheeks. "But that was eight years ago. Why would Lord Hamon wait so long to seek revenge? He'd already cast the Lady Morna off."

Simon shrugged. "Aye, but he still loves her. He knew Guy of Warwick was returning. Knew Morna was waiting for him. Jealousy will rot your soul, Mistress Corbuc, and drive a vengeful man to murder."

Dunback rolled into a sitting position, his legs crossed at his ankles. He rested his hands on his knees and said matter-of-factly, "I hid in the bushes when the horsemen came, they couldn't see me, but I could hear the others screaming. Lady Roselynn begged for her life an' they—"

Her heart sinking, Sybilla raised her hand. "Enough." She raised her eyes to the window and stared at the dark sky.

Guy of Warwick had not returned. Simon reassured her Guy was safe, but the howling winds and Regalo's fading presence felt like a bad omen.

Simon and Dunback finished off the wine, belched, and collapsed into sleep beside the goat.

Regalo barely breathed. She held her hand to his muzzle. No air seemed to come from his nostrils. Sybilla rested her ear against his chest. His heart beat fast, the thready sound barely audible.

A wail of despair erupted from her throat as she pounded on Regalo's chest and rolled him upright. The colt's eyes remained closed despite her prodding.

God's heart! Don't let Regalo die!

Regalo flopped on his side like a rag, his body still warm, his heartbeat fading. Sybilla choked back a sob. Losing Regalo would be like losing a piece of her soul.

She lay her head down on the foal and cried. She cried for the colt, for her lost dreams, and for Guy.

A silver moon shimmered through the narrow window and the great hall stood as quiet as a graveyard. When Sybilla finally awoke, the sky was bright with moonlight. She rubbed her eyes, barely able to remember how long she'd slept, or why. She searched her foggy mind. When she last was awake, Regalo had been—*Regalo!*

She bolted upright, searching the shadowy room. Of the lumpy forms sprawled across the pallet next to her, the goat and Simon, none were equine.

Her heart in her throat, she spun around, her eyes searching, her breath trapped inside her chest. A gust of cold air whisked across the hall and Simon moaned.

Simon rose up and swayed, rubbing his head. "Blessed saints. The bastard hit me."

An egg-sized knot swelled at his temple and the corner of his right eye drooped. He kicked Dunback's empty flagon into the hearth and tried to crawl to his knees, collapsing in a fit of heaves. He swore between gasps. "Damnation, I'll wring his sotted neck when I catch him."

Sybilla hurried to his side. "Simon, where are they? Where's Regalo and Dunback?"

Simon groaned. "I dunno. The little colt was barking an' . . ." His words slurred and he winced before he eased back down on the pallet. "The room is spinnin'. I think my skull is cracked."

Sybilla scrabbled to her feet. "Regalo is alive?"

A feeble voice warbled from beneath the table. "He left."

Sybilla snapped her head around.

Dunback poked his jaundiced face from his hiding place. "He wandered to the foyer, suckled the door latch open and let himself out. I was glad to see the little devil go. I woulda whacked him, 'cept Simon stole my cup . . ." His voice clear and his words coherent, Dunback spoke like a man trapped between two worlds, the world of the lucid and one where men slowly lost their minds.

He scrambled to his feet and huddled at Simon's side.

"I'm sorry, Sir Simon. I didn't mean to hit you." His eyes filled with genuine distress.

Every muscle in her body tense, Sybilla raised her eyes to heaven. "God, help Regalo," she whispered. "He's gone outside."

Her hands shaking, she probed Simon's wound as gently and as quickly as she could. "Simon, I must go for Regalo. Dunback will get you snow. You hold it to your head. The cold will stop the bleeding."

Dunback nodded as he loaded the bucket into his arms. "Yes, yes," he mumbled.

Simon caught her by the hand. "Mistress, you risk your life to go after the colt. Mayhap 'tis best you let him go." He took a deep breath. "If the colt does not come back, you will be free. And Guy could move on with his life. Think about it. You'd no longer be a servant."

Sybilla's heart squeezed. "I cannot let Regalo die. Even if it means my freedom. And what of Guy? Without Regalo, he believes he might never find his sister's and his nephew's killer."

Simon arched an eyebrow, and winced. He rubbed the lump on his head.

Sybilla snapped her mouth closed. That she'd thought of Guy and what Regalo meant to him surprised her. What would Guy do without Regalo? The man would lose all hope.

She glanced at Simon. He'd already slipped back into a brain-addled sleep. She patted his hand. "I'll find, Regalo, Simon. Guy needs the colt."

Sybilla threw a blanket 'round her shoulders and raced to the foyer. The cold night air lapped across the threshold, and she held her breath as she stepped into the yard. The moonlight sparkled on the pure white snow. Shallow

hoof prints shone past the gate and led into the woods, the
trail ambling and weaving.

Mother Mary, where did Regalo think he was going?

A shadow raced across the yard. Sybilla flinched. Her
eyes lifted upward, following the dark and silent forms
that circled overhead. Ravens.

Her heart thumped wildly. Wherever death traveled,
the raven followed. And then came the wolves. The last
breath of many a living soul had oft been given up to the
wolves, witnessed by the lurking ravens. Images of Joan,
the hayman's wife, galloped through her mind.

Sybilla shuddered. She braced herself against the cold
and the fear. Steeling her nerves, she picked up her skirts
and strode through the gate. Her feet sank into the slush,
the icy wetness soaking through her stockings, and she
leapt to clear a puddle. She bounded onward, following
the hoof prints.

Her eyes tearing from the cold, Sybilla choked back
her panic when Regalo's tracks scrambled in the snow,
as if he had stumbled and fallen. He could not have
gotten far. He simply would not have had the strength.

Sybilla passed beneath the snow-piled birch trees, the
tallest in the woods, and icy water dripped from the
branches, spotting her face, her hair. Regalo's prints circled through the trees and tracked along a twisted path
that led Sybilla farther from the manor. Dangerously far.

Surrounded by the ancient forest, and snow that bore a
bluish hue beneath the filtered moonlight, she searched,
undeterred by the night sounds, even those she could not
recognize. Regalo's hoof prints mixed with slush and ice
and became intermixed at times with those from other
creatures. Deer. A hare. A fox. If she didn't find him soon,
she'd lose his tracks entirely. Her feet and toes tingled,

suffering the cold, and the frigid air burned her lungs with every breath.

God's teeth. She needed help. She should have waited for Sir Guy.

She halted.

Howling, a vicious call not far from where she stood, echoed through the woods. The hair on the back of her neck stood straight. That howl was not Regalo's. No, the sound was distinctly canine. Wolvine.

Mother Mary, where was Guy? There was no time to find him, to race to back to the house and see if he'd returned. She'd seen what hungry wolves could do to a foal. They attacked the face first, grabbed on to the nose by the muzzle and held fast, while the other members of the pack ripped at the throat, hanging on until they dragged the animal down. The wolves would feast until the ravens came and claimed their share of the carcass . . .

Her blood racing, Sybilla picked up her skirts and sprinted in the direction of the howling.

The path opened into a small clearing filled with tall stones, some as tall as she. Regalo stood among the rocks, his head lifted, his ears pricked forward. He shot a glance in her direction, snorted and pawed, his nostrils flaring. Sybilla's eyes followed his gaze.

Five wolves, rangy and fiercely ragged, each with their teeth bared, surrounded Regalo. Sybilla sensed a sixth wolf, or more, stalked close by. She dared not turn away and look.

The wolves snarled and the leader, the tallest in the pack with jutting shoulders and a pelt that hung from his bones, growled.

Sybilla searched with her eyes for a stick, or a rock, anything she could use to ward them off. But everything was blanketed in snow and there was no tree limb within arm's reach. Her knees locked. Her chest heaved as she gasped for air. She fought the dangerous urge to run. There was no Guy of Warwick here to save her now. Was she meant to die along with Regalo?

There was only one thing to do that might distract them—attract the pack's attention.

She opened her mouth and shrieked.

Chapter Nine

Settling on Bacchus and pointing the beast toward Baldwin, Guy tugged his cloak tighter around his shoulders; his stomach ached, hollow with hunger. It had taken longer than he'd anticipated to find game. The once plentiful supply of rabbits, boar, and deer had starved to death during the winter, or been poached. He'd tracked a buck so old and decrepit he'd killed the animal out of pity. He tied the skinny carcass behind him. The meat would be dry and tough, but at least there'd be enough for stew tonight.

Guy rubbed his neck and shoulders, the chill settling into his aching muscles. Despite the pain, he relished the solitude of the wood's darkness and the quiet. Sybilla Corbuc had occupied his thoughts and actions too much of late. He could not understand what hold she had on him. Even now, he wanted desperately to ride back to Baldwin Manor and join her in the warmth of their bed. He imagined slipping her chemise down her silken shoulders, tasting the sweetness of her lips . . .

He shook his head and slapped his thigh in self reproach. Nothing could come of this attraction to Sybilla.

His life was dedicated to seeking justice for his sister and her son. Someday Sybilla would marry a good man and have a yard full of children. 'Twas not the life for him. He'd no interest in hearth and home. He'd work harder to keep his lust for her in check.

Guy inhaled, the sharp cold air filling up his nostrils, clearing his head.

He moved Bacchus silently amongst the shadows, much as he'd done the nights after Roselynn's murder. The woods here were as silent as a tomb and just as dark. It'd been six months since her death, six months since last he rode to the place he knew so well, the place where he'd found Roselynn's lifeless body.

He balled his sword hand into a fist. He'd not give in to the grief or to the frustration, but he could not close off the memories. Roselynn used to sit here amongst the stones, feed the squirrels and sing. *"When love abides in home and hearth, 'tis no greater pleasure on all the earth . . ."*

Trees rustled. A branch snapped and low shadows moved quickly through the brush.

Alerted, Guy drew his sword and urged Bacchus to a trot. By God, if Hamon and his men meant to take him here, they would have a fight.

An ear-piercing scream suddenly racked the forest. A woman's cry of terror shrieked from the clearing and nailed Guy's heart to his backbone. Sybilla! A second scream shocked the silence, followed by a frail whinny.

Sybilla! Regalo! Guy wheeled Bacchus 'round and galloped toward the clearing.

What were Sybilla and the colt doing out here?

Then he saw her standing there, with the wolves closing in around her. She had her back to him, and he knew in an instant fear had paralyzed her. Regalo snorted and struck out with his foot.

Guy watched the wolves. "Easy, Regalo. Stay still, Sybilla."

The leader of the pack, snarled and inched closer to Sybilla, one paw at a time. At any moment, he would pounce.

Guy reined Bacchus to a halt and slipped his feet from his stirrups. He knew better than to escalate the confrontation by bolting from the saddle. He spoke in a low voice, but loud enough for Sybilla to hear and not so abrupt as to startle the wolves and provoke an attack.

"Stand up straight and square your shoulders, but don't turn around. Don't turn your back on them."

She did as he said and lowered her trembling arms.

"Now look your enemy in the eye. Lift your chin, like you did when you faced the sheriff, Lord Hamon . . . and me," he added softly. "The wolves are hungry, but they are weak, outnumbered now, and will not attack if challenged by those who show their strength."

Guy silently dismounted. Sybilla stood, now bold and defiant, with her head up and her fists clenched at her sides. He could see her nostrils flare with every rapid breath. Regalo didn't move a muscle and the sounds of the forest quieted, while the beastly silver eyes in the woods watched and waited.

The pack held their place. Each animal, couched and leering, had its teeth bared. Low growls rumbled from their throats.

With one eye on the wolves, Guy sliced a deer leg from the carcass tied to Bacchus' back. Even the horse didn't move, as if he sensed the danger.

Guy moved with caution to Regalo's side; he kept his great broadsword in one hand and the leg of the deer in the other as he stepped in front of the foal. With one smooth toss, he hurled the deer leg over the rocks, into the wood beyond the clearing.

Give the beasts a reason to turn away. Give them what they really wanted. Food.

A lone wolf yelped, his craven gaze following the flight of the deer leg. One by one, the wolves scattered, the largest one with his nose in the air, sniffing. They disappeared into the brush, their gray and silver coats blending into the shadows. Within minutes, their barking subsided, and the sound of a feeding frenzy filled the air.

Turning on his heels, Guy strode to Regalo and patted the foal on the neck. "Well done, my friend. Like a champion destrier. How did you get out here and what were you doing?" Regalo snorted and Guy looked at Sybilla, one eyebrow arched. "And did I not ask you to stay put, Mistress Corbuc?"

Consternation flashed across her face. She let out a long breath and collapsed to her knees. She covered her face, breathing hard into her hands as her shoulders shook.

In an instant Guy knelt beside her and wrapped his arms around her, drawing her into the folds of his cloak. "You are safe, Sybilla, and Regalo is, too." He cradled the back of her head in his hand as her cheek came to rest against him. "Now tell me, Mistress Corbuc, what were the two of you doing out here? God's teeth, have you not the sense to realize the danger? If anything had happened to you—"

Sybilla pulled away, her nose reddened and her cheeks pink from the wind. "I thought he'd died tonight. He had a fit so bad at the manor . . ." Sybilla hung her head. "I fell asleep, sobbing, and when I awoke I discovered *he* let himself out. I came to find him."

"Alone? What about Simon?"

"Knocked in the head by Dunback. He couldn't help me, and you weren't there."

Her words pierced him like a dagger, but he kept his face expressionless. He wrapped her in his cloak and lifted her to Bacchus' back. "You should not have come out here alone. Two lives might have been lost tonight, not one."

Sybilla kept her head down, her body shaking. "And what would you have me do instead, Sir Guy? Wait at the manor until you came back? Regalo could have been dead by then."

Guy opened his mouth to offer a retort, but from the looks of her, her pale face and blue lips, she was in no shape to hear complaints against her.

Guy pulled a rope from his hip belt and tied it halter-like to Regalo. "You must walk with me, Regalo. Three days old and you're as big as a weanling. Morna's nanny goat must make a special kind of milk."

Ravens circled overhead and swooped, and Guy lifted his gaze to follow the birds.

A chill rippled up his spine. The ravens flew eastward beneath the moon—to Baldwin Manor.

Lord Hamon sat on a velvet-covered bench beside the fire, his ankle throbbing. Unused to the never-ending pain, he swore and chucked his crutch onto the table. He pulled his scarlet gloves off, one finger at a time.

"Did you tip them off, my lady?" he asked with quiet anger, holding his gloves to the firelight, inspecting the quality of the dye. Red had always been his favorite color, and this time his wool dyer had gotten the shade right. Deep red, the color of a polished ruby.

He slapped the gloves on the table. "Was Guy of Warwick here, hiding with the little colt and the others, the night you came to bind my wound?"

Lady Morna didn't look up from her spinning, her dark hair falling forward, hiding her deep-set eyes and her thoughts. It irritated him that she never answered quickly. She had the power to control him by simply not responding. Had he not cared so much about the slender, lovely neck of hers, the part he loved the most on any woman, he would have wrung it years ago.

She wound the wool around the spindle before she set the wheel aside. She lowered her dark eyes before she spoke. The gesture, he knew from experience, was a show for men—his men, who fawned over her like she was a princess. She'd won their sympathy by pretending to be demure and gentle. It was all part of her seduction. He suspected she'd wooed more than one into her bed. Sir Gideon mayhap, and Sir Elbert, both fine men who took his orders without question and served him well. He didn't consider their trysts with his former wife a severe transgression. They had no hold on her heart, nor she on theirs as far as he could tell. They kept her safe from zealots in the village and she ordered them around like a general. They were good, fighting men of noble birth and loyal and he allowed them to serve her. But when it came to Guy of Warwick, he had no tolerance.

She raised her eyes, those beautiful rich brown eyes, and smiled. "Good husband, you know Sir Guy and the others were here. How else would I have known that you were injured?"

Hamon's blood boiled. "I am no longer your husband by the law, or in the eyes of the church. You must think me a fool. You have the sight. You knew I'd suffer an accident. Now tell me, did you know that Guy of Warwick would be the cause? Did you wait here for him, and brush your hair until it shone, write love notes to him in your books?"

He reached from where he sat and traced a finger down her elegant cheekbone. "Tell me, my lady. What do you see in him that keeps your heart enamored after all these years?"

She didn't answer. But the scent of the rose water she used to wash her hair filled his nostrils and inflamed him. He leaned close, wanting to possess her, to slip the costly red gown, the dress he'd paid for, from her white shoulders and put his mouth on her breasts. "Renounce him," he muttered against her ear. "And come back with me. Confess your sins before the bishop and my court and declare you love me."

Truth be told, he needed his wife by his side. His grip on his villains had grown precarious, his demesne crippled by poor harvests and high taxes. Civil discord had forced him to deal with his villagers harshly, and he worried that his fiefdom was slipping from his grasp. But if he could unite his starving people in a war against the Earl of Ketchem and regain the fertile southland the man had stolen from him, he would remain the Earl of Cornbury, without contest.

Hamon ran his hand through Morna's silken tresses. He still had no heir and it would be easy enough, with the proper bribes, to set his second wife, the girl he'd chosen to replace Morna, aside. In time, he'd make the necessary arrangements to remarry Morna.

Tonight, sitting here alone with her, in the cottage he'd given her, filled with furniture and comforts he'd provided, he wanted her. He wanted back the days of their youth when his people had gladly served him, when she pretended that she cared for him, at least a little. He wanted back the lusty nights she'd spent in his bed.

She whispered, her voice taunting, "You know I will not go with you. I will always love Sir Guy of Warwick."

He gripped her hard by the arms and nuzzled her neck. "Did you bed him when he was here?"

She didn't answer.

"Then I will kill him, Morna, when next I get the chance. I tire of the impoverished knight who takes things which belong to me. I want him dead. I want the colt he possesses . . . and I want you." He moved his mouth to hers. Her lips parted with a sigh of submission and she rested her hand on his cock.

His fingers tightened around her arms. "I've only let Guy of Warwick live this long because I enjoy the way you beg for his life. But you forget I know you well. Morna, the gifted seer, never gives of her many talents without exacting a price. What do you want this time?"

She didn't wince, didn't move, except to unbuckle his purse belt, and drag it from him. He let her lift his tunic over his head, let her warm hands slip beneath his undershirt and untie the stays on his breeches.

She slipped her hand around his rod and stroked. "You forgot Mistress Corbuc, your bastard daughter," she whispered. "You must add her to your list."

She knelt before him. He leaned his head back and threaded his fingers through her hair, pulling her closer as she closed her lips around his shaft.

He knew from experience jealousy could fester in a wounded heart for years. He intended to let his former wife suffer.

* * *

It was well after midnight before they reached the manor house, the moon as high and as bright as Sybilla had ever seen it. A thin line of dark smoke curled upward from the chimney and the dim glow of firelight that spilled through the narrow window shone on the pathway leading to the door. In the hours since she'd been gone, large patches of snow had melted and given way to the bare earth. By morning, the whole yard, free of trees and shade, would be a slog of mud and slush.

Sybilla sank against Guy's warm chest. He'd said hardly a word and, in the silence, she could hear Regalo breathing, a strong rushing breath, full of vigor. Pray to God, Regalo stayed healthy. If a fit should come upon him at Ketchem, it might cost his life. Peasant folk and priests alike would be suspect of a colt with four white stockings who suffered such a strange malady. Word was sure to continue to spread that she'd been the one who'd attended his unholy birth.

Guy cleared his throat. "Mistress Corbuc, I've been thinking . . ." He reined Bacchus toward the barn. "There are things you and I must discuss before we get to Ketchem."

Sybilla tensed, her back stiffened as did the rest of her, right down to her sodden toes.

"Once we reach the castle, I will call you by your Christian name, as servants are addressed, and you must answer to me as my lord, or Sir Guy."

She twisted round to face him, and opened her mouth, but before she had the chance to utter a word, he placed a gloved finger against her lips.

"Let me finish. If Regalo should have a fit, act as if it is nothing. Say the nanny goat's milk was sour, but do not intervene. Lady Claire would not take it well to learn there is a horse midwife in her house." He reined Bacchus to a halt and dismounted. "Fortunately, Lord Phillip rules the keep. I'd swear my oath to no less a nobleman. You'll be safe as long as you do as I ask and be careful." He helped her down.

Sybilla shuddered. Castle life, though she had little firsthand knowledge of it, did not appeal. Life as a servant anywhere, especially inside the cold, stone walls of a keep, could not compare to the freedom she'd known as midwife, living on a farm in the countryside where fresh, pure air blew across the fields. And she wasn't sure she could refrain from revealing how she'd earned her living. She wasn't good at keeping secrets.

His big hand caught her by the elbow as she gathered up Regalo's lead rope. "Sybilla . . ." He let his hand fall to his side. "I must remind you—no, I must order you—do not raise your chin to me in public, nor to anyone else who is above your rank. Things will go easier there for both of us if you don't."

Sybilla turned away and strode toward the barn with Regalo in tow. "As you wish, my lord."

Be humble and deny my calling. Why not ask me not to breathe?

His hand suddenly wrapped around her upper arm.

"One more thing," he continued as he stepped beside her. "I must always go first. Do not walk in front of me. We should practice this before we get to Ketchem." He strode ahead. "Bring Regalo and Bacchus." He commanded with the voice befitting one who is a lord and master. He flung the barn doors open.

Sybilla pursed her lips. If he insisted on this charade, she would play her part, God help him.

She kept her head down, though she bit the inside of her cheek. "Yes, my lord."

She meant to drop the horses lead ropes right there in

the breezeway, but her eyes fixed suddenly on Addy, her pale body shining in the dim light.

She thrust the leads at Sir Guy's chest and raced to the stall. Addy lay on her side, unmoving with her eyes closed.

The old mare looked thinner than she had a day ago, her body ravaged by hunger, birthing, and time. Her ghostly white form was as still as fallen snow.

Sybilla's heart skipped a beat. She waited for the rise and fall of Addy's chest, the slight flare of her nostrils. When there was none, she knelt at the old mare's head and felt her lips and ears.

Cold. And Addy's gums had turned as white as her hair. The old mare stared unblinking, her eyes dull and sunken.

A lump stuck in Sybilla's throat. Her gaze turned hazy, clouded by tears. Addy had lived longer than most mares, but her death still seemed too soon. Spring was almost here, later than it should be, but the snow had finally started melting. If Addy had lived just another week . . .

Sybilla wiped a tear from the corner of her eye.

Guy heaved the deer carcass from Bacchus' back.

His booted feet stomped into the stall and he knelt beside Sybilla. He patted the old horse on the cheek. "She'd had enough of life on earth. She's earned her peace." He nudged Sybilla and glanced up at Regalo. "I think her colt is not as addle-brained as he lets on."

Regalo nuzzled the mare, his lips nibbling around her eyes, her ears. He snorted and shook his head.

Sybilla rose slowly, keeping her eyes downcast. There was something about Addy's passing that brought back the memory she'd kept stowed away, afraid to discard it, afraid to think about it. Her mother, setting her from her arms, turning to join her husband in the debtors' cart. Spring had been crisp in the air that morning, and the snow had been melting in the fields. Like Regalo, she'd been left alone at dawn by her mother, sooner than she should have been.

Guy kept staring at Addy, his hands by his sides, his face dark. "I know, too, what it was like to be left without a mother. My own died soon after my little brother was stillborn. I was ten. My father'd gone to war and not come back. I give thanks every day Roselynn was there to raise me."

Sybilla glanced at his face. 'Twas the first account he'd revealed about his young life. She wondered what kind of boy he'd been, but she guessed his thoughts had already turned to Roselynn's murder. His eyes had narrowed, his jaw clenched.

She kept her gaze lowered. "I can imagine you missed your mother. I feel fortunate to have had mine as long as I did."

Guy's face darkened, the pain in his eyes quickly replaced by hurt and anger. He strode from the stall. "I'll have the knacker come as soon as he's able." He slung the deer carcass over his shoulder. "There is no life here for me, for beasts of burden, for anyone. 'Tis time we move on."

Sybilla led Regalo out of the barn.

Simon flung open the manor door and stood on the stone steps with one hand on his sword hilt and the other round the neck of the wineskin flagon. "Bloody hell, where have you two been?" He squinted, the morning light clearly painful but the lump at his temple not as angry. "I milked the goat for Regalo, but I fear she's empty now. The little colt has been drinking more than she can make. I'm starving, too. I'll be glad to have some food in my bel—" He shot a glance at the carcass on Guy's back. "A three-legged deer? And a sorry looking one at that. There'll be not much meat on that one. What happened to the mangy beast's other leg?"

Sybilla pushed Regalo inside the hall. "Sir Guy gave it to—"

Simon held his hand up. "Don't tell me, he came upon a family of starving villagers and gave it to the—"

She cut in. "To the wolves."

He raised his bushy red eyebrows. "Wolves?"

Guy dumped the deer at the base of the steps. "They were hungry," he said flatly.

Sybilla shrugged when Simon glanced at her, perplexed.

Guy's sword rattled from his scabbard. "Simon, see if you can find more firewood. I'll dress the deer for cooking. Mistress Corbuc, feed Regalo. As soon as we've all eaten, we'll leave for Ketchem."

Sybilla's mood darkened. By this evening, she would be sleeping in a castle, God knew where, trying to keep her chin down, walking behind Sir Guy, calling him *my lord* and telling no one what she'd done for a living. What kind of life was that? Thank the Lord it would not be forever.

Simon held the wineskin out to Sybilla. "I've got my orders. Guess you've got yours." He set out toward the wood pile.

"You serve because you want to," muttered Sybilla beneath her breath. "I do because I must."

By mid-morning, the hall had filled with the smoky scent of roasted venison, and hummed with talk from men with full stomachs. Regalo rested in the corner of the room, watching all with a contentment that made him seem more settled, almost normal. Dunback dithered on about the fields that needed planting, and how the Lady Roselynn had kept him up all night singing.

Sybilla chewed on a morsel of tough venison and listened while Guy spoke to Simon of the upcoming tourney season, the prizes he'd fixed his sights upon, and lamented the loss of his good horse, stolen by Lord Hamon's men. The mount would have surely won the summer race at Ketchem. The two men mapped out the route back to Ketchem, arguing over which way might be more passable. They would leave within the hour and complete the journey before nightfall, even though Sybilla and Guy had not slept the night.

She took a sip of wine, set down her cup and rose from the bench.

"Where are you going," Sir Guy asked lightly.

"Are we not leaving soon?" She let the question hang a moment before she continued. "Do I have my lord's permission to ready myself for the journey?" She took her newly washed and dried hose from the pegs beside the fireplace.

Looking quite pleased, Sir Guy nodded.

Simon looked askance, as if he thought this exchange rather odd, but knew better than to comment.

Guy swung his feet over the bench. He stood. "I'll get Bacchus. Simon, you get the goat."

Simon frowned. "Who'll be riding the only horse we have?"

A wry grin spread over Guy's handsome face. "This time the goat and Sybilla. You and I will walk."

Simon slumped and Sybilla raced up the stairs, eager to make her transformation before Sir Guy deduced what she was up to.

She went to the chest. Within minutes, she exchanged Lady Roselynn's green and golden gowns for her old blue dress and shift. She brushed the dirt and mud from Lady Roselynn's clothes as best she could, regretting she'd not had time to clean them. She folded the garments and set them back in the chest.

"Sybilla!" Sir Guy bellowed from the foyer, his tone impatient.

"I come anon!" She slipped her hose on and tied them to her thighs with the garters. *I feel like I am stealing from Lady Roselynn. But who would know that beneath the lowly servant's garb, I wear fine woolen stockings and black satin garters rich enough for the queen?*

The hose and garters were no indulgence. Her legs would be cold and her feet would not survive her wooden shoes without protection.

Sir Guy's voice boomed as he strode into the hall. "Hurry!"

She jumped and hurried to his side. "I'm coming," she answered irritably, lowered her chin, remembering no servant would ever speak to her master so.

He took her by the elbow and led her out the foyer, where Bacchus stood waiting at the foot of the stairs with Regalo tied to his side.

If he'd noticed she'd changed her clothes, he spoke not of it, nor did he say a word when his big hands spanned her waist and he lifted her onto Bacchus' back.

He swung up behind her, drew his sword and wheeled the horse around. Bacchus lunged into a gallop, Regalo racing close beside him.

Sybilla tensed, thrown against Sir Guy's chest when Bacchus bolted. Bacchus's pounding gait jarred her words, the wind in her hair and the feel of Guy against her set her blood on fire. "What's happened? Where's Simon? You forgot the goat!"

Sir Guy sat stiffly against her, his arm wrapped

possessively around her waist, and leaned forward, his breath against her ear and Bacchus thundering from the yard. "Hamon's men are in the woods. Simon went ahead on foot to scout. We'll meet him at the ring of rocks. I left the goat for Dunback. She's of more use to him than to Regalo."

Sybilla tensed. Lord Hamon's men on Ketchem land? 'Twas bold and dangerous alike.

Bacchus raced between the trees, surging forward, his head lifting with every mud-sucked stride. The woods were a passing blur of brown and white. Sybilla squinted to focus on the splash of color that caught her eye. Red. The shred of a cloak caught in the bushes.

Her heart leapt. She grabbed the reins. "Stop! There— to the left!"

Guy halted Bacchus, his great haunches sliding far beneath him.

Without a sound, Guy dismounted. His sword drawn, he stepped cautiously toward the brambles where two sets of footprints tangled. The larger set had carved great ruts into the mud. The heels of the smaller pair, too big for women's shoes, but not as large as most men's, had scrambled and skidded.

Guy cursed beneath his breath. He spun around to face Sybilla. "At the first sign of danger, take Bacchus and run. Go north to Ketchem."

Sybilla clutched Bacchus' reins in her fists. Her hands shaking, she gestured to the footprints. "Are they Simon's?"

Guy nodded. He kicked a muddied rock with the toe of his shoe. The crimson color on the sharp stone at his feet was as fresh as new paint.

Blood.

Sybilla bit her lower lip. The feeling of dread rose from her gut.

With the tip of his sword, Sir Guy lifted the shred of a cloak from the bramble. "Hamon red," he said in a low voice, the fury on his face unmistakable.

He flung the cloth aside and parted the bushes with the flat side of his sword.

Sybilla's gaze followed the bloody trail. A chill settled over her, and she shifted, fear rising from her gut.

Staggering footprints led beyond the bramble in the direction of Ketchem Castle. Not ten feet away, the prints merged with mud and slush. The trail of blood faded from red to pink, and disappeared into the rivulets of water from the melting snow. The other set of footprints disappeared altogether.

Guy spun on his heels and strode to Bacchus. He raised his sword over his head, his fist clenched so hard around the hilt his arm shook.

"So help me, if Simon dies . . . I'll . . ." The look in his eyes menacing and deadly, he stood perfectly still for a moment.

He roared, his rage reaching to the sky. "I'll find him. God in heaven, help me find him!"

Chapter Ten

The bloody trail had ended two miles back, Simon's footprints lost in the swirling wood stream that swelled with melting snow. With Bacchus' every step, Guy's hatred for Hamon deepened. Would that the man confront him here and now, he'd make certain this hour would be Lord Hamon's last on earth.

He wrapped his arms around the shivering Sybilla. Dusk fell over the woods like a giant shadow, providing ample opportunity for Hamon's men to attack if they chose. His sword heavy at his side, he was loath to give up the search for Simon, but he needed to get Sybilla and Regalo to Ketchem before nightfall.

He took a deep breath. Ketchem lay not half a league ahead. The four-towered fortress, built with costly gray stones from Tunbridge quarry, sat atop a high hill, surrounded by green fields and a wide, dark moat. Lord Phillip, the sixth Earl of Ketchem, had the good fortune to be rich, to be liked by his people, and loved by his wife. Lady Claire, indebted to God for the five sons and a daughter he'd blessed upon her and her husband, had commissioned stone crosses the size of church steeples, one for each child, to be erected on each side of the road leading to the drawbridge. They marked the way for travelers, and this evening the road was crowded with carts and riders, farmers and peddlers, whores and washer women, and messengers coming and going. The gatehouse drawbridge thronged with servants hurrying to get inside the castle before curfew.

Guy reined Bacchus in line behind a pair of wagons drawn by lumbering oxen. The moat swirled beneath them all, the water fresh from the spring runoff. It was the only time in the year it didn't smell like swill.

A gatehouse solider, a guard with bright blue eyes and lank brown hair, stepped in stride beside Bacchus and took the horse by the bridle. The soldier peered up at Guy. "Ho there!" He suddenly stopped and bowed. "Beg pardon, Sir Guy. I didn't recognize the horse. Lord Phillip has been looking for you. Word has it Hamon's men are at the border near your house."

Toll bells clanged. Sybilla stirred, and Guy eased her from his arms. He dismounted and wound Bacchus's reins around his fist. "Sir Simon. Have you seen him?"

The guard shook his head. "He's not come through tonight, Sir Guy." His curious gaze settled on Regalo. "What happened to your destrier? Who's the weanling?" He glanced at Sybilla, but he did not inquire who she was, worried, it appeared, he'd asked too much already.

"My destrier was stolen. The colt is mine. I bought him and Bacchus here, to replace the horse I lost."

Sybilla's voice rang out. "I am Sir Guy's servant. He was kind enough to let me ride instead of walk beside him." She dismounted, and took Regalo's lead rope in her hands.

The guard arched his thin eyebrows. "His servant?"

Guy shot a silencing look at Sybilla. He would have

to speak to her about talking out of turn. A servant did not answer for her master.

The guard stepped aside. "Lord Phillip wants an audience with you, Sir Guy. Lady Claire is anxious. She's been worried for you."

Guy grunted. Lady Claire considered him a hero-saint, but any man might have noticed how the dog that drank from the king's royal cup that night had sickened. Came as no surprise. The whole court had come from London to the feast and the hall was filled with hangers-on, and hopeful schemers. 'Twas the scent of henbane on the lovely Lady Ingrid's fingers, when she'd raised her hand to Guy's lips for a courtly kiss, that confirmed his suspicions—the king's pretty cousin had mixed the poison.

Guy's gut clenched. Aye, he'd saved King Richard's neck once at Balmont, and then again at Ketchem, along with his liege lord's and lady's. He was good at saving the people who employed him. But when it came to those who were closest to him he'd failed miserably.

"Yield for Sir Guy," yelled the guardsmen to the crowd. He bowed again and stepped aside.

The sounds of the yard, the smith's hammer clanking on the anvil, sheep bleating, and bakers peddling the last of their daily pies and tarts, assaulted Sybilla's ears. Smoke from the outdoor cooking pit drifted in the air and the smell of roast mutton and fresh bread made her stomach rumble.

Sybilla pulled a jumpy Regalo to her side, taking in the sights, the sounds and the tumultuous activity inside the castle yard. Mother Mary, the place was crowded and chaotic.

Guy laid his hand in the small of her back and urged her forward. "This way, Sybilla." He pointed to the stables. "Be cautious. The horse marshal will ask too many questions. Let me answer. You've already revealed too much by talking."

Sybilla stumbled over the rutted path. She staggered to her feet just as a ruddy-faced washerwoman with a basket of wet linens on her hip stepped in front of Guy.

"'Tis good you're back, Sir Guy, and safe. If you've any wash to do, let me send my Mary. Let her have first crack." The woman winked. She grabbed a grinning Mary by the hand and dragged her forward.

With her head wrapped in a beige linen cloth, her bare ankles and shoeless feet poking from a patched gray dress two sizes too small, Mary curtsied at Sir Guy. She smiled and her lips curved upward like a bow.

Guy exhaled. "Many thanks, Ernestine, and Mary, for the offer. But I've no coin to spare."

Ernestine laughed. "Mary would be willing to take your credit, Sir Guy. She does good work."

Mary blushed and nodded.

Sybilla glanced at Mary. She was as fair-skinned and as buxom as her mother, with breasts as big as melons. Mary smiled, her sparkling eyes generous and kind.

A deep voice boomed from the stables. A tall man with yellow hair strode forth and shooed the women away. "Sir Guy!"

The man wiped his hands on his leather apron, but his assessing eyes roamed over Sybilla. She instantly disliked him. Mother Mary, was he was looking at her breasts? She frowned at him and folded her arms across her chest. She'd not be appraised as if she were a new filly come to market.

The man tugged his leather cap over his ears. He took

Bacchus' reins from Guy. "What happened to you, good sir, and to Sir Simon? You missed the first horse race of the season. A knight from Wellington got knocked off his horse and died. Sir Malcolm won, but it was a bloody frackus. He's been bragging 'bout that for weeks, telling everyone you did not ride 'cause you knew his mount would win." He bowed with a flourish to Sybilla. "I'm John of Kent, Lord Phillip's horse marshal. And you are . . . ?"

Guy moved to stand beside her. He thrust Regalo's lead rope to the marshal. "I'll need two stalls. One for my horse, Bacchus, and one for my colt, Regalo."

John smiled. He tugged on Regalo. "I've two stalls ready. God's bones. Where'd you find him? He's what, mayhap, four or five months old? When he grows into that head of his he'll be a giant. He'll suit you, Sir Guy, in size and temperament." He yanked the startled colt toward the barn.

Instinctively, Sybilla reached for Regalo. He'd not been used to such harsh handling.

Guy shot her a warning look.

Sybilla lowered her outstretched arm. God in heaven, it felt like someone was taking away a piece of her heart. Regalo would spend a night, nay many nights to come, without her.

She wrung her hands. "Kind marshal, the colt will need good hay. He's still got a weanling's stomach, not long off mare's milk." Sybilla looked away, unable to look upon Regalo. The poor little horse was befuddled. She could sense his apprehension.

John tipped his head and looked at Sybilla. "You have skill in the care of horses?"

Guy took Sybilla by the wrist. "She does not. She is my servant."

John's eyes flashed with disappointment. "Too bad. She

looks like a horse midwife I once saw in Smithfield market. My Lady Claire's mare is due to foal and has had trouble in the past. I could use the help."

Sybilla's eyes widened, and hope filled her heart.

Guy put his hand on his sword. "She's not a horse midwife. She's my servant." He stepped closer to the marshal. "Her duties are *inside*. I'm leaving you in charge of my horse and colt. The little one has traveled far and been out in the cold too long. If anything should happen to him—if he sickens, send for me."

Sybilla's heart sank. She'd not expected to be excluded from Regalo's care. Heaven help her, how would she manage? How would Regalo fare?

John glanced at Sybilla. "He will be safe with me. I check as often on the horses as the night watch calls the hours. Nothing gets past me, Sir Guy. No horse comes or goes without my knowing about it." He headed into the stables, Regalo and Bacchus in tow.

Guy lowered his voice. "Sybilla, you must be on your guard here. You are far too comely to go unnoticed. John the Marshal has a wife, a string of lovers and four who'd claimed to have borne his bastards. Stay away from him." Guy cast a glance over his shoulder. "He knows more than he lets on. Don't volunteer information. I'd hoped that no one here had ever seen or heard of you. Deny you practice horse midwifery anymore if someone claims to recognize you. Lady Claire would not have a horse midwife in Ketchem Castle. I cannot risk having to send you away."

Sybilla clenched her fists. "Why not? You've cut me off from Regalo. It was not part of our bar—"

Guy inhaled and held up his hand. "I promise, I'll take you to the stables as often as I can. But in three month's time, in June, Lord Percy, a justice from the royal court will arrive at Ketchem. I must be here to see him, Sybilla. I intend to petition Percy with my case against Hamon. Lord Phillip supports me on this. There's no love lost between him and Hamon. They've been at border wars for years."

"And you expect Regalo will reveal his secret in three months time?"

"I do. Providing he has no fits, which he most certainly will if you are arrested. Please, I ask you, lay low and avoid trouble. We share a common enemy, you and I. Together we can beat Hamon. I could not bear to witness you on trial as a Separate. It is a scenario we cannot afford to risk."

Sybilla felt the blood drain from her face. Her hand flew to her cheek. The scent of roasted meat wafting from the cooking pits suddenly made her nauseous. Mother Mary, she'd given up her freedom thinking at least she would be safe, only to discover she was still in danger.

Guy's gentle hand steadied her trembling back.

"Come. And let me answer Lord Phillip's questions pertaining to you, as a master would for his servant." Guy flung his cloak behind his shoulders and urged her along. "Make haste. When the bells ring out the curfew, the yard will fill with drunken knights looking for their beds, a crowd as thick as crows. You'll not wish to be here."

Mother Mary, she never wished to be here anytime.

The smoldering warmth from the center hearth, a fireplace of the old style, filled the cavernous room with haze. The levered vent in the vaulted ceiling did little to help the smoke escape. Sybilla's eyes burned and she coughed. Pray to God the spring would soon fill the hall with fresh air and sunlight.

She scanned the hall. The massive oaken trestle table sitting against the wall was as long as a ship, and silken standards of brilliant red and green, Lord Phillip's colors, hung like sails suspended from the arched ceiling. At the opposite end of the room, costly column candles flickered beside a white-skirted dais and two ornately carved, tall-backed chairs sat in the center of the platform like thrones.

Sybilla sneezed and dust from the fouled winter rushes swirled around her. "Mother Mary, I've been in sweeter smelling stables."

Guy took her by the hand and strode across the hall, leading her to the side of a tapestry curtain which hung behind the dais. He tipped his head at the liveried page in red and green who opened a small door to an antechamber and motioned for Guy and Sybilla to enter.

Guy ushered Sybilla into the chamber. He took two steps, knelt and bowed his head.

Sybilla stood against the wall, her eyes affixed on the stately nobleman standing before her. She should have bowed, she supposed, but she was so in awe. 'Twas the closest she'd ever been to someone of such rank and noble birth. He was not a tall man, but his deep brown eyes sparkled with intelligence and beneath a beakish nose, his lips were red and full. His shoulder length hair was the color of the sable fur that lined the sleeves of his deep blue tunic. He could not have been much more than five and thirty years of age.

Lord Phillip took a seat in a leather chair painted with images of dragons and mythical beasts. "Rise, Sir Guy. I'm glad you have returned to us safely. When next I give you leave, I'll let my Lady Claire know. Your absence took her by surprise. Were she not so pious, I'd think she was in love with you, as are half the women of the castle." He chuckled, arched an eyebrow and motioned for Sybilla to come forward, too.

His eyes creased at the corners as he studied her, but he said nothing. His steward, a wiry man dressed in a black velvet gown with fox fur at the neck and cuffs, and heavy keys on his belt, stood beside him. With his shrewd eyes and pointed chin, the steward looked like a man who wasted not a coin on frivolity or excess, the type to be careful and consider the cost of adding another servant to the household.

Lord Phillip moved his gaze to Guy. "The gatehouse guard sent a runner. I hear you've lost your destrier and Sir Simon, and that you've gained a servant, a scruffy black horse, and a magic colt with four white socks."

Guy rose. "I have, my lord. I fear Sir Sim—"

Lord Phillip interrupted "I've sent a garrison to find Sir Simon. God's bones, you two have a knack for getting into trouble. Were not the both of you amongst the best I have in service, I'd long have given up on him—and you."

Guy took an anxious step forward. "Thank you, my lord. I ask for permission to join the search."

Lord Phillip eased up from his tall chair and poured wine into a pewter goblet. He offered the cup to Guy. "They will find him. I've business with you here. Now be at ease. Winter is at end, thank God. The fighting season is soon upon us. I'm told Hamon is on the prowl again at our borders—and he means to kill you. Am I correct?"

Guy refused the cup. "Old wounds still festering, my lord."

Lord Phillip set down the goblet. "Did you find the proof you need against him?"

"I have not, but I came upon this colt in Cornbury . . ." Guy let his voice trail off.

Sybilla straightened, waiting for Lord Phillip's reaction, wondering what he thought about Regalo.

Lord Phillip tapped the side of his jaw with his index finger. "So I've heard. You've found the mystical horse the legend said would be born in Cornbury. Best not let Lady Claire know you brought the beast into Ketchem. She'll command us all to Mass three times a day and, frankly, I cannot take sitting in the church talking to God any more than I have to."

A small smile upturned the corners of Guy's mouth.

Lord Phillip pointed at Sybilla. "Step forward, girl. Rumors abound and have already traveled from Cornbury to Ketchem. Are you the horse midwife who delivered the colt? You fit the description."

Sybilla advanced. She bobbed a curtsy and glanced at Guy before she answered.

Guy stepped in front of Sybilla. "Sybilla Corbuc is newly conscribed to me. She's quit the horse midwife business and I've long needed a servant. I've yet to find a page or squire who suits me. She'll work in the kitchens when she isn't serving me."

A little gasp slipped from Sybilla's lips. Guy poked her in the ribs with his elbow.

Lord Phillip shot a glance at his steward. The steward made no outward sign of objection, but wrote some figures on his ledger.

Lord Phillip leaned back in his chair and studied Sybilla. He let out a slow breath, as if he allowed this arrangement, but only out of respect for Guy. "Take note, Mistress Corbuc. Lady Claire is a pious woman. She has high expectations of the servants. Especially the women. Stay away from the stables, attend Mass twice a day and do not engage in lewd behavior. You will keep her happy and yourself out of trouble." He leaned closer. "Our priest serves a rigid bishop when it comes to church law. The same rules apply here as they did in Cornbury. If you are caught in the stables practicing your trade, even I will be powerless to help you."

Sybilla shifted. She'd never engaged in lewd behavior, and Guy had warned her about staying far from the stables. But church two times a day? When did servants get their work done?

Minutes passed before Lord Phillip finally sighed and held his beringed hand out to Sybilla. "Swear your fealty to me and promise to serve my most trusted knight, Sir Guy of Warwick, with loyal respect. Make your mark on my ledger. You shall be his servant. Sir Guy of Warwick shall be your master."

Sybilla's stomach churned, but she forced herself to kneel and kiss Lord Phillip's large gold ring. "I swear," she whispered.

Her mouth went dry. She licked her lips, her breath light and shallow. By the saints, she'd not expected this to be so formal. This made it harder, this swearing of oaths and signing ledgers, even though she'd not be here for long.

A trickle of sweat rolled down between her breasts. God help her, she'd sworn to her mother she'd never be a servant.

Lord Phillip rested his hand on her head. "Do Guy's bidding as if it were mine."

Sybilla nodded, feeling like the wind had been knocked from her lungs.

Guy stepped forward. "Many thanks, my lord. I will

see Mistress Corbuc settled. Is there other business you have with me?"

Lord Phillip took a deep breath. He studied his rings. "You have proven your loyalty to me and to King Richard, more than once." He looked up. "Rumor has it Hamon mounts an army and prepares for war. Against Ketchem. Lord Percy is his ally at court, not mine. At this moment, there is no nobleman in England more powerful than Percy. When he comes here on progress in June, he'll ask me to yield four hundred hectares to the south, including Baldwin forest, to Lord Hamon—in the name of the king of course. I will refuse. But I must make Ketchem ready for what is sure to come."

Guy rested his hand on his sword. "I understand, my lord. You have my oath. I stand united with you against Lord Hamon."

Lord Phillip rubbed his forehead. "And you understand by doing so you take a stand against Lord Percy? You risk a fair hearing before the court with him, especially if you ally with me. The likelihood your case will be refused will be much greater."

Guy nodded, the slow rise and fall of his chest the only sign of the gravity of his decision.

Lord Phillip arose. "We've much to discuss. But not tonight. Tonight is the feast in honor of the April Fair. You must sit at the high table. I need good men by my side, now more than ever. Make yourself ready. And as soon as we've word of Sir Simon, you'll be the first to know."

Guy bowed.

Sybilla curtsied. *By the saint's I've walked into a lion's den and know not how to act or what to do.*

She watched as Lord Phillip strode out of the little room. The steward cleared his throat and he glided to a small table, his black robes swirling at his slippered feet.

"Sir Guy, you and your servant must make your marks here. I'll add her to the household ledger. How long is she conscribed?" He spoke to Guy as if Sybilla were a child not capable of answering.

Guy lifted the quill and spoke to the steward. "Three months. A trial period to see how well she does. She needs a gown and a pallet. Can you get them for me?" He scrawled his mark on the ledger. "How much?" He reached for the velvet pouch at his belt.

The steward nodded. "I'll have them sent, Sir Guy. But your coin's no good here. Lord Phillip would not accept it, and I'm an honest man. We need only have your marks." He held the quill out to Sybilla.

Her heart pounding like a drum, Sybilla heard her mother's pleading voice echoing in her ears, *"Never sell yourself to servitude, Sybilla. Never."*

Sybilla trembled. Guy stood there with his hand on his sword, his mouth in a hard straight line. He stared straight ahead, as if he never doubted for a moment she would sign.

Blessed saints I'm honor bound to comply. I do this for Regalo. Pray my mother will forgive me.

Sybilla took the quill into her shaking hand. The pen felt as heavy as a sword. A single drop of ink fell from the point, and rolled down the parchment like a trickle of blood.

Sybilla closed her eyes.

Guy's strong hand rested on her shoulder. "Sybilla," was all he said, the sound of her name reassuring.

With every ounce of will she could muster, she opened her eyes and set the quill tip to the ledger. She made a crooked *X* next to Guy of Warwick's mark.

"'Tis done," she said softly, feeling as if she'd signed the order of her own execution.

God's feet, she needed to sit down, but even she knew a servant never sat in the presence of her master. The room whirled around her and her head felt dizzy.

Guy caught her by the arm. "Sybilla—"

She snapped her head up, trying hard to focus.

Guy released her. His eyes flicked to the steward.

Warmth flooded her neck, her face. She would not cry. She'd known this day was coming. In three months' time, she would be free, as per their bargain. She bit her lip. She'd no reason to doubt the pledge she made today could not be undone—but a small voice inside her warned of those she'd known who'd sold their freedom and never got it back. And Guy had made no mention of what would happen at the end of the three month term to the steward, or to Lord Phillip. What if she'd just signed her life away forever?

The steward dusted the ink with a sprinkling of sand. He closed the book. "Good eve, Sir Guy." He bowed, and swept away taking no more notice of Sybilla, as though she were nothing but wall decoration.

Guy ran his hand through his hair. "A war. Damn Hamon to hell."

Sybilla followed Guy to his private chambers, his feet thundering across the stone pavers, through the labyrinth of hallways and down the stairways. The last turn took them deeper into the bowels of the castle, where the wall torches were posted only every hundred paces.

Guy stopped before a low archway and threw open a small wooden door. Motioning for her to follow, he ducked inside.

Cold billowed from the room like winter wind as Sybilla stepped across the threshold. Guy set his torch into the sconce that hung over his narrow rope bed. He knelt and stoked the small brazier on the floor. Meager light filled the chamber, the room awash in gray shadows.

Mother Mary. Guy of Warwick slept in a cellar in the bottom of the castle. The dank little room was no bigger than a horse stall. A damp chill clung to the stone walls and the vaulted ceiling, so damp the place felt wet. Why would a knight held in such esteem by his lord sleep in a converted storeroom, where the pungent scent of yeast and hops filled the vacuous space? At least the smell of wine and aged beer didn't make her sneeze, but by the saints, except for the bed, the brazier and a chest beneath a narrow window, the room might as well have been a prison.

Did he live here by choice? Mayhap he did not have the means or the clout to keep her after all—or Regalo. Had she bargained away her freedom for nothing?

Guy eased down on the bed. The deep circles under his eyes looked even darker in the shadows. His eyes searched her face. "'Tis not so bad a place. I've privacy here and it's quiet. I have a cat to keep away the rats. I can sleep in peace with no one but my ghosts, as you like to call them, to disturb me."

Sybilla scanned the grim little room.

Mother Mary, he actually chooses to sleep here. Here he can shut himself away.

Guy rested his head in his hands.

She sat beside him on the bed, her knee touching his thigh. The heat from his body made her warm all over.

Guy lifted his head and looked at her, his eyes searching, questioning.

Wanting.

He turned and brushed his knuckles along her cheek, a gentle caress—one she'd not expected.

She closed her eyes, admitting to herself she wanted him to need her.

He spoke in a soft voice, his tone heavy. "Sybilla, I fear for you. You heard what Lord Phillip said. Stay away from the stables. I cannot risk losing you or Regalo. If the colt leads me to the evidence I need against Hamon, I could avert a war. Percy or no, if my proof is strong enough, Hamon could be imprisoned, his campaign crippled. My quest is now more than avenging murder. It's about survival. Ketchem castle could not withstand an attack. Thousands could die. I cannot protect them." Guy lowered his head. "I could not protect you, Sybilla."

Sybilla squeezed his hand. "You are not responsible for me. Fight Hamon in a war if it comes to that. But you cannot hold yourself accountable for lives lost in the past or, God keep forbid, those who die in a war. It will be worse for all of us if you don't stand against Lord Hamon."

Guy's face grew pensive. He said nothing in response, but he entwined his fingers with hers and leaned closer, his sensual mouth just a hair's breadth away.

Her heart skipped a beat. Mother Mary, she wanted to touch his lips, to feel their warmth against her own, but by the saints she could not risk this, this whatever-it-was growing stronger between them. She'd not end up with a babe in her belly. If her life was hard now, poor and without a husband, just imagine what it would be like, pregnant and cast off from Ketchem by Lady Claire.

She scrambled from the bed.

Guy drew back and let his hand fall to his side. Rising, he took a slow breath. "Sybilla, it would be best if you slept in the great hall with the other servants. I'll stay close for a while to make sure you are safe, but—"

His words doused over her like cold water. "The hall?"

He stepped forward and held her by the upper arms, his

eyes smoldering, his chest against hers. "God in heaven, it's been too long since I've . . ." He sucked in his breath. "It's been too long since I've had a woman in my bed. And God help me, I could not sleep here tonight with you without touching you in that way, without showing you all there can be between a man and a woman."

He released her and stepped away, his chest heaving, the space between them as wide as the ocean.

Sybilla rubbed her temple, her head spinning. Hell to the devil, sleeping in the hall could be no more dangerous than sleeping here with him. Mother Mary, she'd not the strength to resist him. She knew she would succumb if he so much as touched her.

She should insist *he* find another place to sleep, but this cellar was too grim for her to fathom staying here all night alone. "The hall will suit me fine, Sir Guy. After all, I am a servant."

A look of surprise flashed across Sir Guy's face, followed by regret. "We've a few hours before the feast begins. I want to check on news of Simon. Wait here until I return."

He strode from the chamber.

The door shut behind him. A peculiar longing, a need for she knew not what, filled the empty room.

Sybilla spun on her heels and paced, her fingers clenched at her sides. St. Genevieve, she felt like she would burst with longing, with the kind of possessive desire that made her more and more willing to give in and love the man, with her body and her soul. What had been once just a spark of desire for Guy of Warwick, was now a full blown fire, raging.

A rap on the door interrupted her silent agony.

A small voice piped through the door slats. "Sybilla Corbuc? Sir Guy sent me."

Sybilla smoothed her skirts and padded across the stone pavers. Through the slats she could see the dark, thick eyebrows and smooth forehead of a woman, a girl really.

"'Tis Mary, the washerwoman's daughter. I've brought your things."

Sybilla furrowed her brow. "My things?"

"Your pallet, dress, and shoes. At Sir Guy's request."

Stepping to the side, Sybilla opened the door and motioned for Mary to come in. The girl swished inside, her big blue eyes taking in the tiny room. She shivered and hugged the bundle to her chest. "I'll never understand why he sleeps down here when he could have a fine apartment on the upper floors. Rather keep to himself, I guess."

She held her arms out to Sybilla, offering her the pallet, a dark brown gown, a clean linen veil, and a well-cut pair of leather ankle boots, serviceable and sturdy.

Sybilla glanced at the bundle. The gown bore Lord Phillip's badge and beneath it, the emblem of a servant—Sir Guy of Warwick's herald, a sword across a sheaf of wheat—prominently displayed on the bodice.

"For you," Mary said, lifting her face, a red slap mark on her cheekbone glaring and fresh.

Sybilla took the bundle and set it on the bed. "Thank you, Mary. I hope it was no trouble for you to bring them." She looked pointedly at Mary's cheek.

Mary lowered her eyes. She touched her fingers to the red mark on her face. "No trouble. Sir Malcolm caught me on the way here. I'd not give him what he wanted. Not this time." She grinned half-heartedly.

"I shall speak to Sir Guy on your behalf. Sir Malcolm hasn't the right to—"

Mary took Sybilla by the sleeve. "No, please. Anything you say will only make it worse for me. Sir Guy

won't be there when the moon is high and men like Sir
Malcolm are still drinking. He's a bad one, that Sir Malcolm. Here's a warning to you, find a place to sleep after
the feast tonight that will keep you safe and hidden. Go
to the darkest corner of the hall, far from the hearth. Be
wary of any sort of invitation. You'll be getting plenty
with that golden hair."

Sybilla stiffened. If what Mary said was true, she
couldn't count on Guy to protect her either. Best be prepared to defend herself.

Mary ran her hand down Sybilla's hair. "Use your veil
and keep your head covered." She patted the dirty strip
of linen she'd wound around her head. "Lady Claire
likes for us to wear it up, but I do it so's I don't get
grabbed by the hair."

Sybilla furrowed her brows. "Lady Claire tolerates
this treatment of the female servants?"

"Oh no. But she can't control what happens when she
goes to bed. And no servant would complain against a
nobleman or knight. It'd do no good. Would only make
it harder on the rest of us." She shrugged. "'Tis our lot
in life."

Mary's words grated on Sybilla's ears. "Who do you
serve, Mary?"

"Lord Phillip, of course. Most of us do, except for a
few knights who've got servants of their own. My
master is a good one, a great lord, though I've never per-
sonally spoken to him. You've no need to worry. Your
master is the handsomest, and the kindest knight in the
castle. He's brave, too, and treats us fairly. Never strikes
or yells. Count yourself lucky to be conscriped to him."
Her cautious eyes roamed the tiny room. "'Tis quiet
down here, but a little cold." She tucked one bare foot on
top of the other and rubbed her arms.

Blessed saints. The winters in the countryside could be harsh, and the work hard, but there you'd not have to worry about being grabbed by the hair or finding a place to hide at night so you might sleep. And you couldn't go barefooted in the winter.

Kneeling, Sybilla picked up her wooden shoes. Old shoes, even those as beaten and rough-hewn as these, were better than no shoes.

She held them out to Mary. "Here. I won't be needing them. If they're too big, stuff the insides with straw."

The girl's eyes widened and her pretty bow-shaped mouth upturned into a wide smile. "I can have 'em? May the lord bless you, Sybilla." Laughing, she cradled the shoes against her chest before she slipped them on her dirty feet. She bobbed a curtsey, as if Sybilla had been Lady Claire herself. "Thank you. I've got nothing much to give you back, except some tricks I can teach you that'll help you get on easier at Ketchem. With that hair and pretty face, you will need them. Find me tonight before you bed down in the hall."

Mary halted. "You *will* be bedding down in the hall. Lady Claire would not want you sleeping here. It would set the servants talking." Her eyes swept over Guy's bed. "Though I couldn't blame you if you did. I'd be happy to have Sir Guy of Warwick warm my bed. Anybody would."

Chapter Eleven

The moon rose against the pewter-gray sky and footsteps passed along the walkway above the chamber window. Excited voices chattered in the night air and headed toward the hall, but none of them was Sir Guy's.

Sybilla pulled the blanket over her shoulders. In the hours since he'd left, the little room had gotten colder. She fed another pile of kindling into the brazier. Mother Mary, where had he gone? Was this delay a sign something was amiss? Had Simon been found? Was Regalo safe and acting normal? 'Twas possible he wasn't eating. What if he'd had an attack?

At the thought of Regalo, all alone in the stables and unattended, Sybilla's stomach heaved. Pain pierced her side, a pain so hot and searing she doubled over.

Mother Mary, I cannot stay here another moment. I must go to Regalo.

Clutching the blanket around her shoulders, she hurried to the door and just as she reached for the iron handle, Sir Guy strode inside, his cheeks pink from the cold and his nose as red as wine. He slammed the door behind him and blew on his hands. He looked relieved to see her.

"Ah, Sybilla, I've good news! Simon has been found. He's wounded, resting in the kitchen now, but with care and time he'll live."

Sybilla's heart lightened. "Praise God."

Guy studied her intently. Disappointment flashed over his face as his eyes fell on the blanket she'd wrapped around her shoulders. He glanced at the door, opened his mouth as if to pose a question, but took a deep breath instead.

"I've been to see Regalo, too," he said softly, his tone reassuring. "By God, he's grown, Sybilla. No need to worry 'oer him."

Sybilla took an eager step forward. "He's eating? Hasn't had a fit?"

"He's fine. Simon's fine, and I—"

Without warning, Guy wrapped his arms around her, pulled her to him, and then he kissed her firmly on the mouth, his tongue slipping past her lips.

He tasted of red wine, and the feel of his chest against hers made her heart race. She breathed in, taking in his male scent—of horses and of leather. His arms around her felt wonderfully strong and warm. She moaned and pressed against him, slipping her arms around his neck.

A throaty sound of pleasure rumbled from his throat, just before he broke off their embrace and stepped away. He ran his hand through his hair. "I'm sorry. I know you do not wish for my attentions."

Sybilla scarcely heard a word, her heart pounding. God in heaven, Guy of Warwick had it wrong. She didn't wish for his attentions? Nay, she ached for him! Desire filled her heart every time he kissed her. How she longed to feel more of this, this whatever-it-was that made her want to forget caution and let him show her everything she wished to know.

She let the blanket slip from her shoulders. "'Twas not I who stopped the kiss. I rather liked it."

She brushed a stray tendril from her cheek.

Guy sucked in his breath. "By the saints, if you knew how much I want—" He cut his words short and his eyes roamed the length of her.

His face suddenly clouded.

"Why are you not wearing the clothes I sent? Do they not fit?" He gestured to the dress still lying on the bed.

Sybilla lowered her eyes. "I don't care for the stitching on the bodice."

"What stitching?" Guy yanked the gown from the bed. He scowled. "My emblem offends you?"

The torch light flickered. Sybilla clasped her hands behind her back. "Nay. 'Tis not your mark. 'Tis hard for me to wear a servant's garb. I fear I cannot play the role of servant with conviction."

Guy let out long sigh, his face softening. "Sybilla, we have a common enemy in Hamon. We must work together, do what we must to achieve our goals. I ask you to please get dressed. Lord Phillip expects us both in the hall for the feast."

Turning, he strode to the chest beside his bed and flung open the lid. He held up a pair of richly woven, dark blue hose and a matching velvet tunic, plain, but elegant and well cut.

Sybilla raised her eyebrows at the fineness. She watched him dress, the sight of him mesmerizing.

He stripped, donned a crisp white linen shirt with a keyhole neck and turned to face her as he pulled a blue velvet tunic over his head. He sat on the edge of the bed and put on his fresh hose without looking up at her.

"Lord Phillip and Lady Claire will be displeased if we are late." He fastened an ornate silver belt low around his waist, the style emphasizing his broad chest and shoulders.

He stood and pinned a silver brooch, Lord Phillip's coat of arms, at his shoulder.

Mother Mary, no woman in the hall tonight would be able to keep her eyes off him.

She lowered her head. "Dressed like that, you should have a real servant. I fear I cannot do you justice."

He folded his arms. "You can. Let me show you."

Sybilla looked up to see Guy snatch a cover from the bed and tie it round his waist so that it fell to his ankles like a skirt. "Now watch how I walk," he said, his voice serious.

He strode across the room taking womanly, light-footed steps. "Walk like this, with a short stride so that your ankles and your feet don't show." He spun around and faced her. "A freeman walks like you do—like this." He kicked his feet up, his "skirt" swinging round his hips like a bell. He halted and planted his fists on his hips. "Try not to walk like that."

Sybilla suppressed the urge to grin.

"And furthermore, wear your veil like this." He tugged his veil low onto his forehead, to the level of his eyebrows. "A servant should cover most of their head, in deference to their master. A freeman wears her veil like this." He pushed the veil back from his face and lifted his chin. "Do you see the difference?"

Sybilla felt the laughter bubble up from her throat. She clapped her hand over her mouth, aware that her shoulders shook.

Guy's wide mouth upturned into a grin. He stared at her with a look she couldn't understand.

"What?" she asked, stifling her laugh. "What is it?"

"'Tis the first time I've ever heard you laugh, Sybilla. I like the sound."

In the silence that fell across the room, she could hear Guy's heart beating.

He pulled off his veil and skirt.

He said not another word but simply held the brown servant's dress out to Sybilla. Her eyes came to rest on the brown bodice.

She felt her chest tighten and she struggled to catch her breath. Remembering. Remembering her mother's talk of whippings and her shredded, blood-stained servant's dress. Remembering the girl who swore to her mother she would never be a servant. Surely her mother would understand this agreement with Sir Guy was necessary and only for three months.

"Sybilla. Are you ill?" Guy held the dress out. "We are already late. We'll miss the first course."

Mustering every ounce of her will, Sybilla snatched the dress, the movement quick, intended to hide her shaking hands. She whipped off her threadbare blue gown and dragged the brown dress over her head, then tied the veil over her head.

She smoothed her skirts. "I am ready."

Guy smiled and swung open the door. He ushered her outside, his hand possessively at the small of her back. "Thank you, Sybilla. Be careful tonight. All of the hall will be watching."

Sybilla fell in place a few steps behind him, remembering her place, practicing her servant's walk. It was harder than it looked.

Music drifted across the courtyard, lifted in the night air over the herbery and reached the tunnels that led away from the cellar. As they approached the great hall, bells tinkled and drums pounded out a festive rhythm. Guy glanced back at Sybilla, his face calm. Not at all like what she was feeling.

"Sir Guy, I've never feasted in a castle, never served a noble."

"I will be there, Sybilla. Watch me. And stay away from Sir Malcolm."

Guy settled at the bench at the high table, his achingly full stomach filled with roasted beef. The hall clamored with the sounds of men and women laughing, dogs barking, music, and the smell of too many sweaty guests. He'd been seated at the high table, next to Lady Edith of Graysbrook, a plump widow with a fondness for salt. He watched while she dipped her spoon in the salt cellar and licked her utensil clean behind her pudgy hand.

Guy leaned away from Lady Edith, and glanced over his shoulder at Sybilla. She stood against the wall behind him, waiting, so it seemed, like the other servants who stood at the ready to fetch a dish, a wiping cloth, or wine. Her astonished gaze roamed the hall, taking in the revelry and the wealth. Dancers twirled around the hearth and the parade of servants carried plates of pork and brown bread, pickled fish, lamb and onion stew. Her eyes came to rest on Lady Claire, who sat dressed in a green damask gown with a white linen veil strapped beneath her narrow chin.

Lady Claire waved to Guy and silently instructed his approach.

Guy swung his legs from the table bench and dusted off his tunic. He took Sybilla by the elbow and ushered her away from the wall. "Lady Claire wants to meet you,

Sybilla. She knows all the servants by name. Try not to stick your chin up."

Sybilla faltered. "Why does she wish to see me? I didn't spill anything, or stick my fingers in the gravy. I've kept my head down."

Guy tugged on her elbow. "You are new here and she wants to meet you, that's all."

Guy made his way around the noble diners and their bored pages. He knelt before the seated Lady Claire and lifted her hand to his lips. The sweet smell of rose water wafted from her sleeve.

Lady Claire smiled. She had keen blue eyes and a waist that hadn't thickened, though she'd blessed Lord Phillip with five healthy sons and a daughter, a round-faced girl with mouse-brown hair who sat quietly beside her and drew lines in the gravy on her trencher.

Lady Claire rested a reproachful hand on her daughter's arm and shook her head, then turned her attention to Sir Guy. "Welcome home, Sir Guy. I hear you've a new horse, an odd little colt in the stables, and a comely servant." Blue eyes twinkling, she craned her neck to get a better look at Sybilla. "Come closer, dear. What are you called and what duties has Sir Guy given you? We've servants a plenty already here. He's never gone wanting for attention," she said too sweetly.

Sybilla stepped forward and knelt. Her face warmed from the tip of her chin to her brow.

Guy cast Sybilla a warning look. Lady Claire used her sweetness with the cunning of an archangel. She knew more about everybody's business in the castle than the priest who heard confessions.

Sybilla's voice cracked. "My name is Sybilla, my lady. Sir Guy has given me no duties yet. I've only just arrived."

Guy held his breath. No harm in that answer. Pray she said no more.

Lady Claire nodded thoughtfully, then her mouth widened into a disapproving smile. "I see. Then I suggest, Sir Guy, she work in the kitchens, unless she has some other God given talent?"

Guy bowed. "She was a horse midwife, my lady. But she's quit the practice. I've no shortage of other tasks for her." He deferred to Lady Claire because decorum required it of him, but Lord in Heaven, she could meddle.

Lady Claire's eyebrows lifted. "Better you should take a page or squire, Sir Guy. But if my husband has approved, then you shall have your servant."

She directed her gaze at Sybilla. "Be a good servant to Sir Guy. You shall find him a fair master. I trust you will attend my chapel twice a day and break no rules of church."

Sybilla nodded. "No, my lady." She looked up. "I mean yes, my lady. I mean I understand."

"I wish to make it clear, I'll not have a pregnant, unwed servant in my court. I will not tolerate lewd behavior. Do not spoil things for Sir Guy, or give him trouble."

Sybilla's face burned. "I will do as he says, my lady."

Guy smiled at Lady Claire. Bless her soul, she had a way of getting to the core of it, of seeing what he wished she didn't. She'd known Sybilla was a horse midwife and he suspected she knew he was attracted to his new servant.

He bowed. "I assure you, Lady Claire, Sybilla promises to be a model servant, and she has a great lady in you to lead her."

Lady Claire's eyes lit up with pleasure. He bowed, strode back to his place at the table, stealing glances over his shoulder to make certain that Sybilla followed. She took her place behind him and stood against the wall.

He eased down next to Lady Edith. She held her cup above her head and licked her salt-speckled lips, then barked over her shoulder. "My cup is dry. Again." She smirked at Guy. "Your new servant needs some training. I suggest you beat her. That'll make her pay attention. I recommend you don't deal with slovenly servants lightly, that's been my approach."

Guy suppressed a smile. "Really? And has it been effective?" Lady Edith's young page slept standing up, leaning against the wall behind her. He snored.

A screech suddenly rose above the din, a woman's voice.

Guy twisted round to see young Mary in the grip of Sir Malcolm. He had one arm around her waist, his hand on her breast. Guy took a deep breath.

He grabbed Sir Malcolm by the shoulder, just as an earthen pitcher cracked over Sir Malcolm's head. Red wine streamed down Sir Malcolm's startled face and Guy's outstretched arm. Sybilla stood behind Sir Malcolm, holding the broken ewer in her hand. She stared at the fragments scattered over the table as if they'd fallen from the heavens.

Mary gathered up her skirts and raced to the kitchens. The crowd fell silent, all eyes on the dais. Guy caught a glimpse of Lady Claire and others shooing their young daughters and children from the hall.

Sir Malcolm bolted to his feet, his eating knife in hand, and wine trickling down his face. His eyes flared like an angry dog's. "You bitch!" He grabbed for Sybilla, but his lunge came up short. A strong hand caught him by the scruff of his neck and yanked him back.

Guy bellowed, "Leave her be, Malcolm."

Sybilla's face turned as white as milk. Her hands trembled as she set the broken ewer down.

Sir Malcolm snatched a drying towel from his page and ran the cloth over his close-cropped hair. "Guy of Warwick, you dare pick a fight over a serving wench? You slight *me* for a peasant? You'll rue the hour—"

Guy's hand flew to his sword hilt. "I applaud her, Sir Malcolm. I cheer her on. You need to learn the manners befitting one who calls himself a knight. Do you wish to challenge me on that?"

The hall fell silent. A hound slipped under the table and whined.

Sybilla's voice rang out. "Sir Malcolm, forgive my ineptitude. I spilt the pitcher whilst I fumbled to pour the Lady Edith more wine."

Lady Edith hiccupped. "Stupid girl. That was the last, I'd wager, of the good wine." She slammed her cup down, the white cloth beneath it saturated with wine. "Mind my advice, Sir Guy, you should beat your servant. 'Twould make her more attentive."

Sir Malcolm cast his furious gaze to Sybilla. His eyes narrowed. A lascivious, gap-toothed smile overtook his face. "This one's yours, Sir Guy? She needs some proper instruction. I'll volunteer to give it to her." He grabbed Sybilla by the wrist and jerked her to him.

His blood racing, pounding in his head, Guy drew his sword and took a single menacing step toward Sir Malcolm. He pointed the tip of his blade at Malcolm's heart. "Release her now, or I will squash you like a louse in front of the whole court."

Lady Claire's shrill voice rose above the crowd. "Sir Malcolm, please. You've been warned before about your rude behavior in the hall. I'll not tolerate this."

Lord Phillip raised his hand. "Sir Guy, Sir Malcolm. Enough! Both of you. Malcolm, you especially test my patience. Release the girl."

Sir Malcolm instantly released Sybilla. He casually adjusted his tunic as if it had all been a great misunderstanding. "My Lord, Sir Guy must really teach his servant some manners. She's clumsy. Needs to learn to watch her step."

Guy seethed. Lord Phillip turned his back on Malcolm and waved at his steward, signaling the night to end. A lone trumpet blared and servants jumped to clear the food from the tables.

Lord Phillip raised his cup and spoke loud enough for the whole hall to hear. "I bid you all good night. Save your challenges for the field." He looked pointedly at the end of the table. "I'll hold Ketchem Castle's horse race in mid-August. The prize this year will exceed all others. A chest of gold and twenty head of cattle. May the fastest horse win."

The guests cheered. Men rapped their cups on the tables. Lord Phillip strode from the hall to the sound of trumpets, his wife at his side and his attendants and his counselors trailing behind him.

Guy watched a page sidle up to Malcolm. The boy spoke in a low voice, but loud enough for Guy to hear. "My Lord Phillip wants a word with you, Sir Malcolm. He bids you come to his chambers. At once."

Sir Malcolm rose from the bench and shot a deadly look at Guy. He tossed his short mantle behind his shoulder and spun on his heels to follow the page. Sybilla pressed herself against the stone as he passed, her eyes lowered, her breath held tight in her chest.

Guy took a deep breath, the blood rushing from his head. "You've made an enemy of him."

"He was hurting Mary. Someone had to stop him."

"I would have, had you given me the chance."

"But what about Mary? Does no one care what happens to her?"

Guy lowered his voice. "I agree with your sentiments entirely, Sybilla. Malcolm deserved calling out for his bad behavior. Mary's treatment tonight was most unfortunate. She wasn't hurt. I'll wager she will keep clear of Malcolm from now on. But now he has it in for you. Mayhap you shouldn't sleep in the hall tonight. I'd rather risk the Lady Claire's ire and have you sleep in my chambers."

Sybilla shook her head. "Nay, Sir Guy, we cannot spend the night together. People will assume worst about us—about me. I'll not be the cause of your fall from favor with the Lady Claire. I will be fine sleeping in the hall. Mary's held a place for me with the other women, far from trouble. I'll keep clear of Sir Malcolm. I promise."

Guy studied three soldiers who rolled dice for the last cup of wine. He spoke to Sybilla in a low voice. "I'll stay close by."

He nodded, then spun around and strode from the hall, leaving Sybilla standing in the midst of the servants who were taking down the trestle tables, and the guests who laid their pallets in the choicest spots around the fire.

Once out of view of the hall, Guy settled in an alcove in a nearby tunnel, a hundred paces from his cellar. He pulled his cloak around his shoulders. He'd give Sybilla less than half the night before she fled the hall. He'd wait right here, ready to escort her to his room. Damn the Lady Claire. He cared too much about Sybilla to leave her unattended.

At the thought of Malcolm standing there with wine dripping down his face and shoulders, Guy let the corners of his mouth upturn into a grin. Suppressing the urge to laugh out loud, he leaned his head against the wall and folded his arms. Malcolm had it coming. Sybilla Corbuc was quite the woman.

Guy shook his head and smiled. Damnation. He enjoyed every unpredictable minute he'd spent with her thus far.

Chapter Twelve

"Don't stand there, Sybilla, help us clear the dais, then we can eat and go to bed." Mary rolled the tablecloth from the far end, clucking beneath her breath when she saw the red stain where the earthen crock had spilled its contents. "Tshh, will take a lot of salt and vinegar to get that out. We'll be toiling over this for hours."

Sybilla collected up the cloth from the opposite end of the table. "I'll help, Mary. It was my doing."

Mary laughed. "Ahh, did you see the look on Sir Malcolm's face? You'da thought he'd been struck by the Almighty himself." She lowered her voice and heaved the big white cloth into a basket. "You should na' have done it, but I can't say I feel sorry for him. He's been pestering me for months. Thank you. And Sir Simon was kind to ask about me." She clucked. "Him, a knight being holed up in the kitchen nursing his own wounds, asking about me? I'll bet he's handsome when he gets his color back. Told me when he gets better, to come find him if Sir Malcolm ever gave me trouble." She spun the basket round and grabbed one handle. "Can you help me haul this to the kitchen? My mam is waiting for the linens."

Sybilla smiled. Simon would be pleased to hear a woman thought him handsome.

She grabbed the handle and made her way with Mary to the kitchen, a cavernous room with two hearths big enough to roast an ox in each. The warmth from the fire drifted over her and the smell of food mixed with smoke hung in the heavy air. Tired servants sat around the tables, eating leftover trencher bread and meat.

At the sight of her daughter, Ernestine wiped her greasy fingers on her apron and rose from her seat. "Lord help us, what a mess!" She pointed to the basket. "Come Mary, we need to get that soaking." She took the handle from Sybilla and waddled with her daughter toward the door.

Mary called across her shoulder. "Eat, Sybilla, and remember what I told you 'bout sleepin' in the hall. I'll find you in the morning."

As she chewed on a slice of sweet-sausage and a cheese Sybilla scanned the room and rubbed her aching neck. Would that she could find a space to sleep in here.

Her eyes fell upon a familiar face, a bearded man resting on a pallet beside the giant hearth. Her heart lifted. "Simon?"

He struggled to sit up, pain twisting his face, his breath rushing from his lungs.

Sybilla hurried to his side. "Simon! 'Tis good to see you." She knelt beside him and laid her hand against his bandaged chest, urging him to lie down. "When Sir Guy lost your trail, I thought—I thought . . ."

He smiled beneath his woolly red beard. "You thought the wolves had got me? 'Twas Hamon's red-shoed sheriff that did this to me." He pointed to his bandaged shoulder. "Chased me down on his horse and poked me with his sword. Thought he had me because I'd been wounded." He laughed, the effort causing him to cough. "He isn't much of a swordsman, your sheriff. I nicked his forearm with my blade. He yelped like a pup, then got back on his horse and went to get the rest o' Hamon's men. They couldn't find me, though. I made sure I walked in the water. Harder to track, but God's hair, it was cold."

Sybilla held a wine cup to his lips. She smiled and wiped his feverish forehead with a cloth.

He pushed the cup away. "I packed my wound with snow, just like you told me to do when Dunback hit me on the head. It stopped the bleeding. I walked in the woodland streams to Forthington, where a farmer found me." He closed his eyes. "Hamon lost my tracks. I lost the feeling in my feet." He smiled. "When Lord Phillip's men stormed into that farmer's hut . . ." He paused. "I thought I'd died and gone to heaven. Guy sent 'em, I know that much. I owe the man my life—again."

Sybilla's heart wrenched. Simon could have died from his sword wound alone, if not from exposure.

She used a cloth to smooth the wiry red hair from Simon's forehead. "Do you need anything?"

Simon didn't open his eyes, but his breathing slowed. He shook his head, and a trace of a smile lifted the corners of his thin lips. "Keep an eye on Regalo, the rascal. He'll go a wandering when you're not looking." He rested his hot hand on hers, his voice so thin and weak she could barely hear him. "Guy needs someone to look after him, too, though he'd not admit it. Stay with him. I think he cares for you, more than you can know."

Sybilla shook her head. "Guy needs no one. He shuts himself away at night in a cellar. He keeps me with him because of Regalo."

Simon dozed, his breathing settled. The thought of Regalo gave Sybilla pause. There'd been no sign that he was in trouble and no one had reported his strange behavior. Mayhap he didn't need her anymore? She wrapped her veil around her shoulders, tucked her pallet beneath her arm and headed to the hall. At least there she was closer to the stables and would get first news if there was trouble with Regalo.

The hall stank of sour ale and sweat. The torch lights on the walls long extinguished, the fire in the great hearth had dwindled and smoke drifted upward to the shadows in the vaulted ceiling. Most of the warmth in the room came from the occupants, at least a hundred guests, mostly those who'd chosen not to travel home tonight.

Sybilla stepped tentatively around the dais, her eyes adjusting to the darkness. The rushes at her feet were strewn with refuse. Dogs rooted for scraps and growled at each other. She scanned the hall. Merchants, tradesmen, servants, and young knights who did not rank enough to win housing in the upstairs apartments, all sprawled on makeshift pallets. Bodies slept on the benches, on the stairs, and in the rushes every which way, dogs curled close beside them.

The place in front of the hearth was especially popular. No matter what course she chose, it would be near impossible to walk without stepping on someone.

Her nose itched and she choked back a sneeze. Blessed saints, she needed to find a place to bed down before her head exploded. But the corners of the hall where Mary had advised her to sleep were already packed with women. There was no space there to accommodate another.

She clutched her pallet to her chest. There seemed to be fewer people sleeping by the entrance than anywhere else. No doubt, the cold and damp from the outside seeped between the cracks in the great wooden doors. At least a little fresh air would be easier to breathe than the stink of the rushes.

She wove her way across the room, offering her apologies to the grunting guests whose hands or feet she stepped on. A dog snapped at her heels as she passed the hearth, and as she turned to free her hem from his teeth, she caught a glimpse of a man's bare buttocks, and pair of woman's bare legs wrapped around his waist.

Could they be . . . ?

Sybilla's eyes widened.

Oh my. The lusty couple were not the only guests so engaged. A servant woman from the kitchen knelt in front of a knight who had his hose around his knees. He threw his head back and moaned.

Sybilla averted her eyes.

"Feast your eyes not on sin, lest you lose your sight," the nuns at St. Bertone's had said, and made her repeat the words before they'd give her bread.

God in heaven, if she'd spent her nights in here, she would certainly go blind.

Gathering her skirts, Sybilla picked her way through the rushes, toward the landing in front of the great doors.

Cold fingers wrapped around her ankle and bit into her skin. Sybilla let out a yelp and, unable to catch her balance, she stumbled forward. She dropped the pallet as she fell, her knees cracking hard against the stone.

The gap-toothed knight wound his hand around her hair and pulled her down, his familiar face stained with wine. She landed in his lap, her head still in his grip, his shaft pressing hard against her buttocks.

Sir Malcolm's voice ground in her ear. "If you scream, I'll tell Lady Claire you propositioned me. Your first night here and you invited me to bed you, then you changed your mind."

Sybilla beat against his chest. "Let me go."

"I've been waiting for your apology."

"You'll get no apology from me." She squirmed, but with every twist, he jerked her head closer. He seemed impervious to her hands pummeling his padded belly.

He ran his hand over her leg, stroking. "What fine hose you are wearing." He threw her skirts back and leaned across her, staring at her legs. He yanked the satin garter from her thigh. "Where did you get these? Too rich for a servant."

Her heart racing, she stammered. "I-I . . ."

He chuckled. "Not born a servant, are you? I've heard the rumors you're the horse midwife who birthed Sir Guy's new colt. You've guts to insult me, a noble knight, before Lord Phillip and his guests. You hold your head too high." He ran his hand up her stockinged calf. "Sir Guy of Warwick gave you the ribbons, didn't he? What did you give him?"

Her skin crawling with disgust, she kicked his hand from her leg. "Release me now, or bear the wrath of Sir Guy."

Long, hard-boned fingers threaded through her hair at her scalp. "I've no fear of Guy of Warwick. We've sparred before." He pulled her head back, his face so close she could smell the wine on his breath. "Are you a spy, sent to Ketchem by Lord Hamon, who plots against my liege? Or are you a whore, masquerading as a servant? Guy of Warwick is a man, not a saint, despite what people think." He leaned close and ran his pointed red tongue across his lips. "I prefer you be the latter. I have coin to pay you. You could buy yourself another pair of stockings." His hand slid upward from her calf, along the inside of her thigh. He squeezed.

White-hot pain raced up her leg. Spy, servant, or whore, whichever he believed her to be, she would not suffer this. She slammed her fist into his jaw. "Release me, Sir Malcolm."

Sir Malcolm didn't flinch but his fist tightened in her hair. "What are you to Sir Guy of Warwick? Answer me."

"His servant!"

She twisted, turning in his lap, fighting back the ragged pain in her scalp. She thrust her knee upward, hit him hard between his legs, so hard his breath left him in a rush and his eyes bulged from his head.

He doubled over, drawing his legs to his chest, shoving her away.

Sybilla scrambled from his lap. But his hand grasped at her hair in a last attempt to haul her back, strands of golden threads trapped between his fingers. She yanked free, her hair ripping from her scalp, the pain cutting to her skull.

She bit her lip to keep from screaming as she grabbed her pallet. "Never lay a hand on me again, Sir Malcolm."

Sir Malcolm, lay curled up in a ball at the foot of the steps and swore a string of oaths.

Sybilla slipped from the hall and bolted into a dark tunnel, not caring where it led as long as it was far from here.

Guy leaned against the wall, his chin resting on his chest, his heavy-lidded eyes drooping, his arms folded. God's bones, fatigue threatened to overtake him. No one had staggered down this corridor in over an hour. The torch lights dwindled. The entire castle would be asleep by now. How he longed to shrug his feet from his footed hose, pull off his velvet tunic, and rest his head on his pillow. Mayhap he'd been overly concerned about Sybilla. She must have found a safe place to sleep.

Hurried footsteps suddenly padded toward him. He jerked his arms to his sides and grabbed his dagger. The lightness of the uneven steps assured him they were female. She was either drunk or lame, he could not be sure which.

He stepped into her path.

With the force of thunder she slammed into his chest, making him lock his knees to keep from stepping backward.

Sybilla cried out. Her tangled mass of hair hung across her tear-smudged face like a tattered veil.

"Sybilla?" he asked softly, sheathing his dagger.

She breathed hard, panting, her breath ragged. Bloody hell, she'd been running as though someone chased her.

She flung her arms around his neck and sank against him, breathing hard.

Her breath slowing, she composed herself and stepped away.

God's breath, how he wanted to draw her back, to hold her close and tell her she was safe with him.

Sybilla cleared her throat. "I couldn't sleep. It's too hot and noisy in the hall."

Resisting the urge to push the tangled hair from her forehead, Guy arched an eyebrow. "So bad it brought tears to your eyes? Why are you limping?"

"I tripped. Please, Sir Guy, I would prefer your cellar to the hall. I know Lady Claire would not approve but . . ." Her body shook as she spoke. She wiped her hair from her face and the blood from her battered knuckles smeared across her cheek.

On impulse, he wrapped her in his arms. To hell with Lady Claire and her rules. "I will deal with Lady Claire," he said softly, noting Sybilla was trembling.

He reached to take her cold hand. Clearly, the hall was anything but too warm.

Sybilla didn't move.

He turned around to find her standing there, looking at him quizzically.

She cocked her head and studied him with narrowed eyes. "Were you out here waiting for me?"

"I couldn't sleep, either," he said, keeping all emotion from his face. He held out his hand again. "Shall we?"

A smile flickered at the corners of her mouth. "Thank you." She hurried past him. "I know the way," she said, her uneven step tapping against the stone pavers. "Once we get there, I'll make my pallet on the floor."

"You shall," he said, mostly to himself. "And there shall be no kissing."

Give me strength, there shall be no kissing.

The cellar door creaked open. Sybilla stepped into the room. The brazier on the floor beside Guy's bed simmered with a fading red glow. Mayhap he'd really tried to sleep and couldn't, the thought a little disappointing.

He strode in behind her, pulling his cloak from his shoulders. He shut the door behind him, then sat down on the bed, and unbuckled his silver belt.

Sybilla swallowed. Staying here with him would prove a challenge. But, as long as they did not touch or share a kiss, she would be safe—safe from her own desires. Heaven help her, every time she was alone at night with Guy, it felt as though she'd lost her wits and all her self control.

Guy hauled his tunic over his head and tossed the garment in the pile with his belt and cloak. He sat quietly on the bed for a moment, then spoke in a tired voice. "Tomorrow mayhap you may clean my clothes. 'Twould give you a good reason to leave the kitchen. I know you'd rather be outside. With the washerwomen around you, Sir Malcolm will not be close at hand."

She lowered her eyes. 'Twas a fitting chore for a servant and he made his expectation clear. She knew where she stood with Guy by day, 'twas the night that had her worried. Still, she'd rather take her chances here than in the hall.

Guy scooted to the edge of the bed and stuck a foot up. "Help me with my hose?"

Sybilla set her pallet on the floor beside the brazier. She studied his foot, not entirely sure how far he meant to go with this game, but her head hurt and her bones ached for sleep. Playing along simply took less effort.

She straddled his leg, his foot between her sore knees, her skirts bunched up. Guy stared down her bodice, but she would not let him know his bold gaze made her stomach flutter.

His fingers suddenly wrapped around her upper arm. "Hold a moment."

He grabbed the hem of her bunched up skirt and hiked her dress higher, the air cold against her legs. Her garterless stocking had slipped around her ankle and goose bumps rippled up her shin.

"Please, Sir Guy," she whispered, her heart thumping hard. "I beg you don't. Lady Claire would not approve of—"

Ignoring her request, he pulled his foot away, still holding the hem of her skirt in his fist. He lifted her skirts, exposing all of her, to the top of her thighs. His face darkened. "Where's your garter? How did you skin your knee?"

Sybilla's throat went dry. If she told the truth, he would set upon Sir Malcolm, and in the long run, it would make things worse for her. The lessons of the night so far had taught much.

"I tripped and stumbled on the steps," she answered. It wasn't entirely a lie.

"You've a bruise on your thigh, Sybilla. And you've lost a garter ribbon. Tell me what really happened."

Sybilla lowered her head. She shrugged, feigning no concern. "'Twas nothing."

Guy reached for the washing cloth on the chest beside the bed. "Sit down. Please." He pulled her to the bed beside him, then raised her skirts to expose her legs.

Gently, he applied the soft wet cloth to her skinned knee. The coolness eased the sting. "Were you hurt . . . anywhere else?" he asked in a quiet voice.

Sybilla sat stiffly while he blotted dried blood. No need to tell him Sir Malcolm kept a handful of her hair as a souvenir. She shook her head.

Pray he does not check my scalp.

Guy tossed the cloth in the wash bowl and stood, then studied her carefully. "I think there is more to this than you wish to tell me, but I'll not press you. I'm for bed. The hour is late. I think it best you plan on sleeping in the cellar from this point forward. The hall is dangerous for you. I'll explain the circumstance to Lady Claire. She knows Sir Malcolm as well as I do."

Sybilla's mouth dropped open. "I never said it was—"

Guy pulled his hose off. "You didn't have to. Who else would dare lay a hand on you? Rest assured, I'll take this up with him. Now get some rest."

Sybilla opened her mouth to protest, but then clamped her jaw shut. She'd never had a real defender, someone who looked after her, or cared. The feeling quite befuddled her.

The fire in the brazier spit and crackled. Guy yanked his shirt over his head, drawing Sybilla's gaze to his broad chest. His skin glowed in the golden light, and the well-toned muscles in his belly flexed and rippled when he twisted to untie his braes.

A whisper of a gasp slipped through Sybilla's parted lips. She'd forgotten his propensity for nakedness. Good Lord. What was it with this man and his clothes? Didn't he feel the cold?

She fidgeted, not knowing where to look. The cloth fell away from his loins and the brazier light illuminated the length of his manhood. Blessed saints, his sword of life was huge.

She ducked her head and stooped to bundle up his discarded garments. Clutching the clothes to her chest, she stepped as far away from Guy as she could. God forbid he see the heat in her cheeks, or hear the erratic pummel of her heart.

"Sybilla, is something the matter?"

Sybilla stiffened. Heaven help the man, why could he not understand? "No. I mean yes. I mean, you've taken off your clothes."

Guy shifted from one foot to the other, the look on his face bewildered. "So I have, as I do every night before I go to bed."

Sybilla bit her lower lip. Blessed saints, he looked like an Adonis standing there, with his long muscular thighs, a broad chest and a thick head of tousled dark hair. She wanted to see all of him, to stare at the place she dare not look.

The room fell silent. Sybilla could hear Guy breathing, his breath deep and slow.

"Sybilla, what's the matter?"

She thrust her chin up, irritated at herself, and at him. "When you take your clothes off when we are alone, it makes me feel—"

His low voice caressed her, though he didn't move. "Makes you feel like what?"

"I-I . . . don't know. But I shall never get used to being alone in close confines with a man I barely know, a naked man at that."

Guy let out an exasperated breath. "Sybilla, this is how we will live for the next three months. Unless I'm sleeping in a battle camp, I never sleep in clothes. Haven't since I was a boy. Too constricting."

"Do you not feel the cold?"

"Obviously, I do." Guy glanced at his quiet cock, his shaft resting against his thigh.

Tingling heat spread from Sybilla's cheeks down her neck, to her belly. Mayhap it was her aching head, but she suddenly felt as if she were standing in an oven.

Guy ran his hands through his hair. "God's bones, Sybilla. Do you think I mean to seduce you, especially tonight, knowing that you've been assaulted? What kind of man do you think I am?"

"I know not. Not really. What I know of you I learned from Simon."

"From Simon?" Guy drew his eyebrows together.

Sybilla took a deep breath. "For some reason, I feel compelled to try and understand you. Why did you rescue me? That night in the barn, before you knew Regalo needed me—why?"

Guy's face grew solemn. He stared at the floor. After a long silence he spoke. "I cannot answer that."

"Then tell me, what happened between you and Lady Morna? Simon told me bits and pieces of the story. You loved her once and she loved you."

Guy looked up. "'Tis private. I will not answer more."

He strode to the bed and threw back the covers. "I'm to bed."

Sybilla flopped down, stretching out as much as she could in the cramped space between Guy's bed and the wall.

She'd not really expected an answer from him. She could see the pain in his eyes. But what bothered her the most was why she cared. Was it possible she was jealous of a woman from his past?

She shivered, her whole body quaking, the cold stone floor against her back and burning thoughts of Guy naked, racing through her mind.

Guy softly called her. "Sybilla, you are cold. My bed is big enough for both of us. I'll not touch you, I swear it. No kissing," he added, "especially, no kissing."

Sybilla squeezed her eyes shut. She couldn't deny how she longed for the shelter of his arms, for the comfort of his broad chest, and his warmth.

The fire sputtered, its last rays of light fading. The stony chamber filled with shadowy darkness. Dampness settled over the room. Sybilla shivered.

Guy stretched out on the bed and patted the space beside him. "There's room for you, Sybilla. Should you wish it." He closed his eyes.

Her knees shaking, she arose from the pallet and crawled into the bed beside Guy. "Just this once," she said. "Just tonight."

His warmth enveloped her and her heart raced at his nearness. She could feel the steady rise and fall of his chest, and hear the solid beat of his heart. His scent set her blood raging.

Wordlessly, Guy wrapped his arm around her and pulled her closer.

She closed her eyes and prayed for blessed sleep.

Chapter Thirteen

Too restless with desire to linger in the bed beside sleeping Sybilla, as soon as the sunlight came streaming into the cellar, Guy quietly got dressed, then made his way to the barn.

John the Marshal came racing from the stables, his cap in his hands and his shirt sleeves rolled to his elbows. "He was there at last watch, Sir Guy, I swear it!"

Guy halted, his face tight with fury, his fist strangling his sword's hilt. "Regalo's got out?"

John twisted his cap in his hands. "Yes, Sir Guy."

Guy grabbed Bacchus' reins from a timid groom and swung into the saddle. "What fool failed to latch the stall gate?"

John the Marshal held up his hands, palms upturned. "It was latched. The colt must have opened it. I've never seen a horse undo one, but he must have." He shot an urgent glance at the stable boy. The boy nodded vigorously, his knees knocking with fear. "I locked him in myself, Sir Guy. I know I did."

John lunged at the boy. "Go search for him! And don't

come back until you have him. Check the gatehouse and see if he got through!"

Guy shot a vicious look at John. "It's you I hold responsible, horse marshal. Not the boy."

Without waiting for a reply, he spun Bacchus on his haunches and spurred him to a gallop, leaving John the Marshal to ponder the consequences of letting Regalo escape.

The gatehouse teemed with tradesmen, castle folk and farmers. Guy slowed Bacchus to a trot and darted around the crowd. The guard stood beneath the portcullis, checking a merchant's papers. His eyes flashed a greeting at Guy.

"Good morn, Sir Guy. Out to check on your little horse?"

Guy reined Bacchus to a halt. "You've seen my colt?"

The guard's brow furrowed. "He went out with the other yearlings. Lord Phillip's horseman took 'em to the east pasture."

Dread rolled up from Guy's empty stomach. He rubbed his forehead, the pain in his temples stabbing. "When?"

The guard looked upward to gauge the position of the sun. "'Bout two hours ago."

Sweat dampened Guy's neck. Without another word, he kicked Bacchus into a gallop, the horse's hooves clattering across the bridge planks.

Damnation. Regalo had proved as cunning as he was foolish. He'd let himself out of that stall. And he'd managed to mix unnoticed with the yearlings, herded out to pasture. God's bones, he should have warned John the Marshal.

His head ached from a sleepless night and his guts twisted with frustration.

He gripped Bacchus with his knees and pointed the horse toward the east pasture. The hoof prints of yearlings churned ruts into the muddy road. Bacchus slogged through, champing at the bit, excited, the morning breeze whipping through his mane and tail.

Guy caught a glimpse of the yearlings running in a frost-dusted pasture. Bays and dappled grays and sorrels pranced and nipped and squealed at one another, while Lord Phillip's horsemen, dressed in green and red, kept an eye on the lot of them.

Guy galloped Bacchus to the nearest of the two men. "Ho there! Have you seen a colt with four white socks?"

The horseman looked baffled. He shook his head. "No, Sir Guy. He's not here."

Guy's white-knuckled fingers tightened on the reins. He scanned the horses in the meadow. No sign of Regalo's four white socks and sleek black coat.

Guy's heart thudded. God's bones. Never for a moment had he forgotten what he owed his sister, and her little son. Their deaths would not go unavenged. He had to find the colt!

A raven cawed from the woods beyond the pasture, an unhappy sound for so early in the morning. Foreboding crept under Guy's skin. His focus came to rest on the rock wall at the perimeter, near the edge of the wood. A large stone had gone missing in the corner section, lowering the fence enough that a horse might jump and clear the wall if he were as tall as a yearling, or nearly so—and prone to wandering.

The horseman's gaze followed Guy's. "Thieving peasants steal the wall rocks for their chimneys. The masons will be here shortly to make repairs."

Alarm shot through Guy like lightning. He dug his heels into Bacchus' sides. "Post yourself beside the wall until they get here. And count your horses!" he yelled across his shoulder, while Bacchus raced across the field. "You left the castle with an extra and he's escaped!"

Bloody hell, if the herdsmen had been more attentive, they'd have seen the colt with four white stockings jump the wall. No telling where the colt would go, what kind of trouble he could find. The river banked the fields to the left, and the woods that surrounded the rest of the meadow were filled with wolves.

Bacchus jumped and cleared the broken wall, his feet landing with a clatter in the rubble. Footprints of a second horse, a smaller horse, tamped down the new grass and meandered from the meadow, toward the woods. Guy sucked in his breath. Regalo had a head start. He'd be deep into the forest by now.

The noonday sun filtered through the trees, scattering shadows and rays of light, but Regalo's fresh tracks had been easy to follow. He'd wandered, then his path veered sharply to the west and straightened.

Guy clenched his jaw. He knew this path. The ancient oak ahead had a branch that looked like the graceful arm of a dancing woman. The rocky-bottomed stream that rippled beside the trail was snow-covered just a few days ago. Now it marked the way to a hallowed place deep in the woods, where 'twas said, druids once practiced their religion.

Sparrows chattered from the clearing ahead, gathered on a patch of unshadowed earth where the grass grew. In the middle of the clearing, the ring of rocks jutted upward, like fingers pointing to the sun. Guy's stomach churned. He hated this place, the very place where he'd found his dead sister, lying by the center stone, strangled, the bruises on her throat black and purple. Her infant son had lain face down beside her, the back of his little skull crushed and shattered. Even now he could sense their restless spirits.

Guy reined Bacchus to a halt. Regalo stood in the middle of the stones, pawing at the new grass.

A tide of relief washed over Guy. He dismounted and with the little halter over his shoulder, he approached the colt.

He stretched out his hand. "Here, here, boy," he crooned. "What have you been up to?"

Regalo lifted his head, his ears pricked, his eyes bright and alert.

Guy slipped the halter round Regalo's head. "Whatever compelled you to come *here*?" He spoke to the horse as if he expected him to answer. Regalo pawed, ripping up the mud and new grass beneath his hoof. He lowered his head and rooted in the dirt.

Guy pulled the colt's head up. "Come, Regalo. If we leave now, we can make it back to Ketchem before nightfall."

Turning, he started toward Bacchus, but the rope snapped taut. Guy spun around to see Regalo, all four feet planted, his head outstretched, pulling back. Just above him, a specter loomed. Roselynn's ghostly form hovered just above the colt and his dark eyes lifted, staring upward, as if he saw her too.

Guy's heart pounded in his chest. He rubbed his forehead and squeezed his eyes shut. God's breath, his mind was playing tricks. Did he really see a ghost in the middle of the afternoon?

He opened his eyes. Holy mother! Roselynn's apparition still floated over Regalo like a gray cloud.

Guy wound his fist around the rope. "Come, come," he coaxed. "No need to fear her, Regalo. Come."

Regalo kept his place, his eyes rolling back in his head. Guy took a step forward and the little horse squatted, sitting on his haunches like a dog.

Guy slackened the rope. He kept his eyes on the form that floated over Regalo, but he spoke to the colt. "Come, Regalo. Mistress Corbuc will be beside herself when she discovers you got out. She will be worried . . ."

The colt pawed, digging a rut in the muddy ground beneath his feet, slinging dirt and bits of grass. Guy bent to knock a dirt clod from the rim of his boot, when he caught a glimpse of metal in the mud.

The key slightly smaller than the length of his palm. The iron shaft and teeth were encrusted with dirt, but the insignia at the neck was clearly discernable despite the grime and rust—an eagle with wheat sheaf in its talons.

The emblem of the House of Hamon.

Guy pulled the key from the mud, his fist wrapping round it, the fury in his heart raging. He'd spent hours on his hands and knees in this place, grieving, searching for a clue to his sister's death, and yet he'd not seen this, a key that bore the mark of Hamon at the very spot where his sister struggled and fought to save her little son before she'd met her death. Mayhap it was a key ripped from the belt of Lord Hamon himself, if not his soldier, but what better proof than this?

Time seemed to stop. A cold blast of air lifted the hair on the back of Guy's neck. He looked up to see Roselynn's apparition fading and the colt nodding, shaking his head.

Guy felt a strange and satisfying warmth swirl around him, then the ghostly figure raised her face to his, her eyes content. Holding her child in her arms she floated upward. Her form vanished like the morning mist in the sun.

The woods seemed to settle. A quiet repose swept over the place.

Guy let grief fill his heart and give him strength. The ghost of Roselynn and her child would not return here, that much he knew. Morna had been right. The mystic little colt, a horse who communed with spirits, had led him to the clue to the killer. Mayhap Regalo had come here two nights ago, intending for him to follow, not expecting to meet with wolves.

Regalo snorted. He backed away from Guy and Bacchus, his lead rope dragging in the mud. He ambled, though not in the direction of Ketchem and slowly enough to allow Guy to shove the key into his velvet pouch and snatch the lead rope.

The colt swung his head around and blinked at Guy, then trotted to the end of the slack rope and waited.

Guy rubbed his neck, his muscles tense. "I know where you are headed," he whispered, gathering Bacchus' reins. He trudged to Regalo's side. "I pray Sybilla will be safe one night alone at Ketchem—and that we don't freeze to death before we make it all the way to Baldwin Manor."

Sybilla awoke to the sound of rapping on the chamber door, the late morning light streaming through the window slats. She bolted from the bed, aghast that she'd slept so late, and surprised Guy had left without her knowing.

Mary's voice called from the hallway. "Sybilla, hurry. Don't be idle. You've missed morning chapel already, and Cook is waiting for you in the kitchen. You've chores to do."

Sybilla pulled her gown hurriedly over her head and flung the door aside. Mary stood staring at her, her eyes as wide a startled deer's. She glanced past Sybilla and her gaze fixed on the empty bed. She lowered her lashes, as if she were not surprised to find Sybilla sleeping in the bed where Guy of Warwick slept.

"You'd better hurry," she said softly. "Don't get on the wrong side of Cook. She can make a bad day worse."

Sybilla turned to fetch her shoes, skipping her hose. "Mary, have you seen Sir Guy this morning?" she asked, straightening her skirts.

"Oh, no. I've been in the kitchen since dawn, helping Cook make food for the men to break their fast."

Sybilla let her shoulders slump. She smoothed her hair as best she could without a comb and wove it into a thick braid.

Mary adjusted Sybilla's veil. "No matter what they say about your high-and-mighty attitude or what you did before you were a servant, one can't fault you for your looks. I can see why Sir Guy wants you sleeping here. You're the lucky one. The rest of them are just jealous." She turned and exited the chamber. "This way." She tittered, and with a coquettish lift of her hip, called across her shoulder, "But I had some luck myself last night, though blessed saints, what I had to let Sir Malcolm do to get it." Mary lifted the yellowed veil that rested on her shoulders. "Said he was sorry for grabbing me, then he treated me real nice. After he tumbled me, he gave me this."

Sybilla bit down on the inside of her cheek. At the back of Mary's neck, laced through her dull brown hair, shone a black satin ribbon—Lady Roselynn's garter.

Bread loaves, golden brown and still steaming from the ovens, lined the kitchen table. The cooking hearth blazed. Cauldrons of stew bubbled and sputtered, filling the room with the smell of meat and onions. Sybilla licked her lips, her mouth watering and her nose tingling.

Then Simon caught her eye. He sat carefully on the bench beside the table and munched on a slice of bread. His wounded shoulder still bandaged, he managed to smile. "Morning, Mistress Corbuc, er, I mean Sybilla."

Sybilla nodded, forgetting all about her hunger, but doing her best to temper the urge to go and sit beside him, to ask him how he fared and if he knew of Guy's whereabouts.

Cook didn't look up from her task of pounding on a swollen round of dough. "So you finally got up, Sybilla? I told Sir Guy I didn't need another servant in my kitchen. Didn't need another idle girl underfoot. Especially one who's never been a servant." She tossed a clean white cloth over the round of dough, and planted her fists on her hips. "He didn't listen to a word I said. Just kissed me and winked, then went about his business." She shook her head and the extra fold of skin beneath her chin dangled like a wattle. "I'm too old for that," she added softly, her cheeks coloring pink. Then she wiped her flour-dusted hands on her apron. "But I'm stuck with you. What can you do in the kitchen?"

Sybilla felt a heated flush creep up her face. She'd never been a natural at cooking, but she knew how to spread the horse manure piles to enrich the earth in the fields and keep the fly eggs from hatching, and how to tell which mare was ready for breeding, which ones would have trouble birthing and which would not. She had no desire to learn how to peel an onion without bringing tears to her eyes, or how to skin a hare and stew it like Lady Claire liked, with eel and entrails. But she couldn't let the cook think her unwilling. No telling what kind of alternate job she'd be assigned—likely one even less appealing. Like spinning, or sewing. God's feet, her stitching looked worse than the holes.

"I've few skills in the kitchen, madam," she admitted, still looking down. "But I'm not unwilling. I am used to hard work."

Cook pursed her lips, and let a long breath out through her nose. "Let me see your hands."

Sybilla held her hands up. Cook inspected her fingers. "Humph. Clean enough for the kitchen. No dirt beneath your nails and you got good calluses. Work hard for me and it'll go well for you here. I've some stature in this house. Served my lord and lady for twenty years. Even have my own cottage, a boon from Lady Claire for my good service. So you come from Cornbury?"

Sybilla snatched her hands away. "'Tis just a small village in the country. Far from any castle, or kitchen as grand as this." She lowered her chin.

Simon piped up. "She can sweep and clean. I can attest to that. She's worked in Sir Guy's manor house for a time." He smiled convincingly.

Sybilla prickled. Deceitfulness made her uneasy.

Cook looked at Simon, her eyes wary. "You and Sir Guy spend too much time in my kitchen, listening and watching. And you've got appetites like horses. I've the mind to send you both out to the hall where you belong, with the other knights. 'Cept you help me with the hauling when my fetching boy's gone missing."

Simon raised his ale cup. "No finer cook in all of England, than you, madam. Glad to help—when next I can." He gestured to his bandaged arm.

Cook's cheeks turned pink again. "Pshaw. Sir Guy's conniving charm is washing off on you, Sir Simon. The two of you could woo a polecat out of its den."

She turned to Sybilla, and pointed to the dough round.

"Quarter this, then quarter this again and make some rolls, then put 'em in the oven. They'll not be done 'afore I get back. In the meantime you can sweep and rub those pots with sand." She dusted her hands on her apron again, then stomped up the stairs. "When I find those boys, I'll cuff their ears. We've got forty knights to feed for supper and the pig in the cooking pit needs greasing."

Cook left the door open. The cool midday breeze caressed the kitchen, the sounds of knights practicing at swordplay echoing from the bailey.

The dough balls readied, Sybilla put them in the oven, then turned to sweeping. "Simon, where is Sir Guy?" She kept her eyes on the dust motes, lest he see her worry.

"Went to check on Regalo." He set his cup down on the table and lowered his voice. "Found the colt missing."

Sybilla halted, her legs as weak as pudding. "Missing? When? What happened?"

"A stable boy came in this morning and said the colt got out. Guy took Bacchus and went to find him."

Lowering herself on the bench beside Simon, she clutched the broom handle to her forehead. She squeezed her eyes shut. "Simon, did the stable boy say anything about Regalo? Did he have an attack? Did he bark?"

Simon rested his hand on Sybilla's shoulder. "Far as I know, he didn't. He just wandered out, like he did at Baldwin. Guy will find him. He rescued you. He'll save Regalo."

"Lord Hamon's men may still be in the forest and Guy and Regalo are alone."

Sybilla sucked in her breath, her sudden realization knocking the wind right from her lungs. She feared for Regalo, but in these last few days with Guy of Warwick . . . she'd come to care for him just as much.

God forbid if something were to happen to either of them. She could feel Guy's absence, as she could Regalo's, the void as palpable as her own heart beating. Damnation. There was nothing she could do.

The church bells rang out, jolting Sybilla. Mother Mary, she was in no mood to pray!

"Simon, give a message to Guy when he returns. Tell him I must speak with him."

"He may not be back for hours. Where can he find you?"

Sybilla flung her veil over her head and raced to the door. "I'll be at chapel, Simon, doing penance with my Lady Claire."

By the time Guy reached Baldwin Manor, dusk had fallen across the pale blue sky. Smoke rose from the chimney, and the yard was marked with footprints. One set followed another, but Dunback's tracks were discernable by their unevenness and stumbling.

At the gate, Guy cautiously dismounted. The second set of tracks was not a soldier's, not even a man's, unless the man was very small and fond of pointed boots. Leading Bacchus and Regalo toward the barn, he thought of Dunback's state of mind, wondered if his old steward might recognize the key. It was worth a try, though his testimony would not hold up well in a royal court.

"You two eat and rest." He shut Regalo and Bacchus in the same stall, worried that he'd have to leave them unguarded. The old mare had died in this very place, but neither horse seemed to notice, both hell-bent on ripping hay from the manger and chewing.

Fortunately, the peasants had made off with the mare's carcass, most likely dragged out the back door. She probably fed a family or two, maybe more.

Guy heaved the great doors to the back side of the stables shut and rubbed the back of his neck, wondering if Sybilla would have recognized the irony. There was a good chance the old mare had fed the widow Margery and her children after all.

He drew the iron bolt across the closed door, wondering if this was what Regalo meant for him to do. To find Dunback and show him the key, or was there something—or someone else here at Baldwin who might yield a clue?

His hand wrapped around his sword hilt as he trudged through the muddy yard to the house, where a voice drifted through the half-cracked window, a woman's voice, vaguely familiar. "There now, have a sip for me," she was saying. "I made your favorite."

Dunback replied. "When Roselynn comes home, tell her we got weevils in the flour again, and the cows got in the turnip field. Two of them got the bloat. Now they'll make no milk for a fortnight."

Edging the door open, Guy stepped into the foyer, the scent of venison and mulled wine filling his nostrils. He walked slowly to the hall, his spurs clinking against the stone pavers.

At the sight of Neda, spooning broth into Dunback's mouth, he let out a slow breath.

Neda turned with a jump, slopping broth onto the floor. Her round pale face alight with excitement, she set the bowl on the table and raced to stand in front of Guy, wringing her hands in her apron.

"Sir Guy!" She bobbed a curtsy. "I knew you'd come back. Word had it in the village you were here. The good folk said the Shadow Rider was back in the woods, chasing down that spooky colt. I came back to take my place in the kitchen, but all's we found is old Dunback and a dead horse in the stables." She lowered her eyes and bit her lower lip. "I think your steward, sir, hasn't much time left on this earth, so I stayed to keep him company. But we was thinking maybe Lord Hamon and his men got to ya, the way they took your sister and her little son." She broke off, the pain in her words apparent. "The rest of the servants went back home. They were ready to go to work, Sir Guy. Everyone is hungry. But when you weren't here . . ." She poured a cup full of wine and held it out to Guy, her hands shaking. "Tomorrow I'll help you set things right, send to the village to bring the men. There's a hole in the dairy barn's roof and I'll need the well repaired—"

Guy interrupted, "I won't be staying, Neda, though I thank you for taking care of Dunback."

Her face paled, and the hopeful look in her eyes died in an instant.

Turning away, Guy strode to the makeshift bed where Dunback lay propped on pillows. His waxy skin still tinged with yellow, he smiled his toothless grin. He'd lost even more teeth than Guy had realized. The poor soul spent too much time drinking instead of eating.

He squatted next to the man and rested his hand on his shoulder. "Dunback, old friend. I'm here to talk to you about what happened. I should have done this days ago, but I couldn't. Wasn't ready." He lowered his voice and locked his eyes on Dunback's. "Do you recognize this?" He held up the key, rolling it between his thumb and his index finger.

Neda stood beside him. "He hasn't said much right since I've been here. Still thinks the Lady Roselynn's gone into the village."

Not answering, Guy winced.

Neda's gaze fell on the key. She gasped, crossed herself

and stepped back. "Where did you get that, Sir Guy?" she whispered.

"Why? Have you seen this before?" He held the key up and before Neda answered, Dunback recoiled. His yellow eyes filled with terror as his mouth gaped.

Palming the key, Guy lowered his hand. "Please, old friend, tell me what you know about the key. Do it for the Lady Roselynn and her little son. I know you loved them, as they loved you."

The words ripped at his throat like knife blades. Guy bit back his anger, the familiar rage he daily fought to keep at bay.

Dunback slumped as if in contemplation, then he suddenly sat up. He nodded, his vacant stare replaced by clear eyes, bright with understanding. "That be one of Hamon's, isn't it? The one who chased my lady with her little son in her arms into the woods, he wore a belt with keys. I know 'cause I heard 'em clinking in my ears when they searched for me. They clanged as loud as church bells. Saw 'em when they dragged her from her room, kicking and fighting. She got away and ran, like me. Into the woods. But the one with them keys went after her." He clapped his hands over his ears. "Found her and little John, but didn't find me." He whimpered, his shoulders shaking. Tears rolled down his hollow cheeks.

He curled into a ball and muttered over and over, "Sorry, Lady Roselynn, sorry. God forgive me. God forgive me." Then he went silent, his chest heaving, his ragged breath uneven and harsh.

Neda covered Dunback with a blanket. Her own face wet from tears, she wiped her cheeks on her sleeves. "You've known all along Sir Guy, it were Lord Hamon. Why did ya come back here to bother him?" She patted Dunback.

Rising, Guy tucked the key into his pouch. "I needed proof, Neda. I needed evidence. I have it now, and until I showed the key to Dunback, he seemed to have no memory of what happened, too afraid to tell me what he knew."

Her eyes downcast, she nodded. "I wasn't here that night. Lady Roselynn gave me leave to tend my mother. But don't blame the manor folk for not talking 'bout what they saw. Lord Hamon once pulled out the entrails of the miller's son, right there before his father's eyes. You can't blame the witnesses for keeping silent. When men like you and Lord Phillip are away, Hamon does what he wants. We need you here, Sir Guy, or someone, to protect us and keep the peace."

Guy winced. If he could change the course of time, he would. He would have been here that night with his retainers, his tenants and his loyal friend, Simon—there'd have been too many men for Hamon to strike against without declaring full-fledged war against Lord Phillip.

He shrugged his cloak from his shoulders, the weight of his sister's and his nephew's death pressing down on his back like stones. "I'll stay the night. He'll not be left alone," he said, stoking the fire. He knew a death rattle in a man's breath when he heard it. "Now go, good Neda, to the village. Fetch the priest to say last rites."

Chapter Fourteen

Sybilla sank onto the bench beside the kitchen table, her legs aching. She'd stood for hours behind Lady Claire and her ladies during chapel, envious of the noble-women's right to sit on the hard wooden bench. Lady Claire had kept a watchful eye on everyone, making sure that no one fell asleep. When she finally released her ladies and the servants, Sybilla's heart leapt at the prospect of returning to the kitchen.

Her mind occupied with thoughts of Guy and Regalo, she'd swept, washed pots, and made marrow pudding from lambs' bones. She'd scraped the grease from the table, and beat the cream until it clotted, all the while thinking of nothing but Guy standing, or lying on his bed, inviting her to join him.

The cellar felt like a tomb when she'd awakened this morning and he was gone. Had she'd known Guy left to search for Regalo, she would certainly have gone with him. But he'd dressed in silence and slipped from the chamber without her.

Ernestine came bounding into the kitchen. She shoved the wine-stained tablecloth into Sybilla's arms and marched her to the well. "We've soaked it all night in fresh cow's milk. Now it's time for scrubbing. A dab of salt and a bucket o' vinegar will get the stain out. Then we'll boil it."

By midday, the table linen shone like snow. Sybilla spread the cloth out to dry on the low garden wall, relieved.

She trudged back to the kitchen, her gown drooping with sweat. She'd tied her veil around her head like a kerchief and kept working, stirring peas and onions into a steaming cauldron of beef broth, careful not to stand too close to the fire and praying for the moment when she would be released from this unsuited life.

Mother Mary, I'd rather shovel out a horse's stall and pick beetles from the hay than spend another hour in the kitchen.

Dusk falling, Cook finally waved her away. "Go find your master. Sir Guy should be back soon. 'Tis almost time for supper and he's never missed a meal if he could help it."

Sybilla hurried from the kitchen without a second thought for the peas and onions.

Her feet hit the cobbled walkway of the garden, and then turned toward the bailey. With the evening breeze on her face and breathing in the sweet smell of fresh cut hay, it wasn't hard to find her way. She could have closed her eyes and made it to the stables. She would wait for Guy there.

Sybilla slid behind the hay stacks. Lord Phillip's stable was the largest she had ever seen, with stalls enough to hold a hundred horses, and an armory with tack and weapons for a hundred more. Knights and squires on their way to supper passed her, men talking amicably of jousting contests and the summer race to come. Harassed stable boys carried saddles, brushes, and buckets to and from the storeroom. Grooms led well-fed destriers and ladies' palfries, meant for hunting, back to their stalls. When the last man was gone and all the horses put away, Sybilla ventured from her hiding spot and down the side aisle. Sir Guy of Warwick's assigned stalls must be in here somewhere.

Horses munched and pigeons cooed from their roosts in the rafters. A moth-eaten dog barked and nipped at her heels while she darted up and down the aisles, searching, hoping she'd not run into John the Marshal on patrol.

Her heart sank. There at the end of the last row, where the rising moon shone brightly through the wooden shutters, two empty stalls bore the emblem of Guy of Warwick. She closed her eyes, her gut sick with worry.

A gloved hand suddenly gripped her shoulder. "Mistress Corbuc, nay, Sybilla-the-servant, a word with you."

Sybilla's eyes snapped open to see the gap-toothed grin of Sir Malcolm. Before she had the chance to scream, his hand covered her mouth, her cries muffled beneath his leather glove.

He sneered. "You left me with a knot in my groin the size of an egg where you kneed me, but Mary made it better. I've been waiting for you, little horse midwife. I know your kind. Couldn't stay away from the stables a minute longer." He yanked her closer. "Mayhap you and I could come to some agreement. I'll tell no one that you sneak into the stables and you offer me your thanks."

An icy streak of terror shot through her. She struggled and jerked her arm away, the sleeve of her servant's dress splitting at the shoulder. Sir Malcolm held her wrist.

"You dare not cry out, Sybilla. You'll be arrested, I assure you."

She cast a glance at the barn door.

"He isn't back yet." Malcolm laughed. "Mistress Sybilla Corbuc, a horse midwife who birthed an addled-brained foal with four white socks, a weanling colt so big he is a freak of nature—or the devil's spawn, more likely. That's what Ketchem's priest would call him, of that you can be sure."

Heat seared Sybilla's cheeks. Pray to God she was not arrested.

A deep voice suddenly echoed down the dark aisle, booted feet thundering closer. John the Marshal bellowed, "Ho there, Sir Malcolm. Lord Phillip wants you in the hall. He said to bring your purse."

Sir Malcolm clapped his hands on either side of Sybilla's head, his fingers gouging her scalp. He held her face so close to his she could see his pinpoint pupils. "Because of you, Lord Phillip has levied a fine against me. You owe me, Mistress. I intend to collect. One way or another."

He shoved her backward, then spun on his heel and strode out of the barn, spitting at the feet of the marshal.

Sybilla sank against the wall, grateful John the Marshal had made his rounds tonight, though he'd not been so attentive where Regalo was concerned.

John leaned against the stall. "I promised Sir Guy I'd be more attentive on patrol. Stay on my watch for anything suspicious. Good for you I did. He's a bad seed, that Sir Malcolm. Good on his horse and even better with his sword, but more trouble than he's worth. I'da gotten rid of him a long time ago, but I'm not Lord Phillip." He turned and smiled at Sybilla. "Then again, none of us are what we seem, are we Mistress Corbuc?"

Sybilla's heart skipped a beat. She backed away from

John, wary of his blue eyes and his angel-yellow hair. The man had a dangerous beauty about him, and instinct told her he was no more a friend than Sir Malcolm.

He held out his hand. "Come. I'll share my supper with you. You've no need to fear me. I used to know your mother."

Darkness fell upon the hall in Baldwin Manor and all went still. Guy sat with his arms folded, his muscles tight as cords. It was the way of this place, a graveyard for the dead and the dying. Life at Baldwin as it used to be was a memory, one that could never be relived.

A bird-necked priest with an honest face crossed himself. "We've done what we could for your steward." He pulled the blanket over Dunback's yellow face. "We are finished here. All the village has suffered at Lord Hamon's hand. He drove your man mad with terror. I gave him a final blessing." He stepped back and slipped his hands into his bell sleeves.

Neda crossed herself and sat down on the bench. She rested her head in her hands.

Guy let his chin come to rest on his chest, bidding Dunback a silent farewell.

Now what to do with Baldwin Manor? Without a steward, the place would fall into disrepair, be looted until nothing but broken stones were left. No one in the village had coin enough to pay rent, or hands enough to work the land and pay tillage.

His gaze came to rest on Neda, a woman in her forties, possessed of wit and health, and a family of ten. He raised his eyes to hers. "Neda, I'm in need of a tenant for Baldwin Manor. I'd not require you to pay me rent or tillage, just keep the house and have your brood work what fields you can. Would you agree? At least until I can find another steward?"

Neda sprang to her feet. "Of course, my lord." She curtsied. "God bless you. The wind seeps through our cottage walls no matter what we do, and my little ones are always cold and sickly. But the big ones can pull a plow and plant."

"See that Dunback is buried properly, then bring your family and move in. As soon as I can employ another steward, I will send word."

Her face elated, Neda tied her shawl at her neck and fled from the hall.

Guy's mood darkened, as if all the goodness in his soul had vanished. 'Twas time to act. He'd the key and a plan to convince Lord Percy and the court to charge Lord Hamon. His purpose now was focused on two tasks, to keep Sybilla Corbuc and Regalo safe, and to see Lord Hamon brought to justice.

Guy turned to the waiting priest. "Is the graveyard beside the village church still well tended? Do you cut the weeds back and keep the headstones clean?"

"I do, sir. We can lay your steward in the plot where Sir Walter, your lady sister and your nephew rest, if you wish. I'll go make arrangements." He edged toward the foyer, as though eager to depart. He halted. "M-my l-lord," he stammered. "I've heard rumors Hamon's men are hunting in your woods."

"It isn't game they hunt. 'Tis me."

He strapped his sword belt to his waist. His anger unleashed, he strode from the hall. "Consider digging a few more graves, my friend. For if Hamon's men dare attack, I'll send them straight to hell."

* * *

Sybilla straightened. God's bones, she needed to get back to the cellar. If Guy should find her here in the stables he would be furious, but how could she resist when the marshal said he knew her mother?

John's face pinched with concern. "You are leery of me. And so you should be. I've a terrible reputation, and Sir Guy forbade you to come here at all. No doubt your absence from the kitchen will be noticed, too. But I only wish to share a bowl of soup and talk. I knew your parents when they were young."

He straightened and smiled. He looked almost harmless when he smiled.

"Mostly, I knew your mother," he said gently.

Sybilla glanced across her shoulders. There was no one within earshot and most everyone had gone to sup.

"Come have a bowl of soup with me while you wait for Guy. Cook always sends enough for two. She'll be back soon to fetch the empty pot." He winked.

Sybilla's empty stomach growled. Gathering up her skirts, she shook her head. "No." It pained her to pass up the chance to hear stories of her mother, but she dared not stay. She headed for the stable door.

"I traded with them," called John. "Your mother knew her horses, could tell a nag from a keeper. Your father . . . well, let's just say he weren't the brightest jewel in her crown." He stepped away from the stall and tipped his head in the direction of a stone house at the end of the stable. "Come and have a bite to eat. I'll tell you about the time your mother rode in a race at Smithfield, and your father bet against her. You were just a girl. 'Bout five or six, I think."

Sybilla halted. She was seven years old the day her mother rode in that race. She'd won a penny and bought her delighted daughter a basket full of honeyed biscuits.

She peered at John, studying his charming smile and tussled blonde hair. He looked harmless and well-intended, but her instincts still advised caution. He was up to something, but on the chance that he wasn't, she might spend a moment or two reveling in his recollections. God in heaven, how she missed her mother.

She stepped beside him. "Only for a minute, sir. I can only stay for a minute."

He grinned and led the way, careful to keep her in the stable aisles that were the darkest.

Inside the smoky cottage, a basket filled with cheeses, yesterday's bread and a cloth-covered pail of soup sat on a small, polished table. There was a large bed in the corner, and two chairs by the fireplace. A woman's cloak hung on a peg beside the hearth.

John ladled the soup into bowls, and held one bowl out to her. "My missus works all day at the miller's an' won't be back for hours. She and I don't get along. She'd see no harm in you being here. Really. Knows I wouldn't lay a hand on a servant who bears Sir Guy of Warwick's mark. Now eat."

Hesitant but hungry, Sybilla took the bowl and lowered herself onto the bench. John sat beside her, close enough that she could smell the scent of horses on his shirt and in his hair. Their elbows touched when he raised his spoon to his lips. Sybilla moved over, though the bench was barely big enough for two.

He smiled before he swallowed. "I tried to get your mother to breed her fine gray mare to one of Lord Phillip's stallions. But she told me she was saving for a stud fee for a Spanish sire. Must 'ave taken years for her to raise the coin. I'd'a let her have any of Lord Phillip's studs for half the price . . ."

Sybilla kept her eyes down. Years, indeed. Addy had turned white before her mother had the stud fee for the Spanish sire. But Regalo was worth the wait.

John set his bowl on the table. "I know a blue blood when I see one, Mistress Corbuc." He shot Sybilla a glance from the corner of his eye.

The hairs on the back of Sybilla's neck bristled.

He leaned back, his fingers interlaced behind his head. "If you think Sir Guy might be willing to sell that little colt," he said casually, "I'd make it worth your while if you put a good word in for me. I've a coin or two saved up and of the mind to make a decent offer."

She set her bowl on her knees, but held her spoon with a white-knuckled grip. "Regalo is not for sale, sir."

John whistled through his white teeth. "Your father lost a sack of guineas to me on a roll of the dice and didn't flinch. Your mother was furious. Like I said, I never understood what she saw in the man." He leaned in, his breath so close she could feel its warmth on her face. "You don't look much like him, and we both know why, but you've got her keen eyes and I've never been the type to snub a bastard. I'll give those guineas your father lost back to you, and pay Sir Guy's asking price if you can convince him to sell me Regalo. It's a fair exchange."

He plucked a sprig of straw from her hair, his fingers grazing her temple.

Instinctively, she jerked back, her hand flying to the side of her head. "Do not—"

A deep voice, joltingly familiar, rumbled across the room. "What goes on here? Mistress Corbuc?"

John jumped to his feet and Sybilla started. Her bowl

fell from her knees, spattering her gown and dotting Guy's boots with soup.

Guy stood with his hand on his sword hilt, his eyes as black as a dark tide.

John bowed with a short nod. "She's been waiting for you, Sir Guy. We all have. Worried for you and the colt."

Guy strode across the room and stopped, standing toe to toe with John. "The colt is safe back in his stall, John of Kent and I've been looking for you. You are paid to keep Lord Phillip and his knight's horses in your care. See that you do, or I'll see we have another marshal."

Sybilla's heart leapt. Regalo was safe. She wanted to throw her arms around Guy's neck and kiss him.

John braced himself against the table, his fingers curled around the edge. "I apologize, Sir Guy. I assure you the colt won't escape again."

"Damned right he won't. Now leave us. I've a word with my servant."

John scurried from the cottage, stumbling out of the door.

Sybilla swallowed. Her throat felt like sand. Guy was angry, and so he should be. But he should understand how afraid she was for Regalo, how worried that he and Guy had been away all day.

The air in the cottage suddenly felt stifling, and the space smaller than the cellar.

Guy squeezed his eyes shut and leaned his head back. "You've no idea how close I just came to throttling the man. Have you no sense of danger? Do you not care about your own safety?"

"I do, Guy. I didn't mean to defy you, but when Simon told me Regalo had escaped and you had gone to find him—I've been sick with worry all day. I only came out here to wait for you. What was I supposed to do?"

Utter exasperation filled Guy's face. "Sybilla, you could have been—"

The cottage door banged open, interrupting.

Cook came flying in with a soup spoon raised above her head like a weapon. "Lord have mercy, Sybilla Corbuc. I knew you'd be out here. John of Kent, if you so much as lay a hand on her I'll—" She stopped dead in her tracks. "Oh. 'Tis you." Her eyes moved cautiously over Sybilla, then back to Guy. She lowered her spoon. "Sir Guy, I've need of your servant in the kitchen if you can spare her. I've got twenty chickens left to dress. I could use the help."

Sybilla buried her hands in the folds of her skirt. "I should like to see Regalo first, Sir Guy. With your permission."

His face grew stern. "Regalo is fine, Sybilla. Now go with Cook back to the kitchen."

His tone was harsh, commanding, and left no room for misinterpretation.

Sybilla's voice caught in her throat.

Unbelievable. He knew how much Regalo meant to her. Could it be he was that jealous of John the Marshal?

She glared at him. Cook cleared her throat and lowered her eyes.

Guy folded his arms. "Cook needs your help. Go, to the kitchen. I'll bring you back to see Regalo later." He drew his eyebrows together.

Sybilla took a deep breath. From the look on his face he was in no mood for a challenge. So be it.

She purposely lifted her chin, picked up her skirts and brushed past him, stumbling on his big, booted foot as she stormed out of the cottage.

Cook hurried fast behind her. "Sybilla, what happened to your sleeve? 'Tis ripped."

Sybilla shrugged and walked faster, hoping Guy hadn't heard Cook's question.

Guy's voice bellowed from the cottage doorway, "Damn the chickens."

Guy swallowed the dregs of his cup. He'd taken his supper in his cellar room, cold chicken and quail eggs, washed down with bitter ale. The meal had suited his mood—vexed and worried that Sybilla was always just one step away from serious trouble. He'd forbidden her from staying in the stables because the place wasn't safe. Couldn't she understand that?

Knuckles rapped on the door, the familiar one-two-three taps Sybilla always used. Bloody saints, his food had barely settled in his stomach. He strode across the room and flung the door open, knowing she'd be ready for a fight, angry for keeping her from Regalo.

In she strode, marching like the Queen of England dressed in a brown dress with a yellowing veil on her head, but the Queen nonetheless.

Sybilla took a regal seat on the bed, her back stiff, her eyes downcast. She picked a downy chicken feather from her sleeve but she said not a word, her pretty lips pressed together.

Guy took a deep breath. He had every right to be angry with her, and he should have, but all he really wanted to do was cover her pursed lips with kisses. He ran his hands thru his hair. "Sybilla. We have an agreement. Three months of servitude and you are free to leave Ketchem. I simply ask that you comply with my wishes and stay away from the stables."

She turned her head to face him. "You cannot keep me from the stables. I must see Regalo. I've a bond with him like I've never known before. Can you imagine how I felt this morning when Simon told me Regalo got away? And then you went to find him, alone and in the midst of Hamon's men . . ."

Guy crossed the room and stood before her. "Sybilla, you will be suspect for every unexplainable mishap in the barn. God in heaven, if you are arrested and accused of midwifing—I cannot protect you from that."

She rose to her feet. "Please, you cannot deny me the right to see him. I will be careful, I promise."

"Blessed saints, woman. Look at your ripped sleeve. How did that happen? I'd wager you encountered some difficulty in the barn. I worry for your safety."

Sybilla took a deep breath. "The dress is old and tore by itself. No need to worry for me. I went to find Regalo and you. I'd had no news and you'd been gone so long— I feared the worst." She stared back at him defiantly. "I worried for your safety, Sir Guy. God in heaven, Hamon's men are in the woods, and you rode out alone. Why didn't you take an escort?"

She had him on that one. It would have made more sense to find a man or two to ride out with him.

Guy softened, his anger giving way. He reached to touch her cheek, his fingers caressing, moving close to her mouth. Devil take her, 'twas such a lovely mouth. "Sybilla, I am touched you thought to worry after me," he said, his voice husky.

She raised her face to his, her pale lips parted. "It's just that you . . . you are all I have . . . you really care about Regalo." She lowered her eyes. "Never mind."

Blessed Mary, it was too much.

He covered her mouth with his, his hand skimming up her arms, he pulled her closer.

She made no attempt to move away. Nay, she leaned

against him and opened her mouth enough for him to slip his tongue inside. Her tongue, warm and wet, danced against his own.

God's breath. She was kissing him back, responding with an urgency he'd not expected.

Her arms wrapped around his neck and her fingers threaded through his hair.

Guy's heart raced. He slipped his leg between hers, pressing upward, his knee against her mons. She moaned a soft, purring sound and wriggled. God in heaven help him, he wanted her. Wanted every bit of her, from her dirt smudged cheeks to her kitchen-chaffed hands. Her feminine scent, earthen and all woman, drove him mad. She'd no idea of the effect she was having on him, and if he didn't stop her now, he feared he could not turn back.

He broke off the kiss and moved his mouth to her temple, holding her close. He breathed in the scent of her hair, pushing away her veil. "Ah, Mistress Green Eyes, I'd not expected such a warm welcome. Had I known this waited for me, I would have herded Regalo home faster. I do enjoy it, but unless you wish me to—" He stepped away, aware that his cock stood beneath his tunic as rigid as a tent pole. He shifted from one foot to the other. No doubt she'd felt his arousal. He licked his lip. "We must stop."

She stared at his groin and blushed. "I'm sorry, I don't know why I . . ."

Guy smiled, grasping for the last remnants of his self-control. Taking a deep, steadying breath, he said, "I'm not sorry."

Once more in charge of his emotions, he took her hand and pulled her to sit beside him on the bed. "Come, I've news to share. Good news. Regalo led me to the evidence. He found this at the foot of the stone where Roselynn died." He withdrew the key from his pouch and held it up.

Sybilla gasped. "He went all the way back to Baldwin Manor?"

Guy nodded, keeping the detail of Roselynn's ghost to himself. Sybilla might think he was losing his mind.

He tucked the key away. "Dunback said it hung from the belt of the rider who chased my sister into the woods."

Sybilla's wide eyes fell upon the key's insignia. "It's Hamon's," she said softly. "Regalo led you to her killer."

Guy stared at the key, turning it over in his hand, his blood pounding in his ears. "In a few short months, I'll make my case before Lord Percy." He looked at Sybilla. "I might settle what there is between Hamon and myself, before he declares a war. I'll celebrate and challenge Malcolm in Ketchem's summer horse race."

Sybilla's cheeks flushed, her eyes wild with excitement. "It's only three months away. Bacchus won't be ready."

Guy reached for Sybilla and took her hand. "I mean to race Regalo."

Sybilla jumped up. "Regalo? You can't! He's too young!"

Guy rose. "He'll be big enough, Sybilla, almost yearling-sized already. I'll bet he grows another inch by then."

"He's never had a rider on his back."

In the awkward silence that followed, Guy stared out the window. "On Regalo I cannot lose. It's our destiny to-gether. Malcolm will never best me."

Sybilla's voice cracked. "You and Regalo could both be killed—over naught but your pride. There are no rules in that race. Everyone cheats. Horses are maimed and men are wounded." She rose from the bed, wringing her hands. "You can't ride him."

Guy stood and caught her by the wrist. "Sybilla, we can train him. You can see him every day, as long as I am with you. You'd not be practicing midwifery, but at least you'd be out of the kitchen. You've three months more to go on our bargain. Our time spent together would not be so bad." He raised her hand to his lips and bent to kiss her pink knuckles.

She pulled away before his lips touched her skin. "No, Sir Guy. I beg you, don't ride Regalo. He could end up broken down and useless, or worse. You could die. And as much as I would like to bed with you, for I admit I would, I could very well be left with a babe in my belly."

Silence filled the room.

It was her last words that stung the most and an icy wall sprang up around Guy's heart. He clenched his fists. Roselynn and her son had been murdered because he could not walk away from his lust for Morna, and in the end even Morna had paid a price for his desire. Damnation. He would not make the same mistake again with Sybilla.

He retreated, suppressing all emotion. He faced Sybilla with the cold detachment of a man who'd shut out any possibility of love. His tone hardened. "Regalo will big enough to ride, Sybilla, and I plan to race him. And if you and I made a child I would see to it."

Sybilla stood unmoving.

Guy stripped his shirt off, then kicked off his boots and hose, but did not remove his braes. "From this point on, don't set foot in the stables unless I am at your side. Now come to bed."

He flung his body down and draped his arm over his eyes.

"Thank you, Sir Guy, for not getting naked."

The cot sank, and Guy could feel Sybilla laying stiffly beside him.

God in heaven. It was going to be a long, long, night.

Chapter Fifteen

Sybilla rubbed her sleep encrusted eyes. Even lying beneath the covers in bed with Guy, the chill of the morning air was too biting for comfort. God's breath, three weeks had passed. 'Twas the first of June, and still the frost settled on the grass at night. Still, Guy clung to his vow to race Regalo, inspite of her objection. He'd taken her to the stables everyday, as he'd promised. Just yesterday she watched with gritted teeth when he started getting Regalo used to exercising at the end of a rope and cantering around a round pen. The boys that gathered in the field to watch made her nervous. Once, when Guy wasn't looking, the tallest one threw a pebble at Regalo to make him buck. Regalo kept a wary eye on the lot of them.

Sybilla frowned. Every week, Regalo had grown another inch or two. Castle folk came to gawk at him. Sir Malcolm watched with a calculating eye. Even John the Marshal marveled at his size. Outwardly, Guy reveled in his success, but Sybilla knew he secretly worried about the attention Regalo attracted.

At night, Guy tossed fitfully in the bed. This morning, the covers were hopelessly twisted round his waist. His long legs covered with goose bumps, he'd nestled close and she could feel his breath against her shoulder.

But never once had he touched her in that way, or even kissed her . . . much to her dismay. She had to admit she was a little disappointed.

Mustn't get use to sleeping with him, she reminded herself. *Soon, my time here will be over.*

Slipping from Guy's arms, Sybilla pulled her brown dress over her head, glad for the warmth. She slipped her leather boots on her feet and turned to leave the chamber.

She halted, unable to resist the opportunity for one last look at the magnificence of the man who made her heart beat so hard it almost hurt. His long legs, muscular and lean, were a sight to behold as was the shaft that lay inbetween, erect, as it usually was in the mornings. Sybilla's hand shook as she covered him with blankets. Hell to the devil, he was glorious in his nakedness, and she couldn't let him freeze to death, even if he planned to race her colt.

Turning away, Sybilla sucked in her breath. She scooped his dirty clothes from the floor and held them in her arms. The scent of Guy, of male musk and sweat, filled her senses and made her close her eyes. *Jesú*, how she would miss him when she had to go. She made her way into the kitchen, her arms piled high with his dirty tunic, his dirty hose and shirt. Washing his clothes did not bother her like it used to.

She dumped the garments on the bench beside the table and shoved a cauldron on the cooking iron. She'd promised Cook she'd set the pottage on the fire first thing.

She stirred the pottage with an iron spoon and kept her eyes focused on the fire, her thoughts consumed with the impending race, and Guy's plan to train Regalo to the saddle. She barely noticed when Simon called her name.

"Morning, Sybilla."

Sybilla startled, dropping the spoon in the pottage.

Simon looked up from the table, feathers floating 'round his head. He held the carcass of a half-plucked goose beneath his bandaged arm. He smiled back at her, then blew a feather from his beard. "You're too late to help us. Mary an' I are nearly finished." He winked at Mary, who sat beside him, her eyes bright from his attention, her cheeks rosy.

She cast a shy glance at Sybilla. "Sir Simon's been kind enough to help me, and he's been telling me stories about a magic horse and the woman meant to raise the little beast." She lowered her eyes. "Helps pass the time," she added softly. "I appreciate the company. Sir Simon is always in the kitchen."

Sybilla smiled, noticing how Simon held Mary's gaze just a little longer than he should have. There was more color in his face than there'd been in days.

"I see," she said, quietly amused. "Sir Simon, how fares your shoulder?"

Simon's smile faded. "Good for nothing but wrestling with a dead goose."

Mary rose, dusting feathers from her hands. "I'll change your bandage. I can find fresh linens for you, too. There are no more chores 'til Cook gets back from the butcher's and my mam strips Lord and Lady Claire's bed." She rested a hand on Simon's shoulder. "Let me help you, Sir Simon. You helped me with plucking."

Simon nodded, looking pleased to have her assistance.

Sybilla scooped the laundry up and headed toward the door.

Cook came bustling in with a basket of turnips on her hips.

Sybilla halted. She knew well enough to give Cook

her due. She could make her life hell in the kitchen if she did not. "Do you need something, Cook? I can return as soon as I've finished Sir Guy's laundry."

Cook set the turnips on the table. "I must warn you, Sybilla, you were late this morning. An' you're looking a little peaked. Aren't sick, are ya?"

Sybilla inclined her head. "No, ma'am. Why?"

"It's none of my business what goes on in that little cellar between you and Sir Guy, but the Lady Claire won't tolerate a servant who's with child without a husband. Even if the father is Sir Guy, you'll get put out o' the castle."

Heat racing to her cheeks, Sybilla lowered her eyes, Guy's musky scent wafting from his clothes and filling up her nostrils. "I've no fear of that, Cook. Sir Guy and I, we . . ." She looked up and drew her eyebrows together. "At times . . . at times we don't even like each other."

Cook snorted. Simon smothered a chuckle.

Sybilla spun on her heels as she pulled her veil over her head. "I'm off to do the laundry and then to chapel," she called across her shoulder.

The sound of Cook's and Simon's laughter echoed from the kitchen.

Guy pulled the blanket tighter round his shoulders. Ordinarily, he'd not have noticed the morning chill, but the hour had grown late and the brazier fire had gone begging. He stretched his legs, his joints aching. He'd spent most of the night awake and tossing. With Sybilla so close beside him, he couldn't keep his eyes shut. When she rolled over in her sleep and presented him her luscious backside, with her chemise wrapped high around her hips, he'd barely been able to contain himself. Lust was hell in the late hours of night.

He massaged his eyelids. The insides felt like sand.

A familiar rap beat at the door. Guy stood, the blanket falling from his shoulders, and unlocked the iron bar. Simon entered, his arm bound to his chest, his face pale but his eyes alight. He looked remarkably recovered for a man who'd almost bled to death just weeks ago.

Guy smiled, glad to see his friend up and about.

Simon strode in with Guy's clean laundry beneath his arm. "Brought these to you. Your servant is detained, late for chapel." He smiled. "Sybilla—she looked a little preoccupied when she came into the kitchen this morning. By the rood, what happens in here between the two of you is not my business, but you should know the castle walls are talking and Lady Claire has expressed her disapproval."

"Let them talk." Guy took the bundle of clothes pinned under Simon's arm. "Nothing happens. I'll make amends with Lady Claire, or the devil take her."

"Lady Claire? The devil'd not take her. She'd taste like pious pie, bitter on the tongue. He'd spit her out and look for a sweet-tasting sinner like you or me." He laughed, then quickly sobered.

Guy schooled his face to stay impassive. He was in no mood for humor. "Nothing is happening between Sybilla and me, Simon. It's what she wishes. I'd appreciate it if you would spread the truth and not the rumor."

Simon suppressed a grin, though not very effectively. "Nothing happening? So that's the problem."

Guy glared at him, then tossed the laundry on the bed. With a snap he unfurled a clean shirt and pulled it over his head, smoothing down the front of the garment before he added his green tunic. "Lord Phillip wants a meeting. Hamon's assembled a cavalry of hundreds." He slipped on his hose and boots. "Can you fight, Simon? I fear another war is brewing."

Frowning, Simon attempted to raise his injured arm over his head. The spark faded from his eyes. "I won't be of much use."

Guy tightened his belt. "Even if you cannot use your sword arm, Ketchem needs you. You know war and what it takes to defend a castle. I'll need someone here to take care of Sybilla and Regalo when I'm away."

Simon eased down on the bed. "Tell me, Guy, if it weren't for Regalo, that infernal little colt who seems hell bound to keep the three of you together, would you free her? Would you let her go? He hasn't barked in a month. You have Hamon's key as proof. What more do you need?"

In the awkward silence, Guy took a deep breath. He raked his hand through his hair. "I cannot. I'm not done yet with her. I need her with me. Soon, I'll put a saddle on Regalo."

Simon arched his bushy eyebrows. "Train Regalo to the saddle? You can't, Guy. You weigh three stone and he's not ready. He's big, he's just not big enough to carry you. I doubt you can convince Sybilla to ride him." He looked away, his eyes staring at the unlit brazier. "As for impending war, I've been close enough to death it makes me take stock. I'm not too eager to return to the battlefield, though I will serve wherever Lord Phillip needs me. I will do my part." He looked up, his face sincere. "But there are things I would like to do before I die, while I'm not too old to enjoy them. Like find a wife and have a son or two. What about you?"

Guy strapped his sword to his waist. "No. I want neither wife nor children. You surprise me with this talk of marriage. Has someone caught your eye?"

Simon grinned. "Aye, there is one. I'll work to earn a demesne of my own. Time to settle down and start living. Why don't you?" He studied the cellar. By the look on his face, he clearly considered the place no better than a pig pit.

"Honor demands I avenge my sister and my nephew. I cannot worry about keeping a wife and children sa—" He stopped, unable to complete the sentence, thoughts of Sybilla racing through his mind. God in heaven, this last month she'd gotten under his skin, made him wonder what he'd do with the rest of his life. Thoughts of his future, or lack of one, kept him up at night. That and the impossible situation of trying to actually sleep next to beautiful woman who set his loins on fire.

Guy swore beneath his breath. Now was not the time for this. His future plans, not that he truly had any beyond his meeting with Percy and his race against Malcolm, would have to wait.

He flung the chamber door aside and strode out of the cellar toward the great hall, straightening his tunic. "Let's go, Simon. Lord Phillip is waiting. We've business to attend."

The hall filled with smoke from the blaze roaring in the center hearth. Lord Phillip and his council sat the high table, their faces dour.

Guy took his seat, Simon sliding onto the bench beside him.

Lord Phillip stroked his chin. "We must ready our defenses. Our spies at Hamon Castle report he is amassing a calvalry and weapons. We cannot ignore the threat." He turned to his steward. "How goes the repairs on the east wall? Are the tunnels filled and the cracks in the foundation mortared?"

The steward cleared his throat. "Not completely, sir. When the fever took the lives of so many summer last, and the spring rains filled the tunnels, we could not find able men who were willing to finish the repairs."

Lord Phillip winced. "Then the east wall is still vulnerable. 'Tis been three years since Claremont tried to besiege Ketchem. His tunnel diggers ran like scared sheep when we smoked them out, and so did Claremont. Time to ready once again for war. Get the tunnels filled and the wall repaired! Call my sons home from fostering and have them organize the workmen."

The steward hurried from the room.

Sir Malcolm slammed his fist onto the table. "We should attack first, Lord Phillip. Why wait?"

Knights pounded on the table. Shouts of "Here, here!" rose over the hall.

Lord Phillip leapt from his seat. "No. We will not start the war. We'll not attack. I wish to keep the peace as long as possible, and be prepared should he go on the offense."

The hall fell silent, not a knight dared challenge the decision, but they were eager for a fight. Many of the men had tasted Hamon's betrayal. He'd marauded over the countryside for years, his attacks coming closer to Ketchem and getting bolder. They'd be itching to ride en mass and make a confrontation.

Lord Phillip put his hand on his sword. "Until you have my orders to assemble in the yard, we'll not attack. In the meantime, prepare provisions. The summer race at Ketchem will go on as planned. You should compete, just as you always have. Best the enemy believes we are not worried. It gives us the advantage. Now go and ready Ketchem."

The men nodded, some appeased, others unable to hide their discontent.

Guy rose and shot a glance at Simon. His friend massaged his injured arm. Simon, ever the loyal knight would do as he was commanded, though it might cost him.

Lord Phillip's voice called out, "Guy of Warwick, a word with you. Come to my chambers."

Evening fell upon the cellar chamber quickly, the fire in the brazier filling up the room with heat and light. Sybilla waited for Sir Guy. After doing his laundry and attending chapel, she'd spent the rest of the day in the kitchen, waiting patiently for him to come and take her to the stables. When all the knights of Ketchem had been called to assemble for a meeting in the hall, she'd taken the opportunity to visit Regalo without the fear of going there alone.

Blessed saints, Regalo kept growing. Even she was forced to admit his size was unnatural. He scarffed down the carrots she'd brought him and licked her hands for more, then whined when she left. The hour was late when she finally made it back to the cellar chamber.

The chamber door opened and Guy strode in, his face smudged with dirt, his shirt stained with sweat and his hose muddied. He carried a bucket of steaming water. Sybilla's heart thumped wildly at the sight of him, as it always did when he returned at the end of the day.

Wordlessly, he set the bucket down and stripped off his shirt and hose. He washed, threw the cloth on the heap of dirty clothes and collapsed on his bed.

Sybilla picked up his soiled clothing and set the bucket aside. She'd not say a thing about his complete disregard of the amount of laundry he created. She could not always tell what he was thinking, but tonight he seemed especially bothered. She took a seat on her pallet. "What was the meeting in the hall about?"

He took one beleaguered breath, and peered at her

from the bed. "Ketchem Castle is under threat of war. Lord Phillip wants his knights trained and ready."

Sybilla frowned.

He eased up on his elbows. "You should also know Ketchem's summer horse race will go on as planned. I will compete. Malcolm will ride against me."

Sybilla fixed her jaw. Damnation. Guy meant to ride in Ketchem's race, no matter what the cost to Regalo, or to himself.

She pulled off her gown and sank onto the bed. She could feel his eyes upon her as she took off her veil and her hair tumbled down her shoulders. She had the chance to wash today as well and her hair felt feather light and as soft as silk against her skin.

Guy reached out and touched a lock that strayed across her eyebrow. "'Tis still the color of cooked honey." His fingers touched her cheek. "Like the night I met you."

Sybilla turned to face him. "Is there any way I can convince you not to race Regalo?"

"No. Let's not quarrel. Now settle here with me and tell me of your days in Cornbury. Did you dance, Sybilla?"

She shook her head, fighting the urge to give in and drop the subject of Regalo and the race. "Not the kind of dances you do at Ketchem feasts."

"Then I shall teach you." He took her fingertips and held them lightly. "There's the Tipton, where the lady holds her partner's fingers through the sets and must never let go."

His fingers danced with hers, sensual and slow, he grazed the center of her palm while he hummed a simple tune.

Sybilla closed her eyes, enjoying the pleasure of his touch, the sensual strokes of his hand against her own, and the richness of his deep voice.

"Why are you doing this?" she murmured.

He lowered his hand. "War is looming. I wish to make

amends, to soothe your complaints against me, though I deserve them."

Sybilla rested her head on the pillow beside him.

He took a slow breath then eased back on the bed. He stared at the ceiling. "I'm not the man I was a month ago—when I met you."

It was hours before Sybilla closed her eyes, her heart beating like a drum and her skin on fire where he'd touched her.

Chapter Sixteen

The morning sun threaded through the iron slats of the chamber window. Guy rolled over and covered his head with a blanket, envious of Sybilla's ability to sleep, her quiet breathing the only sound in the cellar.

A muffled voice calling from the other side of the chamber interrupted his repose. "Sybilla. Please, might we speak with you? 'Tis most urgent."

Guy leaned down and tapped Sybilla's shoulder. "We've visitors."

She moaned, and rolled onto her side. She rubbed her eyes. "Who—"

Cook's voice cracked. "Please, our Mary needs your help."

Sybilla sat up, clutching her tunic to her chest. Guy pulled on his hose and tunic. Sybilla scooted to the edge of the pallet, dragging the covers with her. "Cook? Is that you?"

"Aye, and Mary's mother Ernestine is here, too. We need you to come with us. Quickly."

Guy strode across the chamber and flung open the

door. The two women stood next to each other, their faces anxious and apprehensive.

Cook wiped her hands on her apron. She kept her eyes lowered while she spoke. "Forgive me, Sir Guy, but I've need of Sybilla. I'd not disturb you here, but Ernestine says 'tis urgent."

Sybilla pulled on her servant's dress over her head. She secured her veil and stepped toward the women. "What has happened?"

Ernestine shook her head. She glanced at Guy before she spoke. "Women's business. We need not trouble Sir Guy with the details. Fetch your shoes and come."

Sybilla looked at Guy, her face beseeching. God's bones, he feared what she was walking into, but he would not stop her.

He took a deep breath. "You are free to go."

God keep her.

He swore beneath his breath. Now he'd not get the chance to tell Sybilla he would not be here when she returned.

A wave of panic flooded over Sybilla. She clenched her fists, aware of the sweat on her hands, of the way her heart beat like thunder in her chest. Mary lay pale and doubled over on a pallet spread before the cottage hearth, while her mother stroked her forehead with a wet cloth. Her face drawn, Mary stared at Sybilla through glassy eyes. "Please, don't tell Lady Claire. She'll send me off. And please don't tell Sir Simon. I would rather die than have him know. He cares for me and I for him. I love him and he thinks I am a good girl . . . I only did it once or twice with Sir Malcolm and that was a month ago, before

Sir Simon and I . . ." Her voice trailed off, overtaken by a painful moan.

Cook patted Mary's shoulder. "There, there, Mary. Mistress Corbuc can help you. She knows of draughts and potions to set you right. She's not come here to tattle."

Sybilla laid her hand against Mary's cheek. God's blood, she was burning with a fever!

Cook stepped forward from the shadows, her round form occupying much of the space in the humble cottage. "She's with child, or she was. She went and got a bad elixir from the widow woman in the woods who claimed she had a brew to keep a girl from breeding. She's lost the babe all right, and now she's losing blood."

Ernestine cried softly, her wrinkled hand resting on her daughter's white cheek. "She's a good girl, my Mary. She just had a bit of bad luck." She lifted her watery brown eyes to Sybilla. "There's no one else in Ketchem we can ask, mistress. Please, if you know of something that can stop the bleeding, help her."

Sybilla took Ernestine's hands in hers. "How long? How long has she been like this?"

Ernestine answered quietly, her voice trembling. "She was fine yesterday. Took the potion after we all went to bed. She's been bleeding like this all night." She pointed to the heap of bloodied linens in the corner. At some point, the women must have given up trying to wash them. A large iron pot containing red water sat unattended in the hearth.

Sybilla pressed her knuckles into her forehead. "She is already close to death. I fear it is too late. The only herbs I know of can kill a horse if not mixed right. I don't dare . . ."

Cook took her by the upper arm. "Surely you can try? She will die before the night the way she's bleeding."

Sybilla gritted her teeth, wracking her brain for a way to distill the formula for extract of hazel to the proper concentration for a woman, not a horse. She only used the medicine in the direst of situations, when the mare delivered and expelled the foal and birthing sac too quickly. She'd had some success, but the horses had not been poisoned first.

Cook handed her a pig's bladder filled with an amber liquid, oily and sweetly aromatic. "She's swallowed this."

Sybilla sniffed the bladder. Foreboding filled her heart. "Birthwort—strong enough to kill a cow."

Ernestine sobbed. Mary's eyes closed and her breathing slowed.

Cook knelt beside Ernestine and drew her into her arms. "There, there. If it's Mary's time to meet her maker, so be it. I'll fetch the priest to give her last rites."

Resting her face on Cook's chest, Ernestine sobbed. "He'll not give them and they won't let my poor Mary be buried in the churchyard. Not after this." She turned away.

Mary groaned and drew her knees to her chin, her face contorted with pain. Sybilla's gut wrenched. Mary had had few choices. If anyone had discovered she was pregnant she would have been cast out of Ketchem with nowhere to go, with no food or shelter or the means to care for a babe. She'd done what she did because she was desperate.

Sybilla sat back on her heels and stared into the fire. She'd seen budding swan's neck in Lady Claire's herb garden. The herb eased a horse's birth contractions, and stopped the bleeding, but was wholly dangerous to women. And if she were caught there'd be questions.

Aiding a woman who'd swept a child from her body was
a crime punishable by imprisonment or death. The sentence would be certain for a horse midwife already under
the scrutiny of the law.

Cook said nothing, the look in her eyes pleading.
Ernestine's pitiful cries of desperation tore at Sybilla's
heart.

She took a deep breath. By the saints, she could not
watch poor Mary die and do nothing.

She scrambled to her feet. "I'll try, Cook. Ernestine
keep praying, and keep her warm and elevate her feet
to keep the blood inside her. I'll be back as soon as I
can." She hurried from the cottage.

The midday sun blazed down, warming her back as
Sybilla knelt in the herbery and pulled the leaves from
the tiny swan-necked plants. Newly sprouted, they were
the most potent this time of year. It'd not take but a few
to do the job.

The sound of women's chatter traveled through the
garden. Sybilla glanced across her shoulder to see Lady
Claire and her attendants striding in her direction.
Sybilla drew a quick breath. She shoved the leaves into
her apron pocket.

Lady Claire stopped before her, her pale yellow gown
swirling around her slippered feet. "Sybilla. I wish to
speak with you." She waved her attendants away.

Sybilla bobbed a curtsy, her knees knocking. "Good day,
my lady."

"Come, walk beside me." She glanced over her shoulder at her ladies. They chattered quietly and kept their
distance. "I've need to know what's happening. My husband tells me little of the meetings with his knights. He

does not wish to worry me, but I know something is amiss. Tell me, Sybilla. What does Sir Guy tell you of the meetings? What do the men discuss?"

Sybilla swallowed. "Hamon is threatening a war. I cannot tell you more."

Lady Claire raised her eyes in disbelief. "You spend your nights with him, Sybilla. A man will tell a woman things he shouldn't when it's dark. I've already heard that Hamon threatens Ketchem with a war. Have you other information about what goes on in those meetings?"

"I know no more than you, Lady Claire."

Lady Claire pursed her lips, evidently disappointed.

Sybilla lowered her eyes and added softly, knowing what Lady Claire wanted to hear. "I shall keep my ears ready, Lady Claire, and report anything I've learned."

Lady Claire smiled, the look on her face satisfied. "I thank you. Now tell me what business have you in my garden?"

Sybilla clasped her hands behind her back. She kept her eyes on the path, fearing she might stumble. "Sir Guy asked for swan's neck to settle his stomach. I only took a few leaves, my lady. He had too much wine to drink last night and I thought it might help him."

Lady Claire folded her arms, her eyes staring straight ahead. "Did he? Then by all means, help yourself, Mistress Corbuc, but be careful. You know how dangerous it can be when used to stop a woman's menses."

Sybilla nodded, unable to look Lady Claire in the face. Lady Claire continued. "And speaking of Sir Guy, do you know where he went? He rode from the castle this morning. Alone."

Her chest tightened, Sybilla raised her eyes to Lady Claire's smooth white face. "No, ma'am. I did not know he'd left. I've been busy with my servant's work."

Lady Claire let out a long breath. "God's bones, men vex me. I believe Sir Guy is on some secret mission."

Sybilla's gut sank like it was filled with lead. A secret mission? Guy had said nothing of a mission.

Lady Claire spun on her heels to rejoin her ladies. She stopped abruptly at the foot of a leaf-stripped sprig of swans-neck. She turned to Sybilla. "You will tell me if you've word from Guy of Warwick?"

Sybilla nodded, schooling her face to control her panic.

"Good. Now go and tend to your business, and I trust you will not lie to me again?"

"No, my lady."

Sybilla bobbed a curtsy. She hurried from the garden, but she had the feeling Lady Claire knew exactly where she was going, and why.

Crouching next to Mary, Sybilla huddled low, spooning swan's neck tea into her friend's dry lips.

Ernestine sat at the small wooden table, her eyes red and swollen. She'd cried for hours, taken one exhausted breath and stemmed the tide of tears. She sat silently, her shoulders drooping, her hands folded in her lap. She was resigned, it seemed, to lose her daughter.

Cook strained the leaves from the little pot and stirred the pale green liquid. "'Tis the last of it. No more color's coming from the leaves."

Sybilla wiped her brow. There'd be no need for more, for she dared not give it. Mary hadn't moved or groaned in over an hour, but she rested with her feet elevated above her hips, propped up on a mound of blankets. The soiled cloth between her legs was less bloody than the one before. The blood flow had slowed or else poor Mary had little left to bleed.

Sybilla covered Mary with a blanket. She checked her pulse. The great vein beneath her ear still throbbed, though its beat was faint. Sybilla brushed a stray hair, wet with sweat, from Mary's brow. "I've done all I can, Ernestine. She's a pulse but she's very pale. I know not if she'll live."

Ernestine let out a low keening wail. Cook took Sybilla by the elbow and ushered her to the door. "'Twas brave of you to risk going into Lady Claire's herbery for medicine. Take this for your efforts. You have my gratitude. Whatever happens, we owe you." She pressed two pennies into Sybilla's hand.

Her fingers closed over the coins, two coins closer to her farm, her freedom, to buying back Regalo. With another coin or two, she would be able rent the land she needed, build from there on the first year's crops and . . .

She lowered her eyes. How could she think of farming when the good-hearted Mary lay suffering and close to death, all because of one lapse in judgment? If she died, they'd dig a shallow pit and cover her with rocks, with no priest in attendance.

Sybilla thrust the coins back at Cook. "I cannot take these." She lowered her eyes. "You may need them," she added softly, glancing at Mary.

Cook spoke, her tone grim. "Take the coins. Go to the chapel, light a candle and ask the priest to pray for our Mary here, who's very sick with a *fever*." She said the last words slowly, with emphasis, and pushed the coins away.

A fever would keep the curious villagers away, all fearing some contagion, and if Mary died, there'd be a chance she could still be buried in the churchyard.

Sybilla slipped the coins into her pocket, resigned. "Yes, ma'am." She eased down onto the stool beside poor Mary's pallet and rested her hand on her friend's forehead. Mary's skin was cooling, the fever lessened, though just a little.

Faint hopefulness shot through Sybilla, but she kept her feelings in check. 'Twas too soon to tell. She pulled the blankets over Mary. "I will stay the night, or however long I'm needed."

Bacchus champed at the bit and snorted. Guy settled in the saddle and scanned the horizon. The woods around him were in the bloom of early summer, the thick foliage kept him covered. He'd no fear of being caught, though Hamon Castle loomed in the clearing. Black smoke billowed upward from behind the crenellated walls, curling like witches' fingers.

The castle forgery was engaged in weapon making, that was for certain, and judging by the number of horses, men, and wagons entering the gatehouse, Hamon was indeed gathering an army. By Guy's estimate, three hundred knights or more had ridden in. Just outside the gatehouse, carpenters constructed the spokes for the wheels of a trebuchet. In a month or less they would be ready.

Guy shifted in the saddle. Lord Phillip's spies had reported truthfully. What they hadn't done was given him the names, or numbers of those who'd joined Hamon's ranks.

He focused on the standards, the heraldry and banners that shimmered in the fading sun. Lord Gallagher had sent a contingent, some hundred men and horses. That came as no surprise. Nor were the silks of Lord Nevel unexpected. Both had been at odds with Ketchem for generations.

But he'd not expected who came next. Lord Percy's standard snapped in the breeze, the silken blue and golds waving at the head of the marching column, a cavalry of hundreds. And behind the calvary came the footmen and the sappers—the men who dug the tunnels at the base of a castle until the walls collapsed. Hell to the devil, they carried their shovels strapped across their backs like broadswords.

Guy inhaled, his eyes fixed on the troops below. God's teeth, 'twas almost as if Hamon knew of the weakness in the east wall and 'twas especially bold of him to assemble such an army in broad daylight—bold of Percy to participate. The actions bespoke of the confidence of both men. Lord Phillip would need to call in all his allies, and get the news of impending war to the king.

Guy leaned back and rubbed his forehead. Damnation. A traitor's movement of monstrous proportions was assembling, and more troops would keep coming. The question was how many more? He was prepared to stay the night and watch, but he'd not expected he might be here longer. He'd need more food and provisions, mayhap enough for a week or more.

His thoughts drifted to Ketchem, where his lord would be anxiously waiting for the news, where Regalo would be pacing the stall and Sybilla would be pacing in the cellar. He took a deep breath, and lifted his gaze to the expansive sky. Dusk would soon be falling and the night heavens would be filled with stars.

A strange sensation suddenly washed over him, a once familiar feeling that he'd locked away, long ago.

Longing.

Tonight would be the first time in over a month, he'd spent alone without Sybilla Corbuc.

Chapter Seventeen

Sybilla stepped inside the chapel vestibule and squinted, the darkness a contrast to the late afternoon sun setting against the pale blue sky outside. The cool interior of the church calmed her nerves and the sweet scent of the costly candles on the altar eased the pain in her aching head.

She'd spent the best part of a week balancing between her work in the kitchen and tending to Mary. Praise be to God, her fever had finally broken and she'd taken a little broth from a spoon. Sybilla came to pray and light a candle in the chapel every day as she promised Cook she would.

Relief flooding over her, Sybilla took a deep breath. Mary's close call with death had driven home her fear of getting with child. She'd been right to be wary of Guy, and though she longed to have him home, it felt good to help Mary.

The old sense of gratification spilled over her, the one Sybilla got whenever she delivered a foal. Her presence made a difference to a living being's survival, like it had to Mary. Blessed saints, how she missed the feeling.

Father James appeared from 'round the corner, his robes rustling against the pavers. He wore his red and white cassock with a gold threaded overlay, the garments far richer than the priest's at Cornbury. He moved to sit in the confessional and beckoned for Sybilla to join him. He had a kind young face, but he was known to give harsh penances. Instinct told her to proceed with deference and caution.

Sybilla folded her hands in front of her and knelt before him. "I'm here just to pray again, Father, I've nothing to confess."

The priest pushed the curtains back. "But Sybilla, you've never once confessed at Ketchem. Now would be a good time, before the line gets long." He laughed at his own joke as he studied the gold rings on his small white hand. "Tell me. What troubles you?"

Sybilla's palms grew sweaty. Her dealings with priests had never gone well. "Nothing, sir. I am here to give thanks. Young Mary's fever has broken."

"*Nothing* troubles you?" he asked in a tone that implied her refusal to admit to trouble and confess was yet another sin.

She lowered her head. The priest wore red shoes, just like the sheriff. "I admit I'm here to pray for Guy of Warwick, too. He's been gone a week. I am worried for him."

Father James smiled his wide smile and showed his clean white teeth. He was younger than she was, though not by much.

"Worried for him? Is that it? You can confess all to me, for I understand temptation."

Sybilla felt a scorching blush sweep down her neck. "Temptation?"

Father James thumped his chest. "I traded my nobleman's robes for these priestly garments. I was an earl's son, the fourth in a lusty string of five. Now I am a humble servant to our Lord, though I've been no stranger to sin, Sybilla. There are many kinds of temptation here that I suspect appeals to you, a comely, unmarried woman who hails from Cornbury, and one who has a gift." He grinned, looking like an evil cherub. "Fornication would be bad enough, but I could give you a penance for that." He leaned forward, so close she could smell his fishy breath. "I truly hope you have not practiced your horse midwifery, in any form or fashion, since you've arrived to Ketchem."

Sybilla's toes twitched. She wanted to race from the chapel. "I know the rules. I've not done anything like what I did in Cornbury." *That much was true.*

Father James lifted his eyebrows, his smooth young forehead creased beneath his feathery brown bangs. "See that you don't. The bishop has issued the directive against the practice. I support him."

Sybilla entered the kitchen, her legs still trembling after visiting the church. Best to wait on Guy, whenever he got back, to take her to Regalo. Sneaking to the stables seemed suddenly too risky.

The kitchen's warmth wrapped around her and she settled at the table, resting her head in her hands. The newest servant, a boy from Tillings village, napped before the fire. The smell of burnt pottage rose from the iron cauldron. Cook would be furious when she returned from nursing Mary to find her best iron pot cooked dry and scorched. Sybilla set the cauldron from the hearth.

A low groan coming from the corner of the room caught her attention.

She squinted through the hazy din. Simon sat against the wall, propped up on his pallet, his face pale and drawn.

"Simon," she whispered, as she made her way across

the room. She pressed her hand to his pale forehead, the stench from his shoulder overwhelming.

"Oh Simon, how long has it been since you've last changed the bandage?" She poured a cup full of wine and raised it to his lips. "Your wound is fouled."

His eyes dazed, he rasped, "I've been waiting nigh a week for Mary, she said she'd come and change the bandage, like she always does." His voice trailed off. "I did it myself, once or twice, but not as good. Where is she?"

Sybilla chewed her lip. No need to worry him over Mary. She handed Simon a cup. "Drink this. I'll tend your wound."

Simon sipped from the cup and leaned his head back. The foul smell from his bandage made her retch, but within minutes she'd cut the dirty cloth away. The hole in his shoulder gaped like a dead man's mouth and oozed pus the color of lemon curd.

Blessed saints!

She soaked a clean strip of linen in watered wine and scrubbed Simon's shoulder. Pressing deeper, she cleaned the inside of his wound while he groaned. He muttered Mary's name, his white-knuckled hands gripping his thighs.

She tossed the soiled bandage into the fire. "I'll leave your shoulder uncovered to help the drainage. Let me get some butter to smear around the edges and keep them soft."

Simon grabbed her wrist, his fingers hot and weak. "Don't leave."

Sybilla halted. "I'm not going anywhere. Just across the room to get some butter."

Simon struggled to sit up. "I mean don't leave *him*, Mistress Corbuc. Sir Guy. If you were here with him, I'd feel better about taking off myself."

Sybilla's eyes grew wide. "You aren't going to die."

Simon slurred his words. "I don't intend to die. I'm weary of a soldier's life. This arm will never be good enough for fighting again. I plan to buy a farm of my own and take a wife. I have a little money. I'll be leaving Ketchem—that is if we don't go to war." His eyes captured hers, his look pleading. "Guy of Warwick needs you. He's got no one else." He tried to smile, but coughed instead. "Do you know why he sheds his clothes so often?" he said, wiping his lips.

Sybilla shook her head. "To vex me?"

"No. He wore his brother's pass-me-downs as a boy. His mother stitched his tunics with scraps and pieces, but they were still too small. His brother perished two winters past. Then Hamon killed Guy's sister and his nephew . . ." His voice trailed off, and he stared vacantly at the fire. "I've not seen him show a spark of interest in anything or anyone since. Then along came Regalo— and you."

"He believes the colt will help him vanquish Hamon. I'm his servant. Nothing more."

Simon let his head loll to the side. "You know better, Sybilla. When you are with him, I see glimpses of the old Guy, the one with fire in eyes and passion. And you are in love with him. Stay with him so I might take my leave knowing my friend is not alone."

Sybilla lowered her eyes. How could she admit to Simon she was in love with Guy when she could not admit it to herself?

Simon eased down on his bed, guarding his shoulder. "Am I right? Soothe my conscience and assure me."

Avoiding his eyes, she conceded. Poor Simon. He worried for his friend and for Mary. "On my honor, I'll stay until the end of our agreement."

Simon's eyes drifted shut and he dragged his blanket up to his chin. He snored.

Sybilla settled against the wall, folding her arms around her chest for warmth. No point in going to her room. The place would be far too quiet and without Sir Guy, it would surely feel as big as an empty cathedral.

For the first time in nigh a week, Sybilla lit the little brazier and warmed the cellar. She'd swept the floor and straightened the covers on Guy's bed, though she'd all but given up on his return this evening. Still, it could do no harm to keep the place ready, just in case. Fatigued, she sat down on her pallet and warmed her hands, determined to wait in the place where she belonged, in Sir Guy of Warwick's cellar. Simon was on the mend and, God's breath, there were far too many mice and people in the kitchen.

She closed her eyes. The solitude offered comfort, but sleep would not come easily without Guy.

The cellar door suddenly rattled, shaking as though a battering ram beat against its planks. Sybilla sat upright, her heart racing, her breath held in her lungs. "Who's there?"

"'Tis John the Marshal, Sybilla, 'Tis Lady Claire's mare. She's birthing but the foal is stuck. My arm's too big to help her! Please, come with me."

Sybilla scrabbled to her feet. "I dare not, John. You know I am forbidden."

John pleaded. His voice sounded as if he called from the bottom of a well. "Please, if the foal dies I'll be dismissed. Lady Claire has never liked me. I'm at my wits end. Could you really let the foal die? Or the mare?"

An ache filled Sybilla's gut. Yearning pulled her to the stables, much as it had the night Regalo got away. God help her, if there was something she could do, she could not let the poor beasts die. The hour was late and no one would see. Surely the Lady Claire would forgive her if she were caught.

Sybilla tied her veil over her head and strode across the room. She threw open the door. "We must be quick."

Sybilla slipped silently from the cellar chamber and into the tunnel.

John took her by the wrist. "I am grateful. Forever in your debt no matter what happens." Sweat trickled down his temple.

Sybilla's heart beat hard against her chest.

St. Genevieve protect me, just this one last time.

The quiet sound of horses munching hay and shifting in their stalls filled Sybilla's ears. Regalo hung his big head over the stall and nickered as she passed. She smiled and rested her hand on his muzzle for a moment before she followed John into the birthing box further up the row.

A dun filly lay grunting in the straw, her ears and neck soaked with sweat, her round flank distended. The moth-eaten little barn dog sat quietly beside her head and whined.

Sybilla knelt and examined the filly's ruddy gums. "Heaven help her, John, how long's she been like this?"

John gulped. "Labor came on all of a sudden. Never seen nothing like it."

Sybilla frowned. She moved to the back end of the horse and lifted the animal's tail. She gasped. The mare's hind end was smeared with a blue paste that smelled like pig fat. "John, what have you done?"

"'Tis just a tincture of lapis. 'Twill keep the elves away."

"Did you smear it up inside her?"

John nodded.

Sybilla let out a deep breath. She'd not the heart to tell him she knew from experience it wouldn't work. She would have applied the stuff all over Addy if it might have spared Regalo the affliction.

The little mare at Sybilla's feet groaned a pitiful groan. The rest of the horses in the aisle started whinnying. Prickly bumps rippled up Sybilla's arms. How did horses always seem to know when one amongst them was close to death?

John unwrapped a lump of goose grease from a linen cloth and held it out to Sybilla. "I cannot get my arm inside far enough to change the foal's position. I pray you can right the little beast before the mare gives up or we'll lose 'em both."

Sybilla pulled off her servant's dress and slipped her arm from her chemise. She greased her arm, and slipped her hand into the mare, probing for a hoof, a leg, or jaw. The mare squeezed down, the pressure numbing, squeezing down on Sybilla's arm and sending the foal backward, deeper into the womb.

Sybilla held her breath until the mare's contraction stopped, the pain in her forearm aching. When at last the horse relaxed, Sybilla drove her arm forward, sinking into the narrow passage, past her elbow, up to her shoulder.

The wild-eyed mare grunted and Sybilla felt a tiny hoof. She wrapped her fingers round the foal's slippery fetlock and held on tight.

She shouted. "Help me!"

Jolted into action, John wrapped his arms around her waist and heaved her backward.

The first foot slid out into the light with Sybilla's fist wrapped around the ankle. The second foot appeared behind the first, gushing out in a flood of fluid, followed by the head, and the shoulders.

The foal emerged, blinking, gasping for precious breath through a blue-stained mouth and muzzle. Sybilla hauled the little beast from the birthway, into the straw.

The foal raised its wobbly head, its eyes bright and lucid. The spritely little beast pecked at the mare's leg, already looking for a place to nurse. Sybilla smiled. This one should survive.

The mare rolled onto her sternum, and tucked her legs beneath her. She nickered softly at the buff-colored foal.

His face flushed and his eyes bright with relief, John let out a whoop. He quickly set to drying the newborn. "Well done, Sybilla." He smiled, his large white teeth lighting up his face. "I owe you a favor. If you ever need help you can count on John of Kent." He laughed and motioned at the newborn in the straw. "She's a filly, beautiful and healthy, though her face is stained all blue."

Sybilla nodded, breathing hard. "She's not the only one discolored." She scrubbed at her blue arm with a handful of hay. "Where'd you learn of lapis as an anti-dote for elfshot?"

John dragged the foal closer to the mare. "Sir Malcolm told me 'bout it. He—"

At the mention of Sir Malcolm's name, Sybilla froze. "Sir Malcolm?"

A voice echoed from the stall doorway. "Aye, 'twas me, Sybilla Corbuc."

Sybilla jerked her head around, her heart in her throat.

Her discarded brown dress was dangling from the tip of his sword. Sir Malcolm leaned against the stall door, with a scroll tucked beneath his arm.

Booted feet fast approached. Swords rattled from their scabbards and men shouted.

Sir Malcolm's mouth spread into a malicious grin. "You are under arrest, Mistress Sybilla Corbuc."

"Arrest?" Sybilla asked, even though a part of her had not expected this moment every day since she'd been chased out of Cornbury.

Sir Malcolm unfurled the scroll he was holding. "I have a warrant from the church."

Sybilla felt panic flow over her body, like a wave that meant to drown her. "I shall see Sir Guy of Warwick about this. I answer to him."

"He isn't here, Mistress. Off Shadow Riding, I suppose. Wallowing in grief while his little servant dabbles with the devil."

A Ketchem guard strode in and gripped Sybilla by the arm. Her knees almost buckled. She had not the strength to fight him. "Come with me, mistress," he said, dragging her out of the stall.

"Please give me my dress! Where are you taking me?"

Sir Malcolm smirked. "To the prison in the armory where you will be held for questioning." He flung the dress at the guard who held her. "See that she doesn't wash. Her arm is streaked with blue, proof she committed a crime and used unholy potions to do it. It's a miracle the filly doesn't have three heads."

John the Marshal jumped to his feet. "Sir Malcolm, she saved the mare, Lady Claire's favorite. You know 'tis only a paste of lapis—" He cut his words short, his face alight with comprehension.

Sir Malcolm laughed. "You're a fool, John of Kent."

The great wooden door to the armory prison had iron nails that jutted from the panels. Sybilla took a sharp breath as rough hands thrust her inside, slammed the door behind her, and turned the key.

Moonlight moved across the cell like a ghost, illuminating the only other habitant, an old woman who lay in the corner, stretched out in the filthy straw like a corpse. She wheezed, her mouth agape. She did not turn her head to even look at Sybilla.

Sybilla stood with her back to the door, her eyes focused on the woman's face. Even in the darkness she could see the scar on the woman's cheek, a scar, festering and red. 'Twas a brand in the shape of a half moon—the mark of a woman tried as a Separate, left in prison to wait for the final sentence from the bishop. If she didn't die here first, he'd pronounce her a heretic, have her stripped, dragged into the woods, and left for the wolves.

Sybilla closed her eyes and slid down, drawing her knees to her chest. Saints preserve her, she'd been arrogant. What a fool she'd been not to do as Guy had told her. To think a freeman from the countryside could live as a servant in a castle, ply her trade in secret, and not get caught. Without Guy to help her now, all was lost.

The woman in the corner moaned, the pain in her thin voice as brittle as the winter wind. She gasped, and then went silent. Not a breath followed or even a wheeze, the last of her life extinguished.

Sybilla whimpered. She wrapped her arms around her chest, grateful for what little comfort and protection from the cold her old brown dress had left to offer.

She rested her head against her arms, and in the distance she heard the sound she hadn't heard in months.

Regalo barking.

Chapter Eighteen

In the morning the door banged open. "Sybilla Corbuc," a voice said.

Sybilla tried to rise to her feet, but her legs buckled beneath her. A guard strode in and jerked her up, hauling her along the cobbles. He dragged her through the armory and up some steps, then stopped before another spiked door. He rapped on the door with the hilt of his sword, opened it to a call from within. He carried her inside and dumped her on the stone floor like a wheat sack.

Father James sat at a table opposite the door; Lord Phillip, his steward, Lady Claire, and Sir Malcolm sat to his left, their faces impassive, though Lady Claire's was pale.

The witnesses, castle folk no doubt who'd just been dragged from their sleep, hunkered down on a pew facing the table with their backs to Sybilla, their forms a blur.

Father James motioned for Sybilla to come forward. She couldn't move.

He held a quill in his hand. "Name?" he asked.

She searched for her voice, her throat frozen.

Lord Phillip's steward answered. "Sybilla Corbuc."

"Occupation?" asked the priest.

Sybilla kept her eyes down, her lips trembling.

"Servant," answered a familiar voice, as if it were a matter of insignificance.

Sybilla's heart leapt. She raised her gaze to see Guy of Warwick. He stood from the bench and towered over all as he turned to face her. Dark circles rimmed his eyes, and stubble shadowed his unshaven cheeks.

"She is conscribed to me," he stated flatly.

Sybilla met his neutral look with a stare.

Father James frowned. "The bishop's charge to me is to root out heresy in the castle of our noble Lord Phillip, be it in the kitchens, or in the stables. Your servant is arrested with a warrant on behalf of the church."

Guy folded his arms. "The charge?" he asked, as if he were surprised.

"Caught by Sir Malcolm in the stables last night, practicing midwifery on a mare. She has a skill in witchery and the black arts." Father James spoke to Sybilla. "How do you plead, Mistress?"

Sybilla stammered. "I did not, I mean . . . I've no knowledge of black arts, or witching . . ." she started, her voice trailing off with hopelessness.

Guy leaned his head back. "This is a false charge, Father James, a malicious complaint seeded by the rivalry Sir Malcolm has against me," he said, as if he were bored.

Sir Malcolm jumped up. "She cannot deny it. Her arm is stained blue. She painted herself with a lapis potion to let the elves get in and shoot the foal. She's Satan's lover, and up to mischief. When was the last time she's been to confession, Father? Or the last time she wasn't late for chapel, Lady Claire? Strip her dress away and look at her arm. 'Tis stained with the tainted potion."

The priest hesitated.

Lord Phillip took a deep breath. "I'll allow it."

The guard beside Sybilla grabbed her threadbare dress by the shoulder and yanked, the sleeve and bodice tearing away like wet parchment, along with her chemise.

She stood before the court with her breasts bared and her left arm exposed, her skin as blue as ink.

The men gasped. Lady Claire lowered her eyes, her cheeks flaming scarlet.

Sybilla's chin quivered. She covered her breasts, and stole a glance at Guy. She caught the subtle movement of his arms as he reached for her, then checked himself.

He stood with his fists at his sides for a moment. His fingers unfolded slowly. His face calmed. "This is ridiculous, my Lord Phillip. With due respect, Sir Malcolm has duped my lowly servant to get back at me. She's a woman, and fell for his tricks. Father James was just as easily played. He seeks to rise in the ranks of the church and wants to please the bishop. What could you expect?"

The priest looked up, his face indignant.

Malcolm slammed his fist on the table. "I'll not have you slur against me, Sir Guy."

Guy folded his arms. "Think upon it, all of you. There's no such thing as lapis paste for elfshot. If my servant truly had the knowledge of which she is accused, she would have known that. She's just a woman, witless on occasion, but nothing more, tricked by Sir Malcolm here to do what she should not."

Guy strode across the room to Sybilla, took off his cloak and covered her nakedness.

Malcolm sneered. He pushed away from the table, his chair scraping on the stones. "You challenge me on this, Sir Guy? What reason would I have to make up such an egregious accusation?"

Guy spun on his heels, his hand on his sword. "To get back at me, Malcolm, your only rival in the summer race. You think she has some magic power over my colt. That without her, the beast would lie down and die. She doesn't. He won't. He'll beat any horse you have. This plot of yours nearly killed Lady Claire's favorite mare. John of Kent tells me her labor came on suddenly. What toxin did you feed her?"

Lady Claire put her hand on her heart. "Oh, no."

Lord Phillip fumed. "Sir Malcolm, I've been up all night listening to Sir Guy's grave report on Hamon Castle. If you've concocted this ordeal o'er a rival—"

Malcolm straightened. "I've done nothing of the sort, my lord. Sir Guy is speculating. Did you know last night when we hauled his servant to the prison, his rangy colt barked like a dog? 'Twas unnatural. The little beast is a familiar if I've ever seen one."

The court let out a collective gasp. Father James crossed himself, and Lord Phillip set his hand on Lady Claire's arm.

Father James put his pen to the ledger. "She's a heretic. Brand her as a Separate and lock her up in prison 'til the bishop visits and pronounces her final sentence. Call the smith and have him bring the hot iron."

Sybilla's hand flew to her cheek. "No," she said very quietly.

John of Kent rose from the bench and took off his leather cap. "Permission to speak, my Lord Phillip. I've more information."

Guy of Warwick shot a warning look at John, and Sybilla bit her lip until she tasted blood.

"I'll allow it," Lord Phillip stated before the priest had a chance to answer.

"Sir Malcolm is mistaken. 'Twas not the colt that was

barking. Was him." John pulled the runty, moth-eaten barn dog from beneath his cloak.

The witnesses on the bench tittered. Sir Malcolm's face turned red.

"'Tis true. Aye, Sybilla Corbuc saved your mare, Lady Claire, but wasn't the colt that was barking. 'Twas the mutt. Sir Malcolm and the guard had all left so they saw nothing. They'd heard the rumors 'bout the colt, but I told 'em it wasn't true. Horses don't bark. What kind of marshal would I be if I didn't know that?" John rubbed the mangy dog hard on the back and he yipped as if on cue, wagging his tail. "The pup got excited, that's all."

Cook stood up, along with two washer women Sybilla barely recognized. "And that stain on Sybilla's arm will come off with a paste of salt and vinegar, my lord. It's just blue dye, no magic potion. Must have cost Sir Malcolm a pretty penny."

Malcolm drew his sword. "Silence you old hag." Lord Phillip's guards surrounded him.

All heads turned to face the priest. He raised his eyebrows and looked at Lord Phillip.

Lord Phillip stroked his chin as Lady Claire whispered in his ear.

Guy stepped forward. "My lord, I'll deal with my servant for defying my direct order and going to the stables. I rode my horse into the ground last night to get here, woke you from your sleep to give you my report on Hamon. Does Sir Malcolm really think we've time to squabble over a horse race? We must get on with the business of making Ketchem ready for a war."

Father James gulped.

Lord Phillip nodded. "In light of this further information, I see no evidence of witchcraft, provided the coloring can wash off." He signaled to his steward. "Give my letter to Sir Malcolm."

The steward produced a folded parchment and laid it on the table in front of Malcolm.

Lord Phillip tapped his finger on the letter. "Sir Malcolm, take this message to the king. Tell him Hamon readies to attack us. Go now."

A hard thin line formed around Sir Malcolm's face. He took the letter and bowed curtly. "Yes, my lord. I ask permission to return for the August race." He shot a glance at Guy. "I've never missed the competition since I was old enough to ride and—"

With a wave of his hand, Lord Phillip cut him off. "Leave us. I should banish you completely, Sir Malcolm, but you're too valuable a knight. Do not press me. If you behave at court, I'll ask the king to give you leave to race. Watch yourself and cause no trouble there."

Sir Malcolm strode from the room. Sybilla trembled as he passed her, his cloak billowing around him like a black ghost.

Lady Claire leaned forward and spoke in a quiet voice. "Sybilla Corbuc, you have my thanks for saving my mare, and the foal, but you must stay out of the stables unless Sir Guy is with you. Take the punishment he gives you and ask for his forgiveness. And never be late for chapel again."

Father James scribbled in his ledger. He stood, clasping the great book to his chest. "Sir Guy, take her away. I trust she will be disciplined. Sybilla, I expect to see you in confession when he's done."

Sybilla curtsied to the table, to Father James, to Lord Phillip, and to Lady Claire. Her knees hit the ground with a thud and she found she did not have the strength to stand again.

She slumped, her vision blurry.

Guy of Warwick scooped her up in his arms and carried her from the room.

It was the last thing she remembered.

Guy set Sybilla down. It took a moment for her to realize where she was—in his cellar chamber.

Her legs shaky, she hobbled immediately to his chest, threw back the lid and withdrew the two pennies Cook had given her for helping Mary. She thrust them at Guy. "Take these," she stammered.

Guy frowned. "What for? And where did you get pennies?"

"From helping Mary. There's a woman in the prison who died last night, branded as a Separate and forgotten. Please, Sir Guy, no matter how angry you are with me, please see that she is buried." Her hand shook. The pennies slipped between her fingers, bounced on the stone floor and rolled beneath the bed.

Tears welled up in her eyes.

Guy raised his hand and touched her cheek. She cringed and shielded her face.

He lowered his arm and stepped away. "I'll see that she is buried. Good God, Sybilla, do you think I would actually hit you?"

She kept her eyes down. "I-I . . . I don't know. I thought you meant to punish me."

Guy ran his fingers through his hair and let out an exasperated breath. "Damnation, I would never strike you, Sybilla. Never. How could you not know that?"

He spun on his heels and silently lit the brazier. He stood to face her, the lines around his eyes and mouth deep with worry. "You've no idea, do you? No understanding of how I felt to come riding home last night, racing here to see you, hoping you were asleep and safe. Only to discover you were not."

Sybilla pulled Guy's cloak around her. It smelled of wool and of horses and of him. "I'm sorry. I know you worried for Regalo—"

He rubbed his forehead. "Regalo? Worried for Regalo? Christ's bones, when I learned of your arrest, I could have broken down the prison door with my bare hands. But I was forced to check my impulse, spend the hours explaining to Lord Phillip how Hamon plans his attack, all the while pretending the circumstance of your arrest was just a misunderstanding, one that I could explain when I got the chance."

He stood so near, she could feel his breath on her face. She lowered her eyes. "You are right to be angry, I—"

"Bloody hell! I'm not angry, I'm . . ." He clenched his fists and took a slow, long breath. "I'm not angry, Sybilla. I would have done the same thing, helped the mare and foal. I'm just-just—"

In an instant, he drew her to him, his hands at the back of her neck, his fingers tunneling through her hair. He held her close, so close she could feel his heart beating like a battering ram against his chest.

He nuzzled her temple and scattered light kisses over her eyelids and down the ridge of her nose. His mouth came to rest lightly against her cheek, his voice low and husky. "Hell to the devil, I've missed you." He closed his eyes.

Sybilla shivered, his lips against her skin so divine, so sensual and rich. His touch stirred her heart back to life. She felt like laying her soul at his feet. She found the words to say what she never thought she would.

"Guy of Warwick, I know what I want. I want you to . . . I want you to kiss me like you did in Cornbury, the first night we met. I want to . . ." She inhaled and held her breath for a moment before she spoke. "I want to sleep with you tonight. Naked."

"Sybilla, this is not what you want. I can't let you—"

"It is."

She kissed him hard on the lips, her hands against his chest, moving down to the hem of his tunic. She slipped her fingers into his braes and stroked his shaft.

His cock sprang to life, the skin as warm and as smooth as velvet in her hand.

"Blessed bones," he muttered. A groan mixed with pleasure rumbled from his throat. He placed his hand against her bottom and pulled her against him while he thrust his tongue repeatedly into her mouth. She felt his shaft grow in her hand, and jut against her belly.

Her thoughts scattered after that, along with caution. She cared not for anything but the chance to be with him. For she'd almost lost her life today, and with it might have lost everything. Even if he loved her only as a servant and their union lasted just a night, it mattered not. Even if a babe came from this, so be it. She would survive and love the child.

He rested his forehead against hers and kept his eyes closed. He took her hand gently from his braes, his chest heaving. "Sybilla, I fear this has gone too far. That this is not what you truly want—"

She ran her fingers over his lips to stop his words. "Shhhhh. I am certain."

He peered at her from beneath his heavy-lidded eyes, and took a deep breath. He kissed each fingertip. "You've only to say stop. I will."

His breath hot against her skin, he skimmed his mouth over her earlobe, over her chin, and down her neck. He slipped the cloak from her shoulders and bared her naked breasts, her torn gown and tattered chemise sat at her waist. He stroked a nipple with his thumb, ran his warm hand up her naked back.

She arched against him, her breasts crushing against the rough wool of his tunic. She whimpered, begging him for more, though she knew not for more of what.

Guy stripped off his tunic and his hose. He wet a washing cloth with water from the ewer.

"It isn't warm, but I'll make it as pleasurable as I can." He grinned, and gestured to her blue stained arm.

Heat rose to her cheeks. She lowered her gaze, embarrassed at her filth.

Guy chuckled. "You are beautiful, Sybilla."

He held her hand and ran the cloth along the length of her arm, washing away blue streaks and the grease. He rinsed the cloth and laid it softly on her breast, stroking, drawing circles 'round her nipples. She stiffened, aware that her buds were as hard and brown as cherry pits. The thought of how they looked and responded excited her, and yet at the same time, made her uncertain.

Guy pressed his lips to the rim of her ear, biting, sucking, licking, sending prickly bumps up her neck as he washed her shoulders and her neck, waiting for her to relax. "There are many ways a man can give a woman pleasure without getting her with child. Let me show you."

He tossed the cloth to the floor and lathed kisses over the peaks of her breasts, pushing her gown and chemise down past her hips. The ruined garments fell in a puddle at her feet.

"What of Lady Claire?" she rasped. "If she learns of this."

Guy helped Sybilla step from her clothing. He led her to the bed. "She knows, Sybilla."

He pressed her gently down. He yanked off his shirt. He stood there naked and staring, lust blazing in his dark eyes. "By the devil, Sybilla, you are beautiful. If you could see yourself . . . with one hose tied with a black ribbon around your thigh, a ribbonless hose slipping down the other." He grinned and he lowered himself onto the bed beside her. "I like the thought of you undone beneath your dress."

He brushed a lock of her hair from her cheek. "Let me look at you." He ran his fingers over her breasts, down her belly, lower, and slipped his hand between her legs. "Open your legs for me," he whispered, leaning over her, his mouth close to hers.

Sybilla closed her eyes, relishing his caress, the warmth in his fingers, forgetting where they were exactly, until they slipped inside her. One finger, then two, pressing at her entrance. He stretched her open, and stroked her, a slow, delicious stroke that carried her away.

She moaned, losing herself in what he was doing to her.

He softly kissed her temple, his fingers down below working their magic, entrancing. "More?" he asked, his voice ragged.

She sighed. "Y-Yes." She bent her knees and opened her legs a little more.

"Kiss me," he whispered. He brushed his lips against hers.

She moaned into his mouth, her pulse racing. She arched against him, her chest and belly pressed against the full length of him. She took in his scent, the male musk that rose from his chest and underneath his arms.

He groaned, and slipped his fingers from her cleft.

She clamped her knees together, trapping his hand. "No, please, don't—"

His thumb found the core of her arousal, gently rubbing back and forth. "I'm not done yet."

Sybilla closed her eyes. The incredibly delightful little jolts of pleasure that shot from her center, up her belly and along her spine made her shiver. She moaned, and pressed her mouth against his chest to muffle the sound. Unable to resist his coaxing, she writhed against him, to move as he commanded, giving her direction without words, taking her toward she knew not what. He made her feel as though she was about to burst.

She shuddered, digging her fingers into his arms, and cried out as blessed release shot through her, stealing the air from her lungs.

Panting, and feeling as limp as a rag doll, she opened her eyes to find him staring at her, his eyes ablaze with lust. He climbed over her, poised on all fours. He searched her eyes and touched her lips with his own. "This part may not feel so nice, Sybilla, but it will only last a moment." He nudged her thighs apart with his.

Sybilla pulled his head to hers. "I want to know. Everything." She sucked in her breath.

He placed his rigid cock at her entrance. His upper body braced on his forearms, he thrust inside her.

A gasp slipped past her lips, the sharp stab between her legs catching her off guard.

He withdrew, but only just a little. He thrust again, this time burying himself deep inside her.

She bit down on her lower lip to keep from crying out.

He thrust again. She felt her muscles ease and stretch around him, and the pain began to melt 'way, turning into something else, something altogether pleasing.

"Done?" she asked in a whisper, rather hoping that he wasn't.

He smiled and leaned down to kiss her. "Not yet."

Slowly he moved his hips, his shaft sliding in and out. Pumping.

Instinctively, she lifted her pelvis to grind against him, thrusting upward, in rhythm with his momentum. She gripped his buttocks, her fingers pressing into flexing muscle. "Oh, Guy, I . . . is it supposed to, am I supposed to—?"

Sweat dripped from his temple onto her neck, and his face fixed with passion. "Yes, it's supposed to make you feel like that," he rasped, as he drove himself inside her.

The veins in his neck stood up and he threw his head back. He roared, the sound primal, like that of a wild boar.

She squeezed her eyes shut, pleasure overtaking every thought. Her body arched as she threw her legs around Guy's waist and held on tight. A most exquisite spasm gripped her *there*, and spread from her core to her toes. Devil take her, she'd not known anything could feel this good!

Guy shouted and warmth splattered onto her belly.

She let her legs fall to the bed, collapsing.

He rolled beside her, breathing hard. He held her hand, his thumb drawing circles in the center of her palm. "Done," he said, and a weak smile spread over his damp face. "For now."

Sometime in the early hours of the morning, after Guy had loved her a second, nay, a third time, Sybilla roused from a restless slumber. He was lying with his head cradled in the curve of her shoulder, his breathing deep and rhythmic. It occurred to Sybilla she'd never seen him sleep, really sleep.

Moving quietly, she slipped his head from her arm and rose from the bed to light the brazier. The room lit with a soft glow and Sybilla turned to study Guy, his naked body in full view. He was bigger than most men, the most finely made man she'd ever seen, the kind that turned the heads of noblewomen and villagers alike. In sleep he had the face of a dark angel, beautiful, though the lines around his mouth, the creases at the corners of his deep set eyes and the stern set to his jaw revealed a man whose life was filled with burning guilt. The long puckered scar that wound its way across his ribcage revealed the harsh reality of a year spent at war. She tried to imagine the anguish of a man returning as a hero, only to discover his family murdered.

And yet, he'd walked into a lowly country barn on a wicked winter night and saved a lawbreaking horse mid-wife and the life of a colt that would have surely died. He'd defended her to his lord and saved her a second time from prison. She owed him for that, but it wasn't gratitude that made her heart swell.

She loved him in a way she never thought it possible to love a man.

She couldn't resist stealing a kiss before she rummaged through the chest to find her old blue dress, her servant's gown shredded and her chemise ripped beyond repair.

Guy's sleep-soaked voice broke the silence. "Sybilla?"

Pulling the gown over her head, she turned and joined him on the bed. "I'm needed in the kitchens. I owe Cook a favor. The least I can do is show up to work." She kissed his soft lips, and the ache between her thighs started all over again. "I'll wait for you this afternoon to take me to the stables."

Guy sat up, his eyes red and glazed. "What?" He rubbed his face.

"The stables. You'll take me there this afternoon."

* * *

His mind still foggy after the lovemaking and a stuperous sleep, the words *the stables* and the sound of Sybilla's voice reverberated in his ears.

Guy flung the covers back. Bloody hell. She'd better not be going to the stables without him. Surely she wouldn't disregard his warning, not after she'd just been arrested. Not after what she'd just been through. What *he'd* just been through.

He bolted to the door, his bare feet slapping the floor. "Sybilla!" He raced into the tunnel heedless of the night watchman, heading home.

The man flattened against the wall, his eyes bugging out of his head. He smiled, but quickly wiped all traces of humor off his face.

"Sir Guy," he said clearing his throat. "She went that way." He pointed to the kitchen.

"But you best be getting your clothes on first, sir. Lest Lady Claire and the rest of the world know what you've been up to."

Guy stood there slack-jawed. Damnation. Was there nowhere in Ketchem a man could have a private conversation?

The watchman clucked. "Go on, cover up, for Sybilla's sake," he said, his tone reproachful.

Guy spun on his heels and stormed into his cellar, slamming the door behind him. The breeze from the door slapped his backside.

Hell to the devil. Surely she would not be so heedless?

He snatched his tunic and pulled it over his head.

He never should have kissed her. Not last night, not that first night in Cornbury. Since Morna, he'd bedded dozens of women, some just as beautiful and seductive, but from the first moment he'd laid eyes on Sybilla

Corbuc he knew he was in trouble. Why in God's name had he bedded her last night?

He pulled on his braes and hose, glad to have his rod sheathed and covered. Truth be known, he'd made love to Sybilla because he'd wanted her so badly. She needed him—his protection and all he could offer her as a man. But God's peace, she caused him trouble.

Sybilla Corbuc had courage. He'd give her that. She had a fierce will to survive and she was committed to her values. He'd give her that as well. But she'd no right to intrude on his. Worst of all, now he'd gone and done the one thing he'd promised her he'd never do—steal her virtue.

He shoved his feet into his boots. He felt like fighting. Felt like swinging his sword until he struck something solid that struck him back. He deserved it.

He strapped his sword to his side and splashed water on his face.

Simon had told him once it was time to let his ghosts rest. To find something or someone to care about beside Lord Hamon.

But damned if he was ready. And caring about Sybilla would put her life at risk. Besides, he didn't want the distraction. He could take her to the stables to see Regalo every day if that's what she wanted. That was the least that he could do. He owed her that.

But he would not love her.

Chapter Nineteen

After a long day of training Regalo and a long, sumptuous night of lovemaking with Sybilla, Guy watched her sleeping now. With her golden hair spread out over his chest, her eyes closed and her slow even breaths, she was peacefully settled against him, oblivious to the sound of the crowing cock outside.

For the last eight weeks she'd shared his bed. The May winds had come and gone, melting the last of the Ketchem's snow and the meadows were filled with bright green grasses and white daisies.

Sybilla had spent her days working in the kitchen while he readied Ketchem for a war. And every afternoon, as the sun was setting, she waited for him on the kitchen steps so that he might take her to the stables. If he were delayed or missed their appointment altogether, she sulked. Regalo refused to eat when Sybilla did not visit. Seemed the colt still needed her, though he was close to weaning age and as tall as a yearling.

Guy closed his eyes and Sybilla's soft scent filled his head.

Sybilla lazily wrapped her arm around Guy's waist.

This was how she usually awakened him, stirring silently, followed by a gentle kiss that turned to passion, and passion turned to lust.

Guy struggled to ignore the quiet peace that filled his heart. She wouldn't stay here forever.

Regalo hadn't barked since the night she helped with Lady Claire's mare. He'd be ready for the saddle by the end of the summer.

Sybilla stretched, rolled over, and smiled at Guy.

By the devil, it felt good to see her so content.

Guy slapped her playfully on her hip. "Time to get to work. Today, I'll tether Regalo next to Bacchus and take him for a gallop in the south pasture. This time of year, the grass is as green as emeralds, 'tis the first step to ready him for the—"

Sybilla sat up. "Emeralds get you into trouble, Sir Guy. You aren't planning to ride him are you? It's too soon."

Guy ran a finger over her creamy shoulder. "It's not too soon, my sweet. He's not a colt anymore."

"He's barely three months old."

Guy captured her hand and kissed the inside of her wrist. "Aye, but only you and I know that. I am a knight, Sybilla. I will need a destrier, one that's trained to be one. Bacchus can carry me for the time being, but I will need a horse I can ride on the lists and into battle."

Sybilla's face grew pale. She snatched her hand away. "To battle?" she said, as if she'd not considered that.

Guy stroked her arm. "Of course," he said softly. "Morna said the one who rides him will defeat their enemies. That Regalo has grown so big so fast is proof he is The One for me. His height and size match mine and we struck a bargain, you and I—"

Sybilla slipped from the bed and donned her dress. "It always comes back to that, doesn't it, Sir Guy?"

He slumped against the bed. Sybilla called him Sir Guy now whenever she was angry. The morning wasn't going as he'd planned.

He ran his hands through his hair. "Sybilla, I know you think someday to buy him back, but I'll never sell him."

"Mayhap he doesn't have the temperament to be a warhorse. Mayhap he'll be fearful in a melee."

Guy rose from the bed and donned his hose and shirt. Damnation, the woman was determined. He admired her for that, but her pigheaded insistence on keeping this colt was annoying.

He shrugged into his tunic. "I think you underestimate Regalo. Why must you cling to the notion that you have claim to him?"

Men's voices shouted from the yard below, knights at training. Already the clash of swords rang out across the bailey.

Sybilla turned her head toward the window. "I've lost everything I've known and loved from Cornbury, except Regalo. Do you know what it feels like, Sir Guy, to have nothing much to live for but your freedom and your horse?"

The words hit Guy in his gut. He knew exactly.

He paused, considering her plight. Until he'd met her and bargained for the strange little colt, he'd had no hope, no hope he could avenge his family's murder and assuage his guilty conscience.

Guy strapped on his sword, avoiding Sybilla's stare.

Nay, he'd not release the colt. Though not entirely for the reasons he'd given her before. In these last few weeks he'd grown accustomed to her smile, to the softness of her skin, and her gentle breath against his chest while she slept beside him. He was not ready to give *her* up. He was embarrassed to admit it, but he hoped Sybilla Corbuc would never travel far from Ketchem. If it took the colt to keep her close, so be it.

He grabbed his cloak and flung it round his shoulders. "Need I remind you, the colt refuses to eat if you don't come to see him. You have to stay a while longer, but Regalo will be my warhorse."

He turned on his heels and strode from the cellar.

The late afternoon sun slipped behind a rain cloud, the air crisp with the smell of a coming downpour. Sybilla waited on the kitchen steps and watched Guy storm across the bailey. He headed her direction. He was still put off by their quarrel this morning. She could tell by the way he jabbed his thumbs into his belt and walked with his chest thrust forward.

He stopped in front of her. "Looks like rain. I'll not take the horses to the summer pasture, but if you wish to come to the stables, you can follow me. I've business with the saddler." He looked at her, a challenge in his eyes.

Sybilla rose and nodded, worried if she argued she might lose her chance to see Regalo.

Guy headed toward the stables, and once there promptly deposited her in Regalo's stall. "I'll be back in a moment."

With that he was gone.

Sybilla leaned against Regalo and he sniffed her pocket for a treat. She held a carrot in her open hand and combed his mane while he ate. "We've not much time left together, Regalo. I'll soon be free and Guy will take over your training. You'll be a warhorse, as big and as brave as any." She lay her arm over his neck and rested her head against his withers.

Regalo lowered his eyelids, his jaws munching. He seemed not to care, happy with his carrots.

Sybilla peered out of the stall, making certain there was no one watching. Slowly, she moved her arm down his back, bearing down with all her weight. Regalo never flinched. She took off her veil and draped it over his back, testing, and the great colt didn't move.

Her arms trembling, Sybilla grabbed Regalo's mane and climbed onto his back, waiting to see if he'd object.

Nothing. Not a buck. Not a side step.

Regalo stood impassively as if he'd been prepared for this moment for weeks.

Sybilla slumped over his neck and wrapped her arms around him. Mother Mary, what Guy had said was true.

Regalo was ready.

She pulled on his halter, steering him as he took a few faltering steps. He swung his head around and looked at her as if he wasn't certain what she wanted him to do.

She clucked and jiggled her heels at his sides. He edged forward, walking in circles round the stall.

Sybilla's heart squeezed, in part from excitement, in part from the realization that Regalo would soon enter the world of knights and men, of war and tournaments, and breeding.

She smiled in an attempt to fight back tears. "This will be our secret, Regalo."

"Sybilla!" Guy's voice echoed down the aisle. "Make haste to the kitchen. A storm is coming."

Boot feet approached and Sybilla jumped from Regalo's back.

She dusted the horse hair off her skirts and hands just

as Guy entered the stall. "Come, Sybilla. I've no wish to sit the storm out in here." He waved her out of the stall.

Sybilla patted Regalo. She squeezed past Guy, pleased with her secret accomplishment. He placed his hand at the small of her back, and guided her along. Her stomach fluttered at his touch, his fingers caressing, distracting.

"Did you find the saddler?" she managed to ask, hoping he had not.

"He isn't here, off in Shropshire working for the Earl of Hecton."

Sybilla took a deep breath, stumbling along beside Guy. "Good. Regalo isn't ready."

The dark sky flashed with lightning.

Guy stopped and stared at the sky, his head thrown back as if he dared the heavens to open up and drench him. "Sybilla, we've little time left together. Let's not argue. Not tonight."

He spun around and opened his cloak to her, drawing her inside his warmth. Sybilla let him pull her in, enveloping her in the warmth. Mother Mary, he made her breath race from her lungs.

She walked along beside him to the cellar. Nestled against him she could think of nothing but the wine they would drink together after supper, and the hours in the darkness they would spend tonight exploring each other.

The corners of his mouth upturned into a sly smile. "I'll tell you a secret, Sybilla. But you must tell me one in return."

Her throat tightened. Was he testing her? Had he seen her in the stables on Regalo. "I have no secrets," she replied, keeping her eyes down.

Guy lifted her chin. "No secrets?"

"No," she said evenly, though guilt hammered at her heart.

He drew his head back. "I'll tell you what I've never told another. I've never made love during a storm, Sybilla."

She parted her lips, intending to confess, but his mouth was there and warm against her cheek.

"Neither have I," was all she could say as he opened the cellar door and carried her inside.

God forgive me, I've turned into a practiced liar.

The fire in the hearth blazed like an inferno, the flames too hot for mid afternoon. Not seeming to notice the heat, Lord Phillip paced. He gripped a parchment as though he meant to crush it.

Guy watched the man carefully. He'd been summoned from the yard where he'd been training, and now stood next to the steward and waited for his lord to speak.

Lord Phillip halted. "I've word from the king. We are to receive Lord Percy when he comes to visit, and take no other action. The king is watchful, but he isn't ready to arrest him. Percy is too well-connected. To provoke him now might trigger the uprising we all wish to avoid."

Guy swore beneath his breath. "Lord Percy is a master of deceit. He's been known to turn on his friends. He will betray the king without compunction."

The steward slipped his nervous hands into his bell shaped sleeves. "Surely, my lord, what Percy has done with Hamon is a treasonous offense—to build a private army without the king's permission."

Lord Phillip stared into the fire. "Our king is ill-advised by a squabbling council. Percy and the nobles of the royal court control the law of England. Who'll convict them?"

Guy moved his hand to his sword. Damnation. Hamon and Lord Percy would not prevail. "If Ketchem is attacked we are ready."

Lord Phillip flung open the shuttered window. He lifted his face to the wind, the sound of men fighting, practicing in the courtyard below rising to the ramparts. "The king promises reinforcements are on the way. Fifty archers and two hundred footmen. And he has quietly gone about the business of cutting off the food supply to Hamon Castle. They've no way to feed an army. They may be forced to disband—or they may be forced to attack, sooner rather than later. We watch. We wait. And we receive Lord Percy as if nothing is amiss. The sooner he is gone from here and back in London where the king can watch him, the better."

Standing against the wall and behind Sir Guy, Sybilla watched in awe. Lord Percy was a round man with muttony cheeks and a mole above his left eye. He strode into the hall like Ketchem Castle was his own, his attendants hurrying behind him. His black gown flowed over his massive girth, the gold-edged hem of the garment ending just above his knees. He wore purple hose on his thick legs and chains of gold and silver 'round his neck. The cap on his balding head sported a peacock's feather, its shimmering greens and blues competing with his golds and purples.

Lord Percy even smelled rich—essence of thyme and sandalwood wafted from the folds of his velvet mantle. But Mother Mary, the man was huge. Pity the horse that carried him, better that Lord Percy ride a dragon.

He greeted Lord Phillip with a curt nod and took his seat on the dais, spreading his fingers with his palms down on the table. His bushy eyebrows drew together with the unhappy look of impatience, as Lord Phillip's young page slid half a chicken from a platter onto his silver plate.

Lady Claire, dressed in a gown of white damask and a flowing gossamer veil, smiled. Lord Percy nodded and attacked his chicken with a gold knife. He kept his eyes on his food when he spoke. "So, my Lord Phillip, have you reconsidered? Will you release the southlands to their rightful owner? Hamon is eager to reclaim the lands you stole." He chewed, and raised his gaze to Lord Phillip.

Lord Phillip leaned back in his chair and sipped his wine as if he wasn't bothered. "Yield the southlands to Hamon? Nay, Lord Percy, unless it is the king's request." He leaned forward and looked Percy in the eye. "Is it the king's request, Lord Percy?"

Lord Percy stopped chewing for a moment. "It will be," he said carefully. "His council can be most persuasive." He picked his teeth, took a drink and sniffed.

"When the king sends me his request directly, I will answer. 'Til then, Lord Percy, let's enjoy our meal and talk of other things."

Percy shrugged and speared a piece of eel from Lady Claire's silver plate.

Guy and Lord Phillip leaned their heads together and spoke in low voices, while Lord Percy ate.

Grease shining on his lips, he set down his knife and signaled for more chicken. "So where's this comely little horse midwife who hails from Cornbury? The sheriff there told me all about her. She sounds—delightful. What is she doing here?" He snorted.

Lord Phillip sipped from his cup. He tipped his head toward Sybilla. "She's a servant now. Conscribed to Sir Guy of Warwick. She doesn't practice horse midwifery at Ketchem. We abide by the law of the court and the church."

Lady Claire's face turned pale.

Guy set down his cup.

Lord Percy's gaze moved over Sybilla like that of a man appraising a cow he was considering for purchase.

Determined to ignore him, Sybilla concentrated on serving Guy, careful to refill his cup. She stepped back and stood against the wall without interfering in the conversation, or the drinking.

Guy grinned. "You should really try the beef, Lord Percy. We raise the finest cattle."

Lord Percy grunted. "I only eat chicken. Beef makes a man too fat."

The great wooden doors to the hall suddenly banged open. Instantly, Guy and the other knights sprang to their feet. The guardsmen at the doorway blocked the threshold, their swords drawn.

Lord Phillip's steward squeezed his way between them and strode up to the dais, his traveling clothes spotted with mud, his face mud-stained from a long ride on wet roads.

"On my way home from collecting tillages at Halvern, my lord," he said, breathing hard and without so much as a nod to Lord Percy, "I met a most surprising traveler. Seems we've an uninvited guest."

Lord Phillip wiped his mouth. He tossed his napkin on the table. "Who seeks a place at my table?"

The steward cast a glance at Lord Percy. "Lord Hamon's sister, Lady Avelina, my lord."

Sybilla straightened and glanced at Guy. She couldn't see the expression on his face, but she knew him well enough to recognize the tightness in his back, the slight lift of his head. His fingers twitched and he reached for the dagger at his belt.

Lady Claire rested her hand on her husband's sleeve.

"We have no quarrel with her. 'Tis her brother who disputes our claim to the land to the south of Hewlane River."

Lord Percy stayed seated. He studied the dirt-splattered steward, shot a glance at Lord Phillip and nodded.

With a slow and deliberate movement, Lord Phillip poured himself a cup of wine. "Ask her to join us then."

The steward bowed low to Lord Percy. "'Tis you she wants to see, Lord Percy. She has a petition for the royal court, a claim she says must be settled. She's waiting on the steps with her men. They relinquished their weapons at the gatehouse."

Lord Percy pulled a sour face. Every line around his thin mouth, even the lines at the corners of his eyes suggested he wanted nothing more than to dine in peace.

The hall fell silent, the sound of dogs rooting in the rushes the only noise. Lord Percy set down his golden eating knife as if it were as delicate as glass. He took a deep breath. "Send her in, steward. If she's at all like her brother, I'll get no peace until I see her."

Guy stole a glance at Lord Phillip. Sybilla caught the slight twitch of Lord Phillip's fingers.

The great doors flew open. In came a retinue of unarmed knights, six or seven, leading the way for the woman who walked in behind them with her chin thrust upward and her bright blue eyes surveying the hall like a hawk's.

Her Hamon-red gown, richly appointed with seed pearls on the bodice and ermine on the cuffs of her sleeves, was finer than any dress Sybilla had ever seen. But the golden hair that tumbled from the hood of Lady Avelina's short mantle took Sybilla's breath away. 'Twas the same color as her own—and her murderous father's. With her sharp nose and glittering eyes, she looked just as capable of evil.

Lady Avelina stopped in front of Lord Phillip and lowered herself into a grand curtsy, spreading out the sumptuous fabric of her skirts. "My brother sends his greetings, Lord Phillip. I beg forgiveness for my imposition, but my business with Lord Percy is most urgent. It cannot wait, due to my delicate condition." She rose without waiting for permission, and patted her stomach. A rosy flush colored her smooth cheeks.

The servants' heads snapped up. Guy's didn't move.

Lady Claire stared down from the dais at Lady Avelina. "How dare you come to my house in such a state," she said coldly. "Neither my good husband, nor I, will give audience to a woman so far from grace. Were you a member of my house you'd be sent far from Ketchem castle."

Sybilla flinched. Pray to heaven, she'd not made a child with Guy or she would suffer the same fate.

"Beg your pardon, Lady Claire. I'm not here to see you or your husband. As I've said, I've business with him." She pointed an elegant finger to Lord Percy.

Lord Percy's eyes flickered with annoyance. "Speak your business and be brief. You've interrupted my dinner."

Lady Avelina shot a withering glance at Lady Claire. "I am a married woman, Lord Percy, only just. My husband has been summoned to the north to quell a small revolt. But I've come to see you, sir, to press a charge against Sir Guy of Warwick. He stole my brother's emerald, the very gem that was to be my dowry. Without it, my husband cannot pay his loyal retainers. I've no coin to buy food or provisions." She gestured to the band of knights who stood behind her. "They are loyal and stay with me, though I've not paid them in a month."

Lord Percy leaned back and rested his hands on his belly. "So you've wed, Lady Avelina? To whom and when?" he asked carelessly, as if complaint didn't really matter.

Lady Avelina tipped her chin. "The Baron of Irnmere. We were married weeks ago. There was no time to post the bans."

Lady Claire lowered her eyes and took a large sip from her cup, fanning herself with her free hand. Sybilla studied Lady Avelina's rounded belly, a bit too rounded to have been so recently married. The child, no doubt, would be born conveniently too early.

A wry smile spread across Lord Percy's lips. "Elbert, the ailing Baron of Irnmere? He must be close to seventy. As poor as a pauper, and too sick to put a babe in your belly. He'll not survive the conflict he's been sent to oversee. Any peasant with a pitch fork could knock him from his horse. Pray tell, Lady Avelina, who really sired the babe in your belly and when? Rumor has it you shared your graces with Malcolm of Haverty months ago. I'll wager the babe in your belly will have red hair!"

Lady Claire gasped.

Percy laughed, but a hush fell over the room.

Avelina drew up to her full height, her cheeks blazing red. "The Baron of Irnmere is my child's father, not a lowly knight like Sir Malcolm. The babe was conceived on my wedding night. I'm here to collect what belonged to my brother and which now belongs to me—the emerald that was to be my dowry. Sir Guy stole my brother's necklace. I was there. I saw him do it." She looked at Guy and her eyes filled with the look of an indignant victim and a woman scorned.

Sybilla stood unmoving. Pity Avelina. She was a poor liar and her shrill voice rang out with the falseness of a desperate noblewoman who had no more freedom to choose who she married or where she lived than a peasant.

Guy's fingers wrapped around the hilt of his dagger. "I'm not a thief, Avelina, and you know it. Last I saw, the emerald necklace was in your hands. You took it from your brother's neck while he slept with his head on the table at the inn."

Avelina rested her hand protectively on her small belly. "How dare you accuse me. I would not steal from my own brother."

Lady Claire's clear voice sounded over Avelina's. "The dress you wear, Lady Avelina, is finer than the queen's. The men who escorted you here do not work for free. Did you offer the Baron of Irnmere coin to take you as his wife and claim a child he could not have sired? I'd wager I would find your brother's emerald pawned to a jeweler's shop in London if I looked. If Guy of Warwick said he saw you steal it, I believe him. God knows the truth, my dear, confess your sins and ask the Holy Father for forgiveness."

The hall went still.

Lady Avelina's cheeks turned from pink to flaming red. "I, I—you have no proof!"

Guy faced Lord Percy. "I bear Lady Avelina no ill will, my lord, though I wonder what she really wants. She is a desperate woman with blackguard for a brother. I have the proof Lord Hamon and his men murdered my sister and her son." He pulled the iron key from his pouch. "I found this at the site where she and her babe were killed. Hamon's key. My old steward confessed 'twas Lord Hamon's rider who chased Roselynn into the woods. He kept the secret, fearing retribution if he revealed what he'd witnessed. If I had the emerald I'd declare restitution and keep it, though no jewel could restore what I have lost. I request the royal court to open an investigation."

Avelina strode to the dais. "No! My brother is not a murderer, Lord Percy. Hearsay spoken by a dead steward isn't legal in the court. That key proves nothing. Hamon knights used to hunt in Baldwin woods and could have dropped it. We still hunt there now, but your Lord Phillip wrongly claims the land!"

Knights around the hall drew their swords. Lord Phillip raised his hand, signaling for them to hold their places.

Guy rose from his seat. "Be careful, madam. You insult my Lord Phillip in his own house. Your brother killed my sister and her son. I want justice."

"You distract Lord Percy from my purpose, Sir Guy. My brother wants his jewel back, as do I. If you can't produce it, then we demand your colt to settle the debt. I'll take the little beast back with me to—"

Guy's face turned stony. Sybilla's heart jumped to her throat.

Guy stepped from behind the dais. "If you or your men so much as touch my colt, I'll—"

"You'll kill me? A helpless woman who's with chi—"

Lord Percy stood, his chair screeching on the pavers, drowning out her words. "Hold now," he bellowed. "Sir Guy, the deed of which you accuse Lord Hamon is murder and you've no proof. He is a friend. The key is not enough, nor are tales from a dying man's lips. I'd be laughed out of court if I permitted you a hearing. Don't pursue this. I've heard enough."

Sybilla's blood went cold. This night had gone all wrong, the outcome worse than expected. She glanced at Guy. Mother Mary, the veins in his neck stood out and his chest was heaving like he struggled to get air.

Lord Phillip cleared his throat. "Lord Percy, Sir Guy is not a thief. Take his petition to the royal court. A crime so grievous as his sister's and his nephew's murder deserves consideration."

Tossing his napkin into his chair, Lord Percy stepped

away from the table. "I've ruled on the matter, Ketchem. I'll say no more. Now let me see this colt, Sir Guy. I wish to see if it's truly worth the price of an emerald."

Guy lifted his eyebrows and looked at Lady Avelina. "Why didn't your brother come to plead his case in person, Lady Avelina? What kind of man sends his sister? Does he fear he'll be found guilty of murder on the spot? Or is he occupied with something else?" He let the words linger, hanging in the air.

An anxious murmur rose from the crowd, echoing the sentiment.

Avelina planted her fists on her hips. "His ankle is badly broken and hasn't healed. He cannot ride." She shot a hate-filled look at Sir Guy. "You attacked him on the road outside of Cornbury the night you stole the emerald. You know he almost lost his leg."

Sybilla's blood boiled. She bit her lip to keep from shouting, "No!"

Guy didn't falter. "I'm no thief and I'll not yield my colt."

Lord Percy stepped down from the dais, his knees popping beneath the strain of his weight. "That will be for me to decide, Sir Guy," he huffed, his face pink and sweating. "Let me see the colt. If Hamon's willing to trade an emerald for it, the beast must be something special."

Lord Phillip and Lady Claire led the way to the stables, the path alight by the torches they carried and by the full moon. Guy strode beside them in silence, vaguely aware of Sybilla at his side. To his right, the winded Lord Percy waddled, heavy-footed, the air rushing from his lungs in cadence with his plodding stride. Lady Avelina strode along beside him, holding up her skirts, slipping in the mud.

The horses in the barn hung their head over the stalls and watched while John of Kent trotted down the aisle, pulling on his leather cap. He fell in with the bunch in silence, as if he knew exactly where they were going.

Regalo hung his big head over the stall wall, his eyes alert and curious. He nickered at Sybilla.

Guy's stomach burned.

Lord Percy stopped to catch his breath and mop the sweat from his forehead. "So this is the magic colt?" he stated flatly, walking to the stall. "By the heavens, he's a monster of a yearling. He'll be a giant when he's grown. Mayhap the biggest destrier in all of England."

Guy made no comment. Best let Lord Percy to think Regalo just larger than your average young horse.

Lord Percy addressed John but he kept his gaze on the colt. "I don't believe that twaddle 'bouta white-socked horse born to impart invincible powers to the one who rides him. But what say you, horse marshal? Is this one special? By your observations, has he done anything to make you think he's been touched by God . . . or magic, or worth an emerald?"

John shook his head. "No, my lord. Can't see what the fuss is all about. He's just a horse. A big one, but just a horse."

Impatience raced across Avelina's face. She shifted, and Lord Percy spun around to face her. "Your brother would take this colt in exchange for the emerald?" he asked, his tone incredulous, the look on his face suspicious. "Why?"

She frowned, wrinkling her brow. She shrugged. "I don't know. I avoid the smelly beasts, but my brother made it clear I could have the money from the colt's sale at market."

Lord Percy took a deep breath, his beady eyes edgy and evasive. "You cannot have the colt."

Avelina's mouth dropped open. "But I . . . but my brother said you would—"

"Your brother misjudged me, Lady Avelina, and made an assumption regarding our friendship he should not have made. The matter of the emerald is closed. If you need money, get it from your husband."

Lord Percy faced Guy. "After seeing the colt, and as a favor to my friend Lord Phillip, I'll reconsider your petition to make your case against Lord Hamon. I'll give you the choice, give me the colt and his comely keeper, and I'll grant you an audience with the royal court. I can't say that you will win, but you will get the chance."

The smoke from the torches swirled around Lord Percy's head like demons. Guy cast a glance at Sybilla, her face as pale as milk.

Lord Percy licked his lips. "I want them both. 'Tis a rare horse that's big enough to carry me. I've broke three down in the last year already. This one's got the backbone and the legs I need—and I find the little midwife most attractive. I could use another servant."

Guy clenched his fists and glowered at Percy. The man was a snake and he was ruthless, capable of the kind of betrayal Hamon never dreamed of. The thought of him riding Regalo was bad enough, but if he so much as touched Sybilla, he'd wring the man's fat neck.

Guy folded his arms, pretending a kind of self-control he did not feel. "And if I refuse?"

Lord Percy arched a narrow eyebrow. "Then I'm afraid I cannot help you."

Avelina smirked.

Lady Claire voiced a protest but was quickly silenced by her husband.

"Both of them," Lord Percy repeated. "And you get your chance with Hamon in the royal court."

Guy stood unmoving. He'd waited months for this opportunity, but he'd not expected it would come with such a price. Regalo and Sybilla.

A sheen of sweat dampened the back of his neck. He swore an oath, the pain in his gut as searing as a hot iron. He closed his eyes, shutting out the staring faces that waited for his decision. God help him, he could not part with the colt—or Sybilla Corbuc.

He took a deep breath, the sweet night air sharp and crisp. "I refuse your offer, Lord Percy. I'll find another way to deal with Hamon. Not outside the law, but then again, perhaps not entirely within it. He is after all a murderer. He has no right to fairness."

Percy's face turned a violent red. "No man refuses me." He reached for the dagger at his waist and stepped toward Guy.

Guy drew his sword, the movement as quick as lightning. He pointed the blade tip at Percy's throat. "You are a traitor, Percy. You sit at my Lord Phillip's table and eat his food, drink his wine, and all the while you plot against him and the king. Hamon is a fool to ally with you."

Lady Claire and Avelina gasped, and Ketchem guards closed around Lord Percy.

Lord Percy didn't flinch.

Sybilla laid her hand on Guy's arm. "Let him go, Guy. You could lose your head for killing him."

Lady Claire nudged her husband. She turned her face up to his, her eyes pleading for him to do something.

Lord Phillip kept his eyes on Lord Percy. "Is this true, Percy? Have you allied against me? I've heard rumors you've sent forces to Hamon's camp. I cannot believe a man who leads the royal court of law would get involved in a common border war between me and my longtime rival. Surely Sir Guy of Warwick is mistaken. If not, I must report what I've learned to the king."

"I don't know what you are talking about," Percy stated flatly. "Now call your guards off."

"You deny Sir Guy's accusations?"

"Of course!"

Lord Phillip signaled to his guards. Guy lowered his weapon. He stepped away from Percy. "I beg your leave, my Lord Phillip, and Lord Percy. I must have been mistaken."

Lord Phillip spoke to the band of onlookers who'd collected 'round Regalo's stall. "We are done here. Go to your beds." He smiled at Percy, but his tone was threatening and cool. "Lord Percy, I'm afraid my private apartments are all occupied tonight. I know you'd prefer not to sleep on the floor in the great hall, so I shall provide an escort to take you and Lady Avelina and your attendants to Hartford Abbey for the night. First thing in the morning, they will escort you home to London. To Windsor Castle." He nodded and signaled to his steward.

The steward strode past Lord Percy like the victor over the play yard bully.

Guy shoved his sword into his scabbard. He'd made sure there was a garrison waiting in the armory in case Lord Percy gave them trouble. He'd be glad to have the man and Avelina on the road to London, long before the sun came up, though the abbey, with its dripping, cold, stone walls and its paucity of beds and candles, would be anything but comfortable tonight.

Lord Percy puffed up his chest. "This is an insult. The king will hear of this."

"That he will," echoed Avelina, pursing her pink lips.

Lord Phillip folded his arms. "And he will also hear of

this, Lord Percy. A judge in the royal court who asked for a bribe from Sir Guy of Warwick, the knight who saved the king's life at Balmont, the very knight who saved mine and the Lady Claire's from the poisoned hand of a conspiring cousin." He glared at Avelina. "And if the king and his counselors can be bothered to listen, they will hear the tale of a woman so desperate to keep her secrets, she'd steal from her brother and blame it on the same man, an honest man who is innocent of any crime."

With that, Ketchem's mounted guards appeared, descending upon the barn as if they had been waiting discreetly in the shadows, watching for a signal from their lord. The captain of the guard dismounted. He indicated with his sword that Percy, his attendants, Lady Avelina and her band of ragged knights should follow him.

Slinging oaths at Ketchem, Lord Percy strode to his waiting horse. Three of his attendants helped him mount, and when at last he heaved his great body into the saddle, the horse grunted, and took a step to the side to keep its balance, its back sinking beneath Lord Percy's weight. Avelina climbed into her covered wagon and lowered the flap.

Some fifty horses clattered through the gatehouse and over the drawbridge. Lady Avelina's wagon creaked and bounced along behind them.

Guy closed his eyes and drew a breath. *Roselynn, forgive me.*

Sybilla swept the last of the food-littered rushes into the great hall's center hearth. She stood too close to the fire, heedless of the heat, and watched the smoke carry ash toward the ceiling. She closed her eyes. Mother Mary, she had no control of her fate, or her life. Like the ash that drifted upward in a rising wave of smoke, she was carried along, unable to change the course.

She shuddered, the fear of what was yet to come rippling up her spine.

Seeking comfort from the heat, she leaned against the broom and let the flames warm her cheeks. Tonight when Percy offered Guy a chance in court in exchange for her and Regalo, she'd held her breath. When Guy had refused, she almost fainted. God in heaven, she was grateful. Pray that Guy didn't regret the choice he made tonight and come to hate her for it.

Sybilla swallowed, realizing how much Guy had given up for her—realizing how deeply she was falling in love.

A rude voice shouted from the floor, "The hour is late. Find a spot and settle down to sleep, or give up the space."

Sybilla tucked her broom beneath her arm and picked her way through the crowd that made their pallets 'round the fire. She hesitated, turning to scan the room. Couples lay huddled under blankets, and dogs slept in piles around their masters. A drunken knight pawed at giggling servant girls. The brewess had her back against the wall and her bare legs locked around the waist of her husband. Sybilla turned and climbed the steps that led from the hall. She could sleep here if she had to. After three months working as a servant, she witnessed nothing in the hall that would shock her. But tonight, she longed for the familiar comfort and the warmth of the cellar.

And she needed Guy.

Sybilla hurried down the tunnel that led to his tiny chamber. At the door, she wrapped her fingers round the cold iron handle. She closed her eyes before she lifted the latch and prayed she was still welcome.

* * *

Guy sat on his bed with an earthen cup in one hand and a wine ewer in the other. He'd not bothered to light the brazier, and moonlight filtered through the narrow window, casting a stripe of soft light over Sybilla as she slipped inside the room and shut the door.

Sybilla held his gaze, a look of hesitation in her eyes. She said nothing, but her hands shook at her sides and the rapid rise and fall of her chest told him she was nervous and uncertain.

God's bones. Did she think he'd blame or hurt her for the choice he'd made? Did she worry that he'd reconsidered, changed his mind and any moment would go bolting after Percy?

Damn the woman.

He set his drink aside, stood and crossed the room to stand in front her. She lowered her chin, a gesture he suddenly found irritating. He skimmed his fingers along her jaw and lifted her face to his. "I'd do it again, Sybilla, if I had to. I'd give up my chance in court to keep from losing Regalo . . . and you."

She said nothing, but a storm of emotions raged across her face. Confusion. Surprise.

He ran his fingers over her lips. "I've been a fool . . . about everything."

She captured his hands with hers. "No, you have not."

A laugh rumbled from his throat, the sound harsh and bitter. "I believed I'd have a chance to take my case before the royal court. I believed that justice would rue the day. I believed in Morna's fanciful predictions, but now I—"

"Stop," she said, touching his lips with hers. Without warning, she lashed her arms around his neck and covered his face with fiery kisses.

She kissed him on the eyelids, on his forehead and his

cheeks. She kissed him in that sweetly sensitive spot in the hollow beneath his ear.

Guy moaned. "God's breath, no other woman has ever—"

More kisses.

Hard, urgent kisses. She leaned her head back against the door, took a gulp of air and shot a glance at his shaft.

He was as hard as a rod. There'd be no mistaking the bulge beneath his tunic.

She licked her lips.

Guy closed his eyes and sucked in his breath.

"The devil take me," he whispered. He pressed himself against the length of her body and dragged up her skirts. "I've wanted you since you left my bed this morning. My every waking minute of the day is consumed with longing. I count the hours until I can be alone with you again."

Sybilla gave a throaty laugh. "I've missed you, too, Sir Guy. And yet you keep running off on missions or Shadow Riding in the woods without me."

He growled, a primal sound rising from deep within, all rational and human thought lost to words. He found the slit in his braes and his rod sprang out, throbbing.

Sybilla sank against the door, her heady gaze fixed on his shaft, her chest heaving.

Guy only had to slide his fingers into the silken mound between her legs and caress her and she was slick and ready. He stroked her, his hand moving to the places he knew she loved.

Her breath quick and shallow, she breathed against his lips. "Please."

He grasped her bottom and lifted her up, settling her with ease on his shaft. "Is this what you want?" he murmured, adjusting his stance so that she might have the length of him inside her.

She wrapped her legs around his waist and clutched his shoulders. "I want you, Guy, more than any man on earth."

Her words shot through like a hail of arrows, though he fought to beat them back, and hoped against all hope he could ignore them. He could not love her. Could not take the risk.

He drove himself inside her, withdrew, and thrust again.

She moaned and buried her face against his neck. "More," she whispered, pleading.

Again and again Guy thrust, as if he could pound away all thoughts of caring for Sybilla Corbuc.

Blessed saints, he could not love her. Look what Hamon had done to Morna because he'd loved her. Look what Hamon had done to Roselynn and her son. Nay, any woman who cared for Guy of Warwick was marked for death or ruin. Did Sybilla not understand that?

Guy stormed into her hard, with fierce thrusts that drove his body against hers. Sybilla arched her back, her hips grinding into his. She cried out his name, and locked her eyes with his, her face rapturous and flushed, utterly ravishing.

Blessed saints, her passion filled his parched soul like water.

He covered her mouth with his, his thirst undeniable and raging as he spilled his seed inside her.

What seemed like minutes passed before he lowered Sybilla down. She took deep breaths, her legs trembling, fighting to regain their strength. Her bottom throbbed where he'd gripped her and her lips felt bruised. Spent, she leaned against the door, grateful for its support. In all the weeks she'd spent in Guy's bed, she'd never experienced anything quite like this.

Guy stepped back and fixed his hose, tucking his shaft back into his braes. Save for the dampness on his cheeks no one would have known what they'd just done.

He spun around and yanked his cloak from the bed.

Sybilla tried hard not to sound distressed. "You're leaving?"

Guy flung his cloak over his shoulders and grabbed his sword. "I must. I've business to attend." Keeping his eyes downcast, he strapped on his sword.

"At this hour? With whom?" Sybilla's temper surged. God's breath, the man was always running off.

"Hamon," was all he said, raking his hands through his hair.

Sybilla's knees almost buckled. Her heart rose to her throat. "No!"

Guy pushed a stray lock of hair from her cheek, and kissed her lightly on her forehead. He held her gaze for a moment, his eyes intent. "It can't go on like this, Sybilla. Now more than ever, I feel the need to stop him. He seeks to harm you because you are with me. He plans to start a war. I cannot let that happen." He pulled her away from the door.

"I'm not afraid of him, Guy."

"You should be, but not for long. I will challenge him—to a race. In one week we will race against each other."

Sybilla clutched his arm with both hands. "Please no. Not Regalo. Not the race. You could both be killed."

"I'll be riding Bacchus. The race provides a convenient opportunity for us to fight. No matter the outcome,

Hamon will raise his sword against me. If I kill him there in the spirit of the competition, I'll not be tried for murder. If he kills me . . . so be it. Then he'll have no further interest in you."

"No!" Sybilla felt the blood drain from her face. She could not lose Guy.

Guy raised her hand to his lips and kissed her palm. He pressed something small and delicate into her hand. "If something should happen to me . . . take this. A gift from my heart. 'Tis all I have to give you."

Sybilla opened her hand. Roselynn's prayer beads glittered in the firelight.

He turned to leave.

Sybilla grasped his hand. "No! I want to go with you."

His face suddenly turned stern. "No, Sybilla. 'Tis too dangerous. Don't leave the chamber while I'm gone. Swear to me you won't, so I won't worry. I'll have Simon watch Regalo. If the colt stops eating because you haven't come, then and only then can you venture to the stables— under guard. Mary can get you anything you need. Stay here. Swear it."

With the heel of her hand, Sybilla wiped a tear from the corner of her eye. "I swear it," she said, barely able to speak.

He kissed her, a deep kiss, hard and urgent, the kind that bruised her lips and made her ache for more.

He tore his mouth from hers and he was gone, leaving Sybilla standing alone in his chamber, clutching the prayer beads, her heart ripped asunder.

Chapter Twenty

The morning sun was bright and streaming down. Guy spurred Bacchus to a gallop along the dusty road. The big horse had the heart of a lion, despite his humble origin, and he could run when he made the effort. Guy dug his heels in his mount, eager to make progress. Hamon was a killer. He could count on the man not to refuse a challenge.

A lone cloud drifted in front of the sun for a moment, casting shadows over the path ahead.

Guy slowed his mount and looked at the horizon. God in heaven, they'd made better time than he'd predicted. In the distance loomed Hamon castle, its ominous walls rising to meet the sun, its blue and white banners snapping in the breeze.

He let the corners of his mouth upturn into a satisfied grin as he pulled his hood over his head. Unshaven, and bedraggled as he was, he could ride directly into the camp outside the castle walls and walk amongst the soldiers, horses, carts and tents—and not be noticed.

* * *

Lord Hamon slammed his fist on the table. "Hand-delivered? The man rode into the camp and demanded you bring this to me? Good God, why didn't you arrest him? Could you not tell he was a knight from Ketchem?" Disgusted, Hamon yanked his blanket over his aching foot.

The guardsmen looked at the floor. "Nay, my lord, I could not tell. He rode up alone on a shaggy horse and wore no armor, no badge. Said 'twas a missive from your brother. Said he was a runner from McCullough Castle."

"A runner? All the way from Scotland? You dolt. What Scottish runner carries a sword forged at Balmont strapped to his belt? Who else sits a horse like he was born on one? Guy of Warwick, that's who. I should throw you in the dungeon for a month for this."

The soldier backed away, edging toward the door. "He didn't make no threats, my lord. Looked like a landless knight from the wilds up north. Just handed me the note and left. Said you'd be glad to get it."

Hamon massaged his ankle, his brow furrowed with pain. "You say he rides alone?"

"He does, my lord. He'd not have gotten far."

"Tell Sir Gideon and Sir Elbert to go after him and bring him back. Sir Guy of Warwick and I have business to discuss. Then fetch Lady Morna."

The guardsman bowed and hurried from the solar, his booted feet thudding hard against the flagstones. The hounds in the hall scattering to get out of his way.

Hamon crushed the parchment in his fist. He'd already memorized the message. *To Alfred, Lord Hamon, the Earl of Cornbury: I summon you to Ketchem one week hence to race your horse against me. The loser forfeits a manor house and his horses to the other.*

Hamon stroked the big hound, his favorite, at his feet. Baldwin Manor would be a lucrative piece of property to add to his collection, but the colt Regalo—now there was a prize worth more than any other. Guy of Warwick was insane to think the colt could best his Zephyr, a fleet-footed stallion, born to run.

Hamon laughed and fed the hound what was left of breakfast—a piece of stale bread, dipped in bitter ale. He'd planned to march on Ketchem during the race. Mayhap now he'd do a little schedule rearranging.

Without the meddling Lord Percy issuing directives, the order of command was clear to all. Leave it to Lord Percy to find an excuse to sit in London, while his noble allies fight his fights and starve.

Lady Morna stood outside the postern gate and rapped lightly on the ancient door. The entrance was tucked into the west wall of Hamon Castle and hidden well behind the brush and thickets. Stars glittered in the sky and the bright moon cast a glow through the trees, lighting up the narrow pathway she'd used so many times before.

She pulled the hood of her cloak down over her face and crouched in the shadows. Ordinarily, a Separate caught in public would be flogged, but the power of her former husband saved her from the zealots who enforced the law. Still, she didn't entirely trust him to protect her. He'd failed to protect his favorite knights, Sir Elbert and Sir Gideon, whose bodies, freshly killed, she'd stumbled over in the woods. One had been knocked from his horse and broken his neck, the other had a sword wound through his heart. 'Twas a pity they'd been slain by robbers, and not had the chance to give their lives in war. Hamon would not be pleased with the news and she would miss the lusty, private nights she'd spent with both Sir Elbert and Sir Gideon.

Morna halted at the postern gate. She shuddered at the thought of Hamon's hands on her breasts, of the rough touch of his calloused fingers. He disgusted her. How she hated what she had become—what he forced her to be—his whore. But without him, she could not afford food or wood for the winter. Every time she hinted at refusal, he threatened harm to Guy of Warwick.

Her heart clenched at the thought of Guy, the one man she loved above all others. She'd seen him only once or twice since his sister's death, and no matter how often she'd asked him to come, no matter how she pleaded, he ignored her. Yet, her former husband demanded more and more of her attention of late, complaining his ankle had not yet healed and only her potions could ease the pain.

What he really wanted was her body and tonight, she suspected he wanted something more. She'd already visited at his request three times this past week.

She rapped against the door again, insistent, disturbing the crickets in the vines that snaked along the castle walls. The ancient door creaked open and the darkly menacing guard, Robert Pritchard, stood before her. He smelled like wine and there was food in his black beard.

His beady eyes bore down on her. "Lost your key again, my lady? You're late. There was a willing wench waiting for me on the ramparts. She'll be gone by now." He scratched his crotch and stepped close to her. "Any possibility I could get what I'm wanting somewhere else?" He ran his rough knuckles over her cheek.

Lady Morna pushed his hand away and stepped around him. "You disgust me, Pritchard. I shall have to explain to Lord Hamon *you* are the reason for my delay." She turned and climbed the treacherously dark staircase that led to her ex-husband's private apartment. At the landing, she glanced down to see the soldier standing below with his mouth agape, shaking his head, imploring her to stay silent.

Morna smiled. "Let us hope, for your sake, he's not in a foul temper."

Lord Hamon crooked a finger at Morna without taking his eyes off the fire. "Come in, sweetheart. I've news to share." He closed his robe. He was naked beneath it, but with the blaze before him and the anticipation of Morna's presence, his chambers felt like an inferno.

She swept across the room, her eyes eager. She said not a word, but knelt before him and massaged his bare ankle. The touch of her fingers set his skin on fire.

Hamon closed his eyes. "Your lover has issued me a challenge to the summer race." He peered beneath his half-closed eyelids to see what effect his words had on his lovely ex-wife.

She stopped massaging, but she did not look up. "He means to race you?"

"Hmmmm. He's just that kind of fool. To pit his rangy horse against me on Zephyr."

Morna rose. Panic flashed across her face. "You needn't race him, my lord. You needn't prove anything to Guy of Warwick, or to anybody."

Hamon jumped up and dragged her roughly to his side. He leaned close. "Fearful for him, Morna? You should be. I intend to kill him. I wanted you to know."

Morna jerked free, her eyes ablaze. She grabbed the knot at his waistbelt and yanked it loose, opening his robe.

Her hands roaming, she found his rod and stroked him while she kissed the hollow of his neck. "Don't kill him," she muttered, her tongue touching him, her lips nipping at his flesh. "Spare Sir Guy." She trailed kisses down his chest, down his belly and lower.

Hamon laughed a low, wicked laugh, his shaft as hard as wood and his heart hammering against his chest. "Morna, dear Morna." He ran his hands through her silken hair. "When it comes to Guy, I can count on you to take the kind of action that inspires me. But the game between us all has gone too far. I must kill him. And you will have no one left but me." He gripped her wrists and hauled her to her feet. He locked his eyes with hers. "If you think I cannot best him you are wrong, for I'm prepared to do what I must, whatever it takes, cheat if I have to."

A wad of spittle landed on his cheek. He wiped it on his shoulder and laughed.

Her words slipped from her mouth with a hiss. "Have you no honor?"

"You and Warwick stole it from me years ago. I've no desire to get it back. But do as I ask tonight, I'll make sure his death is quick."

She thrust her chin up, defiantly. "I hate you, my lord. But for Guy of Warwick, I would do anything."

Hamon smiled, his blood pounding in his ears. He leaned away, calling toward the door. "Pritchard! I know you're out there. Come and join us."

He snapped his head around. Unbridled satisfaction made him grin.

Morna's haughty face was as white as a sheet.

Sybilla wrapped the blanket round her shoulders and huddled on the bed. The watchman called out the midnight hour, and the little brazier sputtered, a thin trail of smoke rising from its grill.

Sybilla squeezed her eyes shut. The cellar walls seemed

to close in around her, and the dampness seemed more unbearable than usual. Guy had been gone a day and a night so far, and without him, even the spiced ale Mary brought her tasted bland. God in heaven, she didn't know how much longer she could last. Simon had come to visit and to tell her Regalo had eaten all of his breakfast, but she'd spoken to no one else. There was no comfort here, not without Sir Guy. His absence made the place intolerable.

Rising, she contemplated putting on her shoes to take a walk. She'd sworn she wouldn't leave the cellar—and she wouldn't. Not tonight. But the race was less than a week away—and so was her term as servant.

A week from today, she would be free.

Sybilla took a deep breath. She hadn't counted on the time passing so quickly. She hadn't counted on falling in love with the man who was her master. Mother Mary, how had it come to this? What was she supposed to do? Pack a bundle and walk away—to where?

She flopped down on the bed and studied the shadows on the ceiling. What would it feel like to sleep alone again? To have no one to talk to. To never see or touch Sir Guy of Warwick again.

Mayhap she should consider staying.

She slammed her fists on the bed. Damnation. She could not live as his servant and his bedmate. She had her pride. But since when did a knight marry a servant? It was unlikely to happen, though not beyond the realm of possibility. Simon planned to take Mary as his wife. But *he* was not obsessed with revenge.

Sybilla closed her eyes. Though Guy had kissed her with the passion of a lover and held her naked in his arms at night, he had never mentioned love, or marriage. Nay, Sybilla Corbuc, servant, penniless horse midwife, dared not hope to wed Sir Guy. And certainly, if marriage were forced upon him, she'd be no better than a servant to a husband.

She wanted more than that.

She wanted Guy to love her.

A sinking feeling settled in her chest. The thought of leaving *him,* of leaving Ketchem and of leaving Regalo made her heart feel as though it would split in two.

God in heaven, she was actually thinking about the end of her time with Guy, preparing.

Sybilla suddenly sat up and cocked her head, listening. With no night wind to rustle the trees or rattle shutters, she could almost hear the watchmen talking on the ramparts.

An owl hooted. Someone drew water from the well.

But the single sound she expected—Regalo barking— wasn't there.

Blessed saints, she'd been thinking about leaving. Regalo was supposed to bark!

Sybilla clenched her fists, her mind reeling. Regalo had eaten and she hadn't seen him since the day before. Mayhap he truly no longer needed her. He'd not object if she left. She'd suspected this for days, though she'd not admitted it.

She rose from the bed and walked to the narrow window. The moon was full and bright, shining like a beacon over the keep. She took a long breath, daring to think about her future.

Regalo didn't need her and in six more days she would be free. Truly free. Though the thought should fill her with joy, she winced.

"He's back? By God, Warwick has balls!" Hamon stabbed his eating knife into the table. "By all means send him in—

but he'll not ride out of here again." He wrapped his fist around his sword's hilt.

The sergeant stood at strict attention, his eyes fixed on the quivering dagger embedded in the oaken table. He cleared his throat. "My lord, 'tis not Sir Guy of Warwick."

Hamon narrowed his eyes. "You said a Ketchem knight—"

"'Tis Malcolm of Haverty. He's come in through the spy gate, like you told him."

Hamon kept his hand on his sword. It was hard to find a careful and reliable informer from Lord Phillip's loyal inner circle. Malcolm of Haverty had grown too greedy as of late, but costly information about Ketchem was better than no information at all. The news he'd reported about cracked walls and collapsing tunnels at Ketchem had been most helpful.

Hamon motioned to his sergeant. "Show him in."

His spurs chinking at his heels, Sir Malcolm stormed in from the recessed door at the back of the hall. He halted in front of the table, whipped his helmet from his head and bowed. "My lord," he said with a flourish.

"If you've come to tell me Sir Guy of Warwick plans to challenge me to race, I've already accepted. I'll not pay you for that information. But you can bet on this— Warwick will not beat me on Zephyr—I'll claim his colt as my prize. Now what other news have you from Ketchem?"

"Ketchem is not the reason I am here." His eyes flickered from side to side, as though looking to see who might be listening.

"Then speak your peace and be gone." Hamon folded his arms.

Malcolm suddenly knelt on one knee. "I've secured a post at court. Lord Phillip is sending me to represent him on the king's council. I'll be leaving Ketchem post haste to go to London."

Hamon's grip tightened around his sword hilt. Hell to the devil. He'd lose his only informant from Ketchem, but a spy at court would be useful.

Malcolm rose. "There is more, my lord."

Hamon arched an eyebrow.

"I wish to wed the Lady Avelina and take her with me. As soon as she returns from visiting her cousin I would like to—"

Hamon jumped from his tall-back chair, his heart beating hard. By God, men like Guy of Warwick and Malcolm of Haverty should stick with women of their own class. They'd no right to noblewomen. Warwick had ruined Morna. A baseborn knight like Malcolm would not ruin Avelina. He'd made sure of that.

He slammed his fist on the table. "My sister? You? Why would the sister of an earl wed a lowly, landless knight? You over-reach your station." He grabbed the eating knife and pointed it at Malcolm. "She has not been visiting her cousin. I've married her to a titled goat, old and poor, but titled. Even if the child she carries truly is your get, I'd never let her marry you."

Malcolm's face turned ruby red. "She agreed to be my wife."

Hamon bellowed, "She had no choice."

Malcolm stood there with his head held high and unfettered hatred in his eyes. He was a knight well-known for his skill with a sword, but he had the look of a proud, ambitious man who hungered for more in life than he'd been given—more wealth, more power, and more respect.

Hamon lowered his knife. Malcolm would be useful at court. Best to keep him as an ally.

"Sir Malcolm. Go to London and send me news of

the king. Report to me regularly and I will see you are compensated well. At Windsor, there are many fine ladies looking for rich husbands."

Sir Malcolm nodded once, but the flush on his face and his white-knuckled grip on his sword's hilt gave Hamon pause.

"I understand," he said after a long silence. He bowed and strode from the hall.

Hamon watched him go.

By God, Malcolm of Haverty marched out of the hall through the great front doors, and strode right out into the bailey, his knight's cloak swinging from his shoulders like the robe of a deposed, but still defiant king.

Chapter Twenty-One

Lord Phillip climbed the stairs to the battlements with his sword in his fist. "Damn Hamon. I'll cut his heart out."

He stormed past a startled watchman and jumped onto the wall, his booted feet landing dangerously close to the edge. "You say the workings of a trebuchet will soon be complete?"

Guy suppressed the urge to grab his lord and haul him back. But after two nights with no sleep and a skirmish in the woods with two of Hamon's men, he feared he'd not the speed or strength.

"The weapon is almost finished. And there's a thousand more ready footmen camped outside his castle. I've walked amongst them. They are hungry and agitated. They'll march within a fortnight."

Lord Phillip spoke in a low voice. "They'll attack before the race?"

Guy chose his words carefully. His place of favor with his lord, his future, and his very life depended on his answer. "I heard talk amongst his captains. I believe that was his intent. I think his plans have changed."

Lord Phillip arched an eyebrow. "How so?"

Guy squared his shoulders. "I've issued him a challenge, sir. To the race. I've bet my manor house and horses against his. I will win. I *will* win." He paused, giving time for his meaning to sink in. "Hamon cannot resist the challenge."

The evening wind blew across the ramparts. Lord Phillip's cloak billowed up, swirling round him as though he might take flight. "Will there be a fight at the end of the race?"

Guy smiled, nonplused. "Aye, my lord. To the death. Hamon's. Mayhap this is the quickest way to end this. An army will not fight without their leader."

"The king has arrested Percy and half the royal court. Percy is in the tower." He turned his back to Guy. Staring across the quiet countryside, Lord Phillip planted his fists on his hips and spread his feet apart. "If Hamon loses the race and you best him by the sword, his army will disband. We'll chase them home like dogs with their tails between their legs."

Guy let out a breath. "Yes."

Lord Phillip spun around, jumped down from the wall. "But know this, Sir Guy. The race must look fair, and the fight at the end should be for cause. And don't underestimate Malcolm. He intends to beat you, too. If Hamon is killed and anyone suspects treachery, there's a limit to what I can do."

For you, he means.

Guy nodded. "I understand. I've cause, sir. My sister's murder, and her son's. But there is one thing I ask. If I am killed, do what you can for my servant."

Lord Phillip nodded. "I pray for her sake, and for the people of Ketchem's, that you live."

* * *

Sybilla's heart leapt at the sight of Guy. He stood just inside the cellar doorway with his hand resting on the hilt of his sword, his chest heaving. Mother Mary, he looked as if he'd ridden in from hell. There was dried blood on his tunic. A long scarlet swath ran from the neckline to the hem.

Sybilla gasped, her eyes searching. She could see no wound, but God in heaven, he could have been killed. She covered her face with her hands, as if she could hide from the horror of what happened to him.

"It's all right, Sybilla," he said softly, crossing the room. "I am not hurt." He drew his tunic over his head and flung the garment into the corner.

Sybilla rushed into his arms, burying her face in the hollow of his neck. She inhaled, drinking in his scent. "Three days I've waited for you, not knowing if you lived or—"

She lifted her face to his.

He lowered his head, his mouth covering hers, his hands sliding down her back. His tongue slipped between her lips and probed, his wet kiss igniting sweet sensations that spread from her belly to her toes. She closed her eyes and basked in the feeling, the heady warmth that made her want to melt into his arms and stay forever.

Guy's lips moved from her mouth to her cheek. "Thank God you are safe. If you'd been with me when Hamon's men . . . I was waylaid for two nights in the woods. I meant to be back within a day, not three."

Without further explanation, he kissed her, his lips bruisingly hard.

He swept her up and carried her to the bed.

He tore at her clothing, and almost before he laid her down he'd bared her breasts. "Sybilla," he murmured, his lips devouring their peaks, "Sybilla, you've possessed me." He lowered his head and suckled her nipples hard against his tongue.

She moaned and arched her back, thrusting her smooth, small breasts upward as if she offered him more.

His passion unleashed, Guy rucked her skirts above her waist. Feverishly, he freed his swollen shaft from his braes and thrust himself deep inside her, even though he knew it was too fast . . . too fast . . .

But Sybilla gasped and drew him deeper, held him tighter, her hands clawing at the flesh of his buttocks.

Pleasure gripped him instantly. He cried out, her name on his lips, his need urgent and ungovernable.

She writhed and lifted her hips to meet his, opening herself wider, receiving every thrust. She parted her lips and drew a sharp breath, shuddering.

Torrent after torrent of ecstasy surged through Guy, mighty spasms that made his body shake. He erupted within her, a sweet blessed release that freed him, freed him of days of wanting, of yearning, of needing Sybilla Corbuc.

He collapsed, gasping on top of her.

She lay beneath him, completely still. Her fingers trembling, she brushed the damp hair from his temples, soothing him with her touch.

Wordlessly, he rested his head against her shoulder, her breasts soft and warm against him. He listened to the steady rhythm of her heart for some time, and thought about these last months, reliving every day they'd spent together, every look, every time they'd touched, and laughed and loved. He locked those moments in his heart, hoarding them like a miser hoards his gold.

He hadn't gone looking for this. Since his sister's and

his nephew's murder, grief and hatred had ruled his soul. Then Sybilla Corbuc tumbled into his world and changed everything.

Sybilla slept, the sound of her breathing as soft as a cat purring.

Guy wrapped his arm fast around her waist and closed his eyes. He was not afraid to die. He'd do what he had to to protect her. Hamon must be stopped.

Guy strode into the barn, his cloak swirling round him. He'd been sleeping—quite peacefully, thank you— after their lovemaking when Sybilla burst into the cellar and roused him out bed. Hell to the devil, how was it the servants always learned of trouble before the rest of the castle?

Sybilla shoved her way through the crowd of boys gathered outside Regalo's stall. Sons of laborers and peasants, they parted, but slowly, their attention focused on the colt and the pebbles they were throwing at their hapless target.

"At midnight, he'll sprout horns! You'll see," said the oldest boy, the tanner's son. He flung a rock across the stall door, popping Regalo on the rump. The colt snorted and bucked, his ears pinned back. He charged the door, but veered away just short of crashing into it.

"He'd kill a man if he got the chance," said the same boy. "I'd let him out, but he'd hurt you." He strutted back and forth in front of Regalo's stall as if to prove his bravery.

Guy swore beneath his breath. Damnation, where was John the Marshal? If he was off swiving another wench he'd tan the hide right off the man's sorry arse.

Another handful of pebbles showered the stall door.

Sybilla's voice rang out. "Don't taunt him!" She ducked just as a stone struck her in the face, right below the eye.

"Witch!" a boy yelled.

Sybilla's hand flew to her bloodied cheek. Rage blazed in her eyes. "Leave us alone!" she screamed.

Guy bolted, positioning himself between Sybilla and the boys. God in heaven, they'd hurt her, the little imbeciles! And they'd no idea of the seriousness of their accusations or the trouble they'd invite. "I'll lop the ears off the next of you who throws a stone," Guy bellowed, struggling against the urge to take Sybilla in his arms and blot the blood from her cheek.

Regalo bared his teeth and lunged at the door. The boys leapt back and hooted. Sybilla caught the wrist of the youngest and pried a pebble from his fist.

"Enough!" Guy commanded. He spun around and secured the stall lock. "So help me, the next one of you who throws a stone will know this." He drew his sword and brandished it toward the tanner's son.

A pale boy of nine or ten, with broken teeth and breath that smelled of stolen ale, stumbled forward and pointed at the colt. "He's the devil's horse, Sir Guy. Ain't right between the ears." The boy tossed back his head and barked. The other boys jeered and hooted. Regalo spun around and kicked the door, the wood cracking like fractured bones.

"Stop it!" Sybilla yelled at Regalo.

The colt moved to the far corner of the stall. His head hung low, but his eyes focused on the boys.

The drunken boy peered into the stall, heedless of Guy's big hand on his shoulder. "My father says a colt marked like that grows horns at night, just like a demon—that we should string him up, throw him in a pit

and burn him, send him back to hell where he belongs."
He pointed to Sybilla. "Her too!"

The rowdy tanner's boy cheered in agreement.

Sybilla spread her arms protectively in front of Regalo's
stall door. "No!"

Guy grabbed the drunken youth by his belt and lifted
him until his toes barely touched the ground. God's
breath, he would nip their mischief now before it turned
into lunacy. "You, young pup, are out past curfew and
drunk on your father's ale. Again. I've a mind to tell him.
If I catch you bothering my horse again, or spreading
rumors about him or my servant, your father will answer
to me." Guy let the words hang in the air. The boy's
father could be a brute. It would not bode well for the
youth to have to face the wrath of his sire.

The boy's face blanched. "Nay, Sir Guy. Please." He
shook his head. "Please, don't tell my da."

Guy leaned in close. "If I catch you or your friends
here again, pestering my horse, you'll have more to fear
than your father. Understood?" He shot a warning look
at the already retreating tanner's son.

The boy nodded, his chin quivering. His feet hit the
dirt and he was off, racing in from the barn.

Guy turned to the rest of the boys. "Go home. All of
you. Now."

They scattered.

Sybilla called to Regalo. He cautiously approached
and let her stroke his cheek. His eyelids closed as Sybilla
spoke in a low, soothing voice.

God's breath, the bond between them was unlike any
Guy had ever seen between a horse and his keeper.
Sybilla was the only one who could command Regalo.
The colt had not responded to his pleas to halt his attack.

Guy took a deep breath.

He could not be jealous of Sybilla and her power over the little beast. He cared for both of them too much and as of late, Sybilla had touched his heart in a way no other woman had. Sybilla Corbuc had earned his love and trust. 'Twas right the colt loved her, too.

Damnation. This confrontation with the boys should not have happened.

Guy surveyed the shadowy aisles. Save for the horses who watched curiously from their stalls and the ever present barn dog that finally stopped barking, no one was about. Odd, that so early in the evening John the Marshal had not yet made the rounds.

A cold prickle of suspicion raced up Guy's spine. He grabbed Sybilla by the hand and hauled her into the bailey. "Get the night watch! Now!" He shoved her urgently. "Don't come back without them. I'm going back to guard Regalo."

A stunned Sybilla stumbled as he released her. "What's wrong?"

"Just go!" Guy jerked around, his sword in his hand, every muscle in his body flexed and ready. "Go!" he yelled, racing into the barn.

Sybilla picked up her skirts and raced to the gatehouse.

Entering the barn, Guy drew his sword. The eerie silence in the stables was suddenly broken by the squealing yelp of the barn dog and the panicked whinny of Regalo.

A man shouted a curse. The stall walls shook with the reverberation of what sounded like a well-shod horse pounding against the paneling with both hind feet.

In the corner of his stall, Regalo bucked and kicked, nostrils flaring, his mouth agape. He halted, but only to paw and strike at the figure cowered before him.

Malcolm of Haverty shielded his head with one hand and with the other reached for the sword that lay in the straw beside him.

Malcolm glanced at Guy, but kept a wary eye on Regalo. "Damn your devil's horse! He killed John the Marshal, kicked him in the head. Call off your horse, Warwick! He means to kill me, too!"

Guy bolted into the stall. There in the corner beneath the manger lay John of Kent, blood running from his ear, his jaw shattered. He eyes were closed, but he breathed, though barely. The pool of dark, clotted blood beneath his head indicated he'd been there a while—unseen by the boys throwing stones across the door, or by anyone, except Regalo.

Good God, what had the colt done?

Guy's heart beat hard against his chest. Regalo was out of control and Sybilla wasn't here. Pray to heaven he'd not be forced to kill the colt to save the life of a man he despised.

Guy spoke, hoping he could calm Regalo. "There, Regalo. Be easy."

Regalo snorted and bore down on Malcolm like a lion.

Malcolm staggered backward, his back against the stall wall. With one quick swipe, he lunged and grabbed his sword. "I'll kill him! Then neither you, nor that bastard-maker Hamon will have him."

Guy jerked his head away from Malcolm, his gaze cutting to the crumpled body of John the Marshal. Instinctively, his hands locked around his sword's hilt. Regalo hadn't tried to kill the marshal.

He pointed his weapon at Malcolm. "'Twas you who did this. You who bashed the marshal in the head when he found you here, intending to do harm to my colt. Take your hatred out on me, Malcolm, not my horse. I'd wager 'twas you who spied for Hamon, told him of the east wall's cracks and tunnels. Let's settle this once and for all."

Regalo snorted and advanced on Malcolm.

"Call him off, Warwick, or I'll run him through." Malcolm held his sword poised to strike.

Guy kept his eyes focused on Malcolm's weapon. "Regalo, cease!"

The colt reared and lashed out with both front feet, catching Malcolm across the shoulder, the blow knocking him to the side.

Malcolm fought to regain his balance. "Damn you, Warwick! Call him off!"

Sybilla's voice suddenly called softly from the doorway. "Stop it, Regalo. Guy won't let him hurt you."

Her eyes grew wide as they darted from Regalo to Malcolm, and came to rest on the body beneath the manger. Behind her, men's voices shouted and armor clattered. The night watchmen gathered round, their torches lighting up the stall.

Guy glanced at Sybilla. Malcolm lunged, his sword slicing through Guy's leather jerkin. A flash of hot pain shot across Guy's chest. Blood seeped from the flesh wound, dampening his padded shirt. He glowered at Malcolm. "I should let the horse kill you. But you deserve a slower death." He raised his sword, challenging Malcolm to withdraw from his corner and fight.

Regalo stilled, and in the split second of the quiet, Malcolm's sword sliced through the air. Guy's blade caught the weapon by the edge, a hair's breadth before the sword made contact with Regalo's neck and gashed across the horse's great vein.

Sybilla screamed.

Malcolm fell forward and as his blade went spinning

from his hand, Guy's weapon caught him just beneath the chin.

The gaping gash in Malcolm's neck spouted blood like a fountain.Malcolm stood frozen, stunned in silence, his eyes wide with disbelief and blood flowing down the front of his tunic. His face suddenly contorted into an agonized look of a man whose spirit fled his body. His knees buckled and he crumpled to the floor in a bloody heap, his last breath a mix of gurgling air and gasps.

Sybilla covered her face, her shoulders trembling.

Guy folded Sybilla into his arms, heedless of the wound beneath his jerkin. He stroked her bruised and bloodied cheek. "Shhh, Sybilla," he soothed. "Malcolm would have killed Regalo. He tried earlier tonight, but John the Marshal stopped him. The boys must have interrupted the completion of his plan." He ran his hand down Sybilla's back, drawing her closer. Her heart beat against his chest, the life affirming rhythm filling a void he'd too long ignored. "God, I need you, Sybilla. And Regalo needs you more than ever. Tonight I could not stop him."

Regalo nickered.

Sybilla buried her face in Guy's shoulder, pressing her hand over the slash in his jerkin, the blood from his wound coloring her fingers. "Your wound needs attention."

"'Tis a flesh wound, nothing more." He grinned down at her, pleased by her concern.

She raised her face to his, her eyes watery and red. "You could have been killed."

He ran his knuckles down the side of her face. "Nay, I've too much to do yet, too much to live for."

The realization swept over Guy like an ocean wave. Yes,

he did have too much to live for—and a real reason to care if he lived or died—Regalo, and most of all Sybilla.

Guy planted a tender kiss on her warm lips. God in heaven, if anyone had hurt her, if Malcolm had hurt her, he would have torn the man limb from limb and let Regalo trounce him.

He motioned to the watchmen to carry John the Marshal's unconscious body to the kitchen. With time and the help of God, the man might recover.

"Come," he said to Sybilla, "Let's go to bed. I'll station a guard from the gatehouse to watch Regalo."

A night watchman stepped in front of Guy. He cleared his throat. "Excuse me, sir. But we'll be needing to report this to Lord Phillip. Have your servant tend to your wound. We'll take the news of Sir Malcolm's demise to our Lord. What you did was in self-defense. We'll all atest to that. We'd long suspected Malcolm of spying. We just couldn't catch him."

Guy nodded and let Sybilla take his arm around her shoulder as he leaned against her. It was going to be a long, long night at Ketchem.

Sybilla lay nestled in Guy's arms, their legs entwined. His breath was calm and with his eyes closed and a slight smile on his face, he looked reposed. The bandage on his chest was dry and clean. The wound had not required a stitch.

Sybilla ran her fingers down his arm. "Have you seen the chapel doors? Simon has asked Mary to be his wife. The bans have been posted."

A lazy smile spread o'er his face. "I'm glad for him," he responded, and stroked her upper arm with his knuckles.

Sybilla took a slow breath. Now was as good a time as any to broach the subject that weighed so heavily on her mind.

Sybilla cleared her throat. "The race is two days away, Guy, and in two days . . ."

God in heaven, this was hard.

He kissed the top of her head. "Yes?"

She closed her eyes, hoping he wouldn't notice the heat she felt rising to her cheeks. "In two days my time as your servant ends. Regalo doesn't need me. My time is up. I shall leave Ketchem after the race, unless—"

"You shall have your freedom," he said, his voice low. "Stay and live at Ketchem. Regalo listens to you. What we share doesn't have to end." He ran his hand along the inside of her thigh and nuzzled her ear. "How could you think of leaving when we spend our nights like this?"

Sybilla sat up. "Guy I cannot sleep here—live here—with you, unless we have a more permanent agreement. After the race, the arrangement between us must change." She averted her eyes and added. "that's *if* I were to stay."

Her words were met by silence.

Guy drew his brows up, his face befuddled.

God's bones, did the man have the brain of an onion?

He gently pushed her back down on the bed. "We'll work something out." He traced a necklace of kisses round her neck. "Mayhap after I win the race, I could pay you."

Sybilla's heart almost stopped. The words warmed her cheeks as if he'd slapped her.

"Pay me?"

Her stomach rolled. She felt sick—and foolish, to think for a moment Sir Guy of Warwick might consider her to be his wife. He'd never said he loved her, though he'd saved her life in Cornbury and here at Ketchem. Hadn't he given up his chance before the royal court—for her? Mayhap she'd been mistaken. Apparently, he cared more about revenge and about Regalo.

Sybilla swung her feet over the edge of the bed and stood. Her knees faltered and she braced her hand against the cold stone wall to steady herself.

Guy propped himself up on his elbows. He didn't seem to notice she was trembling. The look in his confident face told her he considered his offer a viable solution. "If I survive the race," he said, "you could work for me and earn an honest wage. You've always wanted me to pay you."

She snatched her gown from the floor and pulled it over her head. She faced him, her heart twisting inside her chest.

"Yes, provided you survive and you win, you'll be rich. You can hire a servant—or a whore." She jabbed her feet into her boots. "But you cannot hire me. I'll be leaving Ketchem."

Guy flung the covers back and bounded from the bed. He caught her by the wrist as she turned to leave. "Sybilla, you know I didn't mean—we can find another way—"

Her hand flew up, the movement swift and unexpected. She slapped him squarely across his stubbled cheek. "I thought myself in love with you and dared hope that you might love me back. I've been a fool." She jerked free, her eyes filling with tears. "The day after tomorrow, on the day of the race, my debt to you is paid, Sir Guy of Warwick. 'Til then, I'll find another place to sleep."

She snatched her old pallet from the floor and raced from the cellar.

* * *

Guy held his head to the side for a moment, and when he finally turned back to face Sybilla, she was gone.

He rubbed at the sting on his cheek. Damnation. He'd never been good at reading women. If she thought herself in love with him, why didn't she just say so? God in heaven, he'd wanted her to stay, why was she so offended by his offer?

Guy yanked on his hose and tunic. Sybilla Corbuc would not leave Ketchem without giving him an explanation. He deserved that much. Hell to the devil, she was more to him that just a servant.

He stormed out of the cellar and headed to the kitchen.

Chapter Twenty-Two

Guy strode across the yard, the sunlight beaming down. He squinted, his eyes searching for Sybilla. He'd barely seen her these last two days, and she would not speak to him when on the rare occasion he could track her down. For the last two nights he'd slept alone, his heart as empty as his bed.

He'd had enough. There were precious few hours left before the race and Sybilla would hear him out. He'd much to say if she would listen.

He entered the kitchen, the smell of freshly baked bread swirling around him like the bustling servants carrying great baskets of fish and beef, barrels of ale, and sacks of early summer apples. If all went well today, there'd be a feast in the hall after the race, but if something went awry and a war broke out . . . a battle in the village would cost the lives of hundreds.

If he could do nothing else, he needed to warn Sybilla, to tell her to run to the safety of Hartford Abbey if there was trouble. Bloody hell, where was she?

Mary tapped him on his shoulder, as if she'd read his thoughts. "She's in chapel with Lady Claire, praying for a safe and fair race." She offered him a bowl of pottage. "I don't know what happened between you and Mistress Corbuc, but she cries herself to sleep at night, curled up by the fire in our cottage with her face buried in the covers. Says she's leaving Ketchem. I don't want her to go." Mary lowered her voice. "She says she is not with child."

Guy stared at the bowl. He'd been so careful, except these last few weeks. He'd worried that she might be pregnant. He could not deny the unexpected tinge of disappointment to learn that she was not.

He spoke to the pottage. "I don't know what's wrong. I asked her to stay."

Mary eased onto the bench beside him. "Maybe you didn't ask her in the right way? But you should make things right between the two of you. Might be your last chance. Lord Hamon brought his horse Zephyr, that white devil. The horse killed a man in the market summer last. Kicked him in the head." She glanced away, then added, "It's not that I've no faith in you and Bacchus, but if you love Mistress Corbuc, you need to tell her. Before the race."

Guy raised his gaze and stared distractedly into the hearth. Love Sybilla? Of course he loved her! How could she not know that? He leaned urgently toward Mary. "Did she say, by chance, what upset her? If I knew, mayhap I could—"

Before Mary had the chance to answer, Cook bustled to the table and cleared her throat. "Mother Mary, why are men as thick as posts between the ears, and still they rule the world?" She folded her arms and glared at him. "'Tis not unheard of Sir Guy, for a knight to take a servant or freeborn woman as his wife. Sir Simon has asked for Mary's hand in marriage. Ask Mistress Corbuc to be your wife. That's what she wants, you dolt."

Guy dropped his bowl, pottage splattering across the floor. He felt as if he'd been struck in the chest by the butt of a crossbow.

Good God, he'd been a fool, an idiot, and as stupid as an ox. He'd been so focused on his single-minded quest for vengeance, he hadn't thought about Sybilla as his wife, a mother to his sons. But things had changed . . .

Cook took a deep breath. "I'll tell you what it's like to live an old life alone, God rest my husband's soul. You'll spend the winter nights worrying if you passed on from the cold, no one would find you till the next day. You'll eat by the fire alone, your old bones begging for the comfort of another person's touch. I had that comfort for awhile, 'til the Lord saw fit to take my Edwin from me. If you die on the racetrack today, you will die without knowing what a life with love can be like. Your sister would have hated that. If it's the difference in your stations, put that aside. Take the Mistress Corbuc to wife. The two of you are suited."

Guy sat motionless, feeling nothing but the pain of a hollow heart. "'Tis not that that keeps me from her, Cook. She's all that I would want in a wife. But I cannot wed her. Hamon would be sure to kill her—and he'd make her suffer as he did it, bastard daughter or not. 'Twould be another way to get back at me for what he thinks I did to Lady Morna."

Cook gave him a pitiful look. "What on earth did you do to her? She spread her skirts for any man who caught her eye, even did it while she was married to Lord Hamon. You were long gone to war. I've heard the stories. He was right to cast her off."

Guy kept his eyes on the floor. Cook's words cut into

his heart, even after all these years. God in heaven, he'd once loved Morna more than life, even after she married Hamon. The night before he left for France, they'd bedded in the woods and sworn their hearts to one another, he newly knighted, and she newly wed to a lord she did not love.

His fingers gripped his sword. He'd been no saint in France, but his love for her had been unfailing. God's breath, he knew the stories about her indiscretions—tales told 'round the army campfires by men just arrived from England. He'd been gone barely a year. He'd written and implored her to remember their vow. *Dearest Guy*, she'd written back, *My bed and my heart are large enough for many . . . count yourself amongst those I chose to love, and if you cannot, I set you free.*

Guy hung his head. He'd been devastated by her dismissal. That she claimed undying love some eight years later, and clung so desperately to the memory of what they once had, was a testament to how unkind the years had been. He could not judge her harshly. He felt only pity for Morna. He'd barely thought of love since he'd been home, so focused on avenging his family's murder. And then he met Sybilla Corbuc.

Guy studied Cook's concerned face. He'd told no one about what had truly happened between him and Morna, not even Simon. Sybilla should be the first one to know the truth.

He would talk to her, really talk as soon as he got the chance . . . if it wasn't too late.

Cook rested her hand on Guy's shoulder. "I can see it pains you, Sir Guy, to think upon the past. I'm not one for prying. Just hate to see you miss your chance at love. Real love."

Guy rose from the bench, his heart resolute. "If you see Sybilla, tell her I was here looking for her and that I wanted to talk to her. Tell her I intend to vanquish Hamon, even if it kills me. He can't hurt her, or Regalo from the grave. And if I should be lucky enough to live, I'll move heaven and earth to keep her near, whatever she wants, whatever it takes . . . tell her that for me, will you?"

He strode from the kitchen.

Sybilla set her bundle on the steps beside the well. She'd packed an apple and two loaves of bread for her trip, though she told no one she would leave this morning. She'd visited Regalo for the last time last night. He'd been agreeable and feisty, nuzzling the filly in the stall next to his. She kissed him on the muzzle and he let out a short nicker, promptly returning to his supper. He was a big colt, and would grow into a magnificent destrier, worthy of a knight like Guy of Warwick. Mayhap someday she'd see him again, in a tourney or on the lists. She hurried from the stables with a heavy heart, and tears in her eyes.

Anxious, she waited by the well for the journeymen, stonemason, a woodcutter, and his young son who'd agreed to take her with them to London. Horse race today or no, they were eager to depart and get the best assignments working on the king's new cathedral.

Sybilla moistened her lips and cast a final glance at Ketchem Castle. She'd been here just three months since she left her life in Cornbury, and yet she felt as if she lived here all of her life. She'd never forget this place. Every event, every sight at Ketchem had been etched into her brain. True, she'd spent some of the most terrifying days of her life at Ketchem, but here she also had found friends . . . and love. Had the moon ever shone so brightly through the window shutters in her mother's cottage in Cornbury as it did through the little window in Guy's cellar? Were the fields as green as Ketchem's summer pastures? Had the nights ever been as filled with stars?

Sybilla closed her eyes and took a deep breath. She was no longer the struggling girl from Cornbury, who worried day to day if she would survive.

She was stronger. She would always find a way to live.

Trumpets blared, stealing Sybilla's thoughts. The stable doors banged open. Horses draped in shining silks, ready for the race paraded out, led by squires and grooms.

The stonemason, the woodcutter, and his son filed out behind them. The stonemason waved as he approached, prompting Sybilla to pick up her bundle and hand it to him.

"Here, good sir," she found herself saying and smiling. "I've packed you food for your trip."

The woodcutter's young son looked disappointed. "Are you not coming with us?"

Sybilla tousled his hair. "You go ahead."

Weaving through the throngs of people and scores of Lord Hamon's tents and horses, she hurried through the field to the village green, her heart beating hard. She stopped and leaned against the gatepost, her breath racing from her lungs. Lines of horses, attendants, and spectators filed past her in a blur, past the Ketchem guards and onto the greens in the center of the town. Guy of Warwick would be out there in the camp of round tents and Bacchus would be resting in the hours before the race.

The church bell tolled, giving warning the race would

soon begin. She squeezed past the castle reeve and his brood, and took a space behind the fence that separated the crowd from the racetrack.

The air crackled with the excitement. The heady smell of spiced wine wafted from behind the stands, where feasting tables waited and musicians played their flutes and drums.

Lord and green, sat on a platform on the opposite side of the track. The awning above the noble couple shone with brightly colored swaths of silks in green and scarlet, and the dais was bedecked with red roses, the first of the summer season.

Lady Claire held her husband's hand while he watched the parade before them, the pole bearers twirling their flags, children throwing rose petals at the feet of the white oxen that pulled a cart filled with the town mayor, the magistrates, and the master guildsmen. For a moment, Lady Claire gazed directly at Sybilla, the look in her eyes worried and apprehensive.

Sybilla shifted, turning to the greens where Sir Guy and Lord Hamon waited in the tents. Pray that no matter the outcome of the race, Guy of Warwick would survive. Pray there was no war.

Trumpets blared and cheers rang out as pages and servants laden with bolts of cloth, stacks of silver plates, and a chest filled with gold coins filed past. Twenty oxen followed, and the crowd gasped as the bull charged a banner draped across the railing in front of Lady Claire.

Sybilla scanned the crowd. Familiar faces caught her eye. Ernestine, Cook, Mary, and Simon stood on the dais steps. Simon slipped his hand into Mary's and smiled. Sybilla waved, her gaze focused on a boy who shimmied up a tall post beside the dais. The beam listed, and the boy—none other than Etienne—swung from the banner flag before he managed to wrap his wiry legs around the post and keep from falling.

Sybilla gasped. "Etienne!" *What was he doing here? And where was Margery?*

Sybilla searched the crowd, desperate for a sign of her old friend. Her heart skipped a beat when she caught a glimpse of a familiar face, partially covered by the hood of a rich mantle—the face of Lady Morna. Her wild, dark eyes were unmistakable, though the tell-tale brand on her cheek had been well-covered with costly face paint.

Saints preserve her, what was she doing here? What compelled a Separate to venture into town?

Lady Morna pulled her hood closer around her face, her luminous brown eyes flashing in Sybilla's direction before she turned away.

Trumpets pealed out the call to order. Lord Phillip stood to face the city gates as the crowd quieted and awaited the entrance of the riders.

A white horse emerged. Zephyr, bedecked in red saddlecloths trimmed with silver bells, danced into the village square with Lord Hamon sitting on his back like a king. Hamon raised his hand in salute to Lord Phillip and the crowd cheered, though the sound was mixed with hisses. Horse and rider danced around the track.

Drums beat and the crowd hushed, waiting for the second horse and rider.

What seemed like minutes passed before Guy appeared at the entrance—on foot. He held Bacchus' reins in his hands, the horse's black and gold saddlecloths shimmering in the sun.

Guy took two steps forward and Bacchus stumbled, lifting one foot off the ground and holding it gingerly in the air. He hobbled, his soulful eyes full of pain.

Sybilla's throat tightened. God in heaven, Bacchus was lame.

Guy's eyes flashed with anger. He tossed Bacchus' reins to his groom and charged past Lord Hamon.

He threw his black mantle back and stood before Lord Phillip. "My Lord, I suspect foul play. My horse came up lame this morning, so footsore he cannot walk. He cannot race and I ask postponement until I find another mount."

A low murmur rose from the crowd.

Lord Hamon dismounted and strode before the dais. "Lord Phillip, the race cannot be postponed. If my opponent cannot ride against me, then he must forfeit the prize, and all he owns. Those are the rules, and rules by which we must all abide."

Guy spun on his heel to face Lord Hamon. "You did this. My horse was sound last night. I know not how, but this is your work, Hamon." He drew his sword. The sound of steel sliding from the scabbard shook the air.

Lord Hamon stepped back, his hand on his sword.

The crowd gasped. Lord Phillip stepped quickly to the edge of the dais. "Lord Hamon, I have allowed you here for an honest race. I extend my hospitality to mend the rift between us, between you and Sir Guy, with honor and fairness and without bloodshed. Agreed?"

Hamon kept his eye on Guy. "Agreed. But the race will go on. Sir Guy must find another horse. I'll not leave Ketchem until this is settled." He kept his eyes on Guy's sword.

Lord Phillip turned to Guy. "The Bedevilar is my fastest and my best stallion. I'll send for him if you'll consent to ride him."

Guy's face turned stony. His dark eyes flared with

frustration. "Agreed, my Lord." He answered in a tight voice.

"I'll tend to Bacchus and wait at my tent." He bowed and strode toward the gates, the crowd parting to let him pass.

Sybilla held her breath. Lord Phillip's great stallion was a fine horse, but not conditioned, or ready for a race. It had taken months to train Bacchus, to build his lungs and muscles so he might sustain the five laps around the course without fatigue. No other horse in Lord Phillip's stables could match the quickness or the stamina of Zephyr—except for one, a horse with four white socks, with legs as fast as the wind, and a heart the size of a wagon.

Her skirts hiked above her ankles, Sybilla scrambled from the fence line, pushing her way through the crowd. She hurried through the gates and headed toward the south pasture, where Regalo frolicked with the other yearlings.

Guy tossed aside the tent flap, his heart pounding, the sweat on his forehead rolling down his face in rivulets.

Damnation. When he led Bacchus from the stall this morning, the horse had such a gimp, lameness so acute, he refused to set his foot down. John the Marshal had sworn no one had ventured past the guards stationed outside Bacchus' stall, but Guy sensed the man was lying, sensed the fear in his voice when he denied letting anyone into the stables, not even the wenches who had come to revel with the stable boys who'd had too much to drink.

All the hot bran packs he had applied to Bacchus' hoof and the ale drenching he had forced down the horse's throat had not set the poor beast right. And unless the Bedevilar had a bigger heart and more wind in his chest than Satan's horse-named-Zephyr, everything would be lost—Baldwin Manor, Regalo. Justice for his sister and his chance for love . . . with Sybilla.

Sybilla.

God's peace, she mattered, more than he ever would have believed that night three months ago when he'd found her. Win or lose this race, he would not let Sybilla Corbuc leave his life. She gave him strength and hope for another way of living, not shut away in a cellar alone at night.

He leaned against the tent post and rubbed his temples, his eyes closed. Hell to the devil, he missed her already.

A soft voice, feminine and light spoke from the shadows. *"Mon cher.* I have missed you."

Guy's eyes snapped open. He spun around, his eyes wide, his hand on his sword. "Morna?"

"I've come to stop the race. Hamon means to kill you. I cannot let him. Just give him the colt." She stepped forward and pushed her hood back, her deep-set eyes filled with tears. "Come away with me, far from here where Hamon cannot find us. I would do anything to keep you safe."

A sudden rush of understanding welled up from his gut. "You lamed Bacchus, didn't you? What favor did you give the stable boy who led you to my horse?"

She shook her head. "It doesn't matter. My sight has shown me what will happen. Hamon will win this race if you ride against him. When you are knocked from your horse by Hamon's sword, he will skewer you. He plans to claim your life, your manor, and your little horse. Surely you know that. He will never forgive you for loving me." Morna placed her willowy hands against his cheeks, and lifted her chin as if to kiss him. "I cannot forget what we once had."

Guy grabbed her wrists. "I do not love you, Morna. And I will face the man who killed my sister and my nephew. This is my day to challenge him before all, and if the price is my life, so be it."

Her dark eyes turned hard and brittle, her gaze touched by madness. "You are a fool, Guy, to think he killed your sister. She was no threat to *him*."

Morna stopped, her hand twitched as if she meant to raise it to cover her mouth. She looked down, her face white, her lips pressed together.

Guy leaned his head back, her words echoing in his brain. He staggered, the weight of his realization bearing down. Good God. Morna, the woman he'd once held in his arms and shared his dreams of knighthood— Morna had killed his sister?

He clenched his fists. "Why?" he asked, his voice tight.

"Because she knew how much I loved you. You were coming back from Balmont and I had plans for us—'tis why I risked visiting the villages and fairs, telling futures, hoping we would meet. She wanted me to leave you alone, even threatened to tell Hamon. Eight years I've waited! I could not risk that she might reveal our reunion. He would stop at nothing to destroy you just to punish me. He told me he would kill you."

Guy advanced on her. "Why my sister's babe? What did the child do to you?"

"It was an accident. Your sister fell and dropped him. He hit his head on the rocks. I didn't kill him."

"The bruises around her neck—those were your finger marks." He caught her by the arm and jerked her toward him. "This is your key, isn't it? I found it at the circle of stones." He held the key in front of her. "'Twas you I saw last winter scratching in the dirt, looking for it."

She knocked the key from his hand. "My key, yes, to my husband's private apartments, to my prison. He will not release me. He uses me in ways that are shameful." She looked away. "Guy, forgive me. I was enraged that night, afraid your sister would tell him about us."

"There was no us! I hadn't heard a word from you in years. Not since the day I got your last letter."

"He would have killed you, Guy," she continued, ignoring his words. "He still intends to and if you manage to survive, he'll kill your mistress. I have seen it. Just give him the colt. Come away with me. I've made arrangements for our safe passage back to France. Forget Ketchem. Forget your little midwife."

Guy stared at Morna. Her red lips parted with pleading. The gift of sight had driven her beyond sanity, into a world where love could justify murder and she seemed to have forgotten her own predictions . . . that a mystical colt with four white socks would lead him to his sister's killer.

Regalo had done just that.

Her fiery eyes appraised him, the look on her sharp face expectant, as if she actually believed he would go with her to France.

Pity rose up from his heart, battling for dominance over his grief and anger, beating back guilt and the urge to do to her what she had done to his sister. Had he not been so foolish as to love Morna, Roselynn would still be alive.

She laid her hand on his sleeve. "Please, Guy." Her blazing eyes told of her desperation.

He let his hand fall away from his sword. He pitied Morna, but he could not let her kill again. "Make your peace with

God, Morna. For you shall be held accountable for the murder of Roselynn and her son, if not in this life, then the next. At the very least you'll spend the rest of your days in a convent or a prison. I will make certain of it."

She folded her hands in front of her. Her face suddenly composed and her voice clear, she said, "You must come away with me. Lord Hamon plans to use Sybilla Corbuc like he uses me, but he'll string her up and kill her when he's finished. All to get back at you. If you love her you will come with me. Hamon will have no interest in her if he thinks you do not."

Guy lunged for Morna and caught her by the shoulders. "'Tis only pity for your sickness that prevents me from breaking your neck, Morna, but if Hamon so much as lays a hand on Sybilla I will—"

"You will what, my love? Run him through? Run me through? My champions Sir Elbert and Sir Gideon are dead, but I've others to take their place. Few men can ultimately resist what I have to offer. I've loyal lovers waiting behind your tent. If I should give the signal, they will not hesitate to put a knife point at your throat. And you will not get the chance to save your little horse midwife from the foolish mistake she is about to make."

"What mistake? Morna, tell me!"

She answered coolly. "Since you have refused my offer, there is nothing more I can do to help you—or her."

The tent flap opened and Simon strode inside, his face red and flustered. "Guy! Come anon! Mistress Corbuc is here and she—" Simon halted at the sight of Morna. "What is *she* doing here?" In an instant, he drew his sword.

Guy flung Morna aside. "Simon, what has Sybilla done?"

"She just rode through the gates—on Regalo. She means to race!"

Guy drew his sword and bolted from the tent. "Watch her, Simon. She's the murderer!" he called as he braced to meet Morna's guardsmen.

Two steps outside and he halted, his chest heaving. He scanned the grounds. Empty.

He flung the tent flap aside and shouted, "And if she tells you she has men to protect her, ignore her. She's bluffing."

He turned on his heels and charged to the track.

Lord Hamon wheeled his horse around to face the gates. Guy of Warwick's colt came charging onto the racetrack, tossing his head and straining against the rope wrapped around his nose. His white-stockinged feet padded on turf, kicking up clods of grass and dirt. On Regalo's back sat Sybilla Corbuc, dressed in the faded blue gown she'd worn when he'd met her on the road out of Cornbury, her yellow hair loose and streaming in the sunshine.

Good God, she looked like her mother. Same bright eyes, same haughty lift to her pointed chin, the features that had attracted him to the free woman who'd given birth to his only offspring so many years ago. He felt his daughter's presence, always, for she reminded him of his greatest failure—to produce a legitimate heir, a son sired by his legal wife, Lady Morna of Darymore, the only woman he had truly ever loved.

Zephyr pawed and struck at the approaching colt. Sybilla reined her mount just out of reach.

Her face determined, she trotted the colt before the dais and reined him to a halt in front of Lord Phillip and

Lady Claire. "Lord Phillip, I wish to race. This colt belongs to Sir Guy, and I am his servant. With all due respect, I've a better chance to win than does Sir Guy on the Bedevilar. There is no law against a woman racing. If Lord Hamon insists on a race today, then let it be against me."

Hamon fisted Zephyr's reins, drawing the horse closer to the dais. "Race a girl on an untrained colt? That would be no contest. I will race Sir Guy, or no other. Knight against knight."

Lady Claire quickly rose and whispered in Lord Phillip's ear. At the sudden clamor of the crowd, Sybilla turned to see Guy thunder through the gates on the Bedevilar, a massive sorrel as tall as Zephyr, but three times as stout and a belly still sprung from his breakfast.

Guy reined his mount to the start line. He raised his hand in salute to Lord Phillip. "I am ready, my lord. Let the race begin—as soon as my servant removes herself and my colt from the track."

Sybilla wheeled Regalo to the start line. She lifted her chin, and spoke loud enough for all to hear. "I will race. The only rule for entry is that a rider has a horse, and all contestants must agree."

The crowd laughed and hooted. Hamon let a sly grin spread across his face. So Mistress Corbuc troubled Guy of Warwick, too? It was clear by the way he looked at her and she at him that they shared more than just a colt. Mayhap he could use that to his advantage in a race.

Guy's face darkened. "Sybilla, do not cross me. This is too dangerous. You'll break your neck."

"I can ride. Regalo is ready and I will not fall. I've tested him already."

Guy's voice boomed above the crowd. "Men have died on this track, and so have horses. I care about the colt. I care about you, Sybilla. Now stand aside." Guy nodded to two of Lord Phillip's men who promptly tried to take Regalo by the bridle. The colt whinnied and danced around them, avoiding capture.

Sybilla's face turned pale, as if the significance of his words took several seconds to penetrate her brain. She shook her head. "Let me ride!"

"No, Sybilla. This is my score to settle and this is no ordinary race. There are no rules here. Whoever makes it to the finish line first is the winner." His eyes blazing, he glared at Hamon. "You've ruined many lives and you know of whom I speak. I hold you ultimately responsible for the murder of my sister and nephew."

Hamon leaned back in the saddle. "I did not commit the murder, though I condone it. You took from me what was mine—who I cared about more than anyone else in the world. You have not paid enough for that." He shot a glance a Sybilla, her beautiful hair tumbling down her shoulders. By God, she was a worthy prize. "I consent to all contestants. To the mark! Lord and Lady Claire, call the race before I set my guards on yours. The melee that would follow most certainly turn into an all out war." He grinned, daring their refusal.

Lord Phillip's face turned red. His hand flew to his sword's hilt. He stood on the dais with his weapon drawn. "You threaten me with war? We are ready, Hamon." His men drew their weapons.

Lady Claire calmly stepped to the forefront. She looked at Guy, pleading. He'd no choice but to obey.

Hamon grinned.

Lady Claire raised her hand. "All riders, take your places."

Guy sidled the Bedevilar beside Regalo. "Sybilla, swear that you will not stop if I am injured. Should I fall, or the Bedevilar go down, ride Regalo to the finish. The lives of thousands are at stake."

Sybilla lifted her chin. "I ask the same from you Guy. Race to the finish no matter what."

Flags hoisted, a single trumpet rang out the start. Hamon dug his spurs into Zephyr. Guy's feet beat against the Bedevilar's sides. In an instant, Sybilla felt Regalo take flight.

The horses raced along the stretch, Zephyr in the lead pounding the turf with his red saddlecloths flying out behind him, and the Bedevilar not far behind, his long heavy strides digging up the earth. Regalo dashed along, three strides behind the other horses.

Sybilla bent low over the horse's neck. God's bones, for every stride the others took, Regalo took three.

One lap around the track and Zephyr, still in the lead by a nose, lost his footing and almost stumbled. The spectators in the stands cried out, and some shielded their eyes from impending disaster.

Guy gripped the Bedevilar's sides with his legs and urged the horse onward. Zephyr's stumble had cost him a length, and by the second lap, he and the Bedevilar raced side by side.

Sybilla held on tight, aware of the crowd's roar as Regalo raced on, though still behind by almost half a lap. Pray to St. Genevieve, he kept his feet beneath him, for she could not have stopped him even if she tried.

Guy glanced over his shoulder, yelled an oath, and flung his arm in the air, signaling for Sybilla to drop back. A sword flashed in the sunlight. Sybilla screamed, just as Guy dodged the blow.

Hamon swung his weapon, slashing at Guy while the horses galloped. Swaying atop the sweating Bedevilar, Guy freed one hand from the reins and drew his blade with the other. Steel clashed against steel and both horses slowed while their riders fought in combat.

Sybilla strained against Regalo's reins. Hamon's sword caught the flat side of Guy's blade, knocking the weapon from his hand, sending Guy reeling backward—enough to throw Bedevilar off balance.

Winded and unsure of his footing, the horse scrambled to stay upright, jolting Guy from his seat, one leg still over the horse's back, his other dragging on the ground. He clutched at the great horse's neck and struggled to throw his other leg back over his mount. Half on, half off the horse, Guy held fast to Bedevilar's mane as they rounded the corner of the fourth lap.

Froth flew from Bedevilar's mouth. He lost speed, first by a stride, then by two. Regalo whinnied as Zephyr dropped back, enough for Hamon to lean to the side—and slice through the Bedevilar's mane as if it was silken thread.

Guy lost his life-line.

Sybilla screamed. Guy's body rolled beneath the horse's feet, the crowd gasping as he covered his head with his arms and shielded his face from trampling hooves.

Dear God! He would be killed, his body broken, bones and skull shattered like splintered wood.

Regalo thundered past Guy's pummeled body and Sybilla fought with her shattered heart to keep from reining the colt to a screeching halt.

She held on fast and fixed her eyes on Zephyr, now only three strides ahead.

Race to the finish. Race to the finish.

She battled back tears and held on tight, all the while her mind reeling, fearing Guy of Warwick was dead!

Much to her dismay, Regalo ran faster, his feet barely touching the ground, his breath no harsher than if he were galloping across a peaceful field. Regalo flew down the track, reaching with his every step, bearing down on Zephyr. The great white horse just a pace ahead, the sound of his thudding stride so near, Sybilla could see the mud flying from his hooves, and hear Hamon cursing.

"Hold on, Regalo." Sybilla crouched low on his neck. "Hold the pace. The homestretch nears, but so does Zephyr. Race for Guy of Warwick!"

Regalo raced ahead, his reed-thin legs beating as fast as bird wings, his small feet skimming the ground like a stag's.

The crowd waved and clapped as Regalo sped past, and Zephyr's head edged into Sybilla's view. She sucked in her breath, squeezing Regalo with her knees. God's bones, only twelve lengths, nay ten, before the finish.

A movement from the sideline caught her eye, a banner post swaying, listing forward, and threatening to fall across the track. Etienne hung from the top, leaned down and screamed at the top of his lungs. "Run, Regalo, run!"

God's breath! Had the boy no sense?

Sybilla sat up straight, hauling on the reins to stop Regalo just as the beam creaked and lurched, falling with Etienne waving, until his face turned white and he jumped free and clear . . .

Spectators scattered. Some dashed across the track, and Sybilla hauled on Regalo's rope with all the strength she could muster.

Too late.

The pole crashed down directly in front of the colt, and without a misstep, he leapt, sailing across the barricade as if it was no more than a fallen log.

Sybilla's stomach flipped. Regalo soared. The crowd roared with approval as Regalo landed, hitting the grass with the grace and lightness of a dancer. Breathing fast and hard, he slowed as he trotted across the finish line to the whoops and hollers of Lord Phillip and Lady Claire and the throngs of people that cheered in the stands.

Then all went silent. All heads turned away from the finish line as Hamon's great white horse thundered toward the fallen post. His striding off, the obstacle too close, and the approach too fast, the great beast threw up his head and slid to a halt, refusing to jump. Hamon roared as he went sailing from his horse's back. He landed with a crash against the fallen post and rolled.

Dazed, Hamon lay moaning in the dirt, wiping at a trickle of blood from the corner of his mouth. His horse snorted at him from the other side of the beam.

The silent crowd began to murmur, a scattering of chuckles, and a few sharply drawn breaths were released.

Sybilla spun Regalo 'round to see Guy clinging to Bedevilar, the horse charging down the track like lightning.

With a great leap, the horse leapt, clearing the post and flying over a dazed Lord Hamon, who squinted and ducked.

The crowd erupted. Men and women cheered and spilled onto the track, forming a wide circle around Sybilla and Guy.

Her breath rushing from her lungs, Sybilla bolted from Regalo and raced to Guy. His body battered and bleeding, he slid off his horse and wrapped one arm around Sybilla's shoulder, drawing her close, his stance unsteady. His other arm dangled, broken at the shoulder, by his side. He winced when she rested her fingertips against his ribcage, but he kissed her lightly on the lips. She could taste the blood on his swollen mouth.

"You have won, Mistress Sybilla Corbuc," Guy whispered, leaning against his horse. "You have fulfilled the prophecy—who ever rides Regalo shall defeat their enemy. Without a doubt he is the magic horse of legend."

Sybilla smiled. "Put on earth to help us both, Sir Guy. I see now why Regalo fought so hard to keep me tied to you. All of this—between you and Hamon," she looked to the dais, "—and Lord Hamon and you, my Lord Phillip must end. No more bloodshed."

Sybilla strode to the fallen post and offered her hand to Lord Hamon. By the looks of him, his broken nose bloodied and flattened, a bleeding gash as long as a dagger down the side of his thigh, he'd fared no better than Guy. He still lay in the mud, as if he were too weak to move.

"I have won, my lord," she said. "I ask nothing of you, except that you go in peace. Put to rest the grievances you have with Sir Guy of Warwick, Lord Phillip and me. End it here."

He turned his dirt-spattered face to hers and squinted. Reaching for her hand, he leapt to his feet and grabbed her by the hair.

Sybilla shrieked, the cold tip of a dagger resting beneath her ear.

"Mistress Corbuc, if you agree the colt is mine and you will be my servant, we have a truce. Say it loud enough for all to hear. I won you, the colt, and Baldwin Manor when Guy of Warwick fell off his horse."

"No!" She twisted, unable to free herself from his grip. Hamon straightened, his eyes focused on Lord Phillip. "Then what say you, Lord Phillip? If you agree to those terms, then I shall collect my due and leave in peace."

Lord Phillip and Lady Claire, descended from the dais and strode past the prize gold and bolts of cloth. Lord Phillip's face was solemn. "I—"

"Release her, Hamon!" Guy's voice boomed. He raised his sword in his left hand, and tossed Lord Hamon his sword with his other, guarding his broken ribs.

Forced to catch his weapon, Hamon flung aside Sybilla and stood battle-ready, his face hot with hatred.

Guy locked his eyes with Hamon's. "You underestimate me, Hamon. I've fought at Balmont with the king and lived to tell the tale. A fall beneath a horse won't stop me. Now fight for what you really want. Me."

The crowd backed away, all too fearful of knights who intended to fight to the death. Sybilla took a step toward Lord Phillip. "Please sir, don't allow this. Guy of Warwick is wounded. His sword arm is broken."

Lord Phillip kept his eyes on the two knights, his face severe. "I'll allow it. There are men on both sides waiting to do battle. I'd rather these two fight here than two-thousand in a war. It would dishonor Guy of Warwick for me to intervene." Sybilla backed away, drawing Regalo to her side.

Guy and Hamon circled each other, the latter just as tall, and lithe, a hardened warrior but older. Guy assumed a low stance, his left arm raised neck-level with his opponent. Swords clashed, and steel grated. Men grunted. Bones cracked and Guy bore the blunt side of Hamon's blade to his ribs.

Sybilla screeched and stepped in his direction. Guards appeared beside her and grabbed her arms, their grips as tight as vises. Sybilla winced watching blow after blow, knowing one man would soon outdo the other. Dirt and blood covered their faces and they staggered beneath the noonday sun. Guy struck with force though his accuracy was lacking, and Hamon rallied with precision, though he was tiring.

A hard clank cracked the air, and Sybilla looked up to see both men face to face, their swords crossed at the base. With the quickness of lightning, Hamon raised his knee, burying it between Guy's legs. Guy moaned, the color draining from his face, his breath trapped in his chest. Hamon broke the contact and stepped backward. Guy doubled over, his sword low.

Hamon raised his weapon, poised to deliver a fatal blow. Sybilla screamed and Lady Claire gasped.

Steel flashed and Guy's sword edge skimmed across the dirt. The flat side of the weapon crashed against Hamon's legs, a blow so powerful his knees buckled and feet flew out from under him. He landed on his back, his arms outstretched, his sword in the dirt above his head. He scrambled to his knees.

Guy kicked the fallen sword out of reach. With both hands, he gripped the hilt of his weapon and pointed the tip of his sword at his opponent's heart, his chest heaving. Guy swayed, his face deadly pale. He staggered, his sword wavering.

Hamon sneered, his fine white teeth glinting in the sun. "I'll not ask for quarter, Sir Guy."

Hamon scrabbled to his feet and whipped a dagger from his boot, the blade's tip directed at Guy's heart. "Nor will I grant it."

Sybilla screamed as Guy lunged, falling forward, driving his sword into Hamon's belly.

Hamon gasped for air, and fell to the ground, his fist still clutching his dagger.

Guy dropped to his knees, the blinding sun beating down. He gripped his head and toppled onto his side, his body slamming to the ground with a force that cracked his skull.

"Sybilla," he rasped. "Don't go."

Guy lay perfectly still, his ribs wrapped and aching, his right ear ringing. He could not open his swollen eyelids, or utter a sound through his lacerated lips. He suspected he was in his cellar room, though he wasn't certain. The room was dark enough and the bed was hard enough, but if he was in hell, it was colder than he'd expected.

He breathed, but only a little, for it hurt too much. He often drifted between consciousness and oblivion. He liked oblivion better. There he could see the face of Sybilla and her golden hair, feel the tender touch of her hands against his battered body.

As muddled as his brain may be, he knew the part about Sybilla was just a wish. She was far from Ketchem by now. But at least Hamon was dead and she was safe.

A door banged open. Someone—Simon or Mary?— crossed the room and wedged a cup between his lips. Beef broth trickled into his mouth. He swallowed, and let the rest of the liquid dribble down his chin.

He wanted solitude, not food.

Someone pressed a warm cloth against his face and neck and wiped away the mess. The door slammed shut.

Alone with just his pain and his thoughts, Guy took a shallow breath, wondering if Sybilla had gone to London. She'd be lost in a sea of people, mayhap impossible to find.

Guy struggled to lift his head and sit up, but his skull throbbed and the room swirled around him. Through the slits of light that slipped beneath his swollen eyelids, he glimpsed a blur of color—shining piles of gold and swaths of blue and red. His head fell back against the bed like a stone.

Damnation. It would be weeks before he'd be well enough to search. Pray to God, Sybilla Corbuc would not be lost to him forever.

For seven days, Sybilla sat on a stool beside him, fed him and changed his bandages. She kept the brazier lit and the cellar as warm as it could be, and the week passed without so much as a whimper from Guy.

She stroked his cheek, her fingers skimming over his eyelids. The swelling had gone down, and so had the bruise on his cheek, though he'd have a scar beneath his eye. Oddly, the wound there had healed in the shape of a small horse shoe.

Sybilla smiled. Guy would be proud of that.

She set the cup down and gathered up the bandages to wash, when a moan rumbled from Guy's throat.

Stumbling over the stool, she hurried to the bed and knelt beside him. She pressed her palm to his cheek to check for fever.

Without warning, he captured her hand with his and raised her knuckles to his lips. "Mistress Green Eyes? You are still at Ketchem?"

"I am," she answered, smiling, relief flooding over her. "I've begun to appreciate the luxuries of castle life. There's a garderobe, if you can stand the smell, and one never need be alone. You can sleep with a hundred other people if you wish in the great hall, and there's always something cooking in the kitchen. I decided to stay. Lord Phillip has hired me to work in the stables."

Guy winced. "The stables?"

Sybilla nodded. "The king overturned the power-hungry bishop's law. Seems Lord Percy shares his tower with a papal guest. I am free to practice my trade. Lord Phillip has earned a duchy for averting a civil war. And you, Sir Guy of Warwick, have been given a post on the king's special council. You will have to go to London for a ceremony. I am going with you to—"

Guy eased himself onto his elbow and clapped a hand over Sybilla's mouth, though his face turned as white as a sheet for the effort. He let out a breath. "Stop talking, Sybilla Corbuc, so I may have a turn. I am long overdue."

Sybilla closed her mouth and folded her hands in her lap.

Guy leaned against the wall. "I wish to thank you for what you did, foolhardy as it was—to ride Regalo in the race. You could have been killed. I am grateful that you weren't. Lord Phillip and the people of Ketchem, I am sure, are grateful, too."

Sybilla lowered her eyes. "It was my chance to climb into the wagon with you."

"The wagon?"

"My mother climbed into the wagon and rode into Gambolt prison with my stepfather. She died there and she didn't have to. I never understood why she went. Never understood that kind of love." She looked up. "Until I fell in love with you."

Silence filled the room. Guy reached from the bed and pulled her to him, wrapping his arms around her shoulders. She could hear his heart beating strong and fast inside his chest.

"I love you, Sybilla Corbuc. I have much to tell you, about Morna, about me. But now, while I have the chance to ask—would you be my wife?"

God's breath, from the first moment she'd met him, he'd made her pulse race and her stomach flutter. This moment was no exception. She loved his battered face and beaten body with all of her soul.

She lowered her chin. "I think Lady Claire had higher hopes for you."

"Sybilla, you are worthy of the king himself. I have loved you since the night we met. And though I am at a loss to explain it, the strange little colt you named Regalo came into the world, it seems, to bind us together. I want you in my bed every night for the rest of my life. Will you marry me, a lowly knight, with a run down manor house and shaggy horse?" He kissed her lightly on the lips. "Say yes, Sybilla."

She pulled away and stood abruptly, wiping the tears from her eyes with the heel of her hand. "No more Shadow Riding? And if I agree to be your wife, will you find a better room for us to sleep in?" She couldn't help but crack a smile, the joy in her heart overflowing.

"Done. No more Shadow Riding. Roselynn's ghost has said goodbye. Life is for the living. And we shall have a large, warm room to sleep in, with a big window that lets in light and noise."

"And now that the law allows it, will you give me leave, as my husband, to work in the stables?"

"As you wish. Work in the stables and birth the foals, though I was hoping for babies—of the two-legged type."

Sybilla could not suppress a grin. "You know what I mean. And when you get angry with me, you'll not beat me, or snub me with silence? I hear some men treat their wives worse than their servants."

"Beat never, but punish you with silence?" he stroked his stubbled chin. "Nay, I cannot promise that. I am just a man, not a saint."

"Then I don't know if I can marry you, Sir Guy." Sybilla laughed, teasing.

A hard knock rattled the door. Simon's voice called through the slitted window. "Guy, I've a message for Sybilla."

Simon strode into the chamber and handed Sybilla a folded piece of parchment. "'Tis a gift from the Lady Claire."

He smiled at Guy. "I see you are back amongst the

living, my friend. Is there something I can fetch for you? After all, it's what I do."

Guy shook his head. "No more. Take Mary and get to Baldwin. Live the life you've wanted. Oversee my demense. 'Tis my wedding gift to you. I plan to buy an even larger farm." His face suddenly grew serious. "What of—?" He hesitated and glanced at Sybilla.

Simon stroked his red beard. "Of Morna? She is locked away in Hartford Abbey, where she will stay unless you press your case against her in the royal court. I'll take my leave now, Guy, and thank you. We'll see you and Sybilla at the harvest?"

"'Tis my hope."

Simon grinned at Sybilla. The door closed behind him with a thud.

Sybilla clutched the parchment in her hand and raised a quizzical eyebrow. "Lady Morna?"

Guy pulled her close. "She killed my sister and my nephew. I intend to tell you all about it. Later. Her life in Hartford will be hard and punishment enough. Now what's in the parchment?"

Sybilla sat motionless for a moment before she unfolded the missive. An emerald as big as a robin's egg tumbled into her lap.

She gasped. "Hamon's?"

Guy nodded.

Sybilla handed him the parchment. "There's a note."

Guy smiled and focused on the script. "Lady Claire found this emerald in a shop in London. Says it is her gift to you. Your dowry."

Sybilla's hand shook. "My dowry?" she repeated, mostly to herself. She looked up. "How did she find this? How did she know Avelina—?"

Guy shrugged. "I know not, but there are few shops

where one could pawn a jewel as rich as this one. Lady Claire probably paid a little extra to learn of its former owner. But her message is clear. Lady Claire means for me to marry you. Is there something else you want, my love? I would like to come to some agreement so we might ask Lord Phillip for permission and be wed within the fortnight."

Sybilla settled next to him. "Before I can agree to marry you," she muttered against his temple, "there is something you once promised me that I've never gotten."

Guy threw the covers back, patted the open space beside him. He pulled her down. "What, my love, is that?"

"A new dress and another ribbon garter."

"Done," he replied, waving at the bolts of red and blue cloth stacked against the wall and the prize gold cup filled with coins sitting on his chest. "Yours for the taking. And we've twenty head of cattle, enough to make you dozens upon dozens of new leather shoes. Now off with this." He tugged her sleeve, and let a wry smile spread over his face. "It's been a week since we last loved. I shall forget how if you and I don't practice."

Sybilla laughed and drew her gown over her head. "Yes, I will be your wife, and I intend to help you practice every night for the rest of my life, and—"

Guy pressed his fingers to her lips. "Shhhhh, listen."

In the distance, a horse whinnied, loud and clear.

Regalo.

Guy smiled. "'Tis your wedding present calling. My gift to you, Sybilla. He is yours. As am I."

Sybilla closed her eyes, her heart and soul given to the knight who held her in his arms and covered her face with kisses.

Author's Note

In England in the fourteenth century, peasant women were intimately involved in farming and the raising of their family's livestock. The practice of veterinary medicine was usually performed by the local blacksmith, but it is conceivable that women attended the birth of valuable animals, much as midwives attended pregnant women. Local laws varied pertaining to how much the church would tolerate a woman of any knowledge or particular skill practicing her trade.

The afflictions I've given the colt Regalo are based on a disorder in horses that occurs when foals experience difficult or prolonged birth. Blood and oxygen flow to the brain are temporarily compromised. The affected newborn foal exhibits odd behaviors that may last for days or weeks. Stargazing, barking, dog-sitting and wandering, as Regalo exhibited, are all real symptoms of the birthing disorder.

There are records of horse racing in England during the middle ages when knights returned from crusade and brought with them fast, fleet-footed horses that were bred for running. King Richard I appeared to be especially fond of the sport.

Discover the Romances of

Hannah Howell